Soul Sanctuary

Susan Faw

Cover Design by Greg Simanson
Edited by Pam Harris

This is a work of fiction. Names, characters, places, brands, media, and incidents are either the product of the author's imagination or are used fictitiously. Any resemblance to similarly named places or to persons living or deceased is unintentional.

PRINT ISBN 978-0-9953438-5-6
EPUB ISBN 978-0-9953438-4-9

Dedication

As I finish the editing of this book and prepare to go to press, it is the blush of a new year. I am excited to be blessed with another year of life, where so many have not made it. For all that this planet can be a scary place I still want to live in it. I hope you do too!

Regardless of who we are, or where we come from in life, we all have an important role to play in the development of our world, for better or for worse. The world is a great stage and every day, we are called to our role, to act our part. Give the performance of your life. Don't let the curtain fall to anything short of thunderous applause.

I'd like to dedicate this book to my family and to my parents who, although they have never read any of my writings (fantasy is not their 'thing') nevertheless gave me the ultimate start in life and have always believed in me. Thank you for your love and support from on high, and here on this lovely blue planet.

To discover additional titles in The Spirit Shield Saga, visit my website at http://susanfaw.com/spirit-shield-saga/

Prologue

This is not your fight. Let them die!

THE ARMY ROLLED OUT of the southern plains and into the short hills, a river of red-coated lava swirling through the valley base. The push of soldiers clogged the narrows, splashing up onto the hillsides and coating the passes in a crimson crust of death.

The Primordial runners peered down at the roiling mass of men from their perch high atop an abandoned eagle's nest, wedged in a towering deciduous tree which clung to the northern edge of the pass. The crown of the treetop camouflaged their lookout while providing an unimpeded view of the undulating scene below.

As one, the runners shimmied down from their perches and ghosted into the dense cover of squat pine, the thick carpet of needles providing silent footing as they ran. Of all the passes to approach, this was the worst, the most feared by the Primordial Chiefs, as the civil war left the defending clans stretched to the limit.

Indeed, some defenders had abandoned their posts, their fear over the rumoured fate of their kin overcoming their desire to fight. Whispers of villages emptied and entire families snatched away by unknown forces had caused a swelling defection within the forward units of tribal defenders. It was so rampant that the Chieftains now arrested those who attempted desertion and handed them over to the priests, rather than admit that the Flesh Clan defenders were cowards.

The Primordial priests were only too happy to receive the disaffected clansmen, as they had their own mandate to fulfill.

In a solitary camp perched high on the side of the Wailing Mountain, deep within the pass, the disloyal were marched with hands tightly bound in front, a never-ending stream of clansmen. The guards assigned to this duty delivered their prisoners swiftly and without delay, wishing to be away from the encampment full of shivering, wild-eyed priests. The priests' camp never slept except during the daylight, the time from dusk to dawn alive with the scurrying holy men.

Late into the night, the screams of the sacrifices howled through the encampment, flooding down to the tents below, the souls of the sacrifices dancing in the flames of their campfires, confirming the transfer to those who would continue the fight.

Primordial High Priests, clothed in cloaks comprised of leathery-patched skins of unknown origins and embedded with eagle feathers, raised bloody knives to the sky and chanted. The bleeding of the sacrifices was a delicate thing. Too little bleeding and the sacrifices would go into shock before the transfer was complete; too much bleeding and the soul would be lost.

A bare-chested apprentice with only one eagle feather bound to each tattooed arm dipped a hollowed gourd into a basin of potion warming on hot rocks at the edge of the firepit. Carefully, he carried the gourd, brimming with liquid, over to the naked, blindfolded woman staked out spread-eagle on the ground at the edge of the flickering light. With one hand, he pinched her cheeks so that her mouth was forced into an *O* shape then tipped the contents of the gourd into it. He plugged her nose, forcing her to swallow convulsively while she thrashed in her bonds. The blindfold slipped, and the woman's furious eyes stabbed into the apprentice. Then, with the last of her strength, she spat the remains of the potion back in his face. With a scream, he stumbled away from the woman, frantically wiping it off. Everywhere the potion landed, it bubbled and hissed. Blisters erupted, large red swellings bubbling under the skin. They popped and oozed, drying instantly. Within seconds her skin withered, cracking and curling into drifts that feathered to the ground, even while the woman's eyes rolled back in her head.

Blood bloomed where the curls of skin had been, to run in rivulets that joined larger flows. The High Priests crowded around the woman's corpse and caught the blood dripping from her body in gleaming bone vessels. Once the bowls were full to the brim, the High Priests began a rhythmic chant, waving a hollowed rainstick carved with runes over the bowls, seducing the spirit of the blood sacrifice and binding it to the blood for transfer into a new vessel.

The woman's heart pumped valiantly as the last of its life force seeped to the surface. With a final shudder, she relaxed in her bonds, sagging limply in the ropes suspending her body.

The priests turned their backs on the empty shell, and the chanting rose in pitch, calling forth the spirit of the dead woman. Wisps of movement danced on the surface of the bowls of blood, thickening then dissipating, and formed once again, a shadowed impression of a red face floating above the surface of the vessels.

They walked past the line of shivering men, kneeling at the edge of the firelight, arms bound behind their backs, awaiting their turn to serve the High Priests. All of them averted their eyes, hoping to not be chosen, hoping that they would be executed in the normal fashion. Beheading was preferable to being bled to death in their eyes. A whimper escaped the mouth of one of the deserters, as his courage failed once again. With a jerk on his bindings, he was hauled to his feet by two burly apprentices. He howled as he was dragged toward the sacrificial pit.

The High Priests paid no attention to the commotion, transfixed on the process at hand. Their chanting grew louder, the rhythm faster as they approached a small animal tied to a metal stake driven deep into the ground. On closer inspection, a bear cub peered up at the approaching priests, licking its lips hungrily. The priests placed the bowls before the cub, chanting in a singsong voice that soothed it.

Once the priests backed away, the cub sniffed at the offering and then began to lap up the blood thirstily. The priests' song shrieked assailing the ears of the watchers as the bear drank until all the blood was gone.

Suddenly, the song ceased. A gong was sounded, once, twice, three times. As the sound faded from the third gong, the cub roared.

A vortex formed around the cub, spinning and swirling, dragging soil into its maelstrom as it arose, faster and faster, tiny bolts of energy sparking within the cloud, which grew into a funnel then into a tornado, which picked up the cub and whirled it about. Bolts of lightning stabbed the ground and the priests stepped back, hands covering their faces as the sand stung their skin, whipping their eagle feathers until they mocked flight.

With a great clap of thunder and a blinding flash of light, everything stilled.

As the dust cleared, a body was revealed, curled into a ball on the ground. Slowly, it unfurled and rose to its feet.

A muscular woman stood before them, ten feet tall with a face that hinted at the bear cub, but fully human in form. A ruff of tawny hair curled past her broad shoulders. She was clad in a tight-fitting leather jerkin and leggings with a sheath for a great sword strapped to her hip.

Artio sniffed the air with a feral toothy grin and rumbled in the celestial voice of the gods, *"Bow to me."*

As one, the Primordial clansmen and High Priests fell to the ground, their faces pressed to the earth.

Artio drew her lips back and bared her long incisors in a parody of a smile and then bellowed with pleasure.

Chapter 1

Witness

AT THE TOUCH OF GAIUS'S HAND on her shoulder, Avery Tiernan slowly released her hold on the leafy undergrowth, allowing it to relax to its normal position.

A ringlet of dark hair snagged on a twig, threatening to shake the bush and alert the watched to the presence of the watchers. She peered at the tangle out of the corner of her eye then unwound the stray lock, silently praying the faces would remain pressed to the earth.

Freeing her hair, she took one last peek at the scene and locked eyes with the giant bear-like goddess. Artio bared her teeth, and a chuckling grunt issued from her throat. Avery broke contact and scooted back to her companions, hiding behind a large boulder with their horses muzzled. Sharisha urged her to mount up beside her father, Gaius, who was already seated astride his big barrel-chested mare.

As one they fled, urging their mounts into a swift trot, eager to put distance between themselves and the Primordial encampment. Reaching the mountain face, they slowed to a walk and allowed their mounts to pick their way along the sheer mountain goat trail that crisscrossed the rocky face of the mountain. The trail was even more treacherous with only the moon to light the descent. Loose shale threatened to slip out from under the horses' hooves at any given moment.

Sharisha's mount clattered over the last of the stones at the base and disappeared down a level path just as Gaius's mount slipped, hooves sliding out from under it. With a crash, the horse fell onto its side and slid the remaining ten feet to the base of the mountain. Gaius cried out at the lurch and kicked his left leg out of its stirrup, but before he could push himself clear of his mount, it was sliding down the scree. His leg, trapped beneath its bulk, carried him down the mountainside with his horse.

Avery screamed and reined in her snorting mount, afraid that they would follow the mare's sickening slide. Gaius came to an abrupt stop at the base of the mountain, unmoving.

Avery rolled off of the back of her horse, Sunny, and slid down the mountainside after her father, a shower of pebbles dislodged in her wake. She stumbled over to the still form of Gaius and dropped down at his side.

Gaius was lying on his back, a long smear of blood on the rocks highlighting the path as though the furrow of rubble created by the slide of the horse wasn't enough to show the route. His leg was bent at an unnatural angle, but the steady rise and fall of his chest showed he was alive.

Avery reached out with her senses and detected a feeble fluttering pulse in the horse. It lay on its side, two legs broken and bent. The horse could not stand, even if it had the strength to do so.

Avery examined her father, feeling along his arms, checking for broken bones. All seemed fine except for the large purple bruise blooming on his forehead and a nasty scrape along one arm, blood oozing through the torn sleeve.

Gaius was partially buried in the scree which continued to trickle down to rest against the back of the horse. She scooped away the stone rubble with her hands, scrabbling in the dirt to determine if his limbs were actually trapped beneath the dying horse. As she cleared the last of the stones away from his leg, Sharisha knelt down beside her and placed her forefingers to either side of Gaius's temple and closed her eyes. Avery sensed a mystical power flowing from Sharisha, a quiet stream of healing waters that flowed from her and into Gaius. The swelling receded and the bruise faded to green. Gaius's eyes popped open. With a gasp, he attempted to sit up. Avery pushed him back down onto his back.

"How do you feel?" Sharisha's hands dropped to the sides of her woolen skirt, a tiny frown creasing her smooth features.

Gaius blinked at her, licked his lips and his hand wandered to the bruise on his forehead. "I have a headache. Why can't I feel my foot?"

"It is currently lodged under your dead horse." Avery began digging around her father's foot, using a smooth stone to scrape away the loose soil. "Lay still while we free it."

Avery dug furiously, heart pounding, occasionally glancing over her shoulder to check the lip of the mountainside. If they were followed, they were in grave danger, exposed as they were at the base of the hill. *Capture would be as easy as netting smelt in a shallow pool.* The foot shifted as she scooped the soil back with her hands. Gaius leaned back on his hands and pulled on his leg, groaning with pain, as it popped free of its imprisonment under the horse.

Sharisha bent back over his foot, examining the bones and tendons. "It is broken. This is beyond my limited ability to heal. We will have to set his foot." Sharisha walked back to her horse and began searching her saddle bags for bindings.

Avery felt a nudge at her shoulder. Sunny snuffled her fallen companion. She nudged her with her nose and whinnied, encouraging him to rise. She did not stir. Avery reached out with her senses once again, searching for the life force of the horse. The mare was dying, the barest essence remaining. She gathered it to her, thinking to comfort her during her last moments before death. She stroked her soft nose and ran her hand down her neck.

Suddenly, the mare rippled in her vision. The body stilled and a blue mist began to rise from it, swirling from the pores of the skin, leaking from ears and eyes, seeping from every aperture. The mist rose and coagulated, brightening into a pure white form, which solidified and stepped away from the dead horse on the ground.

Shocked, Avery stood up and slowly approached the shimmering unicorn. It stood about three hands in height and was an eye-blinding, virginal white with dainty pink hooves and a spiral horn of striped ebony, protruding from her forehead. Avery extended her hand, and the mare sniffed her fingers then allowed Avery to stroke her nose. Sunny, not to be outdone, whinnied and crowded in to greet the unicorn, anxious to make her acquaintance.

"Where did you come from, pretty one?" Avery whispered to the unicorn. She glanced back over her shoulder and opened her mouth to say, "Isn't she beautiful?" but neither her father nor Sharisha paid them any attention. Sharisha had returned to Gaius's side and was kneeling beside the foot. It was like they couldn't see the unicorn. Avery frowned and stroked the velvety nose. The unicorn leaned into the touch, and a peaceful contentment flowed into Avery, drowning the anxiety of a few moments before.

The unicorn stepped around Avery and approached Sharisha, who was still frowning over Gaius's ankle, purple and blue and clearly crushed.

"There is nothing I can do for this foot." Sharisha shook her head. "My powers of healing do not extend to this kind of injury. It requires more healing spirit than I possess. I will try to bind it as best I can, but the outlook is grave."

She walked back to the woods where Avery noticed she had tied her mount. The horse's ears were pricked forward, and it watched the unicorn with avid interest, prancing where she stood, clearly as eager to greet the unicorn as Sunny had been.

Avery followed the unicorn back to Gaius and watched as she placed the tip of her horn against the mangled flesh. Avery's father groaned at the touch and his eyes rolled back in his head as he fainted. Waves of energy washed from the horn and encased his foot, sinking into the skin and flickering over it with a cold blue flame. The foot writhed and reformed under the skin, the bones mending, the tendons reattaching, the skin smoothing as the foot was repaired. The blue light faded, and the unicorn raised her head. Gaius's mouth dropped open and he began to snore peacefully.

The unicorn wandered back toward the woods, her tiny hooves leaving no trail.

"Wait!" Avery cried. "What is your name?" She felt silly addressing the unicorn this way, as though she understood her speech, but then a thought pressed against her mind.

You may call me Deva, whispered the unicorn. *It means celestial spirit.*

How is it I can hear your thoughts?

We communicate by telepathy. For you to be able to see me and hear me, you are a rare human. She stepped closer to Avery, Deva's sky-blue eyes shining. *We know you, Mother.* She nosed Avery's sleeve, and Avery's arm tingled and then burned. She yelped and pulled up her sleeve. Burnt into her skin was the outline of a unicorn.

Chapter 2

Legend

SHARISHA RETURNED FROM HER SADDLE BAGS, her healer's kit in hand, and jerked to a halt when she saw Gaius snoring away on the ground.

"Did you provide healing for this foot?" She dropped to the ground and lifted it, examining the formerly crushed appendage. She even went so far as to peel off his mangled boot and sock, gazing at the torn leather then at the perfectly pink, albeit dirty, foot.

"Uh." Avery was unsure if she understood what had happened herself. She rubbed the tingling tattoo on her arm, hesitant to share the experience with Sharisha. It felt personal somehow, as though the tattoo was connected to the unicorn in some form.

Sharisha rose from the ground "Well? It seems you have been hiding talents from my knowledge." Avery did not reply. "Wake your father. We must ride!"

Avery bent down and shook her father gently. Abruptly, the snoring ceased. Gaius looked up at her, startled. Then he sat up, his confusion evident in the way he gaped at his naked foot.

"Put on your boot. We have to move on. We will have to double up on Sunny."

Hearing her name, Sunny ambled over, tufts of grass sticking out either side of her muzzle.

Gaius pulled on his sock and boot, his eyes studying his dead mount. Avery tried to help him up, but he shook off her hands.

Nothing showed of his tumble except for the torn leather of his boot and rips in his right pant leg.

They scrambled onto Sunny's back and followed Sharisha's retreating back down the gloomy trail, hurrying to keep her in sight.

Gaius leaned over and whispered into Avery's ear. "Would you care to tell me what that was all about? Clearly, I should not be walking."

Avery looked back over her shoulder, eyes searching for the unicorn, then hugged her father around the middle and whispered the events to him, as softly as she could, keeping her tone low. Her father knew all about her strange abilities to sense the souls of animals and to sense honesty and integrity in others. She and her brother Cayden had been born with special abilities to see the spirit world around them. For this gift, they had been hunted since before they were born. There were those who would do anything to capture a Spirit Shield and the magic they possessed.

"And why do you not want to share this with Sharisha?"

"I don't know, Father. I just feel uncomfortable around her. I know it's silly, but..." Her voice trailed away as Sharisha glanced back over her shoulder, checking their progress.

"You have never been wrong before, Avery. Trust your instincts. I know Cayden would say the same thing."

Cayden...where are you, Cayden? Avery wondered, as she swayed on the back of the horse. He had reached out to her a little while ago, telepathically, but they had been occupied with the Primordial camp and strange actions of the High Priests at that time. She buried her face in her father's back, trying to erase the horrific images that crept behind her eyelids, images of blood and flesh and bone transfigured into a beast of unknown intent.

Maybe she could contact him if she tried. *Cayden, can you hear me? Cayden?*

It had been two months since she had last seen him, since they had fled their home in Sanctuary-by-the-Sea. She remembered him riding away surrounded by legion soldiers and being scared to death that she would never see him again.

Obviously, he had had a much easier time of it than she, and his powers must have grown for him to be able to telepathically contact her as he did. He must have been able to keep his magic hidden, much as she had, or he would have been dead by now.

"Father, can you hear Cayden in your head? Does he whisper to you?"

Gaius shook his head. "No, I cannot contact him as you do. Have you?"

"Yes. He tried to contact me while we were spying on the camp and then again, about two weeks past. He was safe at the time. As much as I detest being separated from him, he seems to have chosen the easier path."

Gaius patted the arm slung around his waist. "Let's hope so, dear one."

Sharisha partially reined in her horse as it danced nervously. "We must move faster. We might be followed. Come!" She heeled her mount into an easy trot, and they fell silent as they sped through the gloom of the woods, slowly brightening with the dawn.

They rode through a stand of sage willow, leggy branches heavy with dew, hugging the edge of a bubbling brook thick with copperhead fronds and blue-spotted mushrooms right to the water's edge. With a large plop, a bullfrog launched itself into the water. Sunny's ears flicked as she marked the frog's passage, which was soon followed by smaller ripples at water's edge. Her nervous eyes attempted to follow every splash. Sunny snorted then danced sideways as she attempted to keep all the frogs in sight.

They followed the gurgling brook for roughly an hour and then veered north and up out of the valley floor, climbing once again toward the join of two rounded hills that sliced through the cliffs.

"Sharisha," Avery called over her father's shoulder. "Are you going to explain that scene we witnessed back there? What was that thing the bear cub turned into?"

Sharisha slowed her mount, allowing them to catch up and ride side by side. "The cub is no longer a cub."

Avery twitched with annoyance. "I saw that. Would you prefer I said 'who was that'?"

Sharisha rode on in silence. Just when Avery thought she did not intend to elaborate, Sharisha spoke. "As you know, legends are legends because the knowledge of what actually occurred has been lost with time. It is no different for the Bear and Thunder Clans. Some scholars believe that there truly were clans that could harness the magic of the bear and the elements such as thunder. But what remains to us is the stories passed down, not factual account. It is from those brief stories that have we gained what little knowledge we currently possess of the ancient clans.

"According to Primordial legend, in the beginning of time great bears roamed the land, much as humanity does today. In those days, they walked upright on hind legs and it is believed they had developed a rudimentary language. They lived in family units and communities, not much different than we do today. There are sacred caves that record generations of the Bear Clans, familial lines drawn out in detail on the smooth walls. Our High Priests believe that they once numbered in the tens of thousands. The remains of large stone communal dwellings can be found in the hills, some of which are still in use today as way stations.

"When the Great Cataclysm occurred, legend has it that the Bear Clans packed up their families and moved deeper into the mountain to escape the anger of the Thunder Clans. No one is sure what happened to the Bear Clans, but by the time that humans came to be, the great Bear Clans had passed into legend.

"One particular scroll, however, gives account of a she-bear princess pregnant with cub, who braved the open elements and against the clan's wishes, left their shelter to speak with the Thunder Clan Chieftain to plead her people's case that all peoples had a right to the land under the sky. The Thunder Clans, beings of air and water, believed that their powers gave them dominion and that the Flesh Clans were beneath them, lowly as the earthworm is lowly. Unsurprisingly, the meeting did not go well.

"Legend speaks of an encounter of sorts at the Great Waterfall, a waterfall so tall it soared higher than the cliffs, the summit swaddled in misty rainbows which arched into heaven itself; the home of the Thunder Clan. Artio of legend was a humble bear maiden, blessed with a she-cub who she swore was fathered by the Thunders when they came to her one evening, when she had fallen asleep after eating magical gooseberries. The Thunders have the ability to take the shape of flesh beings, and that evening, so legend tells us, they came to be with her in the form of a man.

"To Artio, a human descending from the bear clans, her daughter was a gift from the heavens and a bridge between their peoples. She gave her daughter her own name and believed that if she could get the Thunders to accept her child, then she could bring peace to their peoples.

"So, she started out on a solo quest to the Great Waterfall, hoping to be granted an audience with the Thunders in the sky. The journey was hard, carrying her child on her back in a papoose, feeding her Thunder-cub daughter magical gooseberries that she found by the path side and jiggling her pack soothed the cub to sleep. All the while she planned her words, knowing she would have but a short time to convince the aloof Thunders.

"She arrived at the Great Waterfall just as the sun was setting, and the waters blazed as though lit from within by a fire. She called to the Thunders, but the roar of the waters was too great and no one heard her.

"Finally, in desperation, she began to climb the rocky face of the waterfall, slippery with moss and water. All the while, she called, 'Thunders, hear my cry. Thunders, hear my plea. Come greet our child, the union of our peoples. We can live in peace and harmony for look what nature has wrought? Thunders, hear my cry. Thunders, hear my plea.'

"She climbed and climbed and eventually she reached the clouds. She was afraid that they could not bear her weight, so she put her papoose down to test their strength. Her cub, well-rested from being carried all the way to the falls and up to the sky, climbed out of the papoose and with a giggle, ran across the clouds and onto a rainbow, laughing the entire way as the rainbows tickled her feet. The maiden called to her daughter to return, but the child cub ran on, the tickling colours creating tones that blended into a tinkling song.

"When the maiden attempted to step onto the cloud, however, her foot sank through the mist. She could not follow her cub. Just then, the last rays of the setting sun pierced the clouds and they vanished as if they had never been. In the blink of an eye, the rainbows faded and along with them, her cub."

Avery waited for more. Sharisha rode in silence, her face pinched in a pensive frown.

"And?" Avery asked "What happened next?"

"No one knows," Sharisha replied. "Legend does not tell us."

"And the princess?" *The story could not end there,* Avery thought.

"No one knows."

Avery drew in a deep, frustrated breath. *What was it that was born in that clearing? Or perhaps the better question is who?*

Chapter 3

The Hunt Begins

CYRUS DISMOUNTED FROM HIS FINE CHESTNUT GELDING, handing the reins off to a soldier stationed at the entrance to Alcina's tent. It was easily picked out in the sea of military canvas. The tent was black, slashed with red, displaying the colours of the now-outlawed Queen's Guard and announcing her presence in the camp. It stood tall enough that he could enter the doorway without bending.

The guards saluted and retracted their crossed pikes, allowing entry. A pageboy, dressed in leggings and livery, announced his arrival in a high-pitched voice that cracked on his name. "The Lord Cyrus attends you, my queen."

The first weak rays of the rising sun pierced the tent as he entered, striping the woven red carpet that formed the floor.

Alcina reclined in a sedan chair covered in brightly woven tapestry, a delicate mug cupped between her palms. She sipped at the tea, watching him approach, then placed the cup on a carved bone table and stretched out one lacquered hand.

Cyrus swept his helm from his head, bent on one knee and lightly grasped her hand, kissing her fingers, then released them. "You have need of me, my queen?"

Alcina studied his bent head, observing the thinning thatch forming on the crown. He, too, showed signs of age; time was making fools of them both. Why, she had found a grey hair that morning amidst her own luxurious mane of ebony. A tiny frown creased her brow at the remembrance.

"Rise," she commanded. Cyrus rose then ran his hand over his bald spot as though he could feel her eyes on it. "I understand we have a captive?"

"Yes, Your Majesty. We captured one of the tree-climbing monkeys they use for scouts."

"And?" she prompted.

"He has been placed under guard and will be questioned thoroughly."

Alcina picked up her teacup and drummed her nails on the side, thinking. "I wish to question him myself."

"My queen?"

"I will not have a repeat of the fiasco with that boy Cayden who usurped my throne. I will know what is happening, every minute of every day. I wish to be present for all interrogations." She glared at Cyrus. "In fact, I should conduct the interrogations myself. It is obvious no one else knows the correct questions to ask or how to ask them. I will crush them like bugs under my heel. They will tell me everything they know." Cyrus bowed in acceptance. "When is the interrogation scheduled?"

"At noon, my queen," Cyrus replied.

She nodded and then, stretching, rose from the sedan chair. "There is one other matter I wish to speak to you about." She waved her hand dismissing the servants in attendance. They departed the tent, leaving Alcina and Cyrus alone to speak in private. As the hem of the last skirt disappeared out of the tent flap, Alcina murmured softly, "The Great Mistress spoke to me in my dreams. She showed me a vision of a girl, one with Primordial features. She travels with two companions, an older gentleman and a woman who could be a Primordial Seeker. We are to find this girl at all costs. The Great Mistress warns that she has the power to unite the Primordial factions. She can undo the chaos we have sown here."

Alcina paced to the far side of the tent and touched a shriveled scalp that hung from a canvas tent pole. The hair was silky, soft, and jet black. "While their eyes are set on each other in suspicion, while they attack and kill their own in religious civil war, they are easy to control and eventually eliminate. United, however, they would become a tidal wave that could crush our armies. Continue with the attacks on the outlying villages, and be sure our elite forces leave a trail of clues implicating the other Primordial faction. Be sure that they are so focused on each other that they are virtually blind to our passing."

Cyrus bowed once again. "I will make finding the girl my personal task. I will take a small group of elites and we will find her. Along the way, we will sow seeds of distrust, starting with the Primordial scouts. If she exists, if she is more than rumour, we will find her."

Cyrus saluted, spun on his heel, and marched from the tent.

Alcina stroked the silky black hair again and smiled.

*   *   *

Cyrus straightened as he released the tent flap. The guards snapped crossed-pikes at his back as he strode away. The Great Mistress had also come to him during the night with the same vision. He saw no reason to share this with Alcina, however. He was unsure if the Great Mistress had communicated precisely the same instructions to both of them or if Alcina was aware that the Great Mistress had begun to visit him. Caution meant he was content to keep his own counsel.

For instance, Alcina had failed to communicate that the girl they sought was the twin sister of the boy Cayden, who now sat on the throne of Cathair, the very throne that had been Alcina's. All this time, they had believed they were looking for one heir, when there were actually two. They were twin usurpers to the throne, a throne that he had been promised to share. It was a pretty large piece of information to withhold.

He rubbed his jaw as he strode along, considering his next move. He was content to allow Alcina to sit in the queen's chair, as in truth, the position was restrictive. As a pretty figurehead, she was always surrounded by fawning servants, counselors, and nobles. She could not do as he did: stroll amongst the men to get the feel of the battle, belly up to the bar in a local tavern and hear the latest gossip, or slip between the sheets in a brothel and find out what the local scheming lords and ladies were up to.

Yes, for now, his position allowed him a freedom to move his chess pieces around the board in whatever fashion brought him the best position, the greatest advantage.

He strode through the camp, acknowledging the salutes as he passed with a lazy wave. His destination was the prisoner's tent. Conveniently located next to the horse lines, the black smithy's tent provided a steady supply of red hot irons, a favourite method of the inquisitors of the legion. The closer Cyrus got to the tent, the greater the smell of burning: burning wood, burning coal, burning leather, burning skin, burning hair. The smells mixed obnoxiously with the odours of horse and human manure from the hastily dug latrines located nearby.

A square grey tent swelled into sight guarded by four sentries, one stationed at each corner. At the flap of the entrance, two more guards stood. Cyrus bent to enter the tent, ignoring their salutes.

He straightened then gazed down at the prisoners staked to the ground. Three men stared back at him, stripped to the waist, hands and feet bound, stretched vertically, and tied to wooden stakes driven into the ground. At the sight of him, their eyes widened. Sweat broke out on their foreheads.

The tent flap opened again and an inquisitor, dressed in a boiled leather jerkin and linen shirt, entered the tent. The ties of his shirt hung loose, the mat of chest hair glistening with sweat. Two glowing tongs were clutched in his hands.

Cyrus grinned. How he enjoyed his freedom. Three men…and Alcina only needed one.

Chapter 4

Cathair

CAYDEN WANDERED THE CASTLE, familiarizing himself with its layout. It was immense. Originally it had been a stone hunting lodge, a vacation home for the first noble family of Cathair. Additions had been built onto it over the centuries until present day where it sprawled over a full acre of land and stood four stories tall.

The wall walk was Cayden's favourite place to be, for he could pace around the upper reaches and see the stretch of land in all directions. Up that high, he finally found peace from the whispers of the dead and the demands of the living, a constant cacophony of noise that intruded on his waking hours.

The original lodge now served as the central kitchens. Even at this early hour, the lodge hummed with activity—cooks frying eggs and bacon, pulling loaves of toasty corn bread out of the hearth, and whipping fresh cream into a soft butter blended with honey. Cayden sniffed as he walked past. His stomach growled, but he did not pause. Breakfast would have to wait.

He entered a covered alcove and pulled open the heavy wooden door that housed the Royal Cathairian Library. Generations of Cathairians had collected and stored the most fragile of works in the library, which was rumoured to have existed before the lodge, as a center of learning. Just as the castle was littered with catacombs so the library had an equally elaborate and wholly uncharted underground.

Cayden pulled the door shut behind him and paused to allow his eyes to adjust to the dim recesses. No candles burned in the building, no open flame, no oil lanterns. Instead, the interior was lit by a large parabolic mirror that hung in the dome of the ceiling and reflected the light of the sun, and was mounted on a clever array of gearings that allowed it to be moved and kept in precise alignment with the sun during the daylight hours, constantly gathering the sun's rays, even on the cloudiest of days, and redirecting them into the cavernous room.

The first time Cayden entered the library in the evening, he carried a lantern that he'd used to light his way. Unknown to him, lanterns were to be left on the hanging peg in the portico. The only thing that had saved him from the wrath of the librarian named Brennus was the fact that Mordecai had already preceded him into the library and was able to fend off the broom-wielding caretaker.

"No flame in the library, you foolish boy!" Brennus had shrieked with a wild light in his eye. The fact that his hair stood on end like the ruff of an angry rooster only enhanced his menacing profile. Cayden ducked, and the broom swished over his head before halting mysteriously in midair. It was then that Brennus truly looked at Cayden. He gaped at the royal robes that Cayden was forced to wear. Brennus's jaw had snapped shut with an audible click as realization dawned.

"Brennus, I would like you to meet our new king. Sire, this is Brennus, archival librarian, at your service." Mordecai snapped his fingers, and the broom in Brennus's hands vanished.

Brennus bowed low to Cayden, hands on knees in apology. "My apologies, Sire. I did not realize that it was you."

"It is nothing." Cayden lowered his hands from the anticipated strike. "The fault is mine. I did not stop to think about whether flame is allowed in the library." Cayden frowned. Now that Mordecai had moved, he saw that the library was lit. While it did not have the full brightness of daylight, it did contain enough light should one wish to read. It was Cayden's turn to be amazed. His mouth fell open in surprise.

Mordecai chuckled. "Perhaps, Brennus, you should show your king through your domain and explain why he doesn't need a flame."

Brennus bowed low again. "Sire, will you follow me?" He tentatively tugged on Cayden's arm and pulled him through the library, babbling away about the mirrors and sunlight and the glow bulbs and the gods providing light in the darkest of days.

"What he means, Cayden, is that the wizards of old were rather good at alchemy. It's a simple enough combination, a mixture of basic elements. Strontium and aluminate come to mind and oxygen, a bit of heat, some tweaking of the crystalline, and you have these—phosphorus crystals. For colour, I like to add a pinch of fruit juice. Gives off a nice aroma when it heats up and the colour is truer. It's quite simple, really." He rocked back on his heels admiring the handiwork as though it was his own.

Perhaps it *was* Mordecai's work. Cayden wasn't quite sure.

The dome structure set into the library ceiling was huge and sat on the stone walls of the circular room like half an egg, the top "whites" made of an opaque glasswork and the bottom "yolk" covered in glittering frescos depicting the gods and ancient wars long forgotten. The never-ending scene morphed from one view to another, and Cayden found himself wanting to lie down on the slate floors and gaze up at the artwork. The reliefs were so precise that they appeared three-dimensional.

Crystalized scenes of forests, rushing waters, and towering mountains, of fishing boats and rolling fields of poppies, all scenes from across the kingdom flowed down the walls and framed the stained-glass windows evenly spaced within the stone walls. These were wedged between large bookcases, jammed with scrolls and leather-bound books and blocks of parchment, each bookcase set with its own rolling ladder.

Tables were scattered throughout the library and some reading nooks with pillowed seating placed under the stained glass. On every table and mounted in the nook was a round sphere encased in crystal, glittering with a fresco of the gods.

After that first rocky introduction, the library became Cayden's favourite haunt. He spent a great amount of time in the library, seeking to learn about his kingdom, its history and its people, especially since his greeting on arrival had been less than thunderous applause. Mordecai set him to reading the history of Cathair and its rulers, trying to catch up on seventeen years of education lost to him, an education that would have been provided by his royal parent. His father Gaius, the only one he had ever known, had taught him and Avery to read, but books had been scarce and he found the older texts housed in the library difficult to decipher. While the texts were legible, the syntax of language used had changed, so that he found himself referencing other writings to try to sort out the convolutions of the language structure and word choice in context. It was laborious and grueling work at times simply to get through a text.

Yesterday, however, Cayden had stumbled across a reference that had made his heart lurch. He'd gasped aloud, reading the text five times to be sure of what it said.

He hurried back to the book and pulled it once again from the shelf. It was heavy, the parchment yellowed and cracked, the pages stiff and bound by heavy leather-wrapped wooden covers and embossed with gold lettering. He carried it to his favourite alcove, the stained glass depicting the Well of Souls. While it did not look anything like the real well, it did manage to capture the essence of the place. The flattened angels faced each other, crowded around the edges of the window, golden horns raised in triumphant call.

He placed the book on the table and ran his hand over the embossed lettering, muttering under his breath, *"Na Déithe de Antiquity Cogadh Chéad"* (*The Gods of Antiquity, First War*). Then he opened the book to the page that had caught his eye and ran his finger down to the spot where he had left off reading.

The birth of four children was a strange twist of fate, for the ancient gods normally abstained from earthly entertainments. It was regarded as the height of folly to intercede in mortal affairs, yet one Ancient could not resist the temptation to dabble in mortal pleasures. Morpheus, the God of Dreams, was captivated by woman named Calleigh, who was fair to look upon. Morpheus began visiting her in her dreams, and there they conceived. In one day, the children were born. The Ancients banned Morpheus from their celestial home and cast him to the earth to wander and learn the folly and futility of a mortal life.

Morpheus and Calleigh did not name their four children until their godly gifts became apparent. Artio was the eldest, a lover of the sky and the celestial wonders beyond the earth. One particular constellation, shaped like a bear cub fascinated her and so Calleigh named the child. She was soon followed by the true twins Caerwyn, the fortress, and his twin sister, Alfreda, the mother of the lands. The true twins shared an affinity and some say a shared soul. Unlike their siblings, the true twins could sense each other at all times and read each other's thoughts. They were said to be one person in two bodies. Alfreda would gift a new people to the earth, a people known as the Primordials. Lastly the youngest, Helga, displayed an affinity for the dead, for things that were ready to return to the earth.

In time, jealous squabbles broke out between the godlings. Morpheus, in an attempt to create peace, separated his children into different spheres of influence. Artio was given dominion over the sky, moon, and stars and was tasked with managing the movements of the heavenly bodies. Caerwyn and Alfreda were sent to work with the souls of the earth, each within their affinity. Alfreda was given charge of the souls of the animal kingdom, for their rebirth was as necessary as a human soul. Caerwyn was given carriage of the souls of humanity and charged with caring for them until it was time for their rebirth. Helga was given charge over the recycling of the earth, the plants, the trees, and the bodies of the dead. As the winter witch, she absorbed the decay of humanity and buried it deep in a blanket of white, one season a year. She created a restful environ for the deceased awaiting rebirth. While it was cold above, it was not so in her mountain home where the fires of punishment burned hot, providing a warm core for the awakening of the world in spring. She was also set as the caretaker of the damned, those souls who were beyond redemption and could not be reborn because of the corruption of their natures.

For a time, they were content within their roles and millennia passed, days fading to years, years fading to centuries. Morpheus returned to the gods on Calleigh's death, leaving the godlings to care for the world.

One day Artio, the moon godling, slumped to the horizon, blood red. Helga found her oozing a bloody light across the heavens. Convinced that she was dying, Helga carried her sister into the bowels of the earth. The dark stilled Artio's light. Helga believed that she would be reborn like the rest of the mortals of the earth, but the godling had no one to care for her rebirth, and was forever lost.

Legend had it that Caerwyn and Alfreda banished Helga to the depths of the underworld, never to return, for the crime of slaying a godling.

Cayden lifted his head from the book and pinched the bridge of his nose. *The names are too close,* he thought, thinking about the legend, *especially knowing now what I know about my own abilities.*

He needed to speak to Mordecai. Surely, he knew the legends. It was time for a serious chat.

Chapter 5

Faylea

AVERY WAS CERTAIN she could not retrace the twisting path taken by Sharisha despite the frequent glimpses of the massive tree that was their destination. It sat on the horizon, towering above the swampy plain, dominating the skyline.

The humidity increased as they traveled through the dense swamp, snaking along drier patches of surface roots that clung to the water's edge. The jumbled matting of the thirsty willows created a boardwalk of sorts, wide enough for the horses to traverse safely. Avery's damp shirt clung to her back as did her father's, sticking to his sweaty torso. Avery's head swiveled as she took in the landscape, her mouth opened in awe. The journey had taken the better part of a week even though they had rested infrequently.

The last bridge they crossed extended longer than those previous, rising up out of the swamp and dispensing the travelers onto a wooden platform that ended in an intricately carved archway and an ironwood gate. The gate stood thirty hands tall and was carved straight through the center of an enormous oak tree the crown of which disappeared into the mists. Carved onto the surface of the door were symbols that Avery could not read.

Sharisha rode up to the door and placed her palm on a circular rune on the right side. The rune glowed, and a cloud of blue and white mist swirled around her hand. She withdrew it, and the door swung open. Avery glimpsed a miniature three-dimensional world, like a view through a magnifying glass, before the rune faded back to wood.

"This is the sacred city of Faylea." Sharisha sat straight in her saddle, her bearing regal. "Humans have not been permitted past this door in over a millennium. Not all will be pleased to grant you access."

Gaius tapped the sides of the horse, urging Sunny forward. Sunny's ears swiveled in interest, then pricked forward. "Is it safe for Avery to enter here? I care not for the politics of the land, only my daughter's safety."

Sharisha frowned at him for the interruption.

"You will be safe for you are with me, but I would warn you that to wander off on your own would not be wise. Follow me." She disappeared through the open doorway of the tree.

Sunny frisked through the opening, her nostrils flaring. She swished her tail and seemed excited about whatever she smelled on the other side. The tunnel ran straight as an arrow through the middle of the great tree and at the end, a shaft of brilliant white light illuminated the exit. Beyond the light a dense wood was just visible.

As they crossed the threshold, they drew rein. The sacred city of Faylea spilled from the hillside and lay cupped in a bowl of vibrant green moss that coated every inch of ground. Great purple-spotted toadstools, taller than Avery's horse, towered like trees above twisting paths creating a polka-dot patchwork of shade across the forest floor. Giant ribbed ferns, planted in curving rows, formed the walls of abodes, the leafy reaches interwoven to create roofs. No house was straight but copied the shape of the ferns, gently bending and curving with the will of the greenery.

Avery was mesmerized. *The houses are alive!* She slid off Sunny and walked to the edge of the hillside to drink in the scene. Waves of harmony washed over her. Tears sprang to her eyes as she felt the first tentative touch from the sentient growth before her. The intertwined ferns acted as a group conscience, as a single entity with millions of parts, all working cohesively. Avery closed her eyes to better hear the whispered greetings and peace flowed over her.

Sharisha watched as Avery's mouth quirked and twitched with smiles, staring in the direction of the city. Sharisha did not smile.

"Avery, I think Sharisha is waiting to move on." Avery's eyes popped open, and she broke the telepathic contact she was experiencing with the plant life and walked back to her father, who gave her a boost into the saddle behind him.

Without a word, Sharisha urged her mount onto the meandering path that trailed to the base of the bowl. The trail followed whatever curve the land chose to take, but it did take them down. As they passed the fern dwellings, Primordial children poked their heads out of the round windows, curious at the strangers in their midst. They tumbled out of the doorways and followed them, a whispering and giggling processional that swelled in number.

Avery smiled at them and waved, and a pretty girl not yet to puberty offered her a flower filled with a shimmering liquid. Avery reached down and took the flower, smiling her thanks. The girl mimed drinking. Hesitant, Avery lifted the cup of petals to her lips and took a dainty sip. The girl giggled and clapped her hands with joy. The nectar was sweet and light with a slight strawberry taste and left refreshing bubbles on Avery's tongue. It quenched her thirst instantly, and she passed it forward for her father to drink.

At the edge of a stream, Sharisha stopped and dismounted. "We must walk from this point. Those who approach the heart of Faylea must do so on their own feet as a display of respect for the sanctity of all life. Leave your things. They and the horses will be cared for." She dropped her reins and stepped onto the rose-quartz bridge that spanned the babbling brook. The children did not follow as they stepped off onto a stone path on the other side.

The rose gravel crunched under their feet. Now that she was walking the earth, Avery felt a vibration through the soles of her shoes, the rhythm of a heartbeat. The path widened and ended at a clearing flooded with sunlight. At its center stood a shimmering white temple which rose from the ground in stacked squares and stood six stories tall. At every corner, a legendary beast was carved, climbing up the wall to the floor of the next level.

Every inch of wall was decorated with symbols and pictures. On the first level, the motifs were of plants and plant life, the second of aquatic life, and the third of land animals including depictions of humans. The fourth level showed the spirits of both man and beast, and the fifth was carved with fantastical creatures of myth. The final level displayed only four images; each image was shown only once on its own wall and the deeply carved relief covered the entire surface. An alabaster spike rose from the peak, soaring into the sky.

Avery's eyes climbed the entire structure, taking in the varied images sunk into the marble façade. A matching marble staircase wide enough for four people to walk abreast completed the structure. Ten steps began at the end of the path and ended at a railed landing in front of two wooden doors. A crystal chime sang out, and the doors opened, inviting them to enter.

Avery, her heart beating in rhythm to the cadence of the earth, walked up the stairs, ignoring everyone around her. The call of the temple pulled her forward in a near trancelike state. Sharisha matched her stride to Avery's, mounting the staircase on her left side while Gaius fell in on Avery's right. Avery felt no fear; what she felt was peace. *This is home. I've come home.*

The minute Avery crossed the threshold of the sanctuary, she felt a surge of contentment. A breeze tossed her curls, and she opened her arms to the wind that called her name. Avery breathed deeply and took another step into the interior. In that instant, with a blinding flash of light, the others vanished.

Chapter 6

The Pact

ARTIO SURVEYED THE PROSTRATE FORMS before her. The smell of blood was thick on the air, coppery and cloying, clinging to the waves of heat emanating from the firepit that lit the clearing. She shook her head, stretching newly formed muscles, exploring the motion and connection of her new body. She raised her arm and examined it. Taut muscles flowed from shoulder to wrist, covered in a short, light brown hair that glistened in the firelight. She flexed her fingers, nails rounded and slightly claw-like. Her legs were similarly constructed, thighs strong, calves rounded and corded. She could run for miles. She knew it.

Ah! This is a great body! she thought, dismissing the cub's sacrifice. *For too long, I have been imprisoned amongst the stars!*

Arthmael, the High Priest of the Bear Clan, rose from the ground, bowing and scraping constantly. He peeked from under his headdress and, in a quivering voice, spoke to his god.

"Great One! We are your faithful servants. We have not forgotten. We woke you from your slumber amongst the stars as was prophesied. The elder scrolls promised this day. We alone of all the Primordial peoples remembered the old ways and have safeguarded the secrets of the origins of the gods. We call upon you, Celestial One, to help us in our time of need."

Artio ignored the mutterings of the human, engrossed in the inspection of her new form. As a goddess amongst the stars, she'd observed the scurrying on the planet below, and she had been an avid admirer from afar. Their lives were fleeting. In a blink of an eye, they were born, lived, and died, yet they believed their lives to be of importance and hurried here and there, building this and tearing down that, yet nothing of permanence remained.

Not like me. I am immortal. I could end their pathetic lives here and now, squash them under my heel, grind them into the dirt they were born of...but no, I must learn more. I must understand why they have summoned me now.

Artio spoke with a voice like a rumble of thunder. *"Why have you called me back from my home in the stars? Speak! I will know the truth of it."*

The High Priest cried out at the thunderous clap of her voice, hands over his ears.

"There is great unrest in the world, Celestial One!" he cried. "Our people are divided. The Spirit Clans have blocked access to the temple and to the gods. We cannot approach and pray as we once did or perform the rituals of your people in sight of the temple. They bar our access to the gods."

"Yet a goddess stands before you. I care not for your petty schemes and squabbles. My purpose is set apart from yours," she boomed.

One particularly bold priest, firelight dancing off his shining bald pate, dared to raise his head and make eye contact. He shivered at the ageless depth, the bottomless pit of black reflected in the eyes staring back at him.

"Great One, the temple is only accessible by the gods. There are rumours of one such as you approaching the temple as we speak. If they enter, they will have control and dominion over the temple. Should you not seize it for yourself?"

Artio glared at the man and crossed her arms, considering his words. *"Where is this...temple?"* she rumbled. *"Take me to it! If it is a temple of the gods, I will have it for my own. There you will worship me!"*

The priest turned to the prostrate men, swiping at a trickle of sweat rolling down the side of his face. "Rise! We march for the sacred city of Faylea."

*   *   *

Artio followed the little men, taking one step for every six of theirs. With her superior height, she could see over the top of the priests, who led the procession through the trees. The winding mountain pass through which they traveled was familiar.

She frowned, trying to capture the illusive memory that tickled within her omnipotent brain. She was somewhat disgusted with the bestial form the priests had recalled her to, despite its efficiency. No thunder god would ever be tied to such a menial form. The gods of the sky viewed themselves as a superior life form to the flesh that crawled beneath them. The body did, however, seem familiar. She searched vast epochs of memory, trying to pin down the thought to a time and place. True, she had virtually slept for eons of time, nestled amongst the stars, but it had not always been so.

The Thunder Clan had once ruled the primitives of the land. They had sent the rains and withheld their blessings in punishment. They had controlled the snows in the mountain watersheds and had filled the primitives' wells with water from underground reservoirs. They had been their caretakers until the rebellion.

Artio and the priests climbed steadily for half the day. By noon the sun revealed a sheltered bowl of a valley, nestled between two curving windswept ridges. Large boulders as tall as Artio were scattered about, as though a giant fist had tossed marbles across the valley in a game of chance.

"What is this place?" Artio rumbled, her voice causing a covey of birds to burst from the treetops and the High Priests to cover their ears.

"It is believed it was a bear community long abandoned, Great One. Little is known about the ancient peoples who lived here, as that history is lost to us, but there are curious drawings in caves set against the sides of the valley. Would you like to see them?"

"It would please me to see these drawings."

The priests led Artio over to a section of rock that formed part of the crater wall. A toppled pillar, long and octagonal, blocked the entrance to a cave. Similar columns were scattered around, as though a child played a massive-sized game of pick-up sticks. Artio craned her neck sideways to study the stones. Stood upright and set back in their proper placement, the ruins would create an ancient stone framework for a doorway.

Artio bent down and rubbed at the face of the rock, scraping away moss and lichens that clung to deep grooves. Pictures appeared along with squiggles and lines. Artio pulled away the rest of the clinging growth.

A carving was revealed. It appeared to be of bears walking about on their hind legs much like Artio did, but these bears were purely animal in form as depicted in the pictures. The bears were dressed in rudimentary clothing and carried pouches that might have contained arrows, although the fine lines had been swallowed by time and exposure to the elements.

Artio straightened back up and approached the dark opening in the rock. Two slabs of granite were wedged together, the right slab having fallen against the left, barring entrance. Artio grabbed the right slab and heaved. With a grinding noise, she shifted the door to the side, leaving just enough room for Artio to pass through. She straightened on the other side and took two strides into the cavern.

Her entrance activated a ring of soft glowing lights, suspended at ceiling height around the perimeter of the cave. It pushed back the darkness, and the cavern was illuminated.

The High Priests paused in the entrance of the cave, unsure whether they were permitted to enter a place where a god was honoured with light.

A heavy layer of dust covered every surface, yet it was easy to pick out the objects in the room.

Stone benches were set in rows, facing a raised platform at the far end of the cavern. On the platform sat a massive granite throne, carved out of the wall itself.

The surface was decorated with leaves and trees and animal shapes that once inhabited the valley. Every carving was crusted with jewels: fat emeralds made leaves on vines flash as if moved by a breeze, flaming rubies gilded butterfly wings, yellow citrine graced the bodies of canaries, and diamonds accentuated the spiral horns of unicorns. In the muted light cast from overhead, the chair seemed alive.

Artio climbed the dais and sat down in the throne, running her hands along the arms of the chair. It was sized perfectly.

The priests, frozen in the doorway, gasped and backed away from the opening, bowing as they did so.

Artio had no need of other temples. The Goddess of the Forgotten Temple had returned home at last.

Chapter 7

The Temple

WITH AVERY'S THIRD STEP, she entered a wild forest teeming with plant life. Great trees soared to the heavens, shading the riot of plant life. It flourished and bloomed in every conceivable colour, covering the forest floor. Great ferns and prickly bushes bursting with sweet red, yellow, and blue fruit; toadstools and tender shoots perfect for nibbling; and snaking vines weighed down by large trumpet-shaped flowers dripping with nectar.

Every inch of space was alive. As Avery took another step, the plant life reached for her. Tendrils of roots wrapped gently around her torso, burning her clothing where they touched her. It did not hurt; it felt more like a caress. Mesmerized, Avery pushed on through the undergrowth, careful to not harshly tread on the living presence she felt all around.

With her next step, the forest disappeared and became open skies and a great plain of waving grasses as far as the eye could see. Every type of grain and grass was present and all burned against her clothing as she passed, causing her to lose more clothing to the brushing blades of grass.

With her sixth step, the plant life faded, and she found herself swimming in an ocean. A dolphin swam up to her. Without pausing to think about it, Avery grabbed onto its dorsal fin and was pulled along beside the dolphin. They flashed over barrier reefs teeming with a kaleidoscope of fin and shellfish, eels and sharks—prey and predators alike. As they paraded past her, they touched her hand in greeting or brushed against another part of her and more clothing melted away, even though the water was cool and pleasant. Avery did not give a care for her growing nakedness. There was no sense of shame in this world. She was mesmerized by the vibrant aquatic life surrounding her. Great whales glided into view, and she reached out to touch them as they passed. Bubbles greeted her, and the bubbles glided along her torso as they passed with the sensation of a caress.

The dolphin glided back to shore, and Avery let go as her feet touched the bottom. The scene transformed into a freshwater lake, teeming with brightly coloured salmon and croaking frogs, salamanders and crayfish. They swirled around her, more fish species than she could identify, trout and bass and catfish, all greeting her as the ocean had. She felt their joy at their reunion, and her heart was full of her love for the creatures of the planet she called home.

She took another step, and the scene changed.

The few remaining tatters of clothing left dried instantly and clung to her body as she stepped back onto land. Giraffes and lions, gazelles and cheetahs all flowed toward her, greeting her with purrs and chuckles and lipped kisses, tugging at the remnants of her clothing. Avery touched them all, stepping into all the areas of the earth and welcoming every form of animal life. The vast plains were now full of animal life, including signs of human habitation.

All approached her except the human life. Avery saw them on the horizon, but they did not come close. She tried to walk closer to them, but they were like smoke, slipping away before her steps. Only one man approached her, a grizzled elder, dressed in nothing but a prayer pouch girded about his loins.

"Elder! I am so pleased to greet you!" Avery said to the short wiry-haired man.

The elder tilted his head to one side, studying her. Avery had the impression she was being weighed and judged.

His face split open in a toothless grin, and he reached inside his prayer pouch and pulled out a handful of odd objects. Four knuckle bones; some smooth rocks; several different kinds of feathers, some brightly coloured, some not; a long jagged tooth; and several jet-black claws, curved and razor sharp decorated the palm of his hand. He showed them to Avery then put them back in the pouch. He took the prayer pouch off and handed it to Avery, who strapped it around her waist.

When she looked up from belting it on, he was gone.

Avery took another step and paused at the sight before her. Fantastical creatures of every shape and size surrounded her. They were not randomly arranged. They appeared to have been waiting for her, as though holding counsel and she was the guest speaker. As she thought this, suddenly she found herself standing on a platform made of rock in the center of a natural arena, the glassy slopes rising away from the center, filled with creatures of myth and legend.

A bronze-winged lion, eight feet tall, stood shoulder to shoulder with an emerald-green dragon, puffs of smoke curling from its great nostrils. Both bowed to Avery as she spun slowly in a circle, taking in her surroundings. Proud manticores and hairy leprechauns; grey-feathered griffins and muscled werewolves; shimmering jewelled fae and ghastly ghouls crowded in around the dais, while flaming phoenixes and Pegasuses soared overhead. Avery even spied a thunderbird perched on the crest of a timbered temple as she completed her circle.

"Hello!" she called to the creatures, knowing, somehow, that they would understand her words. "I am so pleased to meet you!"

The crowd of creatures parted, and an unusual sight greeted Avery's eyes. A snow-white unicorn with a long spiral horn of purest crystal stepped daintily toward the platform, each hoof displacing tiny rainbows of light as it pranced towards Avery. On the unicorn's back was an even stranger sight. At first Avery mistook it for a tree, but as it came closer, the figure dissolved into the shape of a man, green of skin and hair and clothed in a moss tunic and living woven grasses, the tassels of the stalks fringing his boots of willow bark. A beard of curly leaves decorated his face and head and wise old eyes of jet black locked onto hers. Avery's mouth stretched into a broad smile, for this was someone she could understand.

"Uncle!" she cried and jumped down from the dais to greet the Green Man.

"Alfreda. It has been too long!" He swung down from the unicorn and embraced her, smoothing her hair.

A memory stirred in Avery at the name he used. It was a name she was familiar with, one she had not used in a very, very long time. She frowned and released her uncle, who continued to smile down at her.

"Remember!" he commanded and placed a finger in the form of slender branch to her temple.

Memories, centuries and eons old, cascaded into her mind. Images flashed before her, and the room spun. The amount of information was mind-boggling, and she cried out at the rush, the pressure of the intense knowledge transfer overwhelming her. With a scream, she collapsed to the floor.

Chapter 8

A Wizard's Answer'

ZIONA ROUNDED THE CORNER of the hallway leading away from the kitchens and ran smack into Cayden. A startled *"Ooph"* escaped her lips before she straightened, clutching his shoulder.

"Ziona, I'm sorry!" His arm curved around her, supporting her until she caught her breath.

"Why are you sprinting blindly around corners, Cayden?" She rubbed her stomach.

"Mordecai. I need to talk to Mordecai. Have you seen him?"

"Not since breakfast. He mumbled something about 'exorcising the deadwood' and wandered away with a scone clutched in his hand."

"The greenhouses. He is in the gardens." Cayden grabbed Ziona's hand and pulled her along behind him. "This is of concern to you too. Come on."

"Wait for your guard, Cayden! You know you can't go running off without them anymore." She slowed her steps, forcing Cayden to tow her along, allowing the pair of Kingsmen shadowing them to catch up. Cayden glanced back, frowning at the men. "Are you trying to lose them?" she asked.

"No! Well, not intentionally," he groused, "but I wouldn't be sorry if I did. I never have any time to myself anymore."

Ziona matched his stride as they left the castle through a side door and crossed a short courtyard. They entered the walled gardens via an arched stone entrance, pushing open the iron-wrapped gate which squealed in the damp air. A stone path curved right and left off the main trunk, like the limbs of a very organized tree, leading to various branches of plantings. A muffled buzzing sound reached their ears. With a grin, Cayden strode toward the farthest corner where fruit trees were planted in orderly rows. The limbs of the apple trees were dotted with thumb-sized swellings that would in a few months be bright red apples, ready for harvest.

The buzzing grew louder. The leaves parted, and there stood an old man, his flowing white beard and hair standing on end like a fuzzy dandelion, waving his skinny arms at a cross of sticks that hovered above the ground. It was covered in a light canvas material, stretched tightly, and a breeze created by the wizard accounted for the buzzing sound as it moved over the surface of the canvas.

"What is that?" Cayden's eyes followed the object as it floated into the air.

"It is a kinetic instrument trying to escape." He grinned, watching them mouth out the words, their faces puzzled. "It's called a kite." When they still looked puzzled, he waved them closer.

"Look. The air flows over the fabric, and it creates a wind tunnel which lifts it into the air."

Cayden's brow furrowed deep into his face. "But what holds it up?"

"Air."

"But there is nothing to air! It's not solid like the tree."

"Ah. See the leaves on the trees? Observe how they move. The air pushes the leaves when it flows past them."

"That is the tree spirits," Cayden protested, laughing. "Everyone knows trees are inhabited by spirits. You are trying to trick us, Mordecai. It won't work!"

Ziona stepped up beside the wizard, smiling, and touched the string attached to the bottom of the kite, which trailed back into Mordecai's hand. "Which sprite did you beguile into bewitching the branches for you?"

Mordecai looked from one to the other then sighed. He rubbed the side of his nose, sighed again, opened his mouth to speak, thought better of it, and shut it. Shrugging, he pulled the kite down from the air and tucked it under his arm.

Magic truly is in the eye of the beholder, he thought.

"What is it you wished to speak to me about, Cayden? I trust you found something of interest in your studies?"

Cayden glanced around, noting that they were alone except for the two Kingsmen guarding the pathway to where they stood.

"Yes. I need to know everything you know about the godlings."

"So, you have found the passages. Good. Your education begins in earnest, now. But first, we must return to the library as there are scrolls there that need to be consulted." With a swish of grey robes, he strode away, retracing the path out of the gardens.

On exiting the gardens, Mordecai picked up his pace and crossed the bailey, marching right past the library entrance. Instead, he opened the door that led to the staircase of the right tower.

"Mordecai, where are you going?" Cayden huffed, lengthening his stride. Ziona shadowed their progress.

"There is a particular book we need to retrieve from my rooms. A very rare book, one few eyes have viewed. It is a book of history and a book of magic, but it is much more than that. Yes indeed. It has remained hidden within this castle, concealed under a multitude of enchantments, for over a century. Alcina tried to pry its whereabouts out of me; however, such tactics were doomed to failure. Only one person could retrieve that book, and that person is you, Cayden."

They entered the spiral staircase and curved up to the fourth landing, then approached the wizard's chambers. Mordecai passed his hand over the door handle, and it swung open before them. He held up his hand to the Kingsmen, denying them entrance. They took up posts on either side of the door.

Set in a bartizan that overhung the castle wall, Mordecai's apartment consisted of a large circular room, interspersed with narrow casement windows, tall enough to stand in. The room faced east, and early morning sunshine spilled through, striping the hooked rugs that covered the stone floor. Tables were pushed up against the wall on the north side of the room, and on the south side a staircase curved up to a sleeping loft built above the tables. A squashy, overstuffed chair was set beside the cold fireplace.

Cayden shivered and not from the lack of a fire. The room was a reflection of the royal apartments on the west side of the castle. He refused to take rooms in the bartizans even though they were his if he wished. Mordecai had relayed the story surrounding his and Avery's birth and the murders of his parents and grandparents. He had taken him to the room where his mother had died. Even though Cayden had spoken to Gwen's spirit at the Well of Souls under the castle, he found himself dwelling on her and mulling over what it would have been like to have grown up with her in this castle, as prince rather than as a pauper.

It wasn't that he was unhappy about his childhood home in Sanctuary-by-the-Sea. It was more that he felt a huge gap in his understanding of the peoples of this world. His mother, Gwen, had been a Primordial princess who had been betrothed to his father, a prince of Cathair, at the time of her death. Their intended marriage and the children they would beget were meant to forge a bridge between their peoples. With his royal parent's deaths, the Primordial nation had plunged into a twenty-year-long civil war while Cathair languished under the queen's reign. His mother's desperate bid to preserve her children's lives had been successful but at the cost of her own life, a desperate attempt to head off unrest and a war that now spilled over the borders, setting Cathairian against Primordial.

So Cayden avoided the west towers. He did not want the constant reminder of his dead parents. It was bad enough to feel the ghost of their presence in the darkened halls, as the servants whispered to each other that he was the spitting image of his father.

"Cayden, what do you feel? Can you sense the presence of the books?" Mordecai's voice brought him back to the present.

Cayden looked around the curved room, eyes sliding over tapestries and the ragged edges of very old books, extending his senses. He didn't see anything out of the ordinary.

"No, I do not sense anything. How about you, Ziona? Do you sense anything?"

Ziona wandered through the room, eyes unfocused. "There is something here," she murmured.

Cayden frowned, crossing his arms, impatience stamped into his features. "What do we do now, Mordecai? If I am the one that is supposed to find this book, I must know the key. What could I possibly know that no one else does?" Cayden wandered around the room and paused by the window, which looked out over the gardens they had recently vacated. He could see the apple tree in the midst, and his thoughts wandered to the tree spirits. *I wonder if I could get them to appear if I carved a flute from a tree they lived in.* His flutes were great at making animals and creatures appear.

Wait, I wonder if one of my flutes would make the books appear? Cayden spun around and ran for the door.

"I just had a thought. I'll be right back!" He dashed out the door and down the hall to his apartment. Ziona poked her head out the door to observe the Kingsmen guards bolting after their young king, yelling at him to wait up. Cayden didn't even look back.

Grinning, Ziona returned to the room and seated herself in the chair by the fire to wait for his return.

Five minutes later, Cayden rushed back into the room, his satchel of flutes clutched in his hands. His winded and disgruntled personal guards took up their posts again by the doorway, and Mordecai closed the door.

Cayden upended the satchel over the table and out rolled all the flutes he had with him in Cathair. He sorted them through them then selected a knobbly branch that was mixed in with the finished flutes.

The wood was a gift from the ancient oak tree that hugged the pasture back in Sanctuary-by-the-Sea. While he'd sat on the rocks carving and watching over the sheep, the tree had whispered to him. He had completed the snake flute that day, but several other pieces of the rare wood he had tucked inside the bag to be carved another time.

Cayden picked up the branch and turned it over in his hands, wondering if this was the answer. *Could it be as simple as carving the tool I need?*

"Cayden, come sit here on the rug." Mordecai gestured to the thick rug centered on the floor. Ziona scooted back her chair to give him room.

Cayden picked up his carving tools and sat himself squarely in the center of the rug, sitting cross-legged on the starburst-patterned center.

"Relax your mind, Cayden." The wizard brought out his focusing crystal and clasped it between his palms over Cayden's head. Cayden stared at the branch in his hands. Suddenly, the scene shimmered in his view, the tower fading to be replaced by the field where the ancient oak tree sat. No longer was he sitting on a rug, but on the sun-kissed rocks, his favourite spot for carving. He took a deep breath, breathing in the familiar salty tang of sea air warmed by bright sunshine.

He looked over at the old oak tree, and there it stood, just as he remembered.

"Did you really try to speak to me last time I was here?" he asked the oak. It shook its branches as though laughing at the question.

Cayden smiled. Picking up his favourite awl, he began to hollow the branch. It was tough going, the wooden core hard as iron. It resisted any widening as he burrowed so that in the end the center was the narrowest of openings. Cayden frowned at the branch and peered down the hole, barely able to see through to the other end. With that small of an opening, what sound could possibly escape it?

As he turned it over in his hands the branch began to vibrate violently. Surprised, Cayden dropped it. It smashed against the rock, breaking in two precise halves. He picked them up and checked them over for further fractures but couldn't locate any. The wise old oak tree chuckled...and chuckled some more.

"What secrets are you hiding from me, Elder Oak?" Cayden laughed and began hollowing out the fingering on both of the tiny flutes.

Immersed in the moment, Cayden quite forgot about the others, completely at ease in the illusion.

Or was it an illusion?

Ziona walked around Cayden, watching Cayden's lips move. Obviously, by his reactions, he was deep in conversation with someone only he saw. She saw him pick up the stick and begin forming the flute only to have it snap in two. *Instead of becoming angry, he laughs?* She paused in front of him, the final polish of the flutes underway, just as she had observed all those months ago. How far they had come, she mused, and how far they had to go. The future was so uncertain, even for the Lord of the Mists. As she watched, Cayden put down his polishing kit, checked for flaws in his flutes by running his fingers down them one last time, and then raised the first to his lips. He blew on the flute, fingers flitting over the holes. Ziona detected no sound from it.

Cayden frowned and picked up the other flute and put it to his lips. Nothing happened. He stood up and walked toward the staircase and paused before it. His lips moved, but once again Ziona could not hear anything. Hands on hips, he confronted the staircase.

Cayden spoke to the tree. "I can hear the giggling in your branches, Elder Oak. Who is hiding from my presence?" Elder Oak shook with laughter. It wheezed and sneezed and out popped a couple of tree sprites, giggling and holding over their heads like a serving tray a pair of dusty leather-bound books. The sprites, rather than handing Cayden the books, ran around him and over to Ziona. The minute they touched her skirt, the vision faded and they disappeared with a pop. The books dropped to the carpet at Ziona's feet, just as Cayden swung away from the tree.

"Oh!" Ziona picked up a book from the stack on the floor. "Where did these come from?"

"The tree sprites fetched them from the Elder Oak," said Cayden. Ziona raised an eyebrow at this and peered around the room as if expecting to find the sprites hiding in the shadows of the room.

Mordecai chuckled as he fetched the remaining three books and carried them over to the table.

"Come on, let's have a peek inside. Tree sprites indeed!" His eyes twinkled as he flipped open the cover of the first tome.

Chapter 9

Elder One

MAREA TREMBLINGSPIRIT ROSE from the vine-covered dais, gathered her leaf-green robes about her body, and descended with quick, light steps to the audience chamber floor to greet the weary priest.

"Has she returned from the temple yet?" she demanded before he had a chance to rise from his deep bow, arms spread wide to the side and hands open. The light of the firefly globe dangling from the ceiling on a sturdy woven reed chain danced across his bald pate, encircled by a fringe of wispy white hair.

"No, Most High." Eldrid spoke with a small voice as he straightened. "She has not. The temple is still ablaze with light and colour. The rainbow wards continue to encompass it, barring entry to all. We cannot pass through the bands. The rainbow emits pulses of red in warning when we approach, and all who have attempted to penetrate it have received severe burns. We cannot pass."

Marea's mouth twisted, her thin lips displaying yellowing teeth that clacked together in fury. *How dare that young strumpet enter my temple without my presence? The temple of the High Priestess is sacred ground. No one is to enter my temple. No one.*

"What of her traveling companion?" she snarled.

"He has identified himself as her father. We have secured him in the Grass Roots holding cell in Faylea. He is still resisting our questioning," he shrugged, "but it will not be long now before he gives in. If he doesn't, we have other methods of getting the information we need."

"And Sharisha? Where is she? She was to report to me immediately on her return."

The priest opened his mouth to reply, but at that moment the round chamber door swung open and Sharisha strode through, back straight and legs stiff. Seeing who was in the room, her chin raised haughtily. She had changed her clothing back to more traditional Primordial garb. A multi-hued tunic of greens, browns, and purples was belted with woven, purple-dyed hemp. Tan leggings were tucked into soft brown leather boots, which laced up the back to mid-thigh. Flung across her back was a quiver, and she carried an unstrung bow in her hand. Her long hair was tied back by a ribbon adorned with rainbow-hued sequins made from freshwater clam shells.

She strode toward them. Upon reaching the High Priestess, Sharisha gave a deep bow similar to Eldrid's.

"Most High," she murmured on rising.

Marea slowly walked around Sharisha, examining her. "You took your time in reporting to me!" she growled, her anger drawing deep furrows between her narrowed eyes.

Sharisha was not cowed. "Your specific instructions were to return to you immediately, should I have news to share. As your priests had already relayed the news of Avery's entrance into the temple, any 'news' I might have imparted had already been provided to you, Elder One."

If anything, the furrows deepened on Marea's pinched face. "That was only one of my conditions. You have been gone a very long time. You have much to tell me," she snarled, and Eldrid winced at the menace in her tone. Sharisha merely raised one eyebrow and stood tall, refusing to quail or show weakness while waiting for Marea to meet her eyes.

"She is the one we seek," Sharisha said simply, but the words halted Marea's steps. She swung around, her black eyes fastened on Sharisha's, demanding an answer to the question burning in their depths.

"Avery has the gift. She has the ability to read souls. She will be an invaluable weapon." Sharisha smiled for the first time, and Marea's lips thinned even more and curled back into a travesty of a smile.

"Finally, we have captured a Spirit Shield." Triumph rang in Marea's voice as she marched back up to her throne and sat down in the curving branches. "To chain and harness such a one is to have ultimate power. Be sure to collar her when she descends from the temple, and bring her to me. She is destined to serve the Spirit Clans forevermore." She smiled a dark smile, and Sharisha smiled back.

Marea reached under her chair and pulled out a package wrapped in soft deerskin that jingled in her hands. Sharisha mounted the steps and knelt once more, accepting the parcel reverently. She carefully folded back the skins and with a flip of the final corner, a delicate silver collar was revealed, made of fragile, slender links, looping and twisting together into a shimmering rope which caught the light of the fireflies and cast rainbows at the walls. On a smooth bale hung a pendant of polished silver, embedded with a blue stone. The stone flashed and then faded. It could not be looked at directly, seeming to be only partially in this world. Sharisha was careful to not touch any portion of the necklace and thereby interfere with its magic. She gently refolded the cloth and tucked it into the pocket of her shirt.

"It will be done, Most High." Sharisha bowed once more in acceptance of the command.

"Take Eldrid with you. Perhaps he can assist you with penetrating the rainbow." Marea frowned at the puzzle created by this strange event. No rainbow had ever formed around the temple before, not even when she entered it to be raised to Highest. "Eldrid," she commanded in dismissal, "send in the general. I believe he is to be found by the barracks."

"Yes, Elder One." Eldrid bowed low and left the room.

As the door closed behind him, Marea spoke quickly to Sharisha. "Now, before the general arrives, tell me everything that has transpired since you left Faylea. Where is Ziona?"

Sharisha spoke of their wanderings in the human kingdom, the discovery of the twins, the parting of the children by the legion's forces, and her decision to accompany Avery back to Faylea while Ziona went after the boy called Cayden.

"This is a puzzling turn of events." Marea absently ran her fingers over the woven roots forming the arm of her throne. "I never expected to find two children with the gift. What was your impression of this young man? Is he another Spirit Shield? Have their powers been diluted?"

Sharisha shrugged her shoulders. "I do not know. I did not have time to study him. He displayed similar qualities, yet his gift was not the same as Avery's. She has displayed true Primordial bloodlines in the way she interacts with the spirit world. She has a natural affinity for the things of our world." She hesitated, considering her words. "If her brother has the gift, it is a minor talent at most."

Silence greeted her statement, and then Marea's face hardened. "It does not change our plans. We must have a Spirit Shield to champion our fight. The Flesh Clans will come after her, but she is our linchpin. The boy may become a problem, especially if the Flesh Clans learn of his existence." She drummed her fingers on the arm of the throne, a hollow, high-pitched drumming sound accompanying her actions. "I may have to send you after him, in time. We will question Avery closely about him once she is under our control."

Sharisha had risen to her feet as Marea strode toward her. "What of the Flesh Clans? You do know of their plan to recall the goddess Artio back to this world?" Sharisha asked.

Marea nodded. "There have been rumours that the flesh clans have rediscovered an ancient magic of the gods that will bind spirit to animal flesh. It is something that is banned, the knowledge locked away centuries ago. If the rumours are true, then someone has stolen this knowledge and is attempting to resurrect a god. With the return of Artio, there will be two powerful pawns at play in this war. We need Avery to balance Artio's power. She will prove once and for all that the Spirit ways are true, and that Flesh sacrifice is not the only path to appease the gods."

"I had better catch up with Eldrid." Sharisha checked that the collar was secure in the pocket of her tunic and then hitched her bow over her right shoulder. "What would you have me do with her father, the man in the cells?"

"Keep him there. He will be useful as leverage in case our new priestess gives us any trouble. She will not resist us while her father's life hangs in the balance."

Sharisha bowed once more. Then turning on her heel, she strode from the room, pulling the circular door closed behind her.

Marea sat back in her chair and smiled. Soon she would meet Artio. Soon she would meet Avery. Soon she would rule the gods themselves. Her priests were in position and the potions, resurrected from the archives of old, were brewed and tested and working. She would gain control of the Flesh Clans and their leaders without her Clan Chiefs ever lifting a blade against another Primordial. She smiled broadly at her own cleverness then sighed, deeply contented. Soon, the entire world would kneel before her. Soon.

Chapter 10

Cyrus's Plan

CYRUS RODE AT THE HEAD OF A GROUP of twelve legion riders, every man handpicked for his particular skill set. His hands tightened then eased off the leather reins as he pulled his mount to a halt, just shy of the ridge of the mountainside they had been steadily climbing. A mist rose from the ground and swirling opaque fingers intertwined with the horses' legs, obscuring the path.

The last two villages they had entered and "surveyed" had produced only three Primordial males who confessed to having spotted the party he hunted. Not three days back, a group of three riders, two women and a man, had stopped for provisions in their village. With a little *persuasion*, the Primordials had spilled exact descriptions of their quarry and had led him to their aging trail.

Usefulness at an end, Cyrus slew two of them with the curved hunting knives preferred by the Spirit Clans. He was here to sow discord and sow it he would, leaving wounds unique to the curved blades and careful to leave the bodies riddled with arrows fletched with the Spirit Clan's favoured choice of feathers, all of which had been stolen from their villages a few days past. The bodies had been dumped along the path.

The Spirit Clan's villages were to be found in the valleys and open plains where grass was plentiful for their herds of deer and gazelle and the marshes and rivers teemed with fish and frog, while the Flesh Clans favoured hilly and mountainous terrain, prime for herding curly-horned sheep and nimble goats who foraged the steep mountainsides for vegetation. They built stone dwellings that doubled as defensible barriers and outposts to discourage foreign visitors. In the past, the two factions of Primordials worked as opposite sides of the same coin, but now, with the civil war, the Spirit Clans found themselves cut off and isolated by the Flesh Clans, hemmed in by the impassable terrain of the Highland Needle to the south and the Endless Oceans to the north. The few of the Spirit Clans who had created settlements on the human side of the Spine were rumoured to have disappeared without a trace. The Spirit Clans blamed the Flesh Clans, and the Flesh Clans blamed the humans. A few of the elders of both Spirit and Flesh Clan spoke of strange stirrings and signs, but these elders were largely ignored as their traditional views were regarded as not relevant to the modern situation.

Cyrus and his hand-picked legionnaires rode toward their destination under the cover of darkness, a raiding party on the move, with horses shod in the Primordial fashion for silent passage. Reaching the river, they slowed their mounts and allowed them to pick their own path into the swift flowing waters and then headed upstream to rejoin the live trail leading to their quarry. The tracks were fresh. They should reach Faylea and their prey by morning.

The men, halted behind him, waited, the leather creaking as they shifted in their saddles. Cyrus studied the ridge, the undulating landscape changing ever so slightly as his gaze rose to the crest, the vegetation becoming less defined and spookier, its edges blurred as though it was not quite part of this world. Cyrus rubbed his eyes and looked again. It still seemed slightly out of focus and only sharpened when he squinted. Large, perfectly domed tree crowns dotted the horizon, silhouetted by the setting moon, giant feathery pillows resting on a velvety blanket of night. One particularly massive tree towered above the others, its crown sharply defined by the fading moonlight.

"The mists should burn off in the first rays of the sun," the sole remaining Primordial mumbled, his wrists bound to the horn of the saddle, his heavily bruised lips barely able to part to allow the words to escape. He sat tall and proud despite the obvious distress caused by his various injuries. His black shoulder-length hair, matted with blood, stuck to the right side of his head while the left side gleamed in the reflected moonlight. "The mists of the dead only rise in the dark."

Cyrus glared at the man as his men muttered to each other, staring around suspiciously at the mists. Some of the older, superstitious men made a sign to ward off evil. Soldiers they might be, but superstition was a large part of a soldier's life. Few would openly defy the gods and mock the dead. Cyrus nudged his horse forward with his heels. Once alongside the man, he backhanded him with the fingers of his steel-tipped glove. Blood sprayed from the barely crusted lips, and the man's head snapped back with the force of the blow. Slowly, he straightened, returning Cyrus's glare, not a trace of fear in his eyes.

"You will speak when I ask you, not before." Cyrus wiped his gloved hand on a cloth he pulled from inside his tunic. Splatters of blood shimmered brightly for a moment on the dull red fabric with a polka-dot effect before dulling. Cyrus swiped at them, and they faded into the cloth. "We do not care about your mystic Primordial ramblings. The dead are the dead. Mist is mist. Fullmer!" he barked, and a balding pale man with one glass eye nudged his horse from the collective and trotted up to Cyrus's side.

"My lord!" he saluted.

"Take this Primordial popinjay with you and check out the mists. It may not be the dead, but it is a great place to lay an ambush. I want to know all that moves in those mists, and I want you back here before the coals are hot for breakfast. Take two others with you."

"Yes, my lord!" Fullmer saluted once again and with a wave, collected two other soldiers, and trotted away into the mist, leading the captive's horse into the brush. They disappeared within seconds, the mists on the ground rising just high enough to obscure horse and rider. Above the mists, the elongated swelling of a new day blushed across the horizon.

* * *

The soldiers, despite their armour and skill sets, scanned the rising mists with apprehension, pulling their knees up higher and leaving their stirrups behind so as to not have their feet touch the ethereal fingers of fog rising around them. A low moan issued from the ground and a collective shiver passed through the battle-hardened men. They had no fear of facing down another man or an army of them, but how does one fight spirits, if that is what the mists truly were?

The Primordial did not react in any way to the mists. They swirled over his feet and wrapped around his legs, encasing him in a shroud of cloud that hid his lower body from view. The mists drifted higher until only the tips of his shoulders were visible, swallowing him and his horse and his surroundings. Then with a final moan, the mist covered him completely, and he vanished from view.

The men, still leading the Primordial's horse by a rope, paid no attention to him, as they were preoccupied with keeping their own bodies and mounts in visible range.

They urged their horses to the crest of the rise. As the sun breached the ridge, the mists vanished, but so did the Primordial. The lead soldier hauled in the bridle rein, but it ended in nothing. Horse and captive rider had disappeared into the fog.

*　*　*

Achak urged his mount forward, keeping to the mists, working at the ropes tying his hands to the pommel. He slipped a sharp piece of stone from his pocket. The rock was a form of shale that chipped in sharp layers perfect for arrowheads, but this piece was not as sharp as a true arrowhead, as he had not had time to refine the stone. Rubbing his bonds furiously against the leather restraints he slid the leather back and forth across the dull edge, but the thick leather held, refusing to part.

"Thank you, ancestors, for your protection," he prayed as he rode silently through the trees. "Phoenix, aid my blade," he said to his Spirit Guide, not expecting an answer and was shocked when he felt the rock grow hot in his hand. He sawed into the leather and it started to smoke against the glowing edge. The leather parted like melting fat and fell from his freed hands. He clenched and unclenched his fingers, working the circulation back into them as the stone cooled, guiding his mount with only his knees. He pointed her into the dense underbrush thick with the spirits of his ancestors, feeling their welcome and their shelter, as he wound his way toward the ancient entrance into Faylea, an entrance long forgotten by the world.

A stream wound along the base of the cliff and caves dotted the edge of the stream, natural occlusions that swelled with water during heavy storms but now were hollowed vertical depressions in the rock with a trickling stream bed for a floor. He chose a tall, thin cave to enter, the spirits around him brightening, providing him with a glowing blue light to illuminate his way. They whispered at his mind as he rode. He felt their concern and also a great joy that infused their presence. The spirits were very active today, more so than he had seen in a very, very long time. He had a sense that something wondrous had occurred although he could not tell what. Still, it was obvious that they wanted his help, for they guided his horse's steps and showed him the direction they wished him to travel.

Achak followed the cavern for roughly two hundred yards before the cliff face appeared. As he rounded a curve in the cave wall, broad stone steps were revealed, crisscrossing back and forth toward the lighter grey of the exit. He dismounted at the urging of the spirits and began the climb, leading his horse. The stone steps were etched to provide a sure footing in the damp climate. The spirits pulsed around him, cocooning him and his mount in their soft shield. Clicking on the stone, they steadily climbed, passing walls covered in frescoes, scenes of people and clans and animals long forgotten. Some of the animals were clearly creatures of myth, as Achak's eyes had never seen them in the flesh. The elders had sworn they existed and during festivals would call on their particular guardian spirit to share in the celebrations with the clan and commune with the people.

I did see a phoenix one time. I swear it was dancing in the flames of the campfire. It is my guardian, my mother had explained, and a powerful one too—a special guardian to come to one so young. Achak had seen it on his eleventh birthday, when he became a man. But he had not seen it again. Now at nineteen, he longed to know if it really did guide him. Perhaps the phoenix had protected him this day, as he was still alive.

When the queen's elite legion squad descended on the village of Antigonish, the residents at first expected a peaceful trading session with their border village, as was the norm. Many a legion division had passed by their collection of huts at the mouth of the Spine and had traded for goods and supplies to supplement their reserves while conducting their patrols. This time had been different. The elders of Antigonish had been carried away by the men, and the women and children slain. Achak was the only one left that could bear witness to the slaughter at the village. The weapons they bore were of the Flesh Tribes, and yet not one of them accompanied the soldiers.

Where were the Flesh Clan warriors, and why did the legionnaires have Flesh Clan weapons?

Have the warriors been slaughtered, the same as the people of my village, and their weapons stolen? And if so, which village has fallen? I must give warning to my people that the legions are coming. I must warn the High Priestess that the Flesh Tribes may be aligned with the men of the kingdom. If I do not warn them, who will?

Achak reached the summit of the cave wall and stepped onto a stony trail that led to a cut in the rocky ceiling. Light spilled from the crevice and blinded him after the soft glowing of the spirits. As he walked toward the light, he felt ghostly touches along his back. They whispered in his ear. *"Avery…Avery…Avery…"*

Chapter 11

Transformed

AVERY CAME TO, face down on the floor, just inside the door of the temple. Her cheek was pressed against the cold stone, the rough surface biting into her cheek. She blinked. The sideways tilt of the room was disorienting. Slowly, comprehension dawned, and with it a rush of memories that made her head ache. She gathered her strength and rolled over onto her back and promptly screamed as it came in contact with the floor. She sat bolt upright and flapped her arms to put out the sensation of flames dancing across her back. Then, she noticed her biceps. Tattoos covered ever visible inch. As she drew her arms back around and straightened them, she could see the tattoos did not stop there but continued down over her wrists and hands, to the tips of fingers. As she rolled her hands to inspect her palms, it was then that she noticed her legs were also covered in tattoos. Alarmed, she jumped to her feet and hurried over to a floor-length mirror halfway down the ornately carved walls, limping as she walked. She stepped up to the mirror and gasped at her reflection.

She was naked. Naked, but every inch of her skin had been inked with vividly coloured tattoos. They were not random tattoos, however. They marched across her body like a moving panorama, scenes and images flowing from one concept to the next.

It's like the scrolling backdrop for the puppet plays, she thought, remembering the troupes of caravan actors that used to stop at Sanctuary-by-the-Sea during Beltine. She could follow one image of a fellow in battle gear from his house to a great battle scene. Slowly,

Avery turned in front of the mirror, trying to follow his journey, but it was difficult to see every bit of the scene as other scenes intersected with it.

Avery lifted her leg and displayed the sole of her right foot to the mirror. Not even her sole escaped images, although these were of people, seemingly writhing in pain, their mouths open in screams. Avery shuddered at the image and put her foot down. Perhaps it was better that that particular image was on the ground. She frowned, a thought bubbling to the surface and then popping before it fully formed. Frustrated, she continued her inspection.

As her eyes traveled up her body, the reason for the chill on her head became evident. Her hair was gone, as though it had never existed. Not a single strand of her former silky curls remained. Instead, her scalp was etched with images of celestial import, familiar stars and planets that traveled the skies.

She met her own eyes in the mirror and that was the greatest shock of all. Her eyes stared back at her from a silver base. Before, her eyes were set in white orbs, but now they rested in liquid mercury. The effect was frightening, and she blinked several times to reassure herself that her eyes were working properly, rubbing her fists across her closed lids to clear her vision. When she reopened her eyes, nothing had changed. She blinked again and stepped closer to the mirror. Faint lines ran through the silver, and they pulsed in time with her beating heart. She stepped back from the mirror and considered the problem. She could hardly stride around looking like this.

What is happening to me? What am I going to do? Avery leaned in closer to the mirror, tracing a finger over her cheek, examining the swirling patterns that now decorated her skin. *Runes. They look exactly like runes, and they are everywhere. My skin has been imbued with magic, the magic of the temple. These are the markings of a High Priestess,* she remembered. Avery straightened away from the mirror. *There will be no hiding from the world. Friend or enemy, every person I meet will have an agenda. They will seek to control me. I am truly alone now.* She shivered, scared to face the future beyond the temple doors. *It is likely that my entrance into the temple has not gone unnoticed. Who waits for me on the other side? Can the Primordial people be trusted?* Avery thought back to her instinctual distrust of Sharisha and she shivered again. She longed to have Cayden with her. She had never been separated from her twin before, and scared as she was, she missed him intensely at this moment.

At least Father is here with me, she thought in comfort. *It is time to face the waiting crowds*—(for she had no doubt that they waited beyond the double sealed doors)—*but first I need clothes!*

Her eyes wandered over the room, and she noticed another door covered in carvings. She strode over and wrenched it open. A large walk-in closet was revealed, and wooden pegs dotted the wall from which hung robes of varying sizes and shapes. Along the back wall, shelves were stacked with folded clothing, and the bottom row contained boots. Avery strode to the cabinet and wrenched open several drawers. Inside were small clothes, belts, bracelets, and other artifacts. The carvings on the jewellery matched the tattoos on her skin. She disregarded the jewellery and pulled out some soft cotton underthings and slipped them on. Next, she pulled a silvery sleeveless shirt from a stack and slipped it over her head. It fell to her hips and hugged her form like a glove. Avery did not worry about whose clothes they were. The fit was right, almost as though they were made for her. *Perhaps these belong to the High Priestess of the temple? But, if they are clothing meant for the High Priestess, then the Faylea High Priestess should be decked out in this clothing already. Obviously, she is not, which means…these clothes were meant for me, for if she had had access, then the clothing would be gone. I must be the true High Priestess.* The thought rang true in her mind and with it, fear surged causing her heart to race.

Another quick search of a stack of clothing revealed soft black leather leggings with fringes. She donned them and then pulled a belt from the drawer, leather embedded with thick silver links. Charms dangled from the links and tinkled as she pulled it though the loops and tugged the end through a heavy silver buckle in the shape of a bear.

Next, she found a black leather vest with silver buttons and slipped it on over the silver shirt.

From the drawers, wide silver bangles caught her eye, wide enough to cover her forearms from wrist to elbow. She picked them up and saw that they were cleverly jointed with tiny hinges that allowed her to slip her arm inside. They closed with a snap and she was pleased to see that she had full range of movement while they covered the tattoos. All that was visible were the twin birds that ran from wrist to fingertips.

Twin phoenixes? she wondered.

She closed the drawer and then knelt down to inspect the boots. The pair closest to her size, tall boots of black leather, was tooled similarly to her belt with silver buckles and adjustable straps. She pulled them from the shelf and took a closer look. The reason for the buckles became apparent as she opened the boot to find hidden sleeves and pockets built in. The intended use of one set of the pockets was clear as they were already occupied by a pair of matching knives, one per boot.

Avery sat down on the floor and tugged on the boots, buckling them up over her knees. She sighed with pleasure, partially because the ugly images on her feet were finally covered over and also with relief as the cool leather soothed her burning soles.

Strange, none of the other tattoos burns, she thought, *only the images on my feet.*

She stood up gingerly, settling her feet in the least painful position. She was several inches taller in these boots and smiled. *Now, to find a coat that fits,* she thought and tested out her new footwear by walking back and forth before the hanging cloaks. A black one caught her eye, and she slipped her arms through the sleeves as she pulled it down. The cloak was fitted across her chest and fell to her hips. She buttoned it up and then walked out to the main room to the mirror and stopped in front of it.

A woman stared back at her, but this woman was a stranger. A woman in sleek leather stared back at her with silver eyes that imitated the silver on her clothing. The cloak's black hood draped down her back to a point, just shy of her waist and the coat split and cut away over her hips and then dropped to the sides in long sweeping tails that swirled as she walked. The cuffs of the sleeves turned up in a similar fashion, and two large silver buttons held the cuffs straight. More hidden pockets were glimpsed in the cuffs. From the front, her boot tops mimicked the cuffs, with rows of silver buttons marching down the side. She tugged up the hood of the cloak and her face disappeared within it except for her glowing silver orbs.

If I didn't know it was me, I would be petrified! she thought, wincing at what her father would say when he saw her.

She wandered back into the closet, but none of the rest of the garments seemed to be the right size. It was almost as though these particular garments had been waiting for her to come and claim them. She was drawn back to the drawers and touched the face of a thin one that she had not noticed earlier. This drawer whispered as it opened, sliding out and unfolding at her touch. On a bed of softest linen sat a silver necklace. Avery saw at a glance that it was very old. The chain was silver and very long with a flat oval-shaped pendant that glowed. She picked it up and ran a thumb across the polished surface and images sprung to life. Mists swirled and resolved into faces and images of places she had never been to, flashed across the surface. Murmuring reached her ears. As she gazed into the stone, the image of her brother Cayden floated to the surface. He was in a stone library surrounded by books.

"A Seeing Stone!" Avery exclaimed, the first audible words she had uttered since rising from the floor. Her voice was dampened by the magic of the closet. She slipped the pendant around her neck and dropped it inside her shirt to nestle between her breasts. Her eye fell on a matching ring that had been hidden beneath the pendant. She picked this up too and slipped it on the middle finger of her left hand. It molded itself to her finger as though made for her. The phoenix tattoo ended where the ring settled, the flat surface glinting like a fiery eye on her finger.

As she left the closet, the door swung shut with a loud click and, glancing back, she saw that the outline of the door had disappeared, becoming just another arch in the paneled wall.

Avery stretched out her hands to the double doors and grabbed the twin carved handles. This threshold she had crossed *moments? hours? days?* before. Did they still wait for her on the other side? It was time to find out. With a mighty shove, she pushed open the doors.

Chapter 12

Heading for Trouble

CAYDEN LEANED BACK IN HIS CHAIR and stretched his arms over his head, his stiff back popping as he worked out the kinks. He then flipped the thick book closed with a boom that sent the early morning dust motes swirling in the first rays of sunrise to light his apartment. He had rearranged the central room into a proper study, complete with overstuffed chairs, long tables on which to spread out books, and ample lamps to light the interior.

He squeezed the bridge of his nose, the strain of studying all night long resulting in a steady throb behind his eyes. It seemed he always had a headache now. At first, he had put them down to his obsession with reading every work, every tome relating to the history of Cathair and the kingdom, the history of the peoples of both his and the Primordial lands, and back even further to the creation myths woven through the histories of both peoples. Clarity was emerging from the chaos, and he began to understand the motivations of his enemy. But now, Cayden wondered if the headaches had another cause.

He glanced down at the couch located under the brightening window and gazed fondly at Ziona's sleeping form. She was curled into a ball on the soft surface, her toes just peeking out from under a tapestry he had "borrowed" from the wall and draped over her in the middle of the night. Even deep in slumber, he felt her nestled in his head, a residual effect of having saved her life. He smiled at the sense of wonder he felt in her dreams.

He walked over and gently shook her awake. "Ziona. Wake up. It's morning."

Ziona's long lashes slowly fluttered open, and then she peered up at him. "Is it dawn? Did you study all night?"

"Yeah." Weary crescents of darkness painted Cayden's eyes and stubble shadowed his chin. He held out a hand to help her up. She placed her slim left hand in his as he pulled her to her feet. Then, she reached up and trailed her right hand across his burgeoning beard.

"You must rest. You cannot push yourself so hard. What is it you are looking for?" She glanced down at the stack of books. The tree sprites had continued to drop books every few hours, great dusty tomes with a woodsy smell, appearing out of nowhere to thump to the library floor right next to wherever Cayden stood or sat until great stacks covered the table and floor. It had been a few hours since the last book arrived, and that was about the time she had fallen asleep on the settee.

At first, Ziona had been surprised every time a book magically appeared out of thin air, jumping at every deep thump, but after Cayden paused several times in midsentence to speak to the sprites, she had come to understand that he could see what she could not, despite her Primordial heritage. Now that they had been summoned, it seemed that the tree sprites were determined to retrieve and return every book they had ever pilfered from the library for safekeeping. Indeed, it seemed to Ziona that they were determined to return every tome immediately when in actual fact they were only fetching those books on subjects that Cayden specified.

Ziona turned to the stack and ran her thumb down the cracked leather spines, tilting her head to read the embossed gold lettering on them.

Cayden massaged the ache in his neck as he sat back down, arching away from the books. "I don't know, something to help Avery. I have this feeling she is in trouble." Restless, he rose to his feet again and walked over to the window to peer out at the pink candy blush spreading across the horizon above the trees. "She pulls at me through this." He pulled a golden chain out from under his tunic from which dangled a stone. "She always said we would be connected by this stone." He rubbed his thumb across the rough surface, and broken images flashed across his consciousness. He saw an emerald city in the bowl of a valley, a shining white temple and wild images of beasts. Some he recognized, having met a few of them himself via his flutes. "We need to go to her. I feel it."

The bond Cayden had with his twin sister, Avery, had existed since the day they were born. They shared a telepathic bond and could speak to each other over vast distances. It had something to do with their heritage, although he had never heard of the Primordial people being telepathic. Whatever its source, he was sure it was tied into their birth and the magic performed to save their lives…or perhaps the magic that they both possessed. The bond had sharpened suddenly during the night. It was more defined, more tangible than in the past. Something dramatic had happened to Avery.

Cayden studied the castle grounds, watching the servants hurrying and scurrying, going about the never-ceasing chores required in a typical day of running the castle. One thing was for certain. All of his study in the dark hours confirmed his suspicions. The gods were playing a game, and the mortal beings that filled the world were pawns, pieces on a giant chessboard, being pushed to and fro at the whim of the gods. *And where does that leave me as a child of the gods? Am I a pawn or a player? Am I a pusher or being pushed? I would rather be a player and not at the whim or beck and call of the gods. But how? How do I get in the game?* Cayden's face hardened and his hands clenched the window frame, whitening his knuckles with the strength of his grip.

Ziona stepped up behind him and placed her hands on his shoulders and began to gently massage the tight muscles in his neck and shoulders. Cayden groaned with relief, closing his eyes, as she worked out the kinks.

"I will go. She is with my people, and I need to report to the head of my order what has happened here. I will check on her and make sure she is safe. No harm will come to her with my people." Cayden stiffened and grabbed her hand.

"No." He spoke before thinking, his knee-jerk reaction to keep her close. He opened his mouth to say more, but Ziona pressed a finger to his lips, pausing his words.

"The danger has passed for you. You are protected now, safe with your people within the castle and its grounds." Ziona gestured vaguely to the room surrounding them. "And I am needed elsewhere."

Cayden grasped her other hand and pulled her close. "Ziona, I don't think…" Cayden broke off as a knock sounded on the door and it creaked open. A young woman backed into the room, carrying a tray covered in a cloth, chattering away as she ducked under the arm of the guard holding the door open. "Sire, time for you to take a break," she chattered. "Your breakfast is piping hot, and you should eat it before it grows cold and lumpy." She broke off as she swung around and caught Cayden and Ziona in a near embrace. She averted her eyes to the floor and stumbled. "I apologize, sire. I should have waited for you to bid me enter. Forgive me."

Cayden and Ziona broke reluctantly apart, Ziona kissing Cayden on the cheek with the lightest brush of lips. She touched her fingers to her lips, then touched his, transferring the kiss. Her eyes softened with a liquid warm, hinting at a promise unfulfilled. Cayden's eyes widened and, with a grin, Ziona swung away, marching to the door. Ziona spoke over her shoulder as she passed the serving girl, eyeing the woman. She knew that the gossip would spread through the castle like a wildfire. In no time, every servant would know she had slept in Cayden's chambers. Ziona smiled, secretly pleased to stake her claim to Cayden, to send out an emotional warning to all to stay away from him. "We will speak of this later, sire. Enjoy your breakfast."

The door closed behind her with a click, and the serving girl straightened from her curtsy, hurrying over to a side table to put the tray down.

A rapid knock sounded at the door once again. It swung open to admit Mordecai, who did not wait to be invited. The serving girl squeaked at the appearance of the wizard and scurried out through the door before it had time to close behind him.

"Good morning, my boy!" Mordecai boomed, a wide smile creasing the sides of his leathery cheeks. He looked robustly healthy, still skinny, but the pallor of the dungeons had faded from his skin. He walked with a spry step as he strode over to peek at Cayden's tray of food. "What do we have here?" He flipped back the dangling sleeve of his magenta robes and swept the cloth cover off the tray, revealing a pot of tea and a mug, a bowl of porridge and berries, a pot of thick sweet cream, and three buttery croissants. Mordecai picked up a steaming crusty croissant and a knife, slathering it with creamy butter before popping it into his mouth. "Ahh." He rolled his words around hot mouthfuls of food. "You really should try these, Cayden. They are quite delightful. I do believe that Fabian is supplying the castle now."

Cayden's stomach did a funny lurch at the thought of putting food in it. *I still haven't got over that stomach flu,* he thought. Instead, he reached for the pot of tea, pouring a liberal quantity of honey into it, and then took a sip of the blueberry-flavoured brew.

Mordecai *tsked* and wandered over to the table to inspect the recent arrivals. "Well? What have you learned, my boy, for all your nightly vigils?"

Cayden sank into a soft leather chair with a stifled groan and leaned his head back against the cushions.

"I have learned that our true opponent is likely Helga, the goddess of the underworld, goddess of the dead." His head swiveled to Mordecai. "How, good goddess, do we defeat an immortal?"

Mordecai grinned from ear to ear at his words. "Why, with another god, of course!"

Cayden felt the temporary relief from Ziona's massage evaporate as he squinted at Mordecai. "With another god...of course. Why didn't I think of that?" Sarcasm dripped from his tongue. "I will summon one with my flutes. Perhaps Aossi is up to the task." Aossi was a spirit of the world between worlds, an immortal that traveled between realities. She was also a tiny childlike entity that had an annoying habit of showing up just to tweak his nose with what he didn't understand.

"No, no, my dear boy. No need for Aossi, as charming as she is. She really isn't up to the task, in any event."

Infuriating! thought Cayden as he peered blearily at Mordecai's smug grin. *Completely infuriating!* "So, what do you suggest?"

"I suggest you sleep on it. Your brain is stuffed so full of information. You cannot begin to process it all." He walked over and pulled Cayden from the chair and then marched him to his bedchamber, pushing him onto the feathery surface and pulling off his boots. "Sleep," Mordecai commanded, "and we will talk when you are awake enough to process the information."

Cayden's heavy eyelids drooped before Mordecai even reached the doorway. By the time the door closed, Cayden was fast asleep.

*   *   *

Ziona fell into step beside Mordecai as he left Cayden's quarters. Mordecai had snagged another croissant from Cayden's tray and was happily devouring it with quick bites while he strode down the hall, his shoes making a clicking sound on the checkered marble flooring.

"I must leave before he awakens. Cayden is becoming more and more reluctant to let me out of his sight. He will not tell me what is bothering him, but I think it has to do with that last prophecy tome that the pixies dropped. I couldn't read the script, but Cayden picked it out right away. Somehow, he is able to read books written in long extinct languages, languages dating back thousands of years. I don't think he even realizes he is doing it."

Mordecai nodded, swallowing his last mouthful. "I believe it to be a result of his birth lineage, the unique blend of his human royal parents, mixing with his immortal bloodlines. Strange abilities surface when gods and humans mix, and I do not believe this has occurred since the very foundation of the world. A remnant of his immortal existence has been pulled through and merged with his mortal existence. It would explain his natural affinity for runes and his instinctual use of them." Mordecai made to take another bite of croissant and frowned disappointedly at his empty hand.

"Well, so far, he has refused to tell me what he has learned. It's almost as though he is afraid to tell me. There have been times when I have seen him sitting there, shaking with grief. I cannot tell if it is because of something he has read or if it is something he has figured out. Either way, he believes that he must go to Avery, but we both know that would be foolish. He would have to go through Alcina's troops to get there, and that is way too much risk for a monarch." She shook her head at the foolishness of the thought. "What would happen if he were to fall into their hands? He is safer here." She followed the statement with a sharp nod of her head, as though that settled matters once and for all.

Mordecai frowned. "I doubt that you can keep him here against his will."

"That is why I must leave now. I have had the essentials packed for a week." She stubbornly crossed her arms.

"He will not be pleased to find you gone. What will you do to get around the legionnaires' encampment?"

"You forget, Mordecai, that the Primordial lands are my homeland. I know of routes through the Highland Spine that few men have traveled. I will find a way around the legion to Avery."

"Be very careful, Ziona. Alcina is likely with them and she would love nothing more than to capture someone close to Cayden. Be very, very careful."

Ziona patted Mordecai on his shoulder and left him at the next corridor, heading off at a brisk walk in the direction of the castle stables where her horse, Seeker, waited, saddled and ready to ride.

Chapter 13

Power Struggle

BLINDING FLASHES OF LIGHT pulsed from the tiered temple, drawing the eye of every villager in Faylea. Crowds of Primordial clanspeople thronged the edge of the sacred grounds, striving to catch a glimpse of what was causing the sky to flash and dim. Those lucky enough to have a front-row view took it upon themselves to yell out a running commentary on the scene before them.

The carvings that adorned the building were no longer still, but writhed on the sides of the temple, resurrected by the flow of spirit within the temple walls. On the walls themselves, visions scrolled, a diorama of the land and the seas and the creatures that lived within them. Scene after scene played itself out. As one level went dark, the one above it lit up until the front-row viewer's commentary was no longer needed. As the images moved up the temple, a great murmur rose from the throng. Some people wept for joy while others screamed with terror. No one in living memory had seen such a display as the temple was putting out that day.

Darkness descended with the setting of the sun, but the temple did not stop projecting its images. The crowds pulsed and thinned as they gradually drifted away to their homes.

Only the elders remained and with them a contingent of Primordial warriors, who ringed the temple. No one could approach the temple or mount its steps since Avery had entered. An invisible force repelled all who attempted it.

At the foot of the stairs, the High Priestess marched back and forth, scowling at the temple. The elders watched her pacing, secretly amused by her annoyance.

"Marea, why don't you relax? There is nowhere for the young woman to go. There is only one door in and that is at the top of the stairs. She will have to come out the same way she went in."

Marea glared at Elder Hania, her scowl deepening so that he took an involuntary step back from her. "She mocks me. The temple and its secrets belong to the High Priestess. She should never have been allowed to enter it on her own. Obviously, she intends to usurp my authority. I will not allow it for the good of our people. Prophesied One or not, she will obey me." She flung out an arm at the glowing temple. "Look what she has done! She has tripped some ancient safeguard and now the temple is out of control. Maybe she never comes out. She may even be dead. *Baw!*" She resumed her pacing, and Elder Hania opened his mouth to respond, just as the temple went dark.

The darkness was complete and eerie after the display that had lasted the better part of a day and a night. As he furiously blinked away the remaining light image, he noticed the beginning blush of dawn creeping across the horizon as the sun prepared to rise in the east.

Everyone stared at the door, and a hush fell across the watchers. The warriors pulled bladed weapons from their leather scabbards and others notched arrows to the long bows common amongst the clan. A nervous tremor ran through the group. Suddenly, the double doors whispered open, ghostlike. A diminutive figure stepped across the threshold to the balcony railing, just as the first rays of sunlight broke the horizon. The sun flashed over her and the blue glow that initially surrounded her faded in the harsh morning glare.

The archers drew back on their creaking bows, arms straining with the resistance of the wood and sighted on Avery's heart. Marea raised her left hand imperiously, halting the bowmen. She cautiously approached the steps of the temple, feeling for the powerful spirit force, the field of spirit that had been humming throughout the day, but it had vanished. Avery's head rose as she approached, her face masked by her heavy hood, and then she moved to stand centered on the staircase. Marea ascended the stairs, eyes intent on Avery. Halfway up, Avery reached back and drew the hood off of her head.

A collective gasp sighed around the crowd, and then fresh murmuring broke out and a few shouts echoed over the grounds. The elders closed in on either side of Marea, who had paused in midstep.

Liquid silver. Her eyes are liquid silver pierced with celestial blue. What is this creature? Cautiously, now, Marea approached Avery, making no sudden movements. Her eyes narrowed at the tattoos covering her skin.

"Hello, child. I am Marea, the High Priestess of the sacred temple you have been enjoying for the past twenty-eight hours."

Avery stared at her, and then her head swung around to take in the weapons pointed in her direction. "Is this how you usually greet guests? With bows and swords?"

Marea shook her head. "No, child, but none of our guests have commandeered a holy site on entering the city either. They do not know your intentions and are correctly cautious, but no harm will come to you as long as I command it."

Avery's strange eyes swung back to Marea, and Marea shivered, masking the thrill that raced along her pulse as the silvery orbs settled on her. The gaze felt ancient, as though an older soul lived behind the silvery window, a presence older than the temple itself, the age of which had passed into legend. No one knew when it had been built or how or by whom. It had simply always existed, as did the mountains around them, ancient and permanent and unmoving.

"I commandeered nothing. I was bid to enter and I did so." Avery's eyes scanned the crowd, but she could not locate her father. "Where is my father?"

"He is safe. What concerns me is what you were doing in the temple for an entire day and night? Come, we must talk, and you need to be seen by our healers."

"I am perfectly fine. I do not need to see any healers. I want to see my father."

"I'm afraid I cannot permit that right now." Avery's eyes swung back to Marea and their silver centers pulsed angrily. "Come, we will talk," implored Marea. "I do not even know your name. What do they call you, child?"

"I am no child!" Avery struggled to restrain the urge to stomp her foot...like a child. Her eyes glazed for a moment, and she struggled to remember her name. She rubbed a hand over where her eyebrow should have been, now permanently inked to match her body.

"Avery." She tested the name on her tongue and found it to be familiar, if not quite true. "I am called Avery in this age." Memories assaulted her with the thought of her name, and sweat broke out on her forehead, a pulsing pain accompanying the effort it took to remember.

"Come, you need rest." Marea held out her hand, indicating that Avery should join her. Avery stepped down the remainder of the steps, pulling up her hood, joining the High Priestess. The clansmen surrounded them and led them away from the temple and back into Faylea proper, crossing over a second bridge that led directly into the heart of the city.

Two sets of eyes, unnoticed by the Primordial guards, followed the retreating group. One was hostile. One was not. But both followed, slipping through grey early morning patches of shadow, pursuing the assembly.

*   *   *

Elder Hania fell into step beside Avery. "Hello, Daughter. It is pleasant to meet you at last. Sharisha has told us of your journey and the trials you have endured along the way."

Avery nodded but did not reply. She took in the buildings as they passed, larger than the homes that had lined the street from the south. This paved stone road was more westerly, and the buildings had the feel of shops or perhaps meeting places. However, it was difficult to tell as no signs decorated the exteriors to advise of their intended usage. The majority were built from saplings, bent and tied and intertwined as they grew. By the number of stories involved, the age of the buildings became apparent. The deeper into the town they walked, the thicker the trunks became until the houses took on a wooden appearance not that different from the log cabins that were popular in Sanctuary-by-the-Sea. The main difference was that instead of lying stacked on their sides, these trunks stood fused side by side.

Eventually they arrived at an immense central square, which was actually an octagon, each side another road departing the central area.

At the focal point of the octagon rose a spire that twisted into the sky and down into the earth. As the sun struck it, the light bounced off and was sent down one of the darker streets that would have remained in perpetual twilight due to the height of the buildings and the trees involved had this feature not have been present. As they approached the spire, a grinding noise met their ears. A mirrored disc halfway up the tower rotated into alignment with the sun's rays and sent a secondary shaft of sunlight down another street. With a series of clicks and whirls, the remaining mirrors aligned themselves and lit the side streets with morning sunlight.

Avery stared at the contraption. "That is incredible. How does it work?"

"We do not know." Elder Hania watched the machine click over to the next setting. "The knowledge of its construction has been forgotten. It is very old, perhaps as old as the temple or the gods."

Avery's head swung around to look him in the eye. "You know of the gods?"

"Of course. I am an elder. Come, we can discuss more of this once inside the spire." He led the way to a curved arch carved out of the base and onto a spiral staircase, which they climbed in dizzying circles until it emptied onto a landing before a door. The door was carved from a huge alabaster clam shell, and the surface rippled with rainbow hues. It swung open silently at their approach. Inside, arched buttresses soared to disappear into the murky gloom of the ceiling. The pale arches reminded Avery of the bones of a whale she had discovered on the beach one summer, washed up and decayed long ago. Only the bones had remained, and she had wandered around and through the ribcage trailing her hand along the arch of bones in awe that such a creature could exist.

Elder Hania and High Priestess Marea led Avery to a trestle table set with matching chairs and indicated that she should take the chair opposite them. The warriors lined the walls, but they did not put away their weapons.

The door opened again and Sharisha entered, striding up to the table and taking a seat on the other side of Marea. Directly behind her entered a woman bearing a tray with a pewter pitcher with a great curved handle and four pewter cups. She set the cups in front of each of them and poured crimson juice into each cup. Setting the pitcher in the middle, she bowed and left the chamber.

Sharisha met Avery's eyes across the table. Shocked at Avery's transformation, she struggled to keep the fear from her face. She studied the tattoos visible on every inch of skin as Avery lowered her hood to her shoulders and then folded her hands in her lap to keep them from twitching.

I must appear strong and confident. I must not give away my insecurity. I must not show weakness. They do not know what happened in the tower. They do not know who I am. Avery's lips curled into a sneer. "I assume you wish to question me? I will only answer what is appropriate for you to hear."

Marea's glare was quickly replaced by a condescending smile that did not reach her eyes. "Child, what could you possibly say that is inappropriate for us to hear? Simply tell us why you entered the temple and what you found in there." Her eyes travelled over Avery, and she was unable to hide the disgust that flickered in her eyes. "Obviously, you borrowed several artifacts of clothing...which, of course, you will return, as they belong to the temple. Where did you find them?" In all her years as High Priestess, Marea had not found the secret closet, despite searching the temple extensively. *How did she find it so easily?* "You also triggered a dangerous display within the temple. What did you do? I must know so that others do not trip over this trigger by accident."

Elder Hania leaned back in his chair and folded his arms, watching Avery closely. He frowned as his eyes examined the visible tattoos on her head. Whirls and symbols followed a pattern that was familiar to him. He stood up and walked back around the table and stopped beside her chair, his frown deepening, drawing his greyed drooping brow almost into a straight line. Avery watched him approach and pause by her chair, and then she clenched her hands, hidden under the table into fists of anger. The elder did not touch her. He simply studied the array of tattoos, moving slowly around her until he paused on the opposite side.

Marea harrumphed and the elder's eyes flickered to her and then back to Avery. With a sigh, he sat back down in his abandoned chair and waited for Marea to resume her interrogation.

Marea swung back to Avery and did not attempt to hide her displeasure this time. "Well, child? Speak up!"

Avery rolled her tense shoulders and took a deep breath. "I don't know what happened. I entered the temple and after that I passed out. When I came to, I was in need of clothes and there was a doorway in front of me. I opened the door, found some clothes, and put them on."

The silence stretched following these words. Then Marea, in a voice so heavy with sarcasm that it hit the floor with a nearly audible thud, sneered, "And? Is that it? Surely you do not think I believe that story, You were in there *for twenty-eight hours—a full day and night!* You want me to believe you *saw and heard nothing?* That you did not explore the temple? You locked the doors! Why? I will have answers, and I will have them now!" This last came out just shy of a screech.

Elder Hania shot a look at Marea out of the corner of his eye but did not speak.

Avery flushed and stared back at Marea, her eyes glowing with emotion. Her gaze switched to Sharisha, who sat expressionless, watching Avery like a cat who had cornered a mouse, after a long chase.

"Well, obviously, you are not meant to know, if you as High Priestess have never had a similar experience." Avery's smile widened, even as her heart raced. *This will not end well*, she thought. "Perhaps you are not meant to access the temple but merely be a caretaker of it? Hmm?"

Marea's face flushed as bright as the ruby liquid in her untouched cup. She leaned forward across the tabletop toward Avery, and her lips drew back into a snarl. "You, young one, are the one who is sadly mistaken. To enter the temple without permission is an offense, punishable by death. You will tell me everything that transpired in the temple, or you will find yourself staked out as food for the vultures. Chosen One or not, you are still human and die just as easily as the rest of us. Your father thought he could resist us too. He came to understand the truth of the matter…in the end."

Avery shot to her feet, lunging at Marea. Before she could do more than lean forward, strong hands grabbed her arms to restrain her. Weapons were drawn, and Avery was surrounded by the Primordial warriors. A knowing grin spread across Sharisha's face.

Elder Hania frowned deeper and shook his head, displeased at the turn of events.

"Take her to the cells until I choose to question her again. The cell beside her useless father would be a good one. Guard her closely, for if she escapes, you will be very, *very* sorry." Marea stood up, eyes glinting at Avery's struggle as she was dragged out through a side passage.

"You will fail, High Priestess!" Avery yelled over her shoulder. "You were never more than a caretaker!" she spat as she was hauled over the threshold and the door boomed closed behind them.

Chapter 14

Artio

ARTIO ROAMED THE FORGOTTEN TEMPLE, examining the throne room and the attendant chambers beyond the main audience hall. In the private rooms she claimed as her own, she located several trunks with rusted padlocks that broke with a swift tug. Inside the trunks were articles of clothing wrapped in silk. The trunks had been preserved with a spell that kept the ravages of time from harming the contents. Rummaging through them, she found several sets of soft chestnut robes that fell over one shoulder, leaving the other exposed, and dropped to just above her knees. She tossed open the lid of an oaken chest banded with iron and found a sleeveless leather vest and leather-plated skirt with interlocking folds of armadillo shell. Her lips stretched into a feral smile at the discovery. It was more armour than clothing, and she was pleased. She also found leather greaves studded with cabochons of emerald, ruby, amethyst, and tiger's eye. She strapped the greaves on her downy arms and, as a crowning touch, settled a rough circlet of hammered gold on her dirty-blonde curls to complete her transformation.

A bubbled mirror on the far wall reflected a distorted view, but it was enough for Artio to see the warrior goddess in her true form. *I am truly a blend now, thunder-bear and goddess wrapped into one lethal package.*

As she had rummaged for the clothing, pieces of long-buried memory surfaced. Memories of a forgotten past and people, of sibling wars and banishment amongst the very stars she was to maintain. She snarled at the image in the mirror. *I will never be banished again. This time*

I will prevail. My sisters and brother have a lot to answer for, especially the twins. I will hunt them down, and this time I will not fail.

Artio re-entered the audience chamber to find the High Priests exactly as she had left them, standing in the center of the hall with their eyes rolling in their heads. On the floor, scorpions scuttled everywhere, blackening the floor in the circle bound by her magic. One priest whimpered as a scorpion crawled over his naked foot, poised with its poisoned tip raised as if to strike.

"Please, Great One! Release us so that we may serve you. We will find the people you seek. We are sworn to your service!" He shuddered as the scorpion began to crawl under the hem of his robes and out of site. Sweat rolled down his cheek, and his eyes widened at the movements that were now not visible, but that he felt nonetheless.

Artio bent and picked up one of the scorpions, which curled up on the palm of her hand like a dog settling to sleep. *"My pets will not harm you, provided you mean me no harm. Think on that this evening, and in the morning, if you are still alive, you may serve me."*

She strode out the temple doorway and into the night. None followed her. None could, for where she was headed only the dead could go.

*　　＊　＊　＊*

Artio's long legs carried her through the woods. She began to climb a twisting trail that led up to the jagged peaks forming the tip of the spine of the world. The location of the place she sought had come back to her while she'd searched the trunks for clothing. As though awakening from a long sleep, the clouds had lifted and fragments of memory reorganized themselves, solidifying into a solid plan. If the twins did indeed roam the earth again, as the weak priests had suggested, Artio needed to level the playing field. That meant it was time for a little family reunion.

She snarled once again, annoyed at the time lost. Multiple millennia she had been chained. True, she had been unaware of the passage of time (she was immortal, after all)—but still. She checked that the weapon she'd strapped to her left thigh as she left the temple was secure. The long thin blade of obsidian was set in a creamy bone handle that she had been especially pleased to find right where she had left it before her banishment. The blade was impregnated with the deadly poisonous slavering of Cerberus, a very effective poison both in this life and the afterlife.

Memories of her existence as a thunder god blended and merged with her memories of the godling child called Artio. Artio had been a weak creature, barely aware of the world around her. She had been fascinated with the constellations and with the one she had been named after in particular. The irony was not lost on her. Now returned to a physical form, they were bound as one. She should have anticipated that the experiment harnessing the moon that was her home could have dire consequences. She could not remember her name as a cub. Artio would do.

She strode through the night, swifter than a horse could travel the distance, enjoying the journey after eons of time spent watching the world turn. She increased her pace into a ground-eating lope that took her from one end of the Highland Spine to the other. As she walked, steadily climbing, she plucked ripened gooseberries, discovering an intense liking for the juicy red fruit.

Licking the sticky syrup from her fingertips, she paused at the ridge of the great divide and surveyed the lands before her. The vantage point of being at the peak of the world, combined with her extraordinary sight, allowed her to see the entirety of the world. To the south, the foothills of the Highland Needle melted into the grasslands where the Battle of Daimon Ford had been fought. The plains were interrupted by a large swamp enshrouded in fog and then continued on to the coast, where the capital city of Cathair squatted against the edge of the cliffs, the stone fortress flying the king's flag.

Artio's head swung to her left and her eyes followed the coastline to where the great pine forests began, the trees growing taller and taller the further northeast her eyes travelled. When they collided with the eastern terminus of the Highland Needle, a flyspeck village was detected. She growled at the site. The air shimmered with the residual presence of magic in that area. *The home of my now mortal brother and sister, no doubt*, she thought. She turned once again, looking back the way she had come, across the eastern edge of the Spine and down into the lands of the Primordials. She felt a strange affinity for these barbaric people and not only for the fact that they had called her back from her imprisonment amongst the stars. No, she felt a connection to them physically, another mystery to unravel, another puzzle piece to set in place. Her eyes took in the leafy canopy of gumwood and the rounded tops of the mushroom trees, looking ever so much like ruddy faces staring back at her.

As she completed her inspection, her luminous eyes fixed on a convergence of peaks from which issued puffs of steam, cooling and condensing into clouds that drifted away on the breeze. *That's the spot, the entrance to the abyss my dear sister calls home*, she thought. *It's time to knock on the door.*

Ten more minutes of walking brought her to the base of a waterfall that rose impossibly into the sky. The top of the waterfall disappeared into the clouds so that it appeared to be suspended from the sky. It tumbled down the sheer cliff to a frothing pool before flowing away to the south. A tributary wandered away at the base, and she followed the shore of the errant stream. As the water flowed away, it slowed and finally spilled over into a basin of red rock, hissing as it hit the surface. Steam rose from the contact, creating a curtain that she could not see beyond.

Being of thunder blood did have its advantages. Artio threw back her head and roared at the heavens, invoking the air and the water to blend and gather, swirling faster and faster, more clouds forming and thickening overhead. Lightning flashed and the maelstrom darkened, twisting into a thunderhead above the pool. From the midst of the clouds, a funnel dropped, whirling with ferocious winds that whipped the tree trunks, tearing off leaves and branches and sucking them into the vortex. Yet the tornado did not touch Artio. Her clothing did not even stir. The mists parted, and the open maw of a cave was revealed with jagged teeth, glowing red in the flickering light spilling from its mouth. Silhouetted against the opening was a figure encased in long black robes. The hood was drawn up and the face hidden from view. Its arms were crossed, hands tucked into the opposite sleeve. A crow cawed its raucous song from a nearby tree. The figure held out its arm to the bird, which flew down to perch on the outstretched appendage.

"Welcome, Sister. Welcome back. Will you join me in hell?" Helga chuckled loudly at her own joke, then disappeared back into the waiting chasm. Artio followed, leaving the tornado spinning impossibly in the pool devoid of water.

Chapter 15

Alcina

ALCINA, THE FORMER QUEEN OF CATHAIR, strode through the encampment, ringed by her guards. Her cape of blood-red silk fluttered behind her as she marched along. Her heeled boots kept her hem from dragging through the mud, but she grabbed a fist full of skirts and pulled them higher, just in case. She hated soiling her dress in such filth. *No queen should have to live in such primitive conditions. I will have my castle back if I have to eliminate each and every savage, one by one.*

Trotting at her heels was her new Lord General. The departure of Cyrus and the discovery shortly thereafter of the two dead captives had put her in a very foul mood. Her specific instructions had been to leave the captives for her to interrogate. What information they had told Cyrus, what secrets they had shared as they had screamed out the last few moments of their existence on this earth she would never know. It bothered her that Cyrus had done this against her specific command. Furthermore, he had not come to tell her what he had learned before he left, and that was extremely disturbing. Beyond disturbing. It bordered on treason.

One captive was left. Only one. She would have answers from this one or…

"Darius!" she snapped.

"Yes, my queen?" Darius was a young man, barely a man by most accountings. He bowed low, hands on knees. She surveyed his shock of red hair on his head and the line of freckles that trailed down his neck. The lad had proven his loyalty to his queen by befriending the usurper. Then, in an act of betrayal befitting one of her own, delivered the traitor into her waiting hands. Her mistress's pets had dragged the unconscious boy to the cells. If it had not been for that meddling wizard, she would still be safely ensconced within her castle. She had rewarded Darius by granting him a permanent position in the Queen's Guard. His thin frame was now encased in the uniform of an officer, and the only thing identifying him as a Lord General was the insignia that had been hastily sewn onto the breast of his tunic. His pimpled face was partially covered in a thin scruffy beard. Alcina had the impression that he was growing it in an attempt to look older to the men he commanded. He held himself rigidly as he strode beside her, eyes flickering over the men of the camp and back to her. He swallowed, and his Adam's apple bobbled in his throat.

"You were successful in getting close to the usurper as our spy. I want you to perform a similar miracle here. I want you to get to know the Primordial captive. I want to know everything he knows. You are to become his best friend."

"My lady?" Darius frowned at her words.

"I want you to go undercover. I want you to pretend to be a captive alongside him. See if you can gain his trust and find out what he knows."

"Ah, I see." Darius's frown slid into a speculative smile. "The best way to do that would be to have me hauled in and tossed into the same cell."

"Yes, my thoughts exactly. Listen, do you think your men could rough you up? Give you some bruises and such to make it real? How about a cut or two, as though you were in a fight?"

"I can get those on the training field. No need to stage injuries."

"Excellent. Then I expect you to be deposited in his tent before dark. Now, what do we know about this captive? Has he given any information?"

"The only thing we know at this point is that he is some kind of a holy man. He wears strange robes and talks to himself a lot. I am not sure he is completely sane."

Alcina considered the information. "If he is a holy man, he knows a great deal. Did Cyrus question him? Is he damaged?"

"No, my queen. It seems Cyrus chose the men he interrogated at random as far, as we can tell. I believe that he was not questioned by Cyrus."

"A strange stroke of luck," said Alcina, as she paused at the edge of the tent containing the prisoner. "One I intend to exploit to its fullest." One of Alcina's elite protectors stepped between the two legionnaires manning the entrance to the tent and swept aside the curtain. A second bodyguard preceded Alcina into the tent, followed by two additional security guards who fanned out around the fabric walls, but Darius remained outside.

A man, dressed in nothing but the skin he was born with, sat cross-legged in the middle of the room. His hands were resting on his knees, palms up and his eyes were closed. Red abrasions ran around his wrists and ankles where the hemp ropes had cut into his skin when he had been tied to the stakes driven into the dirt floor. Curly white hair flowed over his shoulders and down his back. His upper torso was covered in tattoos that started at the join between neck and collarbone and spread out over his chest and back then encircled his upper arms. He did not stir at Alcina's entrance nor did he acknowledge her presence. His chest barely moved.

The guard, who had preceded Alcina into the tent, raised a gauntleted hand and swung it at the seated Primordial priest with such force that the man was knocked sideways to sprawl on the ground. A trickle of blood bloomed across his cheek and from the split in his upper lip.

"You will acknowledge the queen when she enters a room and bow to Her Highness," the guard bellowed. "There will be no further warnings!"

The priest raised a hand to his cheek, gazing at the blood left on it as he pulled it away. He sat up slowly and then knelt, bowing from his knees to Alcina.

Alcina walked around the priest, examining the tattoos that decorated his skin. "They say you are a man of importance among the Primordials."

He lifted his head from the tent floor and risked a glance at her. "I am a servant of my people. Nothing more."

"Which clan are you?"

"I am of the Flesh Clans."

"And what is your purpose to your people?"

"I am a spiritual leader. It is our duty to serve."

"I am interested in the spirits of your people. Will you tell me of them? And your faith?"

"I would be pleased to speak to you about my people's faith."

"You would?" asked Alcina, so surprised by his words that she stopped circling, pausing between him and the guards at her back.

"Yes, Your Highness. We have much that we need to discuss."

"What is your name?"

"Hototo. I am a priest of the Flesh Clans. I was sent to help you."

Alcina folded her arms, studying the man.

"Well, Hototo, how about you wash up, put some clothes on, and join me for dinner?" Her guards' heads swiveled as though pulled by the same string to stare at her. "There is more than one way to get business done." Hototo bowed his head once again.

Alcina vanished from the tent in a swirl of flame red silk, and Darius fell in beside her as she made her way back to her tents. "You heard?"

Darius nodded silently. "Perhaps he will be cooperative. Maybe Cyrus did us a favour in torturing the other two, helping to loosen his tongue."

"Bring him to me as soon as he stops stinking like a pigsty. And, Darius, I have changed my mind. You will not be spending the night getting cozy with the prisoner," said Alcina. "I wish for you to sit in on this meeting. If all goes well, I will have a mission for you. If not, I will have a body in need of disposal."

"Yes, my queen." Darius left her in the presence of her guards and returned to the prisoner tent.

Alcina entered her quarters, her attendants curtsying low as she passed. "Bring refreshments, enough for three. I am about to entertain," she commanded. More curtsies followed, and then the servants scurried away. Alcina paused by the basin of water under her mirror and dipped in her hands. It was stone cold. "*Water!*" she screamed. *Once again, they have let my water grow cool. Someone will pay for this incompetence. They know the penalty for failure.*

She smiled with grim pleasure. Someone was going to bleed today. Oh yes, indeed.

*   *   *

Darius re-entered the tent and stood, arms folded, looking at the little priest. Hototo's clothing had been returned to him, and he was in the process of pulling on the pale leather-like garments. The clothing had the look of leather and fit the priest like a second skin. Darius's head whipped back, and he squinted to take a second look at the clothing, which disappeared under a cloak made of fur. It was skin, but of no animal he had ever seen on his father's farm. A shiver danced up his spine. *Human skin?* His mind danced away from the thought, not wanting to examine it too closely. The Primordial priest pulled on some soft boots of deerskin and straightened.

Thank the gods I know what that skin is! thought Darius as he studied the priest.

"I have a medicine bag that was taken from me when I arrived. May I have it back?" The old man held out his hand as though he expected to be obeyed.

"I doubt you will need it," said Darius with a smirk.

Hototo dismissed Darius's words. "Oh, I need it all right, and so does your queen. It contains the very articles I was sent to deliver into her possession."

Darius grunted and signaled over his shoulder with a snap of his fingers to the waiting guard. The man left the tent and returned a few minutes later with a satchel covered in seed beading. Some of the designs matched the tattoos on Hototo's skin.

Darius opened the bag and rummaged around inside it, looking for a weapon. Inside was a child's straw doll, a pair of them in fact, along with a couple of broken feather quills that were not useful as weapons, cloth that he took to be articles of clothing, and a pot of clear paste like beeswax. Rolling around at the bottom were several coins, the like of which Darius had never seen before, and some polished stones.

He closed the satchel and tossed it to the priest. "Let's get going. She will be waiting for us."

Hototo shuffled to the door and bent to pass through and was greeted outside by four guards who towered over his barely five-foot height. Quietly he stood, allowing a search of his person. He then followed the entrance guards (another pair closing rank behind him) across the camp to the queen's tents. At Alcina's doorway, Hototo was searched once again and then allowed to enter, followed by Darius.

Alcina was ensconced in her sedan chair, her crown perched on her head. She sipped a steaming cup of tea, recently poured by a trembling maid who attempted to blend into the tapestry hanging between two tent poles behind Alcina, close enough to respond instantly to her summons but far enough away that she hoped the queen would forget her presence. Two places had been set on a low table at her feet. They would be sitting on the floor to eat.

The Primordial stood in front of the table and, with a shove from Darius, sank to his knees.

"Now, now, Darius, show our guest the respect due a dignitary." Alcina gestured to the cushions on the floor. "Sit, relax, and eat. You must be hungry."

On the table before them was a bowl of freshly washed dates, slices of cheese and sausage, peppers, and a crunchy, edible green that grew in the shade of the boulders along the trail, and flat-trail bread baked on open grills. Pitchers of water, beading on the surface of clay with the humidity of the tent, sat next to two squat clay cups. "Come, eat. I assure you none of it is poisoned, or she"—she waved vaguely at the cowering maid behind her—"would already be dead."

Hototo did not need to be told twice and fell to the food with enthusiasm. He rolled meat and cheese and peppers in the flatbread and hungrily bit off large chunks, totally engrossed in his food. His free hand drifted to the pitcher and he poured water, gulping down the contents of a mug as his other hand popped the last of the flatbread into his mouth.

"My, my, one would think you haven't eaten anything in several days." Darius barked a laugh but did not take his eyes off the priest.

Hototo slowed down on his third meat roll and only ate half of the fourth, pausing for another drink of water and then settled back on the cushions, sighing with satisfaction.

"I thank you for your hospitality, Your Highness. Let me present you with a gift from my people." He reached into his satchel. The movements brought the guards and Darius to full attention, their hands on their swords. At the sound of steel being drawn, Hototo looked around and stilled his hand, still buried in the bag.

"I will bring it out slowly. It is a doll...just a doll," he said in reassurance. Darius gave a tense nod for him to proceed. A muscle twitched in his clenched jaw. Hototo's arm moved, drawing out his hand and bringing with it a straw doll. It was about a foot tall with short, cut straw sticking out from the top and woven through the folds that made the head of the doll. String had been tied around the neck, and halfway down the straw was split to form legs and partway up to form arms. The doll was dressed in royal purple robes, and the figure carried a stick that resembled a baton. Along the surface of the baton, small dots were placed.

"A doll? You set yourself up to be captured, endured torture, and have beggared yourself into my presence to give me a toy?" Alcina snapped her fingers, and her guards were instantly at Hototo's side and reaching down to grab his arms and haul him away from the table.

"Wait!" he held up his arms to fend off the grasping guards. Alcina held up her right hand, halting the guards.

"Speak now, and it had better be good, or your head will shortly be bouncing down the side of this sorry mountain." She glared at Hototo as he offered her the doll, which she grudgingly took from him.

"It is not a simple doll. It is a Soul Fetch."

Alcina turned it over in her hand, examining it closely. "What does it do? And why is it dressed in royal clothing?" Her hawk-like gaze pinned the priest to the spot. "If your answer pleases me, I will spare your life. I may even reward you. Now speak."

"A Soul Fetch is a soul-seeker. It is empowered with the ability to search out the soul of an enemy and trap it within the doll, enslaving them to the wishes of the possessor. With that doll"— Hototo poked one crooked finger at the straw figure—"you can control the soul of another and thereby his actions, his thoughts, and his dreams. With that, the victim is your puppet, completely within your control, regardless of where he is in the world."

Alcina's greedy gaze returned to the doll, and the ghost of a smile passed her lips as she considered his words and their implication.

"Go on," she said slowly. "I am listening. Why is this doll dressed in royal colours?"

"That is because, Your Highness, that doll is bound to the current king of Cathair. That doll will control the soul of one Cayden Tiernan, once activated. He is someone who has been a thorn in your foot, if the rumours are correct."

Alcina turned the doll over once again, examining it closely.

"How does it work? And why would you offer it to me so freely? What is your price?"

Hototo's lips peeled back into a toothless smile. "Our price is this. You will help us wipe out the Spirit Clans and their leader Marea, the High Priestess. You will help us establish rulership over those who survive, so that the true faith, the faith of the flesh, is no longer suppressed. Do this, and you can have the doll and your kingdom back. Do this and you will have a true ally to the north. Do this and you will never be challenged again." Hototo stared off into the corner of the tent, for a moment absorbed in some vision that only he could see. His face broke into a huge smile, his eyes shining with the fervour of blind devotion. "With the elimination of the Spirit Shield, we will rule supreme! Forever at one with our goddess, Artio. Refuse to do this and you will never learn the secrets of the doll. Without my help, the doll is but a doll."

Alcina's smiled a cold smile. "A tempting offer. Now show me how it works."

Hototo reached into his bag a second time and this time withdrew a doll with no clothing. "Fetch me a scrap of cloth from the servant's dress," he commanded. The guards hesitated. With a twitch of Alcina's hand, a legionnaire with a shaved head marched over to the cowering maid, snatching a fist full of skirt in one hand and drawing a sharp knife in the other. He sliced off a chunk of the rough-spun cloth of her skirt. The servant squeaked in response, cowering behind Alcina's throne-like chair, then resumed her quivering.

The soldier handed the cloth to Hototo, who wrapped it around the doll like a skirt. Next, he dug into his satchel and removed a smooth stone that glowed with a summer sky blue and tucked it inside the chest of the doll so that it disappeared under the woven strands. "May I borrow your hairpin for a moment, Your Highness?"

Alcina reached back and pulled a long bone hairpin from the back of her hair and handed it to the priest. All heads swiveled to the maid, who was now wringing her hands, eyes darting frantically around the room, looking for a way to escape.

The priest began to chant in a singsong voice that slowly rose in pitch. The stone glowed and the maid's arm blurred as an azure blue mist rose from her skin. The stone pulsed and the mist surrounding the girl throbbed as though the stone carried a heartbeat. She felt the pulsing mist and swiped at her arms, scrubbing at her skin. When this did nothing to halt the binding, she screamed and abruptly bolted for the doorway despite it being blocked by the big burly guards favoured by Alcina.

Before the maid reached the doorway, the priest stabbed the doll where the heart would be in a human. The maid shrieked and stumbled, clutching at her chest. The priest stabbed the doll again, and the maid collapsed to the ground, writhing in agony. He stabbed a third time. She cried out, her body spasming on the floor and then it stilled.

The closest guard bent over her and felt for a pulse and then straightened. "She still lives."

Alcina was transfixed by the doll. The doll was no longer straw but had transformed into a perfect replica of the girl with eyes that glowed with an inner blue light. The priest handed the doll to Alcina.

"She is now yours to command. You carry her soul in your hands. Crush that doll, and she is instantly dead. You need but command, and she will do as you ask. She cannot refuse. Total control."

Alcina's gaze travelled between the transformed doll and the straw doll in her other hand. A cold, malicious smile froze on her face.

"And there is no release from this spell?"

"There is no release short of death. Only a Primordial priest will know how to undo the enchantment."

Alcina's smile widened. Her small pearly teeth glinted in the dim light cast by the lanterns.

"I will pay your price," she hissed, as she tucked the two dolls inside pockets sewn into her skirts.

Chapter 16

Drawings in a Cave

CAYDEN BOLTED UPRIGHT IN BED, eyes wild, and stared around the room at the fading grey light of predawn. He shoved the sweaty covers off his body and swung his legs over the side of the bed, scratching at the itch on his chest caused by the clothing twisted around his torso. What was it that had awakened him? He cast a glance around his room examining his surroundings, but all was still and silent. He frowned and, standing up, strode for the door and wrenched it open.

There, sitting at his study table, sat Mordecai. He sipped his cup of tea. With a tiny clatter, he placed it back on the table and then turned a page in the tome. A toothpick twirled in his mouth, as he worked it side to side, engrossed in the words in front of him.

Cayden ran his hand through his silky hair and wandered over to Mordecai, feeling anxious and out of sorts, having just awoken. Something was bothering him, but he couldn't put his finger on it.

At his approach, Mordecai looked up from his studies and smiled. "Ah, so the king rises from his slumber. Good morning, Your Majesty!" He chuckled as Cayden made a face. While it was the proper form of address, Cayden had spent the weeks after his coronation running about the castle trying to impress upon his subjects that they needn't be bowing and scraping to him constantly and that his name was Cayden, pure and simple. Of course, none of the staff listened. If anything, his constant reminders of what not to do only spurred on the opposite.

So popular was the new king that several entrepreneurial peasants started creating trinkets to sell to the constant stream of pilgrims who now flowed into the castle to see the marvel at the return of the king. Of course, they wanted his royal patronage, and Cayden had spent some initial time blessing this amulet or adding his royal seal to that commemorative coin. The trade was so brisk that the tribunal of judges who had been set up after Alcina's hasty departure, now also had to decide how to place a value on the items Cayden had put his royal seal on. Cayden no longer gave his seal of approval for items, as the furor created by this seemingly innocuous event was way out of proportion to the good he had intended.

Mordecai spun one of those coins between his thumb and forefinger as he watched Cayden's sleepy progress across the floor.

Cayden dropped into the chair beside Mordecai, his eyes on the coins. "Were you able to find them all?"

Mordecai shook his head. "No. The judges did a good job at buying them back from the people, explaining that they would go into a museum for all to enjoy. But ten coins are still unaccounted for."

Cayden grunted. "What are you studying? That looks like the book I was going through yesterday."

"Yes, and a curious tome it is. When your mother died, I asked the tree sprites to gather all the books of magic and any books that referenced you or your sister in any way and hide them where no human could find them. They did an excellent job of it, did they not? I did not know that they had snatched this one from my private library, but it is just as well, as Alcina later stormed the place and burned it to the ground."

Mordecai flipped to the next page and then paused. "See this?" He jabbed a skinny finger halfway down the left page. Cayden leaned in and saw it was the passage he had been reading yesterday when Ziona had awakened.

"Yes, I wished to talk to you about that passage, but then Ziona woke up and I fell asleep." His voice trailed off as it suddenly hit him, what had awoken him. It was silence. The silence of a vacuum, only this vacuum was in his mind. He shot to his feet. "Ziona! Where is she?"

He spun on the spot, looking for her familiar form. He strode to the adjoining room where she sometimes slept when they had late night sessions. He grabbed both handles and flung them open. The chamber was empty, the bed linens undisturbed.

"Mordecai, where is she?" he demanded as he returned to the table. "She has left, hasn't she?"

"Yes, Cayden. Sit down."

He sank slowly back into the chair and cast out with his mind. He sensed she was on the fringe, the link stretched thin. Avery was an even slimmer thread, but the threads were similar. Ziona was travelling in the same direction he sensed Avery to be. She was headed back to the lands of the Primordials.

"Why would she leave without me? I need her. I would have gone with her! I need to join Avery too!"

"She knows your duties are here, Cayden, and she did not want you to leave your people and your responsibilities as king. She felt she was interfering and that a clean break was for the best."

"That is ridiculous and you know it, Mordecai!" he hollered. "I have fulfilled my duties here. The Well of Souls is safe and secure. You heard the spirit of my mother. I have to go to Avery. She needs me!"

"Yes, she does, but not yet. Not now." Mordecai pushed the book to the side as a knock sounded at the door and a Kingsman leaned into the room, holding the door open for the maid who had delivered Cayden's tray the previous day. She backed into the room with a fresh tray of steaming food.

"I have your breakfast, Majesty!" She curtsied, and Mordecai gestured for her to approach. Cayden ignored her. She placed the tray in front of him, removed the covers and curtsied, then left the room. The Kingsmen pulling the doors closed behind her.

Mordecai's stomach grumbled, but Cayden felt nauseous the same as the evening before. He grimaced and picked up the tea, thirsty more than anything.

"You must eat, Cayden. Here, try some of this porridge with the raisins and apples." He pushed the bowl in front of Cayden and added a heavy dollop of cream and a scoop of honey to the top. He filched the crusty roll decorating the edge of the plate and slathered some butter on it then sat back, happily munching his way through the crumbling bread.

Cayden picked up his spoon and shoveled porridge into his protesting mouth. He forced himself to swallow four mouthfuls before pushing the tray away, feeling decidedly green.

Mordecai frowned at him. "The headaches are back? And the nausea?"

"It never really left," answered Cayden.

"Maybe we should have a healer look at you." Mordecai placed his hand against Cayden's forehead.

"Ziona is my healer, and you sent her away."

"I didn't send her away. You will be joining her soon, just not right now. Your place is here, Cayden. There are things we must discuss and plans that must be made. She knows this and understands it. You are the king. Your duties lie here, whether you like it or not. Now come. It is time we added to your education." Mordecai pulled a heavy book entitled *A Comparative Study of the Gods and Goddesses of the Pre-Daimon Epoch* back across the table and began to read aloud.

"Helga, the youngest of the godlings, was perhaps (at least historically) the godling who was most in touch with the mortal world. Ancient cave drawings discovered in the Highland Spine and predating the Battle of Daimon Ford clearly depict the goddess Helga attending funerals of the mortals and assisting the grieving with the passage of the souls of the dead into her brother's care. The drawings illustrate a side to Helga that is rarely reflected in the annals of the gods. This illustration, which has been dated to the earliest epoch, displays Helga in her funeral finery carrying the body of a dying child into the blue mists of the Thunder Falls, one of the most sacred of places of the current day Primordial races. Indeed, to be carried into the falls is seen to be a direct conduit of the soul to the spiritual realm."

Cayden sighed, sliding a hand over his sweating face. He loosened four buttons on his fine red tunic. "Yes, I read that already. So, my godling sibling, Helga, is my nemesis. I figured that out yesterday. It's frustrating that I cannot remember more of my own history. Do you know why I cannot unlock it if I put my own soul into this body? Why is it that I have forgotten everything?"

Mordecai sat back and studied Cayden. Dark half circles formed crescent moons under his lashes, a sign of his exhaustion.

"I think it had to do with my magical interference, or assistance, if you will. When we had to take such desperate measures to save the pair of you, somehow the memory link with your soul was disturbed. Ordinarily, when a soul is delivered to a newborn babe, the memories associated with that prior life cease, as the person they were before no longer exists. As you saw, the memories of that prior life can linger on while they are part of the spirit pool, but it does not carry forward to the new host.

"But you and Avery are unique. Neither of you died to give up your souls, at least not in the traditional sense. I believe that the disruption is temporary, but I do not know how to restore your memories. What you proposed originally, through Aossi, had never been done before. It is magic of the gods. Something I am not.

"You will find your answers, Cayden. I am sure of it. If not you, then Avery will, but I think the knowledge is within the pair of you. You just have to unlock it."

Cayden abruptly stood up and began pacing. "Well, I am not going to sit here and wait for it to pop in my head. I will go mad, Mordecai! I cannot shut down the tug at my soul. I need to go to Avery. I will not delay much longer. The counsel is set up, the courts are working, the people are safe and happy, and the knights Ryder has recruited now guard the Well of Souls. My Kingsmen have swelled in number as the guard of old, and now their adult children have returned to service. There is no need for me to stay here." He paused by Mordecai's chair and stared him in the eye. "I must go."

It was Mordecai's turn to sigh.

"All right. We will go. I can see you are not to be dissuaded from it, but first, let's bring in your captains and plan this venture, rather than bolting out the door on whim and adrenaline. Call them in, and let's find out the lay of the land and what the scouts have to report."

Cayden smiled for the first time that morning. "Now you are talking!" He sprang to his feet and strode to the door, wrenching it open. The two Kingsmen on duty saluted. "Find me Denzik, Fabian, and Nelson. Ask them to report to me in the Shield Room in one hour." One guard peeled away from his post and tapped the shoulder of a companion as he passed him in the hall. The second Kingsman took up his spot at Cayden's door.

Cayden closed the door and pulled on a cord dangling from the ceiling. A bell chimed and a maid slipped into the room and curtsied. "Bring me water to bathe, please." She curtsied again and hurried back into the hallway and off down the corridor. Mordecai had not moved.

"Well? What are you waiting for?" Cayden strode off into his bedroom and slammed the door behind him.

Mordecai frowned, muttering words under his breath that sounded suspiciously like "stubborn" and "pig-headed" and then ran his finger down the page of the book to where he had left off and continued to read. *"Other drawings, discovered deeper within this same cave, depicted a darker, less benevolent goddess. In these drawings of the same age as the first set, Helga is depicted as standing over the bodies of a man and a woman. The symbols painted on the foreheads of these people suggest that they are flesh representations of the goddess Alfreda and her brother Caerwyn. They are depicted as mortals and a blue mist surrounds their bodies. Both historians and scholars agree, that the imagery suggests that Helga is harvesting the souls of the twins, her immortal sister and brother. Why they are depicted in a mortal form is a fine point of debate yet to be resolved."* Mordecai sighed a greater sigh than Cayden's and closed the book, pondering the meaning of the words.

Chapter 17

Remember

AVERY PACED THE NARROW CONFINES of her cell with her arms crossed over her chest, boots scraping across the cold stone surface. A weak light spilled in from the street from a window set high in the cave wall. She knew her father was next door, but she was unable wake him no matter how much she called out to him.

The guards had attempted to remove her jewellery and clothing before depositing her in the cell, but it was as though there was a forged link between her and the garb. It refused to come off regardless of how much they tugged. At first, they thought she had resisted, but after a few good slaps and pinning her to the ground with a knee in her back and lots of tugging that arched her back to painful levels, they saw the light. She could not resist, and they quickly discovered that the clothing was fused to her physically and would not come off. The same held true with the jewellery and the lone weapon that she carried. In fact, when they tried to remove it, the blade cut them despite their precautions. It was almost as if the blade had a mind of its own, fighting back against capture. Avery shivered and gingerly touched the knife, which grew hot in her hand now and seemed to hum. She sensed it was *happy*. She felt a welcoming warmth from the blade. *It almost seems alive.*

The end result of this unfortunate discovery was that triple the normal guard was placed around her cell, but she was grudgingly allowed to keep all of her acquisitions in the cell with her. What else could they do short of killing her to take it?

Marea will be thrilled to hear about this! She is probably planning my execution by morning.

Avery grew tired of her pacing and sank down on the stone bench that doubled as a bed and shivered from the dampness of the cave. Discouragement washed over her in a wave. *Some welcome this is. I did not ask to come here. Why is the magic of the temple working in this fashion? What is so important about these things?*

Curious, she shrugged out of the coat. It slid easily from her arms, and there was none of the prickling and pulling and biting of the cloak that had accompanied the tussle of a few minutes ago. *Interesting. It seems to know to whom it belongs. Now how to figure out why it's decided it's me.* She stood up and rummaged through the pockets, seeing if there was anything in them she had not noticed before. The pockets on the outside were extraordinarily deep but yielded nothing. She laid the coat open on the bench beside her. She ran her hand over the smooth, seamless interior. To her surprise, she felt a lump in the armpit stitching. She felt along the seam, and there, tucked where no one could possibly find it, was a small pocket. It looked like a spot where the stitching was missing. In the pocket was a piece of parchment. Gingerly, she pulled it out, checking over her shoulder to be certain she was not being watched.

The parchment was furled so tightly it was nearly impossible to unwind. She carefully unrolled it on the stone bench, using her knife to weigh down the one edge as she flattened it for reading. The script was in her personal handwriting. The ink was faded with time but still legible.

Avery's heart leapt into her throat and started to race. She scanned the letter but quickly became lost and had to force herself to slow down and go back to the beginning. She fetched the stub of candle sitting on a wooden tray and carried it back over to the stone bench to better illuminate the fragile parchment. A thin edge crumbled in her shaking hands as she attempted to position it better. She leaned in and began to read.

If you are reading this, then you have successfully entered the temple and found the secret closet containing the garments of the gods. If you are reading this, I have to assume you are me, for no other could enter this room. It is for the offspring of the gods only and has been set aside for time without end for our use. You are one of only four godlings who can enter the true temple safely, for it is not located in the physical mortal realm but in the celestial. No true mortal could cross its threshold and trigger its secrets. You have visited the realm of the gods.

I ramble, and time is short. I fear that with the plan we are about to instigate I may forget my heritage, so I write this note to my future self. I—that is, you—and my brother Caerwyn have, after great debate and weighing of the odds, decided to become mortals. If you are reading this, we obviously succeeded, which probably makes this letter moot, but I write it for my (our) peace of mind and as a safety precaution should something go wrong with our plan. By the time that I (you) read this letter, Helga will have had eighteen to twenty years to solidify her hold on the world. The mortals, both animal and human, who have been Caerwyn's and my charges since our father died, are in grave danger of being enslaved by Helga for all eternity.

Helga has set in play a plan to capture the Well of Souls in Cathair, which the royals of that land have long guarded through a combination of physical presence and through Caerwyn's influence. I have heard rumours of an assassination plan, but we have been unsuccessful in uncovering its details. Needless to say, to lose the physical Spirit Shield of Cathair would give Helga the opening she needs to seize the capital and take dominion over the souls of the dead awaiting their rebirth. These souls have not been condemned to her realm. My sister grows more and more greedy and jealous of our positions over the earth's inhabitants.

But for me, personally, the stakes are even higher, for the lives of the non-human population are also at risk. The great spirits of the animals are disappearing. Daily, I stroll through my beloved Faylea and the surrounding forests, and they grow quiet. The animals are disappearing, their voices silenced. But even more shocking is that their spiritual forms are also growing quiet. I (we) are their caretakers and yet, they are not coming to me to pass over. I can only conclude one thing, that they are being snatched away before death and enslaved in the underworld. Twisted to Helga's desires, it can only bode ill for the world, for they could be unleashed as powerful weapons against all mortal existence. Soon, all life within our dominion will cease to exist.

We are Spirit Shields. We maintain the River of Souls. We are the guardians of the rebirth, the reincarnation of all mortal kind. This is our fight: to free the captured souls in Helga's clutches. We can do nothing for those already twisted and turned to evil, but I cannot abide the idea that all souls are lost. I have set certain plans in place to slow Helga down, but they will not last forever. I pray that they will last just long enough.

I dare not say more in this letter, lest it fall into the wrong hands, as even in Faylea, I fear that Helga's spies are in our midst. I have been forced to abdicate my position as High Priestess amongst great discord. I believe that Marea will be the next High Priestess, yet only a godling can be a Spirit Shield. I (we) have worn many faces over epochs of time, but this time I see Helga's handiwork. Beware of the Flesh Clans, for they worship a dark spirit that can only be Helga.

I go into exile now and will travel to our brother, Caerwyn, to prepare for the transformation. There is a wizard named Mordecai, who can be trusted in all things. He is but a child now, yet he is the only one that Aossi has spoken to, other than the prince and princess whose twins will become our host bodies.

Something desperate is about to happen, and I am powerless to stop it. I can feel the storm approaching. The only one who was ever able to control Helga was our sister Artio, but she has been lost to us for a long time now. Her focus is on the stones and the experiments that she conducts with the moon. I do not believe her plans to be harmful, yet she will not hear a word against Helga.

You must bind the Primordial people together. Civil war is inevitable, and I fear what will have transpired by the time you find this letter. Understand that Helga will stop at nothing to divide all peoples. Her plans work best when humanity is fighting against one another. Divided, they are easy pickings for her minions of the underworld. Remember always, those souls she enslaves are possibly enslaved forever. Twisted over time, they could become an army impossible to defeat in the human realm. We must succeed in our mission.

As mortals, we have a chance to save this world. As mortals, we can have an influence that was not possible as godlings where our influence could not be known. But as mortals, we can take control and lead the living back to the light and into war, if it must be. We are their caretakers, their Spirit Shield.

Choose your path wisely. I say this as a reminder to myself. Although I cannot see into the future, I can see that much death and pain lie along the path before the end. Remember our bond. Remember our people. Remember our strengths. Remember that we are godlings. Remember.

The last word reverberated inside Avery's skull like a thunderous gong. For the second time that day, she found herself on the floor. The enchanted word sprung the hatch of her memories, and a closed compartment in her mind burst open like a flash of lighting in a stormy sky. The crush of eons of memory made her cry out, and she let go of the paper, which rolled back up and flashed into flame, burning instantly to a fine white powder.

She remembered...she remembered *everything*.

*   *   *

Achak leaned against the wall of the potter's studio and studied the prisoner cell building, counting the number of guards and patrols. So far three had entered the building but only two had come out, so one guard remained inside and possibly more. He would be wise to assume there were other guards within the building.

It was strange to see any guards, for the Primordials rarely imprisoned anyone. In fact, when Achak had left Faylea a few months ago, this building had been used for grain storage. The Primordials were a direct people. Punishments for crimes or infractions were dealt with immediately and publicly and then forgotten. They considered it barbaric to cage anything, including animals. It was the highest of insults to imprison a person, a severe slight that did not escape Achak's notice.

It was probable that there was only a single guard left inside, as there was but one exit from the building. The stone exterior was periodically pierced with small round windows, too small for a child to squeeze thorough. *No possibility of escape from those,* he thought as his eyes continued to study the structure. On the top of the building, grass thatching provided a waterproof roof, yet he knew the ceiling of the cells were thick-beamed timber and mud plaster. Maybe with years to work on it, one could chisel out enough wood to create an opening, assuming one was allowed a knife or other sharp tool. No, he would have to break the woman out by going through the cell door. So, the only question that remained was how to get that door open.

His eyes ran over the thatch once again, and suddenly an idea came to him. He stood up and glanced at the sun, judging the hours left until dark. He would return when it was night to implement his plan. He shoved his hands in his pockets and with stomach rumbling strolled away in search of a meal.

*   *   *

Cyrus pulled the hood of his robes tighter around his face as the Primordial who had recently been his prisoner walked by within spitting distance. At least he thought it was the same one. To his eyes, they all looked the same.

The woman who had come out of the temple was now being held prisoner inside the stone hut, and that interested him greatly. Regardless of who she was, she was important enough to hold in a cell. He recalled the adage from his early legion training: "The enemy of your enemy is your friend." Whether or not she was a "friend," she was certainly a form of leverage. *How can I use her? That is the question,* he thought.

"Do you have any idea who the woman is?" he whispered to his second-in-command. Fullmer grimaced painfully through the disciplinary injuries he had received after allowing the Primordial to slip away from him in the mists.

"No, Lord Cyrus. Although I have seen her before."

Cyrus's eyes narrowed at the words. "How could you have seen her before?"

"She was in that flyspeck, sheep-loving village out on the cliffs. Sanctuary-by-the-Sea I think it was called. I remember seeing her there when we rode into town."

"She comes from the same village as the usurper? Cayden Tiernan?"

"Yes, my lord, I am sure of it." Fullmer glanced around to make sure they were not being watched.

"Well, isn't that interesting. I wonder what a Primordial would be doing in Sanctuary-by-the-Sea." Cyrus rubbed a hand across his jaw, considering the possibilities.

"I believe she lived there. She was dressed like the rest of the commoners."

"Even more interesting. Now I definitely want her. Come on. I don't want to be noticed in the area." He slipped between two buildings, heading for the woods with Fullmer at his heels.

Chapter 18

Captured

CAYDEN RACED DOWN THE STAIRS, taking them two at a time. The maidservant in the hall at the base flattened herself against the wall, soapy water sloshing over the side of her mop bucket and a bemused expression on her face as she watched the young king run past her like a child in a game of tag.

Ryder's sword clanked against the railing as he launched himself over the side, rather than taking the last few steps, hoping to gain on Cayden's retreating back.

"Cayden, wait!" he bellowed, his boots pounding down the flagstone. He rounded the corner where Cayden's flapping coat had just disappeared to see the door at the far end of the gallery hallway swinging shut. Shouldering the partially closed door aside, Ryder took the next five steps in two giant leaps. Landing on the sunny gravel path leading to the stables, he crunched the remaining distance to the barn, halting just inside to allow his eyes to adjust to the dim interior.

"Cayden!" he bellowed. In response to his call, a head poked out of a stall midway down the length of the barn.

"Yes?" Cayden's head turned in his direction for a second and then disappeared back inside the stall.

"You're mad, you know that?" Ryder walked up to the stall and leaned his arms on the railing, watching as Cayden tossed a blanket onto the back of a deep-chested stallion with one white sock. "There is no way you are going to be allowed to leave alone. We are going with you."

"Fine, but you better be ready when I leave because I am not waiting for you. You will just have to catch up." Cayden tossed the saddle onto the back of the chestnut and tightened the cinch, eliciting a grunt from the horse as he tugged it tight. Cayden tugged on the girth strap once more when it exhaled.

"You won't leave without me." Ryder smirked over the stall wall. Cayden glanced up at him, and his eyes caught on an object in Ryder's hands. Ryder was holding his satchel in his beefy grip, swinging it back and forth. "I know you don't go anywhere without this."

Cayden made to snatch it from his hands, but Ryder stepped back, grinning. "I will be back in thirty minutes, and you will be right here." Ryder walked out of the barn, whistling for his knights, who materialized out of the shadows. "Thirty minutes, gentlemen, and then I expect you saddled and ready to ride!"

Thirty minutes later, the clop-clop-clop of horseshoes on cobblestone and clanking armor announced the knight's arrival. Cayden stood by his mount, impatiently twitching the reins back and forth in his hand. He peered between the stone buildings to where the knights' horses were housed, the stable located at a side gate out of the castle grounds. Spying Ryder, he barely restrained himself from running over to him. Instead, he crossed his arms and glared at him, Ryder rode up beside Cayden, refusing to meet his eyes. Cayden swung up into his saddle and said, with a low growl, "You know, Ryder, you can be a royal pain."

"Of course, Your Majesty, it is my duty." Ryder bowed low, hiding his smirk. He held out Cayden's satchel to him. Cayden took the satchel then clouted Ryder on the back of his head. Ryder's yelp followed him as he walked the big chestnut out into the courtyard and he smiled. Ryder rubbed the back of his head and, still smirking, heeled his mount to follow Cayden.

At that moment, Denzik appeared with twenty grizzled, battle-hardened Kingsmen. As soon as he saw Ryder and the newly minted knights assembled looking as though they intended to ride with them, he pulled Ryder off to the side. The two men began to argue, hands waving and pointing at both the castle and the distant mountains, each man frowning and shaking his head until finally Ryder rolled his head skyward as if praying, cracked his neck to each side and then nodded his acceptance of the instructions with a grimace.

Satisfied, they rode over to the king. "Sire, a change in plans," said Denzik. "Young Ryder here believes the knights could use more training and are reluctant to leave the castle with minimal fortification. They have volunteered to stay behind and continue their training and see to the defence of the castle in your absence."

Cayden studied Ryder's sour expression as Ryder grimaced then echoed Denzik's words. "We cannot leave the castle undefended, and Denzik and his men know the hills better than I, having fought many a campaign in those mountains. They will be of better service and protection on this venture."

Cayden nodded acceptance of the change in plan, his thoughts already drifting back to Ziona. "Where is Mordecai?" he muttered, impatiently. His words seemed to produce the wizard as Mordecai sauntered around the edge of the garden wall, leading an old mare as grey as his beard. She was painted with symbols that Cayden could only wonder at. The saddlebags bulged with large square objects. Mordecai refused to be parted from his books.

Cayden refused to show curiosity and studiously ignored them all, staring off into the distance in the direction he sensed Ziona to be. She was headed directly for Avery. Ziona was not answering his silent call, but perhaps Avery would.

Avery, can you hear me? Where are you right now? I am coming to you.

He waited a moment, and then a voice whispered in his mind: *Cayden! It's so good to hear your voice! Do not come to Faylea! They are not friendly to outsiders, and I fear your reception will not be what you expect. I am being retained by the High Priestess right now, although I do not know why…well, maybe I do…but she is no friend to us.*

Where is Father? Cayden asked through the bond.

He is here but hurt. I will take care of him. Do not fear. I have so much to talk to you about, but we need to meet face-to-face. Do you remember the path leading to the Thunder Falls? There is a wayfarer cabin there. Meet me there in five days. I will figure a way to get out of this…place.

Are you sure you do not need help escaping? Why would they detain you? What is going on?

I cannot say, Cayden. Not now. There is too much to tell. I will find a way out. They will not hold me forever. They do not dare.

OK. Be careful! There are enemies everywhere.

I know. See you in five days.

Ryder rode up beside Cayden and examined his blank expression. "Talking to Avery? Or Ziona?" Ryder had learned of the bond from Ziona during one of their discussions after the battle and had been amazed to know that a form of telepathy existed between them. His childhood friend had morphed into royalty and something more. They had all changed. "Sending her telepathic love notes?" he ribbed, chuckling. "Just imagine, you could say anything to her, and no one would know what you said unless you gave it away by blushing." The colour rose in Cayden's neck at the thought of saying anything suggestive to Ziona. The very thought heated his blood. "See? Just like that. You are turning as red as a—"

"Ryder, shut up."

Laughing, Ryder gripped Cayden's shoulder. "Be very careful, Cayden. Watch for enemies. It is difficult to tell friend from foe right now."

Cayden looked back at him and squinted against the glare of the sun. He raised his hand and rubbed at the persistent headache. Ryder noted the darkening circles under his eyes and the fine lines of strain in the creases.

"Avery. I was talking to Avery, not Ziona. She is in some sort of trouble. It follows her like a swarm of mosquitoes." Cayden's head swung back to where he thought Avery to be. "We will meet up with her in five days at the wayfarer cabin by the path to the Thunder Falls. Let's get going," he said in a louder voice. He nudged his horse into motion, and the Kingsmen fell in beside and behind him, the gates to the castle grounds opening at their approach. They clattered over the drawbridge and into the cobblestone streets of the city proper. A great cheer arose as they trotted out into the city. Ryder watched them depart then swung back toward the castle, dragging his feet to his duty.

Cayden did not look back. His concern was all ahead. Ziona had a three-day head start on him, but he would find her. *Nothing will stop me, short of death.*

* * *

Ziona crept through the bushes, silent as a hare, and froze at the snap of a twig nearby. She listened, cocking her head to one side, slowing her breathing, and lowering her heart rate. After a time, she resumed her stealthy retreat from the edge of the Flesh Clan's encampment.

Why are they so deep into this side of the Spine? she pondered as she slunk silently back to her cold camp. When she'd left Faylea with Sharisha three years ago to search for the prophesied children, she'd not believed it would take so long to find them. Much had changed since they'd left their home. Ziona had heard rumours about the unrest between the two Primordial factions, but if this was any indication of the severity of the split, it was more like a chasm.

Reaching her camp, she checked on her mount, finding him tied where she had left him, munching happily on the sparse grasses at his feet. She stroked his nose and then rummaged in the saddlebags for some dried fruit for a quick meal.

Taking a bite, she examined her options. *Should I stay and observe the camp longer, or should I push on for Faylea?* The decision weighed on her mind as she considered the problem. Knowing what the Flesh Clans were up to would be handy information, but she was not sure it outweighed her need to report to the High Priestess in Faylea and inform her order of the return of the Spirit Shield, of the return of a god, albeit in human form. She still marveled at this, that a god now walked amongst them.

And then there was Avery. Cayden would be angry with Ziona for leaving this way. He had wanted to accompany her in the search for his sister, but his place was in Cathair as the current monarch. He could not be traipsing all over the known world like some common courier.

She felt his pulse in the corner of her brain where the bond nestled, protected by blood and bone and tissue, that ethereal essence that was the blended portion of soul they shared. She had tried not to think of the bond and what it meant for them. In very un-Primordial fashion, she had hidden from the truth. In very un-seekerly form, she had avoided confronting the issue. Instead, she'd taken this excuse to flee, to put distance between them and the overwhelming desire to move past a sisterly relationship to something more...adult. As she pondered the situation, the bond surged, and she physically took a step back from the wash of emotion that flooded her. She stepped back again and abruptly halted as she bumped up against something solid…and warm.

Instinct drove her to her knees, and at the same time she tucked and rolled, pulling knives from her boots. Springing to her feet, she froze in mid-throw.

She was completely encircled by Flesh Clan Primordials, each clutching the wickedly curved knives they favoured. Ziona spun on the spot, trying to keep all eight men and woman in sight at once. She half turned, and froze. The pair closest to her horse parted for a tall, straight-backed woman in a burgundy wool dress that hugged her curves. A cape of black silk, trimmed with ermine, topped the dress, the hood framing an austere face, set in a frown. She held up a regal hand, freezing the combatants.

"Well, well, what do we have here?"

The circle closed on Ziona, tightening the ring, narrowing her focus until the only person she could see was the woman standing directly in front of her. Rough hands relieved her of her knives and others grabbed her arms, winding a rope around her wrists and binding them in place in front of her body. She did not resist. It seemed ill-advised, given the fact she was alone and surrounded. The jute ropes bit into her wrists as the man tying them gave a sharp tug.

"A Primordial woman, all alone in the woods. Spirit Clan too. Now tell me, what would possess such a person to wander unattended through heathen-infested forests?" The Flesh Clan warriors surrounding her shifted their feet at her words. "A foolish one, I think." She drew the finely woven riding gloves off her hands, revealing a large signet ring on the middle finger of her right hand that flashed in the fading light.

Ziona's heart sank at the sight.

Alcina walked slowly around her, examining her. "You would be the Primordial woman I have heard so much about." Ziona's eyes widened in surprise. "Oh yes, I know of you. You are the seeker who left to look for the usurper, and it seems you found him before I did." She laid a lacquered finger up against Ziona's cheek, turning her face to look directly into her eyes. "You have inconvenienced me greatly." Her eyes glinted with malice as Ziona's locked onto hers. "And finally, I have someone who will answer for this crime. You do know that the penalty for treason is death?" She cocked her head to one side, waiting to see what affect her words would have on the woman before her.

"Although you are Primordial, your treacherous actions occurred within my realm. You will be tried as a traitor and hung, as is the penalty for such crimes. *Take her away!*" She dragged her lacquered nail against Ziona's cheek as she flung it away, and the nail cut deeply, leaving a stinging, red tear that welled with beads of blood.

The rope tying Ziona's hands was jerked tight, and she stumbled to keep her balance as the holder of the rope mounted up on his horse. Heeling it into motion, he trotted off toward the camp. Ziona was forced to run or be dragged all the way to wherever they were going. Twice she stumbled in the darkening woods and was roughly pulled to her feet then made to run again. Maintaining her balance was difficult given the uneven terrain, but still she ran as she had been trained to do.

The last rays of the setting sun disappeared just as they arrived at the camp, cooking fires guiding the way to the Flesh Clan encampment just as full dark descended. Eyes followed her as she was dragged and shoved along the pathways to the center of the camp.

They came to a halt in front of a tent clad in skins and reserved for prisoners. The guards pulled aside the flap and shoved Ziona inside. She tripped over the threshold and fell to the floor, catching herself on her bound hands just before her face struck the ground. When she raised her head, a familiar face greeted her.

"Hello, Ziona. Welcome to the combined legion and Flesh Clan camp. Being as you are Primordial, you must already know that they eat their prisoners here." Darius's pitiless eyes were as cold as Helga's dark hearth.

Ziona straightened to her knees, her eyes impaling him with hatred. "Traitor!" she spat. "Cayden trusted you! I trusted you! I hope you are fed to the Charun someday. You are not fit to die a hero's death in battle." Darius snarled. He could not prevent the memory of the Charun, the shadow-formed monsters that had attacked Cayden's escort six months ago, from flashing into his mind. The grizzly aftermath of their rampage through the legion was not easily forgotten. Darius shivered involuntarily. Then, angry that she had witnessed his fear, he back-handed Ziona, with a vicious clout that sent her toppling onto her side. This time she smacked her head on the ground, hard. Darius bent down and pulled her upright by her hair, bending her neck painfully.

"Alcina is the queen, and you are nothing but a dirty Primordial. If you wish to retain those teeth for another couple days, I suggest you shut your mouth." He shoved her back to the ground and retied her bonds so that her hands now stretched behind her back and fastened them to her bound feet. He then ran the length of rope through an iron loop welded to a stake in the ground. Satisfied she was secure, Darius stood up, gazing down at her prone form. "Maybe I will get a chance to enjoy your charming company before you are executed." His gaze wandered across her body, leering at her feminine curves. "I'd keep a civil tongue, or I will cut it out in advance of your hanging."

He left the tent without a backward glance.

Ziona shivered on the cold floor, flexing her fingers to encourage some circulation into her cramping fingers. She closed her eyes, consciously closing off the connection with Cayden, placing a mental wall between them. She did not want him to feel her fear or her pain. She did not want him coming after her. It was her own foolish lack of attention that had gotten her into this, and she would have to figure a way out on her own. *I will not become bait for a trap for him. I will end my own life before being used in that way. My duty is to protect Cayden, now and always.*

Chapter 19

Descent into Hell

ARTIO MATCHED HELGA'S STRIDE, her damp footsteps flashing to steam as the heat of the stone floor evaporated the moisture on contact. Helga led her along a twisting path, lit by glowing fissures in the stone that made their shadows dance wildly on the slick walls as they passed.

A low moan whispered around them, then faded away. Artio's head swiveled in the direction of the sound, and she sniffed the air. It smelled of sulphur and ashes, acrid in her nostrils. The sound of running water echoed oddly around the chamber, the noise coming from the deep cracks and crevices in the rock. Some glowed red and some glowed blue, but the sulphur smell predominated. She rubbed at her nose then refocused on her sister.

"Why do you persist with using that foul odour? Don't tell me you are still pretending that this place is roasting the remains of people?"

Helga chuckled as she reached up and pushed back the hood of her cape. "It amuses me. I push the smell out the exhaust ventricles, and the smell of roasting flesh keeps the mortals from coming too close. It feeds their superstitions and discourages the curious from investigating too closely. Of course, a few well-timed disappearances never hurt. This mountain is cursed. Did you not know? *Tsk, tsk.* You really should have tried harder to escape your starry prison."

Artio glared at her.

"Tea. I think a nice cup of tea and some of those tasty salmon sandwiches you always favoured are in order. Yes, tea on the promenade. Come."

Helga took a fork to the right, and the path pitched down into the center of the mountain. Five minutes of walking brought them to the end of the tunnel, which opened abruptly into a cavern flooded with sunlight. At first it appeared that there were multiple suns, but upon closer inspection, the suns were revealed to be parabolic mirrors suspended around the curvature of the opening to the sky.

The cavern was immense, and a riot of tropical colour assaulted Artio's eyes from every direction. Pink roses climbed the rocky walls, and purple, red, and yellow hibiscuses grew in clumps along the pathways. Date palms heavy with fruit flashed with hyacinth macaws, jumping from cluster to cluster to gorge on the bounty. Their red and green cousins soared around the cavern, alighting on nests wriggling with fledglings. Lovebirds whistled and chirped, and canaries sang joyously from the shrubbery as they passed.

Artio sniffed again, and this time smelled the heady scent of jasmine and honey orchids and the earthy smells of growing things. The air was heavy with mixed perfumes, so strong they made Artio's senses swim. Helga smiled and gestured for Artio to precede her into the hidden paradise. The path twisted here and there, a meandering route that emptied onto a springy moss floor. A river passed through the center of the cavern. Bright blue, it glowed as though lit from below. Fog floated just above the surface.

Helga led Artio to a wooden table set with tea for two, tucked against the stone wall and giving an unimpeded view of the cavern.

"How do you like my garden? It has been millennia in the making, acquiring the seeds and soils and eggs of unhatched birds. They have no natural predators here, so they live long lives in their volcanic home." She picked up the pot of tea and poured two cups from the bone china pot into large mugs. "Honey? But, of course, you want honey!" She dropped a dollop of honey into one cup and stirred it with spoon before passing it over to Artio.

Artio picked up the cup and took a drink. It was as good a tea as she had ever tasted. The smell of the salmon sandwiches made her stomach rumble.

"Sandwich?" Helga passed a plate of sandwiches but did not take one herself. She sat back and studied Artio as she wolfed down several, smacking her lips in satisfaction.

Artio wiped a sleeve across her lips, dislodging a few crumbs. "Still not able to taste food?" she sneered, eyeing the lone sandwich remaining on the tray.

"No, nor can I smell the flowers in my garden. Sometimes, I think I can. I feel it tickling the edge of my memory. What I wouldn't give to smell flowers or taste the tea. I remember I didn't like honey, but I cannot remember what honey tastes like." She sighed and put her tea down. "You did not come here to talk of tea and my gardens. What do you want, Artio?"

Artio leaned back in her chair and considered her sister.

"First, I want to know what happened, millennia ago, when I was locked away in the stars. And secondly, I want to know where to find the twins…to kill them." Her fierce eyes flashed yellow for a moment, the bear rising to the surface. "And thirdly, I want to know why you did nothing to rescue me. Answer all three well, and I might let you live. Answer poorly and your garden will shortly be absent an owner."

Helga threw back her head and laughed. Her blatant display of unconcern did not fool Artio. The sibling godlings all knew it was possible to die as she had. It was not possible for a mortal to kill a godling—the feat was beyond a mere mortal's capabilities—but another godling or one of the gods themselves could accomplish the task. *The twins killed me, and I will have my revenge! Helga will not stand in my way.*

"You were always one to bite first and later wonder if the prey might have told you something useful," said Helga, holding up her hands to hold Artio back. "I will answer your questions. Yes, I will! But first you must answer some of mine. What do you remember of your banishment?"

Artio frowned, thick brows drawing together in concentration. Her nose wrinkled, while she sifted through the memories that were slowly returning to her.

"It was a cold, clear night. We were experimenting with the moon, trying to harness the latent power of its orbit and bind it to the stones. With the moon's power and the healing set up in the medicine wheel, we believed we had found the key to lengthening the normal lifespan. We—well, I—wished to prolong my time with the mortals or one particular mortal. How they fascinated us both! Especially the man named Genii. So tall and so dark! Do you remember him?" Artio stood up and began to pace, suddenly annoyed with the tea-time setting, and prowled around the enclosure, restless. Startled birds squawked into flight. "Genii was special, unique amongst humans. Handsome, broad-shouldered, and brooding, I think his dark features set him apart. He could have been descended from the gods. Could have been, but wasn't. The resident bad boy!" She barked a laugh. "He was always getting into trouble in any town he passed through. I remember him being quite the ladies' man. I adored him. He had two friends who were always with him." She frowned, dragging the names from her memory. "I think the blond one was named Julio, and I can't remember what the weedy one was called. Do you remember them?" Artio glanced over her shoulder at Helga and caught a fleeting look of smugness fade into pinched concern.

Artio frowned, wondering if she had imagined the flashed expression. Helga's face was studious, as though she was hanging on her every word. Artio stopped pacing and planted her feet, crossing her arms. She would not give Helga further opportunity for evasion.

Helga picked up her cup of tea and took another sip, her cup rattling on the saucer as she returned it to the plate. "I remember him. Genii," Helga stated flatly. "He was indeed quite beautiful to look at, but in the end a mere mortal, unworthy of our attention."

"What happened to him?" Artio demanded. "We were trying to harness the power of the moon. We were trying to bring them a sampling of immortality, elongating the span of their lives. Something we have done a thousand times before with lesser creatures."

Helga tilted her head to one side, clearly considering how much she should divulge to this fierce version of her sister. The bear combination had certainly given her a backbone she had not possessed before. "You have changed since you merged with the bear cub. I do not remember you being this aggressive in the past. In fact, you acted more like the

Thunders than your bear heritage. Clearly, your time amongst the stars has aged you." She dismissed the thought with a flick of her hand. "What does it matter? It is ancient history at this point. They were mortals and are long gone from this earth."

Artio didn't hold back the snarl that curled past her lips. She growled and her nostrils flared as her red-hot temper coursed just below the surface of her skin, heating her blood. Her fingers curled into claws as she fought to stay in control. She would have answers or Helga would live to regret it.

Helga stood up and walked around her sister, examining the changes. "If you must know, they all died when the link to the moon's energy snapped and rebounded. They were incinerated on the spot, but you would not know this, for the rebounding knocked you senseless. The twins were responsible for the feedback problem as they disrupted the transfer that you had initiated. Then, believing you to be dead, they sent you to the very moon you were harnessing to be kept in limbo forever."

"Just like that? That's everything? You stood around and did nothing? *We were in this together! These were our boys!*" The last words came out in a roar and more brightly coloured birds took to the air and began to circle high above the trees, a swirling mass reminiscent of bats leaving a cave to feed. Artio grabbed the front of Helga's robes in clenched fists, jerking her to a halt and immediately, darkness fell in the cave and black-hooded beings melted out of the crevices of rock, their forms wreathed in black mist that made it impossible to look directly on them, as though they were not quite in this world. Artio saw them coming and released Helga, who stepped back and straightened her robes, her eyes flashing with anger. The swirling figures crept closer, and Helga halted them with a raised hand.

"Touch me again," she snarled, "and my Charun will kill you. You are here because I allow it, but my pity only extends so far. Touch me again and it is you who will die, dear Sister, and this time it will be forever."

"Tell me where to find the twins, and I will leave you, never to return," Artio hissed.

Helga picked a pen from the tea table and scribbled instructions on a piece of parchment impressed with flower petals. She rolled the parchment and handed it to Artio but did not let go. "You will find them in two different locales, but both are headed this way. You see, I have something they want very badly. They were foolish enough to become human, thinking they would be better equipped to stop the wars occurring amongst their beloved humans, but they are fools. Humanity belongs to me." Releasing the parchment, she sat back down and poured more tea. "I have one last gift for you." She reached under her robes and withdrew a heavy gold chain. Hanging from the chain was a slender bone carved with shapes. She drew it over her head and handed it to Artio. "A piece of your love to carry with you."

Artio reached forward and took the chain, her eyes locked on the slender knuckle bone. She stroked it with one finger and then slipped it over her head.

"My pets will escort you out. Do not return here, Sister. If you do, you will die."

Helga did not notice the person who watched her intently from the shadows. Tall and dark, his eyes followed her retreating figure, unseen. His brow pinched into a brooding gaze. He did not look away from her vanishing form until she had faded from view, then silently retreated back into the obsidian recesses of the underground fortress.

*　*　*

Helga watched her sister's retreat until she disappeared from view over the rim of the bowl and then stood, clapping her hands together. Tea, cups, and table instantly vanished to be replaced by a waist-high stone basin perched on stone columns carved with faces. Liquid silver danced across the sheen of refracted sunlight reflecting off the mirror's surface. Helga peered into the basin, and the face reflected back at her morphed into a serpent, eyes narrowed and tongue flickering, testing the air. Annoyed, Helga swiped the surface, and another image appeared: that of Avery astride a fine golden mare with creamy mane and tail, following a Primordial man through the deep jungle undergrowth. Helga smiled as she watched them push their way through the thick plant life.

It would be fun to watch everything unfold from the basin and even more fun to watch the meeting in person. She was bound to the cavern, however, and could not step out into the real world, a backlash of her and Artio's experiment all those years ago. Artio had been imprisoned in the stars, and Helga in her underground fortress. Try as she might, she could not leave the confines of her gilded prison. She was every bit as trapped as the birds swirling about the bowl. That did not mean she could not touch the world, however.

Abruptly, Helga marched back through a cleft in the rock and down the tunnel, lit by glowing rocks along the ceiling. The tunnel sloped downward, ever downward, into the bowels of the earth. Heat began to rise in waves, and Helga sighed with satisfaction. The caves were cold and damp, but once she reached this depth, they warmed considerably and became moist and humid. She fed this air into the bowl, which accounted for the growth of the plants.

Side tunnels branched off periodically, maze-like, with nothing to distinguish them from the branches before them. After about ten minutes of walking, the floor of the tunnel flattened and widened, and a fresh humid breeze laden with the scent of the sea wafted past her nose. She waved a hand in front of her face to chase away the offensive odour and then raised the front of her tunic to cover her nose.

She paused to glance over the side of the short stone wall that opened into the cavern. A set of steep steps had been chiseled into its side, winding down and around, clinging to the wall like moss to a tree trunk. The staircase emptied onto the floor of the cavern, a thin oblong sliced in half by a ribbon of quartz from which a bluish glow emanated. The cavern stretched as far as the eye could see, and skeletal figures with elongated pickaxes chipped away at the surface, their glowing faces covered in sweat and grime.

Men, women, and children—all were bound in groups of three and four, chains shackling their feet to the person next to them. The slaves of Primordial birth lined the ribbon, pecking away at their section of rock while Charun floated above them, keen eyes watching the slaves and the lack of fervour for their work. Incentives to work harder were plentiful. Whips whistled through the air and snapped, eliciting a cry from the unfortunate Primordial on the receiving end. Here and there, Primordial children scurried, dragging large leather bags of water to the slaves. The Charun carried away the weak with no more regard than for a beast of burden whose usefulness had ended. Most of the slaves who collapsed in the heat, died.

At one end of the cavern, the surface of the quartz had cracked and a faint wailing hiss slipped from the fissure. Helga strode down the steps on the wall with an assurance of long practice and over to the crack, her black robes fluttering in her wake. The workers fell away as she approached, kneeling on the heated floor and pressing their foreheads to the stone, trembling. She knew that they would not gaze on her.

Helga knelt down at the edge and ran her hand over the crack. The wails increased, and the blue swirled faster and faster under her hand. She closed her eyes, the fingers of her right splayed over the whirling mass, ruby lips murmuring soft words. Her hand closed into a tight fist and she pulled. Up through the crack, blue mist melted around her hand and stretched like thin taffy, following her hand as she stood.

With a piercing wail, it snapped away from the crack and the swirling soul bound itself to her hand. Eyes still closed, she chanted and waved her left hand over the closed fist. The celestial blue darkened to indigo then to midnight until all colour fled. The blackness remaining expanded, and a shape twisted in the air, expanding beyond Helga's five-foot nine-inch frame. Helga's eyes snapped open, her eyes dancing with a remnant of blue flame that faded back to black. Her lips curled in satisfaction. "Welcome, my pet. Take your place amongst your kin. Serve me well." The newly born Charun drifted over to join the others swarming around the edges of the cavern.

Chapter 20

Jail Break

AVERY WOKE TO THE SOUND OF…well, she wasn't sure. At first, her dreams had interpreted the tapping as a woodpecker in a tree, high up in her beloved woods out back of the farmhouse in Sanctuary-by-the-Sea. But as she fully woke, her eyes told her the truth and the dream faded.

"*Tat-tat-tat…tat-tat-tat*" went the sound, and her eyes travelled up toward the ceiling of her cell. Small bits of dust and dirt puffed from the ceiling with the impact, creating a fine dusty rain of debris. She walked underneath the spot and, shading her eyes, peered up at it. A hole roughly the size of two fingers appeared immediately above her, large enough to slide an object through. With a pinging sound, the object dropped to the floor. She bent over and picked it up. It was a key.

Startled, Avery looked up in time to see a scrolled parchment drop through the same hole. It dropped to the floor, and then the hole disappeared, covered over once again.

She picked up the scroll and walked back to her bed to read by the flickering light of the candle once more, the key disappearing into an inner pocket of her tunic.

The message was short and sweet. *Second hour. Be ready.*

She glanced at the height of the full moon out her cell window and the angle of the patterns on the floor. She judged it to be first hour or a little after. She got up and crept over to her cell door and placed her ear against the thick wood, listening for sound on the other side, but all was silent.

If someone was going to break her out, why give her a key? What did this mean? And who had it come from? Nervous about the implications, she began to pace. *Is this someone aiding me or setting me up to be killed?* Either way, she had little choice in the matter. She had to get out and she wanted to be ready. She packed her few meager belongings and checked the placement of the weapons she could not be relieved of. Everything was in order. She strode back to the door and bent down to check the keyhole. She saw the dim light of a flickering lantern, and then something blocked the light. A guard paced back and forth just on the other side of the door. She considered putting the key in the door, just to be ready, but if the guard decided to put his in to check on her, then he would discover she had a key.

She glanced at the window once again, judging the time.

Suddenly, an explosion rocked the ground. With a roar and a brilliant flash of light, a powerful fist of wind blew bits of stone and thatch through the bars of the window. Avery was knocked to the ground by the concussive air and threw up her arm to shield herself from the heat of the flames that roared just outside of her window, licking at the wall. Avery smelled the thatch on the roof as it began to smolder. She pushed herself to her feet, rubbing her bruised shoulder. She could either wait to see if someone came for her or use the key clutched in her hand. She chose the latter and leapt for the door, jamming the key in the hole and twisting it viciously. She prayed silently that the guard had not slid the wooden bars in place. The lock scraped and then clicked, and she wrenched on the handle, dragging the door open. She nearly tripped over her guard. The guard she had seen pass the keyhole earlier lay in a pool of his own blood. His throat had been cut, and blood seeped and puddled on the stone floor.

Sickened, Avery ran across the hall to her father's unguarded cell and pushed on the door in a panicked attempt to reach him. She was surprised when the door swung open easily, and she rushed inside. His cell was empty. Avery spun on the spot, double-checking the shadows, but her father was not there. Avery dashed outside and then quickly searched the other cells. All were equally vacant.

Alarmed and close to panic, Avery coughed and threw a sleeve up in front of her nose. The smoke was thickening and the air turning toxic. She had to get out. She heard distant screams and shouting and knew that a crowd was gathering at the entrance to the cells, attracted by the flames. She dashed toward the back, racing down the stone steps that led to the rear of the building. At the end of the hallway was an old wooden door that opened into a broom closet. As she ran up to it, the door swung open and a man stood in the opening. Avery reached for the knife tucked in her boot and then paused when she saw who it was. Elder Hania stood in the doorway, a finger pressed to his lips warning her to be silent. He motioned for Avery to follow him, then turned and lifted a trap door in the floor. He disappeared into the opening without a second thought, dropping down into the dirt cellar and pulling the trap door closed over her. Darkness descended, but the air cleared immediately. Avery sucked in a great lungful of the blessedly clean air. Without a word, Elder Hania strode off down a low passage, lantern bobbing in his wake, leading the way. Avery followed without hesitation. Smoke curled around the edges of the trap door, drifting down toward where she crouched in the passageway.

They ran, hunched over like a pair of armadillos, keeping to the shadows lest they come across another Primordial. The tunnel was short and emptied into a cellar of a building across the road from the cells. The owner was a weaver and seller of carpets, as was evidenced by the bales of yarns and large vats of dyes and shelves stocked with shuttles and weavers' needles of varying sizes. They slowed and slunk through the bales until they found a staircase, then cautiously crept up the steps into the silent shop.

As Elder Hania stepped out from the top of the steps, a youngish voice said in an urgent whisper. "Did you get her out?" Elder Hania stepped aside to reveal Avery standing in the opening at the top of the staircase.

"Thank the gods! Come, we must go." The hooded figure tossed a large cloak at Avery which she caught and pulled on over her own clothing, drawing the hood up around her face. It was deeply cowled and hid her from inquiring glances, but nothing could dim the glow of her eyes. The men ran off toward the rear of the shop, and she followed, slipping out the door behind them and pushing up against the wall to gain her bearings. She was in a narrow alleyway behind the store, rather well-lit for the time of night due to the glow from the flames. She glanced over her shoulder to where a bright glow lit the sky. As they ran down the alley, Avery glimpsed crazed shadows cast by running villagers backlit by the glow of the flaming thatch. Men and women ran back and forth, tossing buckets of water on the inferno, which hissed angrily and flared anew as they ran back for more water.

Avery pulled her hood tighter to her face and glided from shadow to shadow, following the tall elderly Primordial through twisting alleys until they reached a barn on the edge of Faylea. Elder Hania paused under the overhang, checking to see if they were being followed, and then pulled open the door and pulled her inside.

She found herself facing ten Primordial men and women of varying ages. They were all dressed in white tunics embroidered with images of birds and beasts climbing the hem of their garments and twisting around sleeves. Avery recognized many of the images from her journey in the temple, flaming phoenixes and rainbow-hued thunderbirds, werewolves and sabre-toothed tigers, unicorns and Pegasuses, creatures of myth and legend. Except she now knew they were real. Very real.

Elder Hania eased the hood from his hoary head. "Welcome, Ancient One." He bowed over his hands.

Avery's voice, still winded from their run through the dark streets of Faylea, came out harsher than she expected. "Did you kill the guard to get me out? Why would you do that? You could have just knocked him out. Why did you kill him?"

Elder Hania bowed once more over his hands. "An unfortunate accident, Mother. I intended to do exactly that, but he struggled and the knife slipped. I regret the loss of life. All life is sacred. He would likely have died in the fire in any event, as you saw, lighting a thatched roof is usually fatal for all inside the building. It burns so quickly and so hot, most do not make it out alive."

Avery glared at him, but the elder turned her attention to the others in the barn. "I would like to introduce you all to Avery Tiernan, who comes to us from the village of Sanctuary-by-the-Sea. Avery, may I present to you the elders of Faylea, the Spirit Temple guardians."

The elders bowed, hands pressed together. Avery returned the ritual greeting, straightening just as the door of the barn opened again, admitting the young man who had aided her escape. Elder Hania caught sight of the man and smiled. "And this is my son, Achak."

Achak stepped forward into the light and Avery's eyes widened. The light glinted against straight black hair that framed a rugged face with high cheekbones and hollow planes. A straight pointed nose ended at full lips, which were curved in a smile of greeting. Avery met his eyes and a thrill passed through her. Keen intelligence was reflected in his eyes. Broad of shoulder, his cloak was slightly parted and displayed a tattoo of a phoenix in full transformation, a flaming herald of rebirth. His shirt was tucked into soft deerskin pants that hugged his body as though made especially for him, and likely were, now that she came to think of it.

Avery jerked her head in greeting, not trusting her voice to speak, and his smile widened at her reaction.

"We wish to welcome you to Faylea properly," yelled a woman from the midst of the crowd. Avery refocused on her, glad for the interruption, as she blushed slightly. "Marea believes we are traitors for supporting you in your quest, but we know that the spirits have spoken to you. It is obvious that you are the chosen one." Heads nodded, and Avery sensed from their words that they did believe.

Avery smiled in return and lowered her hood. The collective eyes of the elders widened, as did Achak's, taking in her fully tattooed form and glowing eyes.

"May we approach?" the woman asked. "I am called Sarea, and I am a guardian of the equestrian spirits."

Avery nodded. As the woman approached, the other guardians quickly followed. Avery shrugged out of her coat so that her bare arms were revealed. The guardians crowded around Avery, exclaiming at the number of tattoos that covered every inch of skin.

"You are blessed beyond women, Avery Tiernan," said Sarea. "We, who are guardians, are blessed with one or maybe two tattoos when we go through the trials. I even heard of one elder who had three. But this"—she gestured to the landscape of tattoos marching up Avery's arms—"is unheard of. Legend tells us that the only people so blessed were of the gods." Murmurs arose at her words and heads nodded.

Avery shrugged back into her coat and then raised her eyes to meet the gazes of the elders.

"You are correct, Sarea. I am of the gods. I am born as Avery Tiernan, but my true name is Alfreda."

The elders gasped at her statement, their eyes widening in shock and sudden fear. As one, they dropped to their knees, palms pressed together, heads bowed.

"Forgive us, Mother! We did not know!" They bowed, pressing their foreheads to the straw-covered wooden floor.

Avery, embarrassed, quickly reached down and pulled Sarea to her feet. She did the same with Hania, helping the elderly man back to a standing position.

"Please! Stand! I have only just learned this myself. My memory had been lost all these years since my human birth. I am still absorbing the truth. Believe me, it is as much of a shock to me as it is to you. Please stand."

They regained their feet but refused to meet her eyes.

"I need your help," said Avery, "if you are willing to give it. I and my brother Cayden willingly chose to be reborn as hybrids. You see, our mother was the Primordial princess Gwen, and our father, the human prince Alexander. Hunted since the beginning, we nearly died before we were born. It was only with the aid of a dear friend that we survived. Our souls transferred to these bodies just before birth.

"We have returned to stop the war that has been brewing between the nations, Primordial and human, but even more there is a blackness that is creeping across the land. I can feel it. Can't you? It spreads like a plague, the sickness creeping into the minds of men and turning them against one another. Jealousy and greed follow in its wake. Tell me, why are the Primordial people fighting each other? Why is there this divide between the Flesh and Spirit Clans? How did this come about?"

"It started with a legend, as all things do." Elder Hania gestured for them all to sit, and they sank onto bales of hay set in a rough circle, others sinking to the floor, all eyes focused on Avery and Elder Hania. "Legends are the children of myths, and myths are birthed from partially forgotten truths. And truth, well, that is tainted to reflect the perspective of the storyteller. Nevertheless, I will aim to be truthful in this retelling.

"This legend involves two warriors, who both loved the same woman. One warrior was of the Spirit Clan and one was of the Flesh

Clan. In order to win her hand, she set them both a task to perform, to prove their love and show her how much they desired her. She set them a task that was known only in myth and legend. She set them the task of capturing a ray of moonbeam, for love born under the moon is eternal.

"The Spirit Clan warrior, being a spiritual fellow, desired her love not just for this life but for life eternal. So, by the light of the moon, he captured the spirit of a dying caterpillar, knowing that the spirit of the butterfly is beautiful and free, as was his love for her. The moonbeam immortalized the transforming caterpillar. He placed the spirit butterfly in an enchanted cage and carried it proudly back to the maiden.

"The Flesh Clan warrior, being a man of the flesh, desired her to see him as the mighty warrior he was and that he could provide for her for all time. He captured a wild, pure-white mare, and, by the light of the moon, sacrificed the poor beast. As he bled the mare, the spirit of the horse arose, a shimmering soul of a unicorn at rebirth. He captured the spirit of the unicorn in an enchanted cage and brought the spirit to the maiden at the appointed time.

"By a full moon of the vernal equinox, the warriors presented their gifts. The maiden burst into tears and wept for the poor souls trapped within their gilded cages, for she had not believed the warriors were capable of such cruelty. She broke open the cages and absorbed both spirits into her own soul and vanished. You can find her still, wandering the world by the light of a full moon, searching for her true love.

"This legend explains the split of the clans. The Spirit Clans believe that the way to approach the maiden, the Mother Goddess herself, is through spiritual communion. The Flesh Clans believe that physical sacrifice is the path to pleasing the Mother Goddess. The division of beliefs between the clans has ever been a sharp divide, but of recent date, a dark presence moves through the Flesh Clans. They have rejected the preordained right of the Spirit Clan to choose the High Priestess. The Flesh Clans no longer abide by the rules and precepts of the temple. They have resurrected the old ways and now practice open sacrifice and the harvesting of souls as a way to appease the gods. *To appease you.*"

His dark-eyed gaze pinned Avery. "Perhaps now that you have returned to us, you can tell us who is correct."

Avery stared at her fingers, which she had twisted together during the course of the story. She looked up, meeting eleven pair of eyes, all staring at her keenly.

"I cannot tell you what you want to hear, that the Spirit Clan is correct. The truth falls somewhere in between, but I do not believe you are yet ready to hear it. What I do need to know, is where I might find the ancient scrolls? Sharisha mentioned them many times, and I believe there are truths to be found in them that may shed some light on how to bring peace to the Primordial peoples."

Sarea spoke up. "They are hidden in a secret cave deep in the Highland Spine. We have a map that will take you there." Sarea rose from a bale of straw. "Now, you must go—quickly! You are sure to be pursued. I can hear them hunting for you right now." The cries of the searchers were indeed coming ever closer to their location with every passing moment.

"We cannot show you the way. We would be missed immediately," said Elder Hania, "but Achak can accompany you and provide you with protection. We have prepared provisions." Another elder separated from the group and strode over to a pair of saddled and waiting horses, tucking a packet of parchment into Avery's saddle bag. Elder Hania stood and gave Avery his hand, pulling her to her feet. Achak sauntered over to Avery, smiling down at her.

"The sooner we depart, the better." Achak motioned to the rear of the barn where the two horses stamped their hooves, impatiently. Avery nodded and followed him, eager to mount up and to put distance between her and Faylea.

"Ride with speed, Mother. And may the gods protect you!" The barn doors flung open. Putting heel to side, Avery and Achak leapt out into the night, chased by the flickering light of the burning jail.

Chapter 21

Ring of Shade

AVERY AND ACHAK RODE HARD down the narrow trail, under the bright light of a nearly full moon, afraid to stop for the night. Safety lay in creating distance between the searchers and themselves, so they kept a steady pace. They also rode silently, neither one venturing into conversation as the stillness of the night carried sound like a trumpet blast. The pounding hooves of their horses rang in their ears, inordinately loud despite the soft earth of the path.

They climbed higher into the evergreen threshold, leaving behind the tropical paradise of the Spirit Clans. The trail at this altitude was covered in soft pine needles, and other than the occasional click of a hoof on a loose stone, their passage was virtually silent, even to Primordial ears. Non-human eyes followed their passage, the nocturnal scurryings of the forest dwellers the only sounds to reach their ears.

At first, Avery was content to let Achak lead, but toward dawn, she heeled her mount and rode up beside him. "Where are you taking me? What is our destination?" The words came out in a croak. She lifted her waterskin to her lips, taking a drink to ease the dryness in her throat, then let it drop back beside her saddle. Achak glanced over at her, his perfect teeth glowing in the waning moonlight as he smiled.

"We are going to a crystal cave, known only to the priests of the Primordial people. It is a holy place, a depository of sacred things."

"The Shakra Caves?" she asked, the memory floating to the surface of her mind.

"Yes!" Achak jerked with surprise. "You know of them? I thought you were new to Faylea." His eyes travelled over her face and head, examining her tattoos.

"It is true. I have never been to Faylea before, at least not as a human." Achak frowned at her and opened his mouth to ask a question, but Avery cut him off. "And not recently either, as a Primordial. It was a very long time ago. We can chat more about my history once we are out of danger. How much longer till we reach the caves?"

Achak's head cocked to one side as he examined the night sky. "Dawn will be here in about an hour. It is three more hours to the caves. When the trees end, we will have to leave the horses as we will be climbing to reach them."

They rode along in silence for a while and then Avery asked, "Why is Marea so hostile to my presence? I thought that I was expected. Sharisha originally told me that she and Ziona had been sent out to find me. I felt the truth of her words when she spoke them."

Achak shifted in his saddle. "Marea was appointed High Priestess after the assassination of the previous High Priestess. Her predecessor was a Flesh Clan guardian and much beloved by the Flesh Clans who had not had a High Priestess chosen in hundreds of years. They had great hopes that their High Priestess could bring back some of the old ways and give them an equal voice amongst the Primordial people. For as long as anyone can remember, a Spirit Clan High Priestess had been chosen. They proposed that Princess Gwen be sent to the humans to negotiate for peace along the border with the humans. When she was captured and not returned despite repeated requests, the Flesh Clans blamed the Spirit Clans. They saw treachery in the negotiations. They accused the Spirit Clan liaisons of not trying as hard as they would have, had the High Priestess been born of the Spirit Clans. When the assassination of the Primordial princess and High Priestess occurred, the tribes fractured and began to fight amongst themselves. They blamed each other for the assassination. You see, she was born of the Flesh Clans, and on her death the Flesh Clans took it as proof of the treachery of the Spirit Clans, in not guaranteeing her safety. The Spirit Clans, on the other hand, were angry that they were set up in such a fashion and outraged at the accusations. The assassin was never revealed. Her body was not returned to her family. There were rumours that she was to be married to a human prince. But they were only rumours."

It was Avery's turn to frown, digesting the information. "So Marea…she volunteered? How are they normally chosen?"

"It's something like that but not quite. This time, the Flesh Clans were not consulted. They were not invited to present another candidate. They were shut out entirely from the process. You can imagine their reaction when they were shunted aside. Marea was a young priestess who had surprising access to the temple when for many years the doors had remained frozen and inaccessible. No one understands exactly how the temple chooses. But she was the only one who could get past the front doors. There was really no other choice. A High Priestess must be able to enter the temple to contact the gods."

"So, the infighting between the Primordials is a result of the choice of High Priestess?"

"In part. That was the triggering event, I think, but things had been brewing for a long time due to their ideologies clashing." His eyes slid to look at her out of the corner of his eye. "But now that you are here, you can fix things. I saw you enter the temple. *You were gone for days!* Only a chosen one could have done that. Marea is jealous as she has held the power for the last twenty years and has been very vocal about her chosen status. Then suddenly you show up and without so much as a by your leave you march in and occupy the temple."

"Then why search for me? Why send seekers to find us? She would have been better served to leave us lost."

"Well, from what my father has told me, it is precisely because of the prophesies that she wanted you found. I think she intended to control you, use you as puppet to enhance her own power and position. Sharisha has been her right hand ever since she rose to High Priestess. It is not a coincidence that she was the one to find you, I think." Achak twisted to check their back trail, examining the trees. "We are entering the Ring of Shade."

Avery peered around at the trees. The straight-backed trunks of the lower valley were now bent and twisted, as though a large hand had pressed down, squashing them towards the earth ages ago. Yet even in their twisted form, they towered above her, a curly leafed labyrinth of shade and shadow. An owl hooted. From the corner of her eye, Avery saw an ethereal form pass between trunks.

She reined in her mount, curious but somehow unafraid. The woods were calm, and a peace rested on the forest unlike any other place she had passed through. Achak, realizing she no longer followed, halted.

"This place is ancient," Avery whispered, breathing deeply. She felt the body of the woods and the bones of the forest, the spirit of the trees, wise and all-knowing. She also felt the spirits that dwelt in the woods. "Can you feel it?"

Achak nodded and slid off his horse, walking back to her. "I can feel my Spirit Guide. He is near. Would you like to meet him?"

"Very much." Avery dismounted also, and Achak took her hand to lead her off the trail following a path known only to him. He pushed through some waist-high ferns, the early morning dew dampening his coat and slapping wetly against Avery's shorter frame, leaving her dripping from neck to knees. Her ears caught the sound of a brook bubbling over rocks, and she licked her lips, suddenly thirsty. The ferns petered out, and the stream came into view, cascading over rocks in a meandering path. Avery knelt by the water and scooped it up in her cupped palms, bringing the cool liquid to her lips, and drank deeply. As she lowered her empty hands, she noticed Achak standing, eyes closed but lips moving silently. As he mouthed his words, a red glow from the region of his heart pulsed to life and then travelled down his extended arm until it swirled around his curled fist. The suspended flaming glow brightened, and then from the night sky appeared a flaming phoenix, spiraling out of the moon to alight on his outstretched arm. Avery rose from the stream and approached the bird, which flickered with fire but did not burn. Achak nodded his head in introduction.

"My Spirit Guide, Pyrrhos."

Avery heard Pyrrhos's thoughts although his beak did not move. *Greetings, Mother. I have heard whispers of your presence here in the shade of the mountain.*

And I have felt your presence and that of your companions, Avery thought in greeting. *Why do the others still hide? Bring them forth so we can become reacquainted.*

Achak tilted his head, aware that a nonverbal exchange was occurring.

Faint rustling met their ears as the shadows solidified into creatures of every description. Legendary creatures. Achak gasped and gazed around him in wonder.

A werewolf, tall and tawny parted the ferns and knelt to drink, eyes reflecting in the moonlight. A great mane of grey flowed from muzzle to chest and down its forearms, tapering to muscular thighs and calves, which ended in paws with curved grey claws. It straightened upright like a human, towering over them, fixing his gaze on Avery. The werewolf spoke aloud, the human speech partially swallowed in growling tones. "Greetings, Mother. I have met your brother."

Avery's eyes widened in surprise and then crinkled with joy. Achak started at the human-like voice issuing from the creature, and then his mouth dropped open when he realized he understood the werewolf.

"You saw Cayden? Where? Is he well?" Avery touched his arm and stared up into his furry face. "Tell me. Where is he?"

"He is well, Mother. Can you not sense him? He travels this way. My she-alpha shadows his human companions."

Avery nodded, knowing it was truth.

Avery greeted the other creatures emerging from the shadows. Fae folk peeked out from around rocks and roots of trees, male and female, wings a whirl of emerald and ruby and their motion a tinkling song. A kelpie poked its head out of a deep pool, amethyst mane and ears flicking her direction. As she climbed out of the pool, her body shifted into a human form to greet Avery. Her skin cast a pearl reflection on the surface of the pool.

"Greetings, Mother. We are glad of your return. The woods grow silent. Our kin are disappearing. A great shadow moves through the forest, and any who fall under it are not seen again. We hide continuously for this shadow moves in both the day and the night. It is never seen directly. There is no warning, no sense of where it comes from, but..." She gestured to the mountain, wreathed in clouds, just visible above the trees. A continuous cloud of vapour billowed as though a volcano slumbered beneath the rocky tip. "I believe the shadows are from the mountain." The pixies nodded, chiming their agreement.

At that moment, the ferns parted and a familiar form entered the glade. The pristine white unicorn picked her way over the rocks, her horned head bobbing, but it wasn't the horned head that caught Avery's attention but the figure seated on her back. A small child sat astride the unicorn, her rainbow-ribboned skirt fluttering in an imaginary breeze and a large orchid nestled in her tight blond curls and tucked behind one ear.

"Aossi!" cried Avery. She ran over and plucked her off the unicorn's back, swinging Aossi round and round till they were both dizzy. They collapsed, giggling.

A bemused smile tugged the corners of Achak's mouth as he watched their childish display.

Avery sat up and Aossi stood, their heights about equal, and they hugged.

"It has been too long, Mother. It is so good to see you again, although you are much changed from your days as Alfreda." Aossi grinned, deep dimples creasing her cheeks. Surrendering to an impish impulse, she tweaked Avery's nose. "Welcome home!"

"It's been too long. I am still sorting all my memories, but it is wonderful to be home, to remember everything. What news do you bring?"

Aossi's smile faded and an uncharacteristic frown settled on her cherubic face.

"Dark news, I'm afraid. Time grows short. Helga extends her powers further into the world, and it is she who is behind the shadows that have been stealing the living." She waved her hand toward the waiting magical creatures. "They are correct. The shadow looms, and they are taken without warning. Neither the souls of the living nor the dead are safe. Cayden has done his part, but now you must do yours."

"You have seen Cayden? How is he? Where did you see him?"

"He was well when last I saw him. I dropped in on him to enjoy the music of his flutes. His ability is truly magical." Aossi grinned, thinking herself clever at her own joke. "He has secured the Well of Souls in Cathair, but that is only one outlet, as you know. Helga moves to capture the souls of the dead awaiting rebirth and enslave them to make them her own, a part of her dominion. If she can take control of the souls awaiting rebirth, it will spell the doom of humanity and Primordial kind. She hunts the good, those souls worthy of a rebirth, worthy of another chance at a mortal life. She strives to enslave *all* mortal existence. I fear her plan is nearly complete."

"Can you see what is happening, Aossi? Where is she going to strike?" Avery tried to keep the note of pleading out of her voice. "You maintain the veil. What do you see? What do you feel?" Avery shifted onto her knees in front of Aossi and caught a glimpse of worry in her normally gleeful face.

Aossi sighed. "I cannot see unless she touches the veil directly. But holes are appearing, and the threads are weakening. It's like moth's larvae are chewing at the weave, but the hole doesn't appear until later when it's laundered. But eventually, the holes appear, and when they do there is no predicting what comes through the holes. She is planning something." Aossi placed her hands on Avery's shoulders, and she gathered Achak in with her glance. "You must go to the Crystal Cave and recover the box hidden there. The cave is protected by magic that you should be able to defeat, but be warned, Helga is also watching the cave. She will have spies, or worse, waiting for you to approach it." She reached into her pocket. Picking up Avery's hand, she pressed a small crystal bottle with a cork into her palm, curling her fingers around it.

"This potion will hide you from view should you need it. There is only one dose, and the effects will wear off within five minutes, but that may be just enough if the situation is dire."

Aossi turned to Achak, who knelt in front of Aossi with his head bowed. She placed her hands on his head and murmured, "You are now appointed as Avery's guardian. You are her protector. This is a grave charge. Swear to me, on your belief in death and rebirth that you will guard her life as your own."

Achak swore his oath. When Aossi's hands lifted, he looked up. "You have magic at your command. Use it in her service. Your phoenix will add to your strength."

Aossi stepped back, and her impish smile returned. "This will be a *great* game! Play well, and you might just save the world." With a skip and a jump, she sprang onto the unicorn's back. "Farewell and good luck, Mother." Aossi and the unicorn left, their images blurring and fading within three steps.

Avery stood up, brushing leaves from her knees. She walked over to Achak. Taking his hand in hers, she led the way out of the glade and to their waiting horses.

Chapter 22

Sleepwalker

CAYDEN WOKE WITH A POUNDING HEADACHE. His rest had been disturbed and troubled, filled with dreams he could never recall upon waking but that still left him sweaty and shaking. His muscles were stiff, locked up tighter than a saddle girth and he only managed to relax them after a few minutes of stretching in the tent. None of it touched the pain of his headache. He grimaced and pulled on his clothes, stamping into his boots and then belting on his sword before flinging his cloak over his shoulders.

The dawn was cold and crisp as an apple but already warming as the sun crested the horizon. Restless, he stepped out, intent on a walk around the camp. Four guards dropped in behind him before he could take two strides. He ignored them. He was getting good at that. He had no place in mind to go other than he wanted to stretch out the remaining tightness in his thighs and hips before spending the day confined to a saddle once again.

He had walked about a quarter of the distance around the perimeter of the camp when his head throbbed with pain so intense that it felt as though a white-hot iron was thrust into his temple. He cried out, clapping his hands to the sides of his head and fell to the ground writhing, screaming at the top of his lungs. His guard rushed up, hollering for help and tried to restrain him, but Cayden jerked out of their grip in a spasm of agony. His eyes rolled back so that only the whites could be seen. His screaming went on and on, and suddenly Mordecai was there. The guards parted, allowing him to kneel beside Cayden. Mordecai took Cayden's head in both of his hands and gripped it tightly, chanting in a singsong but commanding voice. Cayden arched his back, and drool dribbled out of the corner of his mouth. Mordecai did not let go. Gradually, Cayden's twisting slowed and his body stilled. With a final sharp command, Cayden sagged, body limp and still on the ground.

Mordecai took one hand away and retrieved a polished stone from his pocket and placed it on Cayden's forehead. Still chanting, he drew a line with both hands from temple to stone, repeating the motion three times to establish the link. He stopped chanting and then removed the rock. Cayden's eyes popped open, confusion evident on his face. He turned his head to see the crowd of Kingsmen bending over him and tried to lift himself. Mordecai helped him to sit up. Cayden grimaced and placed a hand on the swelling lump on the back of his head. It came away red, slick with blood. Cayden said nothing but motioned for Mordecai to let him up. Two Kingsmen stepped forward and helped Cayden to his feet. A Kingsman reached into his pocket and handed him a fold of cloth, which he took gratefully, pressing it to the abrasion on his scalp.

"Thank you," Cayden said. The Kingsman nodded and stepped back. *So much for loosening my muscles,* Cayden thought. *I think I know why I did not get any rest last night.*

He hobbled away, Mordecai at his side. "What happened?" Cayden asked. The headaches were increasing in frequency and strength.

"Another attack. I was able to repel it. It is a powerful magic. Cayden, I have been doing some research."

Cayden rolled his eyes. "When are you not doing research? Never mind. What is it you wanted to tell me?" he said, rubbing at his temple. The headache was always present.

Mordecai shook his head and grabbed his arm to stop him from walking away. He lowered his voice. "Listen to me. This is serious!" he hissed. "I believe that it is a form of Primordial magic being used against you! I think someone has created a Soul Fetch."

He snorted. "A Soul Fetch? I have never heard of such a thing. Besides, I have had these headaches ever since I moved into the castle. I think it is more likely that someone has been trying to poison me."

It was Mordecai's turn to frown, then he raised his hands and delved Cayden's body with a quick spell designed to determine the health of an individual. His brows drew together when he detected poison in his body.

"It would appear that your instincts are correct. I do detect a small quantity poison, although it is fading now. As it is weakening, that would confirm your theory that the source of the poison is at the castle. However it does not explain the headaches that are occurring now."

"What is a Soul Fetch?" Cayden asked, his eyes clouded with worry and the residual pain of the attack.

"It is an ancient magic held by the High Priests of the Flesh Clans. I think someone is trying to build a link to you and the link is getting stronger." Mordecai paced off ten steps, feet kicking the hem of his robes, hands clasped behind his back as he thought. "The possessor of the doll is trying to take control of you and I fear they may be able to do it. I am researching ways to block it, but until I find a way, all I can do is assist you when an attack comes. For that I need to be close."

"I don't believe it," snorted Cayden. "I have some headaches, a residual of the poison in my system. That is all. It's probably stress." Mordecai shook his head, negating Cayden's theory. "So what if I have been feeling sick. Everyone has times of illness. Besides, I have never even heard of a Soul Fetch."

"All the signs are there, Cayden. Soul Fetches are extremely rare. Think. The headaches started up just after the recall of the coins. Remember how you could not locate them all?"

Cayden laughed. "Coins? You want to blame the coins? There were not enough missing to bribe a guard."

"The coins are not a bribe. They are a connection to you, a solid connection. A Soul Fetch needs something personal, something important to the victim, in order to bind them. Not only do they bear your likeness, but you imbued them with your will, by making them the objects of such an intense search. It is precisely the type of magic that a Soul Fetch utilizes." Mordecai paused in front of Cayden, knowing his next words would not be received well. "I do not think it wise for you to sleep unattended any longer."

"What? I am not having the entire camp standing in my tent when I am trying to sleep!" As Cayden's voice rose in anger, the guards behind him dropped back a pace. When a king and a wizard argued, it was never good to be close by.

"Well, what do you suggest, Cayden? I could sleep in the same tent with you, and then I would be there to assist you immediately."

"And listen to your snoring all night long? And those spooky eyes that never close? It won't matter if I am attacked. I won't fall asleep with you there." Cayden rubbed his temple, grateful that the headache had lessened with Mordecai's assistance and annoyed at feeling grateful at the same time.

Mordecai sighed with frustration. "Cayden, this is for your own good. Someone wants you desperately, and we do not need to form a long list before we arrive at the most likely culprit. Alcina must be in possession of the doll. She will know you are near. This is why I counseled you to stay in the castle to remain safely away from her machinations."

"It would not have mattered if I was here or in the castle, she would still have attacked me."

"True, but there, it would have been easier to care for you."

He is treating me like an invalid, like I am sick or diseased. Cayden's heart hardened despite his gratitude. He would not be controlled by Mordecai, or anyone else for that matter. He knew that Avery needed him. He felt the pull of her soul. He had to reach her and Ziona. Somehow, that bond was muted, fuzzy as though it had been tossed under a heavy cover of blankets, muffling the connection.

Mordecai sighed and put out an arm, stopping Cayden. "If you will not allow anyone within your chambers, then I insist you take this." He reached inside his robes and pulled out a simple stone and placed it in Cayden's upturned palm. Cayden examined it, turning it over in his hand. It was exactly what it appeared to be, a smooth stone embedded with clear crystal, covered in dirt as though Mordecai had just plucked it from a river bed.

Cayden looked up, puzzled, and in a flat tone said, "You want me to have a rock."

"Yes, I do."

"Did anyone ever tell you that you are a bit strange?"

Mordecai chuckled. "Oh yes, I have been told and by stranger men than you."

"Do you mind me asking why you want me to have a stone?"

"Ask away." His eyes twinkled, enjoying the game.

"So I can remember you always?" Cayden's tone dripped sarcasm.

"Yes! Yes! Very good!" Mordecai clapped his hands together, gleefully.

Cayden rubbed a hand across his forehead as it gave a painful throb. "So I can remember you? I do not see any engraving."

"It's not a party favour. It is a memory stone."

"A memory stone," Cayden said in a flat voice.

"Yes, a memory stone. This is how it works. Before you go to sleep at night, tuck it under your pillow. The stone will remember everything in your head right up until you fall asleep. In the morning when you wake, put it back in your pocket. You will pick right back up where you left off the night before.

"So…what happens if I forget to put the stone in my pocket?" Nervous about the answer, he shied away from Mordecai's gaze.

Bleak clouds drifted across his eyes. "Then…you will be lost."

Not reassuring, Mordecai! Lovely…just lovely. Now I am supposed to trust everything to a bloody stone?

* * *

Cayden tossed and turned and his blankets twisted around his sweat-soaked body.

Cayden, come to me. Rescue me.

Cayden mumbled, his head thrashing on his pillow

Cayden, rescue me. Rescue me.

Cayden sat bolt upright on his cot. His eyes, glazed and unseeing, were wider than a full moon. The memory stone tumbled from his fingers to the floor of the tent, forgotten.

He rose with the jerky motions of a puppet and pulled on clothes and then, taking up his sword, he slit the back of the tent. With the silent but sure tread of a sleepwalker, he disappeared into the night.

* * *

Cayden struggled to wake. Vaguely, he knew that something was wrong. The dream would not end. It was as if he were peering at the world through a spyglass, everything distorted and blurred around the edges. The tents of the camp faded away and trees overtook the narrowed view. He floated through a hazy but amazingly pain-free world. That, in itself, was a vast improvement from the last week. *Maybe now I can get some real sleep…if only I'd stop dreaming. Or maybe I am asleep and this is part of the dream?* He reached out to the horse that swam into focus in front of him. It felt real enough under his hands.

An undeniable force clamped down on his mind, steely and commanding. "Get on the horse."

Obediently, he put his foot in a stirrup and swung onto the horse. It started off, and the swaying of the beast pulled him. He fell into a deep sleep, rocking gently in the saddle.

*   *   *

Cayden woke with a start. The forest of his dream had vanished. In its place, striped canvas walls filled his vision. He was kneeling on a plush carpeted floor on which sat the legs of an ornate chair. The chair was not empty. Groggily, he lifted his head to see Alcina, dressed in a low-cut green gown that clung to her curves, seated in a throne-like chair. Cayden blinked and shook his head to clear it, trying to gain control of his senses, but it was like trying to grab the shifting sand of an hourglass. Thought and memory trickled through his fingers until Alcina spoke.

"Look who we have here. The mighty king of Cathair." She stood up and walked around him in a circle, twitching the drag of her hem out of the way of her pearled boots. "How I have waited for this moment. You have done well, my pet." She stroked his hair, trailing her fingers through it as she passed behind him. "You have come as called, as I commanded."

Cayden's low ebb of panic bubbled ever higher, struggling to free him, but he could not take command of it to make it his own. It shifted away and drowned, leaving him groggy and semiconscious once again.

"I will enjoy controlling you, I think." She completed her circuit and sat back in her chair once more. "Before I kill you, I am going to use you to regain my throne and take control of this miserable world. Before I kill you, you will restore me to my rightful place. I will squeeze your mind and your soul, until you beg for release. The torture of your mind will be delicious! In your lucid moments you will remember what you have done and weep for it. The first place to start is with these pathetic Primordials. You, my pet, will be the key to their failure and to their surrender."

The words registered in Cayden's brain, but somehow, he could not muster the will to care.

Alcina reached over and picked up a doll that resembled Cayden in form. A crude approximation of his clothing dressed the straw. A pin was jabbed into the temple. "See this? I am now your master. When I locate the other doll, I will also control your sister. Soon you will be my playthings, and those you love will never see it coming. Not one of your Kingsmen would lift a finger to harm you, and it will be your undoing." The fingers of her left hand tapped on the arm of her chair, head tilted to study Cayden. She bent over and grasped his chin in her hand, tilting his face up. His eyes flickered with the wild element of a trapped animal. With the other hand, she twisted the pin and Cayden's eyes widened and crazed with pain. He gasped, a scream ripping from his hoarse throat. His hands gripped the sides of his head, and he toppled sideways on the lush carpet, tearing his head from her grasp.

"You will obey my every order without hesitation, my pet. You can't imagine the torture I can inflict on you by this lovely doll now that I have control of your mind." She released the pressure of the pin, and Cayden squinted through watering eyes, trying to bring the swimming doll into focus.

"For your first task, I'd like you to meet an old friend. I promise you will enjoy it," she purred.

Chapter 23

Deepest Desires

ZIONA SAT UP, rubbing the itching abrasions on her wrists from the fibrous ropes. The thin blanket they had left for her slid to her lap as the heavy wooden door of her makeshift cell was flung wide open with a crash. There was no light in the decrepit stone hut, nor was there a source of heat. She shivered with cold, blinking at the sudden glare of light from a lantern held aloft, and her eyes fell on a man stepping across the threshold. Tall and broad-shouldered, his sky blue cloak was flung back to reveal a royal purple tunic was matched with tan pants, tucked into tall suede boots. His face was hidden by shadows as he paused while her two guards pulled the door tight and locked it from the outside.

He raised the hand holding the lantern higher, the light pushing back the dark and illuminating his face. Even without the light, Ziona knew who this was. Cayden stepped toward her. As his face became fully revealed, she saw that his brow was pinched with pain, deep furrows of strain puckering his skin. He swallowed heavily, Adam's apple bobbling. A trickle of sweat rolled down the side of his face from a forehead beaded with moisture. Her momentary spike of joy at seeing him flushed away, replaced by a feeling of dread. He was in pain. Great pain.

He appeared sick, but from what, Ziona couldn't tell.

Cayden, what is wrong? She spoke through their link, only to find that the link was damaged. She could sense him there, but it felt as though a solid brick wall had formed between them. She sensed cracks in the emotional mortar, allowing occasional glimpses of the man she knew, but always the wall repelled her attempts to breech it. She could sense him struggling to find a way around the wall and reach out to her but to no avail.

Suddenly, he jerked into motion as though someone else controlled his steps. He hung the lantern on the peg on the stone wall then removed his purple cloak and hung it beside the lantern on a second peg. He shivered as the cool of the cave touched his fevered brow.

Ziona stood up and walked over to him, placing a hand on his chest. *Cayden, can you hear me? Come on, Cayden, fight it! Speak to me! Use my strength through the bond. I am here. Reach for me.*

Cayden shuddered at her touch, and she felt the burning heat of his body against her hand. Ziona's eyes caught his fevered gaze and recoiled at the wild look about them, as though he was teetering on the edge of madness. His crazed eyes frightened her, and she nearly backed away, but then she remembered how he had saved her and that he did love her. They were bonded mind, spirit, and soul.

Whatever comes of this, I trust him. I swore that my life was his to do with as he chose. Ziona took a deep, shuddering breath to slow her racing heart, then reached out and enclosed one of Cayden's hands in hers. Gathering his wild eyes with her warm, welcoming ones, she spoke to him aloud in a soft voice. "Cayden, you know that I trust you. Do not be afraid. I am not afraid. I am yours, remember?"

Cayden's green eyes flickered with the memory, and just for a second, the madness receded. He gasped, "Alcina! She…she is controlling me…by a doll! I cannot fight it for long. Ziona! I don't think I can stop her from doing what she wants with me. I cannot get past the doll." He grimaced with pain and cried out, clutching at his back and stumbling, falling to his knees at the stab of pain that pierced his back. "She is taking control again, Ziona, bond with me, quickly!" Ziona grabbed his hands, and they merged their minds before the wall closed again. The madness returned to his eyes, but the core of him, the gentle man that Ziona had come to care for so deeply, remained.

Cayden stood back up and jerked Ziona into his arms, his mouth coming down on hers in a crushing kiss that forced her lips back from her teeth. She did not resist but instead wrapped her arms around his neck and melted into his hold.

His tongue darted into her mouth, the kiss thorough, long, and sweet. He pulled apart and then scooped her up into his arms and carried her back to her cot. He placed her on the bed and then began to remove his clothing with jerky, halting movements as though he still fought the control of the Soul Fetch.

Do not resist, Cayden. This is not a bad thing, Ziona whispered to his mind. She held up her hand to him. "Come to me."

Naked and shuddering with relief, he followed her down onto the bed. In a corner of Cayden's mind, the part that realized what he was about to do, he was ashamed. Not for the act of loving Ziona. Never that! But that he was being forced to make love to her in this fashion. He had dreamed of this privately, of being with Ziona, but not in this way. He was revolted that he could not fight back and that a part of him didn't want to. Guilt raged in him as he pulled her shirt off and slid her small clothes from her body. His eyes widened as his eyes slid over Ziona's perfect body, and he groaned aloud as he struggled to resist Alcina's command. She was the most beautiful thing he had ever seen. Suddenly he had no desire to resist Alcina's manipulation, as it was perfectly aligned with his own desires. Pleasure raged in him, and the combination became a different type of agony. A tear he did not know he'd shed, rolled down his cheek as he kissed her.

Ziona wiped the errant tear away and kissed the corner of his eye. She trailed a hand up his strong arm, the muscles rigid with tension, and then let it wander over his bare chest. Cayden shuddered violently. Ziona's last coherent thought was if she was to die in the morning, there was surely no better way to go.

* * *

Alcina looked up as Darius re-entered her tent and bowed deeply. "Well?" she barked, ignoring him in favour of adding an extra dollop of honey to her tea.

"He has been placed in the Primordial's cell. We have doubled the guard on the tent door as commanded." Curiosity flared in his gaze, but then his face blanked. Alcina smiled knowingly. She knew he was dying to know what she had planned.

"You are wondering why I put the two of them together, rather than letting you have your way with the seeker wench? Perhaps you resent it?" She picked up her cup of tea and studied him over the rim, eyes taking in his lithe form, the breadth of his shoulders, his narrowed hips. She took a sip then placed the cup down on the small spindle-legged table beside her chair.

Darius stood, hands clasped behind his back, freckle-faced and red-haired, a slight sunburn brushing his cheeks. He strove not to fidget under the queen's intense gaze, but he felt a blush creeping up out of the collar of his uniform despite his tight control.

Alcina's smile widened as she witnessed his embarrassment. "Perhaps I have better uses for your talents." Darius kept his eyes fastened on a point beyond her chair up and over to the left.

Alcina stretched, observing the way his eyes unconsciously followed the arch of her body and the way the tightening of her dress outlined her breasts. She stood and walked around him, trailing a finger across his chest and up over his bulging bicep and then along his back as she slowly inspected him, like a prime cut of beef in a butcher's shop. Darius gulped and shivered slightly when her finger trailed up over the exposed nape of his neck where the blush betrayed his desire.

Alcina laughed at the shivering shudder that wracked his body. "Yes, I can find better ways to test your talents. Let Cayden rut with the Primordial wench. He will despise himself, for his honour will not allow him to seek simple pleasures in the arms of a woman. And as for the Primordial, she is nothing more than an object on which to test my control over him. Pleasure can also be torture. A sweet kind of torture, but it is still torture for those who it is inflicted on. She will hate him, and it will crush his will. He still fights the Soul Fetch, and I will have his soul fully in my grasp before I unleash him on his people. Now, I tire of politics. Come entertain your queen." She tugged on Darius's hand and led him back to the secluded room at the back of her tent. He did not resist.

Chapter 24

Genii

HE WATCHED HER CLIMB the stone pathway to the entrance to Helga's lair, careful to remain hidden in the shadows, even though he knew there was no way to hide. The dark of the cave was as daylight to the dead. For those like him, the undead, well, it was perpetual twilight wherever he went. Yet, he longed to rush after Artio, to grab her hand like in days of old; to hold her and kiss her like he once had. Occasionally, a flash of poignant memory would surface, usually prompted by an emotional trigger. Those very human longings were still a part of him, part of the memory of who he once was, who he had been before the change, before the betrayal of the moon.

He could not disobey his mistress though, for she had bonded him body and soul. He could not run after Artio. His mistress had forbidden it. He vaguely remembered the desire of his mortal days, the longing to be with this godling yet he was held by another, her sister. He'd managed to cage away a small section of his mind and of his heart, and when he was truly alone, he would take it out and examine it, turning it over and over. The pull was still there, deep down.

He watched her vanish over the lip, and he twitched, his body actually taking a step in her direction before the impulse abandoned him, submerged under his mistress's command.

He felt a presence, and then Helga materialized beside him with a purr. "Doesn't she look fantastic? Why, my sister is lovelier as a bear goddess than she was as a human hybrid." Helga drifted around in front of him. Reaching up, she pushed back his dark hood to reveal his still classically handsome features, unmarked by time.

Genii remained silent, accustomed to the leading questions, the digs in an attempt to get a rise out of him, to make him respond. Helga had tested him from day one, and initially he had resented the questions. How could his mistress doubt his loyalty or his devotion? In the early days, he could think of nothing else but how to please her, how to win her favour. There had been nothing he wouldn't have done, including dragging the body of his former love out of the circle of the sacred stones and staking it out for the vultures to pick clean. There had been no one to compare with Helga's magnificence or with her beauty.

Eventually, he had come to see that she was driven by fear, a fear that he would no longer love her, that he would somehow walk away from her love. Absurd as it was, he knew she still harboured these thoughts and so she once again tested his loyalty, and he once again gave her the answers he had learned by rote.

"She is nothing compared to your beauty, my love. She was never anything but a lover of humans, too weak and paltry to be a goddess. Yours is the only face I wish to see. You are my moon, my universe." He reached down and took Helga's face in his hands and kissed her, deeply. Helga wrapped her arms around his neck and pulled him to the ground with her.

"Time to reinforce the reasons I command your loyalty, and pleasure is so much more effective than pain." She nipped at his earlobe, biting down until a moan rose in his throat. "Come, forget the outside world." And for a time, he did.

* * *

Genii took the right fork, and the path began to ascend, twisting this way and that before eventually widening, spilling out into a cavern dimly lit by twitching flames flickering on the eddies of fresh air drifting by. Genii felt a refreshing breeze stroke his cheek, cooling his blood and bringing sanity and self-awareness to the surface of his mind. He paused for a moment and pressed his fevered cheek against the moist stone wall, then drew a deep steadying breath.

When the insanity took over, he lost all sense of himself. His fractured memories were commandeered by Helga's will and drowned before they had a chance to float to the top. He came here, to this special cave, as the distance from her lair weakened her hold. Sometimes he'd surface enough to grab a gasp of air he did not need and regain a fraction of his lost soul.

Well, not his soul—*he was undead, after all*—but a fraction of his consciousness as a human. Flashes of distant memories teased his mind, and snippets of images rushed along the long disused pathways. The urge would occasionally overtake him. When it did, he climbed the final passage that emptied out into the light of the outside world. But his steps always faltered at the last moment. The light was blinding and he was unwilling to test what it might mean to be exposed to it. Yet he longed to try. Artio was out there. For some reason, that was important to him. Gut-wrenchingly deep, the truth of that bubbled inside of him, although he could not say why.

Genii pushed off the wall and strode down the long passageway, firming his resolve. A circle of light shining on the far wall showed the exit to the light of day. He walked to the circle, careful to keep out of the direct rays reflected on the stone floor. The brightness made his eyes water, or at least they would have watered, had there been any moisture to form tears. He blinked but his eyes could not process the light. He looked away and instead stared at the distorted reflection shimmering on the water-slicked rock wall.

A wriggling reflection of trees just outside the shadowed opening zigzagged up the wall, impossibly green and brown and alive. He ran his hand over the image and suddenly a memory of striding under trees—real trees—floated to the surface, and a voice, tinkling on the breeze, laughing.

"Genii! Isn't it a glorious day? Look at how the sun makes the seeds sparkle in the air! Dance!" she commanded, giggling as she spun on the spot, dislodging more seed pods that burst with the force of a mini-explosion, tossing more winged seeds into the air until she twirled in a feathery maelstrom. Genii laughed out loud, both in his memory and for real. The sound was odd in the dark cave, his voice rusty from disuse.

Unbidden, her name rose to his lips. "Artio, my love," he rumbled. He clutched his chest, fingers curling into his shirt at the sharp spike of sensation where his stilled heart lay. Pain lanced through him with the acute throb of longing and despair.

*   *   *

Artio stood at the base of the falls and recalled the tornado. The mists parted and the swirling mass of water collapsed into the rocky pool. The falls resumed their normal coursing, tumbling into the basin and splashing over rapids as they roared away, destined to join the meandering River Erinn. Artio plucked a leaf and tossed it into the waters and watched it bob and spin, thinking over her encounter with Helga. She had thought to find an ally, not an enemy. She had thought that Helga would champion alongside her, but something was off. Artio looked back at the dark mountain fortress, and a crease formed between her brows. She strolled along the bank and gazed at the rock, willing answers from its stony face, but it remained silent—silent as the grave. She stared at it for several long minutes, arms folded across her chest. With a growl, she opened the furled note and read the words scrawled on the paper.

You will find Alfreda riding toward the Crystal Caves, formed when the moon collapsed. She rides with a mortal you should find interesting. Caerwyn is a guest of my puppet, Alcina, and it amuses me for him to stay with her for the time being.

Artio crumpled the note and tossed it into the waters. The second it hit the water, it flashed into flame then sputtered, sinking below the surface and out of sight.

So, I must return to the scene of my demise, but is this by accident or by design?

It bothered Artio to blindly follow Helga's instructions, but the desire for revenge overshadowed her caution. She turned her back on the cliff face, and a shadow slid across a cave opening several stories above her.

Friend or foe she did not know, but it was past time for lingering. She strode away from Helga's realm without looking back.

Chapter 25

Decisions

MORDECAI PACED THE CONFINES of the squat circular tent set up as the meeting hall for the Kingsmen. In one hand, he held a book and in the other, his focus stone. It glowed softly and provided the only source of light in the otherwise dark tent.

In the early morning hours after Cayden's disappearance, they'd searched the surrounding woods for his trail. Scouts followed his faint path until the trail became unmistakable, trampled by the hooves of many horses. It was a simple matter to follow the all-too-obvious trail to the outskirts of the legion before turning back. No attempt had been made to disguise their passing. There was no sign of a struggle, no sign that Cayden had not joined up with them willingly.

Denzik stood on a raised four-square wooden platform that put him about half the height of the crowd taller, his hairy forearms folded across his chest, and stared impassively at the milling, muttering Kingsmen. The scouts fidgeted, their feet shifting at being the center of attention in the camp and the object of their fellow Kingsmen's displeasure.

"But, Captain, if the king joined them willingly, would he refuse to leave if we mounted a rescue?" They knew where he was being held, but how to get him out was still a point of argument amongst the Kingsmen.

"Don't be daft!" snapped Fabian, brandishing a towel snatched from over his shoulder where he had flung it as he dashed away from the camp kitchen. "Cayden would no more join them than I would volunteer to cook for the former queen." He smirked, as he had done that exact thing to originally assist in rescuing Cayden, but it was unlikely to work twice. Denzik's lips twitched at the comment and then settled back into their straight line.

"Then he was taken!" shouted another from the crowd.

"There were no signs of a struggle," volunteered a red-haired scout, "and no one came into the camp. No one got past the guards. He simply walked away."

"Maybe he was invisible!" shouted another.

Nelson growled deep in his throat. "Listen, you lump-heads! Cayden cannot turn invisible any more than you or I can. He is as human as any of us and can die just as easily. He would not give himself willingly to the enemy, especially an enemy that wants him dead. He wouldn't do it." Nelson divided his silver-browed glare equally amongst all present. He brandished a long-handled spoon as he would a sword, challenging anyone to doubt his words.

Muttering arose from the Kingsmen, each man talking to his neighbour and waving his arms to make his opinion heard, divided on how to approach the rescue of the king. Denzik heard snatches of "guards asleep on the watch" and "the king has magic—I saw it" and "Alcina is a witch and can turn herself invisible"; but the most outlandish one of all was "Cayden became the eagle. He can transform, you know."

Denzik unfolded his arms and held up his hands, shouting over the din. "If you will all quiet down, there is someone here who knows what happened." The murmuring trailed away. Once silence descended, Denzik motioned Mordecai forward.

Mordecai sensed Cayden through the stone. He had found it in Cayden's tent, whether abandoned or forgotten he did not know, but it had performed as expected. The stone was meant to provide interference against the Soul Fetch to allow Cayden to retain control of his mind, but now that he had been taken and the stone abandoned, it provided a perfect beacon, a link that only he could trace. Mordecai had no need of the Kingsmen to locate Cayden. Since the beginning—*the real beginning*—he had been able to find the Spirit Shields by the stones. It was not because of any special ability he had, but because of a stone he'd possessed.

Once, Mordecai had owned many such stones, but the very first stone he had found as a child, he'd kept inside a special box, black as coal, from which light did not escape. The rarity of such a box had escaped his understanding as a child, having been passed down from mother to daughter, daughter to grandson. He had always had it but had never seen its like in the kingdom in all the hundreds of years spent serving the royal family of Cathair. His father was long dead, and all of those who now lived had forgotten that he was also of the royal house, a sidelined branch of the family tree.

One can always locate family.

Mordecai mounted the platform and stood before the assembled Kingsmen, expectant faces staring at the rarity of a wizard. Silence fell.

"My good fellows! Locating the king is not the difficult part. Rescuing him is a possibility, yet it is fraught with danger which you do not understand. Cayden is a captive of mind and soul, not of body. What you seek to free is his person, yet what holds him captive is his mind. This is not a foe you are equipped to battle. Swords will not free him, nor will stealth be able to sneak him away. He is enslaved. To free him, we must break the bond that holds him. But mark my words, the breaking of that bond could kill him as well as any blade."

The Kingsmen shifted their feet and more than one face crinkled in bewilderment. Men of action rarely knew how to respond when the foe was not brandishing a sword in their face.

"Alcina knows this and made no attempt to hide their actions for this very reason. If we are foolish enough to challenge her hold on Cayden, to boldly attack her and the legionnaires, she can snuff out his life before we set the first blade to throat. We would never reach him in time, and we would find a lifeless corpse when we did."

Angry, frustrated voices flashed between the men, fingers flexing on sword grips as they fought the urge to draw blade and dash out to engage the enemy.

"No, we must be very wise in what we do." Mordecai held up his hands to indicate silence, but Denzik bellowed, *"Quiet!"* and silence fell once more.

"We are working on a plan to rescue the king. Do not worry. We will get him back and safely too. But for now, we need to turn our attention to one we can help. General?" Mordecai stepped back, and Denzik stepped forward once again.

"Avery is the king's sister." Heads bobbed in acknowledgement. "She is still out there, and every bit as much of a target as Cayden. Alcina hunts her and will stop at nothing to capture her. I suspect it is why she has stationed herself as she has, knowing that she has travelled to the Primordials with the other seeker. You all know Ziona. Well, there were two seekers sent to find the Spirit Shields, and one returned to their holy city with Avery. We will focus our efforts on finding and guarding Avery, lest she suffer the same fate as Cayden. We know the king was on his way to his sister, which was his primary purpose in leaving the castle. We can pick up his quest where he left off and be the physical shield as we always have been. We *will* secure Avery's welfare. We will reunite Cayden with his sister. While you are aiding Avery, know that we have a plan to rescue the king and will ensure he is returned to us." Expectant faces stared at the general.

"We will leave in two hours. It is time to break camp. You are dismissed." The men filed away in groups of twos and threes, talking softly between themselves.

Mordecai and Denzik stepped down from the landing and joined Nelson and Fabian.

"Somehow, I do not believe that you intend to join us in locating Avery," said Nelson, as he paused beside the wizard.

"Indeed, I do not." Mordecai gestured toward the retreating backs of the Kingsmen with a bony hand. "They need to reach Avery as soon as possible, or we will lose her too. She is vulnerable, and she does not know it. That is, if she has been successful in reaching the Primordial leadership. She is even more dangerous in the wrong hands. You must protect her with your life. *All* of your lives." Mordecai's blue eyes flashed around the circle of faces with the intensity of a bolt of lightning. "When you reach her, give her this." He pulled an object the size of the palm of his hand wrapped in a soft cloth. He folded back the cloth and revealed a Soul Stone, identical to the one he had given to Cayden a short day ago. "Tell her that it works in the same manner as the stone from Daimon Ford. She should understand if she has been reunited with the temple." He folded the soft cloth back around the stone and placed it in Denzik's hand. Denzik tucked it into a pocket sewn inside his shirt, against his chest.

"You will find Avery in the Highland Needle. You will need to get past Alcina's legion and into the mountains. Look to the Primordial forests where the creatures of myth are said to dwell. You will find her there. I will go after Cayden. Only magic can save him now."

Denzik grabbed the elderly wizard's hand in his and shook it, and placed his other hand on Mordecai's shoulder. "Go with the favour of the gods, Mordecai. Rescue the king. We will find Avery and protect her with our lives."

"I will prepare food for your departure. I might even find a sticky bun or two to lighten the journey." Fabian's eyes crinkled at the look of pure joy that lit the wizard's face.

"Oh yes, that would be a delectable twist in what is sure to be a nasty-flavoured journey."

As Mordecai strode away, the Kingsmen were already forgotten. Cayden's stone pulsed angrily in his pocket, flaring with heat. This time, it was Cayden calling to him, rather than the other way around. *Hold on, dear boy. I am coming.*

Chapter 26

Sharisha's Hunt

SHARISHA RODE AT THE HEAD of a long column of Primordial warriors, the High Priestess Marea at her side. Of all the warriors of the Spirit Clan, the dedicated of the temple were the fiercest, bound to the High Priestess by oath, both verbal and physical, the magic of the binding rune running deep under the skin. The seekers were the highest level of the dedicated, their lives bound to the will of the High Priestess.

Sharisha smiled a dark smile. *The strongest soul binds are not made by blood, but by spirit.* Imbibing of flesh and blood created mindless drones, creatures who could no longer think for themselves. But a true spirit-binding bound *the will* of a soul, and left the recipient a thinking, reasoning individual, his will aligned to the purpose of the binder. This kind of soul-binding was unbreakable; a soul-binding was for life.

Sharisha had been bound to Marea as a child, and her feet set on the path of a seeker from the earliest of days. Her purpose had always been to search the world for the Spirit Shields, to find the prophesied children, and bind them for all eternity to the High Priestess, as she herself was bound.

Word arrived from Alcina's legion camp by their spy's pigeon in the early hours, reporting that the alleged king of Cathair was now soul-slaved to a Fetch, a spirit doll.

With that news, a force of forty warriors, Sharisha, and the High Priestess set out on the trail of the fleeing Avery. Marea's singular focus was to catch up with her and bind her in a similar fashion, once she was within her grasp. This time, it would be the necklace stored in their saddle bag that would assure Avery's allegiance. She would soul bind her and bring her to heel at last, in service to the High Priestess, as was her duty.

Sharisha, riding at Marea's side, frowned and glanced back over her shoulder at Elder Hania slumped over in his saddle and tied in place by thick ropes. *He should not have betrayed Marea. He should have obeyed. He should not have resisted. Now look at him.* A dark bruise bloomed on his temple, and the cheek below was split open and hastily stitched. Blood seeped between the stitches and trickled down his slack face. A strand of his white hair stuck in the oozing, stained pink. His right arm was bound, having been broken in two places. They had hastily healed it, but neither of them had the power to fully mend the break. One other man accompanied the elder, slung over the saddle of a second horse. Gaius lay on his belly, tied in place so he did not slip off. He was unconscious.

It had been a simple matter to track the fleeing fugitive to the barn at the edge of Faylea and a simpler matter yet to determine she had fled with assistance. But no matter, if the trail faded, one of the pair would be able to provide the answers they needed to track Avery to her final destination.

"If you are correct, and Avery is headed towards Helga's realm, how do you plan to gain entry? It is deep within Flesh Clan-held lands, and Helga herself does not encourage visitors. Even from those who profess loyalty," Sharisha said softly, speaking for the High Priestess's ears only. She peeked at her from the corner of her eye, trying to gauge her reaction to her statement to gain a hint of Marea's thoughts.

Marea ignored Sharisha, her eyes scanning the path ahead, searching for any sign of movement amongst the trees. Seeing nothing of interest other than a couple of lovebirds flitting from one branch to another, she finally rewarded Sharisha with a glance. "The former queen believes she is in control, that she steers events, but she is as much a puppet as is the young whelp Cayden," she sneered. "This journey will net both Spirit Shields and never again will anyone doubt who rules the Primordials. The Flesh Clan will be brought to heel. The Spirit Clan will take its rightful place in the world and push back the Cathairian infidels. The Spirit Shield's blood will be purified by fire, and their wills harnessed for all eternity." She sniffed and glanced back at the unconscious elder. "Even amongst our own, traitors are discovered."

"Do you mean to march right into the main Flesh Clan encampment and demand their surrender? There is no love lost between Flesh and Spirit Clans. They will not bow to a Spirit Clan leader, even one in control of a Spirit Shield. It is true the main force battles Alcina's legion, but they will not have left their priests undefended," said Sharisha. "Besides, there is nothing to say that the boy is still in Alcina's camp."

"Of course not! But a small strike force can be enough to steal a prize with the right distraction. I want those dolls and the priest who makes them." Marea smiled a grim smile. "The boy is a bonus. If I have the doll, I control him regardless of where he is. He will come to me." *I will recover the boy and his doll, all of the dolls. I will see Spirit and Flesh Clans united under my reign.* Marea smiled grimly, and a vision of the Spirit Shields kneeling before her in the shadow of the temple amused her thoughts for the next few minutes.

There were only three people important to her plans: Avery, Cayden, and Hototo. Alcina was an annoyance. The puzzle was Hototo. Marea did not understand why Hototo had given away the dolls in the first place, unless he thought he could not get close enough to the boy to place the binding. But if that were true, why give them to Alcina? Surely, she would not have had access to the boy, or he would already be dead. No, something else was at play here.

Alcina would have to be disposed of as she possessed knowledge of at least one of the dolls, an additional complication. The knowledge of the dolls in non-Primordial hands was a crime punishable by death. Marea snarled under her breath. Hototo's treason was nearly as deep as the bouncing elder behind her. How could he give away Primordial secrets to an outlander?

Marea rode on in silence, and her introspection made her blind to the details around her. Had she turned her head and looked back, just once, she would have seen the faint smudge of dust in the sky. But she did not.

Marea was not alone in her interest in the prophesied children. The Spirit Shields, now returned to the world of men, were sought by many parties, and one such party shadowed the Primordial clansmen at a discreet distance, biding their time.

*   *   *

Hototo's escape from the prisoner tent was a silent but non-bloody affair. Despite the queen's promise, she'd immediately returned him to the prisoner's tent and promptly forgotten about him. She had spared enough energy to double the guard but left instructions for him to be left unbound, given clean clothes, food, and water.

But Hototo did not have time to waste waiting on Alcina.

Close to midnight, with the camp quiet around him and the campfire coals banked toward morning, Hototo rose up silently and went to the tent door. There, two guards manned the entrance, swaying as they fought sleep in the quiet of deep night. One raised a hand to his mouth to smother a yawn.

Hototo took a reed from his pack, which had been returned to him as part of the agreement for the handover of the Soul Fetch. He prepared several sleeping darts, by dipping a sharpened bird-feather quill into a small pot of paste then slid the drugged quills into a hollowed tube pulled from his pack. Spying his first target, he put his lips to the other end of the reed and blew. The dart flew from the end and struck the neck of the guard with no more force than a mosquito bite. The guard swatted at his neck and yawned again.

Hototo repeated the process and shot a second bug bite into the neck of the other guard, who jerked and slapped the spot.

Less than a minute later, the guards were sinking to their knees and then gently slid sideways to ground, snoring softly.

Hototo returned the reed and the darts to his pack, slung it onto his back, then slipped from the tent on silent feet. He disappeared into the dark, carefully stepping over the sleeping guards, then sliding from shadow to shadow through the main camp to the horse lines. He paused to let a patrol pass then crept up to the horse line, untied the rope of the last horse, and led the animal away at a slow, quiet pace into the trees. Once out of sight of the camp, he swung up onto its back, twisting the horse lead into a makeshift bridle.

With a gentle touch of heels to flank, he urged his mount deeper into the forest and began to climb. He left behind the foothills of the encampment with the fading of the night, and the path became steep and slick with loose scree from the mountain face. The sky lightened with the blush of dawn. As he rounded a corner of the cliff face, he halted abruptly.

The trail was blocked by a recent stone fall. Only the narrowest portion of trail remained passable. He dismounted and continued on foot, leading his mount around the fall, acutely aware of the precipitous drop of hundreds of feet to his left. He glanced down as he walked along, and his eyes were caught on the body of a horse, lying on the rocks far below. There was no sign that the horse had come from the trail, but rather it appeared to be partially buried in scree that had swept past his ledge and down into the beginnings of a shallow valley below.

Hototo frowned at the bloated carcass. His eyes swept the scene below, still partially cast in the gloom of night. The horse was either white or pale grey, or he would not have detected it at all.

It has been there for days, maybe the better part of a week…and the timing is worrisome, he thought. This was the valley bowl where the Flesh Clans had been camped. The presence of a dead horse indicated the presence of spies. Spies who may have witnessed things they should not have seen.

The blockage ended, and Hototo regained the main path. The Crystal Caves were still a day's ride away. The mountain rumbled, and the scree shifted, pebbles and rocks slipping over the side of the trail behind him, to disappear below.

The god who resides in the mountain is stirring. The souls of the mountain call to me. It is time to seek out Dark's Mistress, to warn her. It is time to prepare the Shakra Cave, for her enemy approaches. Artio will be pleased. Serving two mistresses was a fine line to walk, but walk it he did. The Flesh Clans must be victorious. With the power of two goddesses to throw at the Spirit Clan, there was no possible way to fail. They will be crushed once and for all, the temple returned and the true faith restored. He would see these things happen, or die trying.

Chapter 27

Freedom

CAYDEN AWOKE WITH A SPLITTING HEADACHE and groaned as he unstuck his eyelids. He blinked, stirred, and attempting to stretch, only to find himself curled around a soft body. Not simply curled, but spooned together in the most intimate of positions. His eyes shot open, and his groan became audible, the soft something stirring in his arms.

With a stretch, it sat up, blanket dropping to waist. Ziona rubbed sleepily at her eyes, and then they wandered slowly over the astonished man at her side. She smiled and leaned down to kiss him full on the lips.

"You are having a lucid moment, I assume? You have the eyes of a startled fawn."

Cayden passed a hand over his chest then glanced down at its naked expanse. "If I were to peek under the covers, would I be embarrassed at the state of my undress?"

Ziona grinned, her gaze growing bolder. "You are as naked as a tree in winter. Thankfully you are not as cold…although the heat you generated last night would have sparked a forest fire!"

Cayden's face reddened right on cue, and Ziona laughed. He grimaced as a sharp spike of pain flashed across his temples, and his hand rose to the side of his face.

Ziona's mirth fell away, and her mouth sagged in distress. "The pain, is it back?"

"It is always there, a dull throb that turns white hot until it wipes away all ability to think consciously, to react, or take any independent action. Ziona, she can get inside my head, and she steals my thoughts and replaces them with her own. She sabotages my will."

"Tell me." She slipped into his arms and placed her ear on his beating heart. "Tell me what happened."

Cayden filled her in and when he got to the spot about the straw doll, her hand clenched into his chest so hard that the nails bit into his skin as she sat up.

"*Ouch!*" he cried, pulling her hand away.

"She didn't!" Ziona hissed, fury thinning her eyes to catlike slits. Her irises glittered with anger.

"What is it, Ziona? Tell me!" Cayden sat up too, facing her.

"She has a Soul Fetch! Where did she get a Soul Fetch?" Ziona shook her head and then flung her feet over the edge of the bed, pulling the lone blanket with her and draped it around under her arms, tying it off in a twisted knot over her chest. Cayden shivered in the sudden cold and reached for the blanket, but she stepped out of reach. "Your people know nothing about the making of a Soul Fetch. It could only have come from a Primordial. My people have betrayed us. The question is, was it someone of the Spirit Clans or the Flesh Clans?"

"You mean *our* people. I am half Primordial, remember?" She grunted in agreement. "What is a Soul Fetch? I mean, Mordecai did tell me, but I thought you might know more."

"It is a doll that uses magic to bind the soul of the person to the possessor. It captures your will, your very soul." She gazed at the tiny window of her room. "I must get out of here. I cannot protect you from a cell."

She spun back around then bent and picked up his discarded clothing, tossing them onto his lap. "Get up. We have a short window to prepare for the next possession. We must get that doll."

Cayden picked up his pants and pulled them up his legs, standing to complete the process. "And then what? I smash it? Burn it?"

"*No!*" she shouted, and her hands rose in panic. "No," she said in a softer tone. "Whatever you do to the doll will happen to you, even to death. No, we must break the bond…and that comes back to…"

"Mordecai." Cayden finished the sentence for her.

She nodded unhappily. "Yes, Mordecai is the only one we know of that we can trust to break the spell and not kill you in the process. Everyone else is suspect, I fear. We must get you back to Mordecai."

"I would not be surprised if he is on his way here already," Cayden mumbled through the fabric of his shirt as he pulled it down over his head.

"But we cannot rely on him to get us out of the middle of a legion with you bound to the doll. Come here," she commanded, the Ziona of old, now the seeker, the lover of the evening before vanishing. "We have the Soul Bond from when you saved me back in the spring, but now, I am going to put a tracer on you that Mordecai can follow. The only drawback is that any Primordial seeker will be able to track you with it too. I am going to put a seeker bond on you as was placed on me by the temple."

She dropped her blanket and stepped up to him, naked as the day she was born. She seemed unaware of her nakedness and completely at ease, but sweat broke out on Cayden's brow at the sight and he dropped his eyes. How he wanted to ogle her! Cayden fought the urge to stare. She laughed then put her hand under his chin, forcing him to look up. Once his eyes had travelled the distance from toes to her eyes (a journey that took much longer than it should have taken!) she raised her right hand. He had never noticed it before, but just inside her palm at the fleshy join where the thumb connected to her hand was a tattoo of an oak leaf, shot through with an arrow. It looked strangely similar to the oak leaf on the banner of Cathair, the royal seal.

"Place your right hand flat against my hand. That's it." She placed her other hand against his cheek. "Now reach out to me with the bond, Cayden. Merge our minds. Keep your eyes on mine. Do not close them. I must be able to see through the windows of your soul."

Cayden locked his eyes on hers (a tough thing to do with so much flesh available for viewing) and reached out for her soul with his. She was the most beautiful woman he had ever seen. Now that he had really seen her, *all of her*, it was all he could do to concentrate on her instructions. He wanted to forget the war and where they were. He could almost ignore the danger they were in. He wanted her so badly. Yet the constant throb in his temple warned him that time was short. He stamped down on his longings and concentrated on her instructions. They merged with a tingling sensation, and then he heard her voice in his head.

Hi, there, she whispered softly. *Now, I am going to transfer the magic of the rune along our bond. When it is complete, you will bear an identical rune on your palm. It will burn, but do not pull away until the transfer is complete.*

I understand, he whispered back as his temple throbbed painfully, *but hurry!*

The link flared and magic coursed along the ethereal connection, like steam on ice or lava on snow. The ice smoothed the path and the lava burned, his palm burned, skin to skin, until he wondered how she did not flinch away. It took every ounce of focus for him to remain locked in the transfer, but he held himself rigidly and did not move.

Someone moved him.

With a jerk and an inaudible screech, he was flung backward onto the bed and his mind snapped, as the haze of possession rose within him with a sickening lurch. His vision blurred, and Ziona vanished behind a white haze of pain. Cayden jerked upright and walked toward the door, knocking once. The door was flung open and the guard standing in the light of the open door leered at the sight of a naked Ziona before Cayden blocked his view. Squeezing out a last act of defiance, he grabbed the door handle and slammed it shut behind him, smacking the guard's nose as he leaned around him for a better view.

The guard snarled and clouted Cayden across the back of the head in a glancing blow. Cayden grunted and stumbled forward. He did not pause. He could not pause. His will was not his own. He stumbled toward Alcina at her command.

A sensation like a whip slashed across his torso. He cried out, his back arching in pain. His feet sped up, and the guard behind him chuckled at his jerking, faltering jog, amused to see him dance on hidden strings.

Cayden stopped resisting, and the pressure lightened until he could walk normally. The scenery around him was blurry as though he peered through infected eyes. But this time, he felt Ziona, nestled in the corner of his soul, her heart beating alongside his. Their merged souls kept him grounded and kept him sane. His will was not his own—Alcina controlled that—but his heart belonged to Ziona. It would have to be enough until help could come. *It will have to be enough.*

He was pulled along, past tents of guards and legionnaires, past tents dedicated to the kitchen and medics, past smithy and farrier. No one approached him. No one guarded him. Yet he could not flee. He could not turn from the path his feet trod.

His legs carried him once again to the entrance of Alcina's tent. He bent, pushing aside the flap of canvas serving as a door. His feet carried him to the carpet in front of her grand chair, and his knees sank onto the medallion as they had the night before, the first time he had visited this tent. His head bowed, and he panted with the exertion of running and resisting. A lock of hair fell into his eyes, and he didn't bother to swipe it away. He stared at the carpet, trying to make sense of the pattern in shades of crimson and periwinkle.

A slender hand with red-enameled nails reached down and gripped his chin, tilting it upward.

"I trust you had an enjoyable evening?" she purred, searching his eyes. "Every condemned prisoner should have one last pleasure before facing the ferryman. Don't you agree?"

Cayden stared at her, consumed by an overwhelming desire to please her. The command seeped into his head, and he found his lips moving. "Yes, mistress." He licked his dry lips. The words caught in his throat.

"She is going to die...but not quite yet. I sense that you need more incentive to do my bidding. She may have a use yet. If you are a good puppet, I will keep her alive. I might even allow you to visit her again. You now know of her charms. It would be a fitting reward, yes?" She dragged the forefinger of her right hand down his cheek, and it made a rasping sound under her nail. "You are quite pretty with a day's growth of stubble." She dragged her nail down his cheek once more, but this time it curved under his chin and across his throat. Cayden swallowed as the sharp nail scratched across his bobbing Adam's apple.

"But, if you disappoint me, I will end your life and hers by personally cutting both of your throats. You will watch each other die, spilling your life's blood onto each other. That is a promise, my puppet."

"Yes, mistress," Cayden rasped as she dropped his chin and straightened.

"Now, I have a task for you." She bent down and placed her lips against his ear, whispering her instructions.

Cayden's eyes glazed over. The next thing he knew, he was no longer in Alcina's tent. The fog lifted from his brain, and he was startled to see he was standing outside of Ziona's door. There were no guards present. Alarmed, he shoved open the door and stumbled into the room. "*Ziona!*" he screamed, eyes frantically searching the room. He found her bent over her satchel, packing her few possessions into its depths and then tugging the leather thongs tight to close it. She straightened at his sudden appearance and smiled. Relief flooded through Cayden.

"You're safe!" He strode over to her and dragged her into his arms and kissed her, hard. Suddenly, realizing what he had done, he pushed away and mumbled, "Sorry," as colour crept up his neck.

Ziona laughed, eyes sparkling. "Will you ever stop blushing around me?"

The colour crept higher still.

"I have been released. Do you have anything to gather?" Her smile wilted, seeing his surprise. "They told me that you had been released too. Alcina has pardoned both of us. You know nothing of this, do you?"

Cayden shook his head.

"Alcina said all we had to do was swear allegiance, and we could leave. She indicated you already had."

Cayden frowned. "I do not know. I was kneeling in front of her on the carpet and...I don't know. Perhaps I did and I don't remember it?" He shifted, looking around the chamber as though something there would jar his memory.

"Well," Ziona brow wrinkled into a worried frown "you must have convinced her somehow. We are now free. Let's get out of here before she changes her mind."

Ziona took his hand and led him out of the tent and down to the horse lines where they found their horses saddled and awaiting them.

"Wait till Mordecai sees us! He will be so surprised!" Ziona swung into her saddle.

Cayden mirrored her movements then shifted in his saddle as he gathered his reins. Something did not feel right, but damned if he could figure out what it was.

With a slap of reins, they trotted away from the legion encampment.

From high on the hill under the arch of canvas of her tent, the queen watched their departure, an amused smile on her lips.

Chapter 28

Love Lost

THE BOULDER-STREWN VALLEY was filled with Primordial warriors, their tents dotting the ground between the rocks. A clear space like an invisible barrier curved around the entrance to her temple, Artio was glad to see. With a snarl, she left the mountain pass and entered the valley and a wave of Primordials prostrated themselves, arms straight and extended as she passed. Mutterings reached her ears, prayers offered to the gods mixed with an occasional sob, so soft only her ears would have heard it.

She ignored the warriors, her focus on her temple and the High Priests gathered at its entrance. They bowed as one and offered her trays of succulent blueberries, strips of salmon, and a shining goblet of crystal clear water in welcome.

Artio strode past them and into the temple, and they followed. She mounted her throne and sat, motioning the priests to place the food on a table at her right side. Picking up a plump pink slice of salmon, she tossed it into her mouth and chewed.

"Well?"

The High Priests shuffled their feet, uneasy and puzzled by the question. No one wanted to be the first one to answer such a vague question, lest they be in error. The silence stretched.

"*What is happening? Where is the girl? Do not tell me you are not spying on the Spirit Clans. Has she taken the temple?*" Artio roared in her celestial voice.

The priests fell to their knees, and Arthmael raised his head, lips trembling. "Yes, Holy One, the girl known as Avery has taken the temple. Our spies report that she has left Faylea where she was imprisoned after taking the temple. They say she escaped."

Artio popped another slice of salmon and a handful of blueberries into her mouth and chewed, considering. She picked up the goblet and drank half of the icy water then placed it back on the table, swiping her arm across her mouth.

"Where is she going?"

Arthmael gulped. "Holiness, she is headed toward us. She is coming this way. I do not know her destination. She is followed by the High Priestess of Faylea and a guard. One of the seekers travels with her."

"I know where she is headed. You will give orders to break camp in the morning. Your warriors now serve me and me alone," Artio rumbled. *"Leave me!"*

Arthmael bowed low and backed away with the other priests and left the temple to pass along the orders to their recently assembled camp.

Artio stood and walked back into her rooms. *There is only one thing my sister could be seeking…and it belongs to me…but first I need to eliminate those who follow. This false High Priestess chases a prize to which she has no right. It is time to deal with the temple puppet priestess, so that I can confront the true one.*

And then there is Helga.

She frowned, perplexed at her sister's reactions when she visited her in the grotto. *She may believe she is the master of the mortals on earth, seeing as Alfreda, Caerwyn, and I have been absent for so long. But Helga is not in control of events. She has not considered the heat of my anger.* Artio wandered over to the chest and flipped back the lid. Her eye fell on a velvety bag of softest deerskin, a bag that had once contained a box. That box had carried her hopes and dreams. Dreams she had shared with the image of a man, taller than she, with ebony hair touching his sun-heated flesh, corded muscles straining against a massive stone. *Genii.*

Shock froze her to the spot, her body locking as realization flooded through her. She remembered the fleeting shadow that had watched her depart. *Helga has Genii!* White hot anger surged within her, unlocking her limbs. She struck out at the chest, pounding it with her fists. She did not feel the pain, for it was overshadowed by the pain searing a hole in her chest, in her heart. The heat of the betrayal burned along her nerve endings, raw and searing. *Helga will also pay,* she snarled. *I will slay them all. This I swear on the soul of my lost love, Genii.*

Artio spoke the name aloud as the name floated to the tip of her tongue. Memories long buried resurfaced and with it the anguish of a pure love lost for not simply for a lifetime but *for eternity*. Images flashed into her mind of a former time, of hands clasped and knees touching, bodies cradled in the soft grass of the sacred clearing, minds blended, souls touching, bodies uniting. And then a searing, wrenching pain as her soul was torn from his—then the empty nothingness of space.

Artio sank to her knees, bloodied hands clasped in her lap. She threw back her head and roared at the heavens. Her bellow of anguish brought the camp to a complete standstill, and silence fell. After a moment of frozen silence, they crept back into action, resuming their tasks, but they walked with the softest of tread, lest they bring the full fury of Artio down on them all.

*   *   *

Artio did not leave her chambers, nor was she seen at all, for the remainder of the day. The food brought by the priests remained untouched. They tiptoed in and tiptoed out, not wishing to disturb their goddess when she was angry.

Instead, they oversaw the packing up of their potions and instruments and gathered together the supplies for their dolls. They would not leave behind anything to fall into the hands of the Spirit Clans, should they rediscover the Bear Clan temple.

Just before dark, Artio summoned Arthmael, and he entered the temple on trembling knees. They gave out just as he reached her presence. He let them carry him to the floor, kneeling with his bald head lowered.

Artio was seated in her throne, absently turning over a deerskin bag in her hand. She did not seem to notice his presence.

He remained silent. Artio looked up from the bag, and her eyes fastened on him.

"How many dolls can you make, and how quickly can this be done?" she demanded.

"Highness, we can make as many as you want. We can make about fifty a day if we concentrate all of our people on the task. Forgive me, but may I ask what you intend to do with them? I might be able to provide some guidance as to their use." He bobbed his head, lowering his eyes.

She studied him for a moment, and then her voice boomed, echoing strangely in the throne room, *"I wish to control a large group of people. Can this be done?"*

Arthmael bobbed his head once again. "The dolls work by the trigger of a binding object, usually something of the person you wish to bind. The soul binding works between the doll containing the object and the person it belonged to. But to bind a large group of people, you would need a very special object of great personal value to them all. It would then have the strength to bind all those sworn to the possessor."

"An object of great personal value," she rumbled, considering the trembling priest. *"Bring to me the swiftest and stealthiest person in the camp. There is a service I require."*

"Yes, Your Highness. Right away!" He stood up and, still bowing, backed to the entrance and left.

Chapter 29

The Sacred Slopes

CYRUS STEPPED OUT from behind the rock watching the dust plume drift away, a cloud of dirt borne on lazy winds as the last of the Primordial force dropped below the horizon.

Marea was leading him directly to the primordial, blindly assuming that she was the only one interested in Avery's whereabouts. They did not check their back trail, a mistake they would soon regret. Cyrus was outnumbered three to one, but his elite force was more than capable of handling the rabble of Primordials.

Ahead the mountains of the Highland Spine stretched toothily toward the heavens, a wreath of dark clouds obscuring the summit. Shadows slid down the face of the peak, as though a mountain giant stood blocking the sun. A rumble of what he took to be thunder reached his ears. The giant frowned down at him, angry at their encroachment on its sacred slopes. Cyrus shook his head, squeezing his eyes closed, then looked at the mountain again. The shadows were only shadows once more. *Stop giving into Primordial fancies! You are allowing them to bewitch your mind!*

"Do not look at the mountain!" Cyrus commanded his force as they joined him, leading their horses. "The Primordials are laying their lures and traps. If we are not careful, we will ride off after an illusion. Everyone take a partner, who will ride by your side. If you see anyone acting strangely, it is your responsibility to stop them before they get into trouble. Count off!"

The men divided themselves into pairs and mounted up. Cyrus swung into the saddle, and Fullmer took his place beside him, eyes averted from the mountain.

"Follow the trail, but ignore the mountain." Fullmer put heel to horse, and his mount broke into a fast walk. An eagle soared overhead, circling on updrafts. They crested the ridge, the trail sloping gently down toward a break in the dense evergreen forest that hugged the base of the mountain. As they rode, the path of their quarry narrowed as the brush became shrubs and the shrubs were swallowed by the trees. The dirt track became stony, and the boughs overhead blocked out the sunshine. As they entered the forest, the sound of birds vanished and the woods were silent. The soft needles underfoot deadened the sound of their mounts. Nothing stirred.

The forest holds its breath, waiting to see if violence will be done this day. The grim thought floated through Cyrus's mind. Out of the corner of his eye, a face slid behind a tree trunk. He stared at the spot, and out of the corner of his other eye, the figure reappeared, only to vanish before he could swing his head back around.

Fullmer swiped a hand down his arm, then slapped at it. The sound cracked the silence.

"Stop that," Cyrus commanded.

"Ants! There are ants under my shirt sleeve." Fullmer hauled up his sleeve, but there was nothing there.

Cyrus glanced back at the other men and then reined in sharply.

The men were gone. Not a track showed that they had entered the forest.

Fullmer's eyes widened in shock. "My lord! Where have the men gone?" He swung his horse about and started back down the trail but Cyrus's hand shot out and halted him.

"Stop!" he commanded. "Do not move!"

Fullmer froze, eyes darting frantically to locate the missing men. His horse stood placidly, tail swishing, and reached out its nose to snuffle at…nothing.

"Close your eyes, and slowly open them," commanded Cyrus.

Fullmer did as he commanded. When his eyes focused again, everyone was there, pair by pair, staring at him in a puzzled manner.

"My lord!" Fullmer gasped. "Where were they hiding?"

"They were right behind us, all along. The illusions are strong in the trees. It is part of the warding of the mountain. It is designed to keep strangers away. The Primordials would say non-believers, but what they really mean is non-Primordial folk. Come."

Cyrus guided his mount back to the trail and continued on up the path, a nervous Fullmer riding tight to his side.

They rode in silence for a period of a half hour or so, the forest oppressive and forbidding.

The evergreen trees grew taller and widened until six men linked hand to hand could not encircle the trunks. The lower limbs, long-shorn by age and a lack of sun light rose higher and higher until they were riding clear under the great trees, devoid of any brush and thick with pine needles and cones of every shape and size. Sticky resin ran down the trunks and along the branches, and brown ropes stretched from the tree limbs, drifting softly in the silence.

A soldier riding three rows back brushed against one of the dangling cords as he rode under a tree. With a violent thrash, the tree came to life and the resinous ropes snaked around the rider, jerking him and his horse into the air. Shocked, his partner grabbed for his horse's hoof, a gut reaction, attempting to hold him down as more resinous ropes twisted around him and his mount. Additional ropes dragged the screeching soldiers higher and higher into the trees, and then they vanished.

The shocked soldiers froze, afraid to move a muscle. Resinous trailers swayed innocently, seeking the next victim.

"Touch nothing!" spat Cyrus harshly, then jabbed his mount into motion.

Frightened of attracting the attention of the great trees, the men cowered in their saddles.

"Let's move!" Cyrus heeled his snorting mount and pushed on deeper into the forest.

Signs of the passage of their quarry surfaced as the great forest thinned. Cottonwood and birch saplings sprouted here and there in the soft soil, and burgundy ferns thickened and replaced the pine needles. The air moistened; humidity increasing as the sound of running water reached their ears. The horses pulled eagerly at the reins, hoping to dip thirsty muzzles into the approaching stream. Their riders, however, kept a leery eye pasted on the trees as they passed.

The trail led straight to a bubbling brook, tumbling over rocks and splashing into tiny rapids. Smiles broke out on the men's faces, and they slid gratefully to the ground and dropped down to their knees at the water's edge, cupping the crystal-clear liquid in their hands and splashing it over their faces and hair, allowing it to drip back into the swift stream. The horses' muzzles sank into the froth, and they drank deeply from the cooling waters.

Standing back up, the first batch made way for the second set of soldiers, who happily splashed into the water, knee deep.

"Look!" A soldier named Billy motioned frantically to his partner urging him over to where he stood. "There is gold in here!"

"Where?" Billy's partner splashed over to where he pointed. Sure enough, scattered on the bottom of the brook was a glittering ribbon of gold with nuggets as fat as a thumb.

"Good Lord!" Billy plunged his hand into the water, and his fist closed on the largest nugget he could find.

Suddenly, he jerked and was pulled into the clear water. His fist was pulled into the bottom of the bed, and his arm was swallowed. With a strangled scream, his head was pulled underwater, followed by the rest of his body. Before their very eyes, he disappeared under the surface. A stream of bubbles broke the surface and then they too, stopped.

"Billy!" his partner called and began to scrabble amongst the shallow waters. His hand brushed up against the glowing nuggets. Suddenly, a great jaw rose up from the bottom, the gold sparkling off knobs on its pebbly head, and a pair of glowing green eyes blinked once at him before the jaws closed on his arm. His shriek of pain and panic ended abruptly as he was pulled under the water, the creature sinking back into the stones, pulling him with it. A stream of blood pooled on the surface of the water for an instant when it stilled then was swept downstream by the current. Within the space of few seconds, there was nothing left to show anything had occurred, except for the fact that both men had vanished.

"*I said, touch nothing!*" roared Cyrus from the shore. He drew his sword and spun around to the men, brandishing it at their faces. "The next one of you lump-heads that *touches anything* in this accursed forest will die by *this*! Mount up!"

They mounted again and crossed the stream, continuing down the trail, towing the two empty-saddled mounts behind them. The forest thinned and a sheer rock face came into view, forcing the trail to swing around its base. Another rock rose on the left, and the trail narrowed until it was impossible to ride two abreast. They dropped into a single file, keeping nose to tail, every soldier afraid of being left behind. The last soldier in line glanced back over his shoulder so many times that he mimicked a metronome.

The walls of stone pressed ever closer until their legs brushed both sides as they rode. One barrel-bellied mare caught her rider's leg against the stone, and the man swore and lurched in his saddle, dragging his opposite leg up across his saddle just in time to keep his legs from a dual crush between horse and rock.

With a growl, a grey-and-white sabretooth, the size of a small pony, launched itself from a cleft in the rock overhead and landed on the final rider. Great jaws with long fangs that extended well past the lower lip sank into his throat and, with a shake of its head, the unfortunate soldier's neck snapped. With its second bound, the cat launched off the back of the panicked horse, which reared and came down on the horse and rider in front of him. His partner's scream was drowned by the screams of the crazed stallion, and he was trampled under its hooves. His mount kicked back at the deranged horse and the rest of the mounts also panicked as more snarls and yowls echoed down the passage. Cyrus kicked his horse savagely, driving it forward, and it raced down the narrow passage, heedless of its rider. The panicked legionnaires heeled their mounts, and the narrowest stampede in history ensued. Cyrus glimpsed other cats of different colours with long dripping fangs, swishing tails, and yellow eyes picking out their prey. He did not stop to see how the others faired. He gave his horse its head and let it run.

Suddenly, he spilled out of the cleft into a grassy bowl, and his mount plunged three-quarters of the way across before Cyrus could pull it to a quivering halt. It hung its head, sides heaving, eyes rolling, as the surviving men gathered around him, some calming bucking mounts. Cyrus's eyes scanned the survivors. Horses with long, ragged claw marks shook with shock. One limped, favouring a rear leg dangling from a flank with a chunk of rump missing.

Equally bloodied men, whether from direct injury or from their wounded mounts, he could not initially say, staggered around, eyes darting in every direction in search of the next attack.

Half. Cyrus counted half of his original force. He swore loudly, shook his fist at the mountain. "You will not defeat me!" he screamed at the skies.

The wind chuckled as it swept through the valley, carrying the collective laughter of all creatures mythical and magical, who called the forest home.

Cyrus was not amused.

Chapter 30

Friend or Foe?

ACHAK TWISTED OUT OVER THE EDGE of the trail, leaning precariously to the side to peer around the edge of the curving rocky slide blocking their path. Craning his neck, he saw that the ledge was blocked for a good two hundred paces, to a height taller than his stature while mounted on his horse. There was no possibility of crossing it, even walking the horses.

"We must go back," he said, taking his reins back from Avery's hand.

Avery's stomach rolled. Reluctantly, her eyes slid over the side of the mountain. She hated the thought of passing by the bloated carcass of her father's dead horse. The odour of decaying flesh was heavy in her nose, coy and clinging. Not for the first time, she wondered where Gaius was and what had happened to him. Although she knew he was her mortal parent only, it did not stop her from loving him. Fear pricked her heart. *Surely Marea would not have killed him! If she has harmed him…!*

"Then we must go back," she sighed. She dismounted and leading her horse, doubled back to where the cliff-side path split into a Y, the trail zigzagging down the hillside a little more than a goat path. She led her horse, testing her footing as she descended. Loose shale and tenuously anchored vegetation made it too treacherous to ride, as she knew by recent experience. They picked their way slowly, stones slipping and sliding underfoot, the temperature of the air increasing the deeper into the depths they travelled until, an hour later, they reached the bottom. A hot wind gusted down the ravine, carrying with it the odour of putrefying flesh.

Avery wrinkled her nose and pulled the flap of her cloak over her face to mask the smell. Anxious to get by the area, she swung up into the saddle, but her mare tossed her head, dancing nervously, balking at the direction she asked her to go. Avery kicked her mare into a trot and then a run, as anxious as her mount to clear the area. They rounded the base of the rock face, Achak riding tight to her side. Avery closed her eyes as she passed past the dead horse, allowing her live mount to choose the path ahead. The horse ran well past the carcass then slowed as the sharp odours faded. Avery opened her eyes…to a wall of Primordial warriors.

Swords drawn, men and women with painted faces spread out in a wall. Avery hauled on the reins. From the corner of her eye, she spied more men coming out of the trees, circling around behind her and Achak. She recognized the masks, Spirit Guides personal to the bearer, and many of the masks were reflected in the images that covered her body. She pulled her hood tighter around her face to hide her tattooed features. She had no intention of displaying them to the warriors.

The Flesh Clan warriors tightened the circle and then one stepped forward, separating himself from his companions. He was garbed as a Flesh Clan Primordial priest in leather comprised of dried human skins. Avery's mind flashed back to the scene she had witnessed during her first journey through this area. The priest bowed deeply. As he rose, a dart gun appeared in his hand. With two quick *phuts*, he shot a pair of darts at herself and Achak. One pricked the skin of her arm and the other pierced Achak's thigh.

Drat, she thought, as she slid off her horse. She was out before she hit the ground.

*　*　*

With a jerk of his arm, Hototo ordered several warriors to pick up the unconscious woman and her guard. They slung them over the backs of their horses like sacks of grain. Following Hototo's lead, the guard led them into the valley at the edge of the Crystal Caves. It was a bowl-shaped, verdant-green clearing with gently sloping sides surrounded by steep cliffs on one flat side, and a semicircle of scrubby brush on the other, before emptying into the trees of the Sacred Forest. The narrow path they traversed was the only entrance or exit. Tight up against the cliff a series of cavernous openings dotted its face.

They laid Avery down in the shadow of a circle of tall stones, ancient and knowing, that graced the pasture. Her hood fell back, and the Primordial who had carried her yelled as though burned. The stones by which she lay bore symbols that matched those revealed on her hairless skull. Murmuring broke out. The warrior backed away, afraid to touch Avery, afraid to be near her.

A second warrior placed Achak on the ground beside Avery, and then his eyes fell on her.

"A goddess! She bears the markings!" he gasped, stumbling backward, and grumbling ignited and spread amongst the circle of warriors. "Is she a goddess? A goddess! Where?"

Hototo pushed his way through the crowd to the front of the circle and halted abruptly when his eyes fell on the sleeping woman. He walked around her, gazing at the tattoos, and then examined the pillar above her, comparing the symbols. He did not answer the warriors.

"Pick up her and her companion and follow me," he snapped, striding off toward the caves. The warriors looked from one to another. No one made a move. "Now!" Hototo roared over his shoulder. The men who had originally carried Avery and Achak gingerly picked them up again and followed the priest.

Hototo strode well ahead of them and disappeared into a rift running vertically up the face of the mountain. It was barely wide enough for two people to walk side by side, yet the shade of the bowl disguised the opening. Only by training their eye on where Hototo disappeared could they see the spot. They entered the crack, staring uneasily at the tilted stone that towered above them. After about one hundred paces, the crack widened and flattened into a cave glowing with a soft internal light. The mouth was encircled with jagged stone teeth that caught and absorbed the muted light of the passage, leering at the intruders with a frosted, rocky grin, as they crossed into the cave. The great maw seemed poised to snap shut at a moment's notice.

Shivering, they carried the pair to a stone table at the back of the cave, beside which stood Hototo, gesturing anxiously for them to hurry with their delivery. Gently, they deposited the still forms on the slabs of unpolished crystal and, bowing, backed out the cave. As soon as they were past the mouth, they ran, as fast as their moccasined feet could carry them.

Hototo ignored Achak, his attention focused entirely on Avery. He studied the runes and, lifting a finger, traced the swirls and patterns on her head and over her ears, murmuring to himself. Blue light followed his finger, and the runes glowed. Then with a gasp, Avery sat straight up. Her silvery eyes fixed on Hototo.

Hototo stepped back, shivering in reaction to her unusual eyes, and bowed, palms pressed together, and arms raised so that his fingers steepled, dividing his face. "I apologize, mistress, for our treatment. We saw intruders. We did not know."

Avery swung her legs over the side of the stone slab and swayed as the last of the paralyzing dart faded from her system. She slowly surveyed her surroundings. The walls were a smoothed milky white with shallow pockets as though the walls were made of cheese. Inside the glowing pockets, objects of various shapes and sizes were displayed: glass vials and small leather-bound books, carved wooden trinkets, a bracelet of twisted copper strands with charms, and the mummified bodies of what she took to be small animals. Even an ebony box graced one alcove. The box absorbed all light that touched it.

Avery's eyes drifted down to Achak and then to Hototo. "You have attacked us. Wake him!" she commanded, and Hototo bowed once again then hurried over to the prone form. He traced his temple in a similar fashion to how he had awakened Avery, and Achak's eyes drifted slowly open. Groggily, he rolled onto his side and pushed himself up on one arm, head hanging.

"This is the Crystal Cave. Why are you guarding it? And from whom?" Avery demanded.

"We have always guarded the cave, mistress. It has been our sacred, secret duty for longer than any of us can remember. From the beginning, it has always been so. No one may enter the caverns except the chosen ones. Similar to how the Spirit Clan's High Priestess is the chosen one for the spirit temple, the Flesh Clan priests serve the Crystal Cave. We guard the cave and keep it safe for the return of the Chosen One of the gods. It is here, look." Hototo pulled a scroll from amongst the books in the alcove that housed them. He unrolled the parchment and held it in front of Avery. "See here? The prophecies state that the Chosen One will bear the markings of the temple spirits and will be a priest above all High Priests." He let go of the parchment with one hand, and it rolled back up. He lifted his hand to point at her tattoos. "You are marked by the spirits." Hototo returned the scroll then tugged at the ties of his shirt, pulling it open to display his chest, covered in tattoos. "And so am I. The prophecies say that when the Prophesied One appears, the gods will be reunited with the people. One has already returned to us, and now you appear, mistress."

Avery stood up, frowning. "Who is this other?" she asked, her tone sharp and demanding. "Who else has come to the cavern?"

Hototo shook his head. "No one, mistress; the Chosen One I speak of was returned to us by the gods themselves. She has descended from on high. Artio is returned to us, blessed of the goddesses."

"Artio!" Avery shot to her feet, and Achak, seeing her alarm, forced his knees to straighten, wobbling over to Avery's side. "That's impossible. Where is she?" she demanded, suspicious that a trap may have been laid for her and Achak.

"She is in her temple, mistress. Surely you know of the Bear Clan temple? I must admit, the knowledge had been lost to us, but with the return of the bear goddess, all is being restored, and the timeline reset, as prophesied." He frowned at Avery, hesitant to challenge her.

"Bear goddess?" Avery and Achak's eyes met and then Avery walked over to the alcoves, letting her fingers trail along the wall as she strolled by them. Some of the objects brightened as she passed, others darkened, but all reacted to her presence.

Eventually, she paused at the last of the objects. The black box hummed and rattled, as though a beetle scrabbled inside it. She reached her hand forward, but Achak caught her wrist before she could touch it. "Mother, let me retrieve it."

She shook her head. "You don't know what it will do. Hototo, can anyone touch these objects? Come on, man, speak up!" she demanded in an imperious tone.

"We do not handle the objects, Mother. They were placed here by the gods eons ago. They are not for humans. We would not dare."

Avery tsked. "You mean to say that no one has ever been tempted to handle these things?"

"You misunderstand, Mother. We cannot touch them. See?" Hototo strode over and reached out for the black box. Along the vertical plane of the front of the alcove his hand abruptly halted. An invisible barrier prevented his hand from entering the cavity.

Achak reached out his hand, expecting resistance, but instead, his hand sunk through the barrier. Startled, he stumbled forward, thrown off-balance, and his hand settled on the box. It was cool to the touch and all vibrations ceased. He grasped the box and withdrew it. Behind the box, pushed further back into the cavity was a black leather purse. Achak pulled it out too and slipped the box inside it. The box caught on an object already inside it and would not go in. Achak gave it an extra hard shove, and it slid partway but would move no further. When he looked up, he saw they were both staring at him.

"Well, that is resolved then." Avery swung back to the priest. "I still do not understand the reason you are here. Why are you not with the Flesh Clans? Are they not at war with the men of Cathair?"

Hototo shifted, eyes jumping from one to the other, and then his eyes focused on a spot over her shoulder. "Yes, they are. I had business to attend to elsewhere. I returned here," he gestured at the cave, "to retrieve an object, just before warriors alerted me to your presence."

The runes on Avery's scalp danced as she shook her head, lips flattening in dissatisfaction at his answer. "You cannot touch the objects. What could you possibly have expected to recover?" Avery's eyes shifted to the box in Achak's hands and opened her mouth to speak once again when the light of the cave darkened as though a dark shelf cloud rolled overhead and the ever-present glow of the cave dimmed. Shadows formed in the rounded corners and the temperature dropped. Alarmed, Avery drew her knife just as a slimy hand clapped over her mouth from behind. Strong arms wrapped around her torso and she bucked angrily, fighting to free herself.

Achak found himself similarly restrained, as a pair of Charun slid from the shadows. Thick strands of black stretched like warm taffy to warp an underworld portal into the cave. The box tumbled from Achak's grip and bounced away across the floor, falling clear of the leather bag.

Hototo bowed low to the Charun, backing away from of the spill of dark ooze that was the magical passage to the netherworld, as it spread slowly across the cave floor. He was afraid to touch the soul-sucking blackness. He bent and scooped up the bag as he backed away. Once he reached the doorway, he spun around and ran from the Charun, fleeing the cave, racing down the narrow passageway. He had his prize. He shook the bag as he ran. Out tumbled a straw doll. The last doll. He grinned then stuffed the bag back under his tunic.

Once clear of the passage he slowed to a walk. He had all the time in the world now. No need to hurry. The Charun had the fake High Priestess now. *One problem solved. My mistress will be well pleased. I will be rewarded above all others.* His cheeks creased into a fleshy grin.

Chapter 31

Mordecai's Plan

MORDECAI WAS A PRACTICAL WIZARD. He was also a patient one, and prided himself on his ability to wait out any problem. Often a solution would present itself without having to actually formulate a plan.

So, when he spied Ziona and Cayden riding out of the legion's camp spread out in the valley below him, he was only mildly surprised at the turn of events. He stepped out from behind the big tree he had been hiding behind, observing the comings and goings of the camp, and hollered down to them, waving his arms in the air to attract their attention. His sleeves flapped like the wings of a bird, his grey wizard robes shot with silver thread sparkling in the sunshine.

Ziona spied him first, and tapping Cayden on the arm, pointed up the hill to Mordecai. She reined her horse in his direction, trotting up to his location with Cayden on her heels. As they approached, Cayden swayed in his saddle, slipping sideways as though drunk.

Mordecai frowned and grabbed hold of the bridle, halting the horse as it moved past him. Cayden patted the horse's neck and grinned at Mordecai. "Alcina freed us with a pardon. Wasn't that kind of her?" Ziona frowned back at him, twisting in her saddle.

"Kind? Alcina is never kind." Ziona grimaced. "Focus, Cayden. Fight the doll." She had grown more alarmed the further they had ridden from the legion camp. While they were free, Cayden was obviously not. Strange phrases and thoughts spoken aloud that would never have come from him normally proved that Alcina still controlled his mind. *I do not know what to do about it. While I am with him, I can monitor his activities, but what do I do if she takes him over? What is Alcina's plan?* Mordecai's face echoed the expression on hers, as he frowned at the young king. "She did release us with a pardon, however," she said.

"A pardon, you say? A pardon. I have never heard of Alcina granting pardons, unless they were posthumously. You both look to be alive. So, the only conclusion, my boy, is that she did not pardon you. But now is not the time for that discussion. You are free and away from her camp and that is what matters, for now."

"How did you know we were being freed?" asked Ziona.

"I had no idea."

"So why are you here? Surely you were not intending to come rescue us alone?" Her eyes searched the trees but located no one else with Mordecai.

"I am quite alone, Ziona. I am not powerless, you know. Sometimes one can do what an army cannot, especially when stealth is required. I came to recover the doll, not to free you two." He waved a bony hand at the pair of them.

Cayden snorted, glaring at the wizard. "I suppose you brought the stone too? Fat lot of good it did."

"Actually, it did a lot of good, Cayden. It has led me directly to you."

"Anyone could follow the trampling of two thousand legionnaires. That did not require the stone."

"No, but it still points to you and only to you."

Cayden shrugged, unimpressed.

Mordecai ignored Cayden's grousing. "Ziona, I want you to join up with Avery. Can you still find her?"

Ziona nodded. "She is not far away."

"I thought so. A day's ride at most I would say. Go now." Mordecai's attention swung back to the legion camp. "I am going after that doll."

"The odds of you being successful are low," Ziona muttered. "She keeps it with her at all times. She never puts it down. And there are at least two dolls, not one."

"She will have them together and on her person. No matter. I will figure out a way to recover them."

Ziona gathered up her reins, and her head swiveled in Avery's direction. Her sense was vague, but then Cayden spoke up. "I can ask her where she is."

He closed his eyes and reached out to his sister, mind to mind. *Avery, I am coming to you. Can you show me where you are?*

He felt her touch his mind. Into his vision swam an image of a narrow trail with tall mountains and around and in the distance, a smoking summit. "She is in the Highland Needle, near the Thunder Falls."

"Then let's go. Good luck, Mordecai. Be careful. Be very careful."

"You forget that I have been a guest of Alcina's in the past. I do not fear her. But I also do not underestimate her desire for revenge. I have no intention of falling into her clutches again."

Ziona smiled and, with a slap of the reins, set off, Cayden at her side. Mordecai watched them until they were swallowed by the trees, and then his attention shifted back to the encampment.

He would wait till nightfall and then slip in at the perimeter where the guard was thinnest. They patrolled the edge of the camp but did not venture any further than a couple spans from the set perimeter, and always patrolled as a pair. One hundred paces, square the sword, bow, pivot, one hundred paces back. But in that time when they bowed, there was a point when all eyes were pointing at the ground. That was his window.

Mordecai settled down under the tree, pulling a couple apples from his pocket. He shined one on his robes then took a big juicy bite. *Nothing to do but to wait till dark. Wait and observe.*

* * *

Cayden took the lead as the terrain became rockier and the trail less sure. Birds twittered and cawed and occasionally a squirrel chittered at them as they passed, scolding them for disturbing the quiet of their forest dwelling. Ziona relaxed as they rode. The further away from the camp they travelled and the deeper into Primordial lands, the more relaxed she became. By midday, the trees changed to evergreens, the leafy deciduous of the lower foothills thinning as the soil turned poor.

"Soon we will be entering the Sacred Lands. Here the magic of the mountain will take over, and the guardians who walk it allow only the worthy to pass." Her eyes darted in his direction. "I believe your father tried to enter with the Kingsmen, back before you were born. They were turned away. Sometimes it is done gently. Sometimes it is deadly. It depends on the perceived threat. But you"—she looked at him fully this time—"are a god. I have no fear that they will let you pass."

Cayden yawned and rubbed his eyes. He was having difficulty focusing on her words.

"Cayden, are you all right?"

"Yes, but the doll is still working on me. She may have shelved it, but I think she takes it out to play with it like a child. I think she can't resist. I need rest." Another yawn cracked his jaw. "Where do you suggest we bed down for the night?" He blushed when he realized what he had said.

Ziona grinned at him. "So eager! Don't worry. I have a place in mind."

Several hours later, at the edge of the Sacred Forest, Ziona led them to a clearing containing a small pond. Sunlight sparkled on its surface and bugs skimmed across the surface. Every once in a while, a fish would jump out of the water and snap at an insect, then fall back with a splash. A third of the circumference of the pond was edged with a tangle of raspberry bushes, the branches bending low under the weight of ripe berries.

Ziona dismounted with Cayden, and they hobbled the horses then pulled off their saddles. Retrieving their bedrolls, they made a rough camp. Ziona knelt by the water's edge and gave a blessing to the waters, asking for them to share their bounty. She placed a hand in the water and caught a fat trout with her bare hand, tossing it up on the shore where it flopped and flailed.

Ten minutes later, the trout was grilling over an open fire and they gathered berries to complete their impromptu feast. Before the sun was fully set, they snuggled in each other's arms. Ziona smoothed Cayden's brow with tiny kisses that trailed down the side of his cheek. Cayden gasped and rolled Ziona onto her back, as his hunger for her ignited into a more robust version of her kisses. The stress of the day vanished, and passion flared white hot as they fell under the spell of their love.

* * *

In a camp, a long way away, Alcina grinned as she stroked her doll. She ran her finger down the side of the doll's neck and could feel the doll trembling in her hand in response. *What a wicked boy you are, Cayden! Who knew such passion ran through your veins? Maybe I should keep you for myself.*

The bond was just as strong as it had been when he was in the camp. Alcina was pleased with the total control she still had over him, at any distance.

Now, lead me to your sister, like a good soul slave.

Chapter 32

Brimstone

A MIST DESCENDED INTO THE CLEARING, shrouding the pond and creeping across the ground. Fingers of fog ghosted the trees, wrapping around limbs and clouding the space between trunks. The mist cast a bluish hue in the rays of a nearly full moon, filtered and weakened by its passage through the mist overhead.

Cayden rolled over in his sleep, twisted up in the blanket he shared with Ziona, and his face smacked up against a soft muzzle that snuffled and snorted, ruffling his hair.

The horses…have wandered over, he thought in a sleep-drugged stupor. He pushed the muzzle away. The horse snuffled him again then took the blanket in its teeth and tugged it off.

With a shiver, Cayden woke, as the cold vapour touched his exposed skin. Cayden's eyes popped open, and he sucked in a surprised breath. It was not the horses.

Slowly he sat up and the creature stepped back, eyeing him steadily with pitch black eyes that shone in the filtered moonlight. A mane of thickest black curls flowed from sharply pointed ears. Cayden's eyes slowly followed the flow of its neck to its body, from which sprouted long, feathered wings tipped in white. The Pegasus snorted once again. As Cayden rose to his feet, it nudged him hard in the chest with its velvety nose. Cayden stroked the muzzle, hand curving around his lower jaw.

"Brimstone!" he breathed, knowing the name to be right, running his hand down Brimstone's sleek neck.

A hidden lever in his mind clicked, and with it, a rush of memory assailed him. Eons of memory of ages past flooded his mind, and he cried out under the crushing weight of the images flowing through his mortal brain. He sank to his knees, clutching at his head. This pain was not like the doll, which was external. This pain was the pain of memory, the pain of loss and remembrance. Tears streamed down his face, and Brimstone snuffled him once again, smearing the tears with his nose.

Ziona sat up abruptly, woken by the sound of Cayden's sobs. Her training kicked in, and knives appeared in hand as though she had slept clutching them. She sprang to her feet, then paused at the sight of Cayden and Brimstone. "Oh, Cayden!" Seeing his distress, the knives disappeared, and she knelt beside him, putting her arms around him to hug him. "Shhh," she mouthed. "It's OK. I know it hurts."

As she rocked him, she examined the Pegasus. She had never seen one, but the ancient texts spoke of the Pegasuses that the godlings had ridden. They had disappeared with the godlings themselves. No one knew why, but she suspected they were tied to the gods in some way.

Cayden calmed and wiped his sleeve against his eyes, drying them.

"*I remember*," he boomed, then paused, startled at the sound of his voice. The voice was of a distant Cayden, the voice of a godling. Ziona's eyes widened and she backed away in surprise. "I'm sorry, Ziona. Don't be afraid." He stood up, rubbing a hand across his temple and then strode over to the Pegasus who tossed his head, nostrils flaring and flapping his silky, ebony wings.

"Hello, Brimstone, my old friend. Thank you for the gift of my memory."

Brimstone bowed to him.

"Brimstone has returned my memory," Cayden said in his normal voice. "All of it." His gaze swept around the clearing. With eyes suddenly ancient, he focused on her still form. "I remember everything, Ziona." He reached out a hand to her, and hesitantly she took it.

"Mordecai said this day would come. Brimstone carried the key to my memory block. He was waiting for me to come to him in the Sacred Forest to be reunited with him."

Cayden stroked the sleek neck. "Where are Moonbeam and Sandstorm?" he asked Brimstone.

Brimstone shook his head, tossing his mane, and then whinnied and from the mist two more Pegasuses approached. Cayden smiled at them, greeting each of them in turn as they crowded in. "Moonbeam was Alfreda's—Avery's—and Sandstorm was Artio's. Although at the time of the cataclysm, they were with me. They were a gift from our father…" He trailed off, exploring the memory. When his eyes refocused, Ziona was on her knees again before him.

"Ziona, I thought we had settled this. Do not kneel before me." He reached down and pulled her to her feet.

"You are a child of the gods. I am mortal kind. I must worship you." She kept her face downcast.

"No, you are my soul mate now. You will not bow to me. Worship the gods, but not me."

He raised her chin with a finger, and Brimstone crowded in to nuzzle her cheek. She laughed and stroked his soft muzzle. The other two, not to be outdone, shoved their noses in for pats, trampling their blankets in the process.

Cayden and Ziona both laughed, and the laugh was echoed by fairies that flashed out of the reeds at the edge of the pond and flashed around them, jewel-coloured and chuckling with a tinkling sound as they flitted above them.

"Caerwyn! Caerwyn!" they called, their tiny voices the peeping of baby birds.

Cayden reached up, and a turquoise fairy with snow-white hair lit on his finger. "Aossi said you would come soon," she pipped, her iridescent wings sparkling in the moonlight.

Delighted, Ziona said, "Do you have a name? I am so happy to meet you!"

"Laila," she squeaked.

"Laila, Laila, Laila," the other fairies tinkled.

Brimstone tossed his head, and the fairies scattered, bringing attention back to him. He nudged Cayden with his shoulder.

"I think he wants you to go for a ride," said Ziona. Brimstone snorted agreement.

"Oh! Well…" Unsure, Cayden patted Brimstone on his shoulder, and Brimstone sank down on his forelegs, making it easier for

Cayden to mount. With a shrug, Cayden swung a leg over onto Brimstone's back, just behind the withers where jutted the massive wings, and tucked his knees under the huge muscles. He then twisted his hands in the thick black mane. Brimstone stood up and within a couple of strides launched him skyward. Cayden yelled as he cleared the trees, the beats of the wings stirring their leaves. Sleepy birds twitted angrily. Then Cayden was above the trees, above the mist, and soaring in the pure light of the moon.

The ground below sank away as the Pegasus flew. There was only the sky and the moon. If it were not for the cold night air streaming past his face or the heavy beat of Brimstone's wings, Cayden would have thought they were standing still. The peace of the flight helped him sort through the tumbling images in his head. He took a deep breath, settling himself, sorting and filing the information. *I am transformed. I finally remember who I am.*

It was not as comforting as he had thought it would be before he knew. With the return of his memory also came the return of the worries of the world, a return of ancient anxieties and problems. While it cleared his focus, it also complicated his path. With a sigh, he patted Brimstone on the neck. "We need to go back down, Brimstone, and rejoin Ziona. Can you find her?" Brimstone twisted his neck, and a snort of disgust issued from his throat. Cayden smiled. "That's my boy."

Brimstone banked and sank back into the mists, touching down with a lightness that disturbed nothing on the ground. He trotted back to Ziona, who was stroking the other Pegasuses and feeding them leftover raspberries from the palm of her hand. She looked up as they approached, a huge grin of pleasure on her face. Her eyes sparkled.

Cayden slid off and walked back to her. "I know what we need to do."

"I'm glad," she said simply. "I will follow wherever you lead, Cayden."

Cayden smiled at Ziona, shoving his hands in his pockets. Brimstone nudged him hard in the back, pushing Cayden into Ziona. Cayden's arms came up around her. Ziona laughed and hugged Cayden back. Brimstone tossed his head, as though saying, "Now, that's better!"

Cayden eyed Brimstone. "Don't you start getting cheeky with me!" he growled in mock anger. Brimstone shook his head, curly mane flopping into his eyes. Cayden's lips twitched with amusement.

Cayden checked the position of the moon, which was sinking below the crown of the trees.

"We need to get some more rest...if these great louts will let us. I would like to be on the trail as the sun rises."

As he and Ziona crawled back under their blankets and settled in, the Pegasuses wandered over to greet the horses. Cayden's last thought as he drifted off was how happy Avery would be to see Moonbeam once again.

Chapter 33

The Second Doll

MORDECAI WAITED UNTIL THE DEEP OF NIGHT to slip into the legion's camp. As the guards neared the end of their shift, they stifled yawns behind hands. Their paced patrolling slowed as the night crept on. Keeping to the shadows, Mordecai drifted from one dark trunk to the next with each pass. Now fifty feet of grass separated him from the comforting blackness of the nearest tent. He counted…sixty-five, sixty-six, sixty-seven…and on the stamp of seventy, he ran, crouching low across the open space. He slid into the overhang of the tent, which turned out to house supplies for the horses, and paused, listening for any hint of alarm. Hearing none, he stealthily made his way toward the ornate tent located at the center of the camp. He avoided the low-burning firepits that dotted the landscape, and none saw him pass, night-blind by the flickering flames. His hand drifted to the breast of his robes. Yes, the package, his backup escape plan, was still there. He would use it, but only as a last resort, should his escape be…impeded.

Alcina's tent rose up out of the encampment, twice as large as any around it and heavily guarded. Like a moss-covered rock, it was draped in guards, sprouting here and there. It was separated by a cleared circle of trampled grass that left the tent isolated, even though it was surrounded by a legion full of men. The sounds of the encampment around it were muted, and the croaking of crickets filled the air.

He paused, crouching down beside a tent at the edge of the circle and checked the placement of the guards. Two helmeted men stood at attention at the entrance to the tent, and Mordecai counted four others around the exterior; one leaned up against a tree, another lit a cigarette with a splinter of wood from a firepit. Two more played cards by the light of the low flames, and coins jingled as one laid out his wager.

Mordecai pulled the stone from his pocket and clutched it in his right hand and closed his eyes. His lips moved, and a thin probe of spirit whispered up from the stone attuned to Cayden's will. It drifted across the intervening space and then slipped past the guards and through the crack of the tent opening without attracting notice. He commanded the probe to explore the tent, searching for the doll that held Cayden's will. The probe melted around the tent, searching until it paused beside a sleeping person. Cayden's will pulsed, a strong throb that warmed the stone in Mordecai's hand. Mordecai urged it to look for the second doll, and it moved on, wandering around the tent, but it could not find the doll. Frustrated, he recalled the wisp, opening his eyes to break the spell. He had not expected it to. Without the tie of a soul, there was nothing to sense. It was just a doll, after all.

Mordecai made to stand. As he attempted to rise to his feet, he bumped into a solid object. Scarlet-slippered feet peeked from the hem of a grey, rough silk gown. Mordecai's eyes travelled upward to meet Alcina's victorious ones. In her hand, she held a doll, dressed in grey robes. Attached to its chin were several strands of beard, his beard. She picked up a long needle and locking her eyes on his, stabbed the doll in the chest. Pain shot through Mordecai, and he grabbed at his chest, his eyes widening and his mouth opened in a silent scream. His nerveless fingers dropped the stone clutched in them, and he toppled sideways, writhing on the ground while Alcina stepped around him, snapping her fingers to call her guards.

"So," she purred in a soft voice dripping with menace, "we meet again, Mordecai. This time, you will not escape. This time the only possible escape is death. It was useful to cut your hair all those years ago. I kept them, you see, as the mage promised me there was magic to be had in your graying locks." She reached down with a knife and cut a strip of cloth free of the sleeve of his robes and draped it around the doll. "Your will is mine. Your soul is mine. You will obey and serve me until death releases you. But first, I will enjoy torturing you. Oh yes, this time I will find the time." Her pitiless blue eyes stared down into his. "Finally, the will of a wizard is at my command." With a predatory twist of red lips, she commanded, "Pick up this filth and carry him to my tent. I intend to have some fun with him. Gag him first. I do not want to disturb the rest of my troops."

The men bent down and shoved a soiled cloth into Mordecai's mouth, tying it roughly behind his head then pulled back his arms, binding his wrists behind his back. They hauled him to his feet. Still bent double in pain, he sagged in their arms.

Alcina withdrew the pin and scraped it along the chest of the doll. Mordecai groaned, as his chest registered the sensation of a sharp knife slicing across his chest. Blood bloomed under his shirt and trickled down, fine rivulets that quickly soaked through.

Alcina was panting with pleasure as the blood blossomed on the grey robes. A powerful lust consumed her, flaring in her eyes as she called over her shoulders, as the guards hauled Mordecai into her tent. "Darius, attend me," she purred, and followed the soldiers inside, the flap dropping back as the guards released it after she had passed.

Darius grinned and, strutting like a prized peacock, followed his queen into the tent, already loosening the ties of his shirt, sweating with the heat of anticipation. He grinned at the jealous stares of his fellow guards. *They should be jealous,* he chuckled to himself. *Oh yes, they should be jealous.*

Clearing the entrance of the tent, Darius saw that the guards had dumped the wizard on the gaudy carpet, so recently decorated by Cayden. He had laughed at his former friend, the "king" of Cathair reduced to a drooling puppet. Now he grinned at the old man, his queen's nemesis, a rival she had fought her entire life. He walked up and kicked the old man in the stomach, and Mordecai jack-knifed around the blow, his air going out with a whoosh. He thought he heard something crack and shook his head. "He will not last long under torture. He is too old." Darius spoke the words aloud as the guards left the tent, leaving just the three of them.

Alcina placed the doll on the table beside her judgement chair, as he had come to think of it, and then sank down onto its overstuffed surface.

Steepling her fingers, Alcina studied the wizard. He lay panting on the ground, groaning softly.

"Well, Mordecai? You never did have any tolerance for torture. Do you remember the old days? When the Queen's Guard went at you with those hot irons? You would faint as soon as the iron touched your skin, then I would have to wake you to heal yourself. It's no fun torturing an unconscious person. I finally had to give up and forget my plans to extract information out of you. Instead, I left you in that dungeon to die. But you refused to, you stubborn old goat." Her grim smile widened and her teeth gleamed, feral and deadly. "But with this doll, I can fine-tune it, can't I?" she paused, but Mordecai did not answer. He could not answer. With a slippered toe, Alcina dragged the gag from his mouth and down onto his chin.

"As much as I like seeing you bleed, that is hardly going to work with you, is it? No, the torture I intend for you is of a mental nature. You will not be able to shut it off or escape because it will be all in your head. I intend to force you to listen to your friends screams as they die…at your own hand. When I eventually release your mind, you will kill yourself. It will not be of my doing or by my hand."

"You know that I have Cayden under the same control, or you would not have come here. You hoped to recover this." She twitched a doll dressed like Cayden in front of his face, then tucked it back into a pocket in her skirt. "He did not escape. I set him and his seeker free. But he is still completely under my control. From where I send him, he will not return. He has a mission to complete that he has no knowledge of. It will be triggered when he reaches his destination. And then he will die, after he chokes that useless seeker to death. You will never see either of them again, wizard."

Mordecai straightened, fighting the pain of what felt like broken ribs and took a shallow, tentative breath. "Once again your delusions lead you into realms of impossibility. You cannot control me with that doll. *I…will…not…submit!*" he ground out through clenched teeth. "I will stop my own heart before I hurt either of those kids. And as for Cayden, he is stronger than you can possibly understand. He will find a way to undo the damage you have inflicted on him. You will lose again, Alcina."

Alcina reared up from her chair, her temper flashing to the boiling point, then ran at Mordecai. She snatched up the doll and stabbed the pin into the straw head. Mordecai's temple exploded with pain. He screamed, clutching at his head, and collapsed to the floor, thrashing as crushing waves of pain washed over him from head to foot, so strong his toes curled in his boots. He cried out once more then stilled.

Disgusted, Alcina tossed the doll back on the chair and stepping around the unconscious wizard, then grabbed Darius by the arm and dragged him unresistingly back into her private chambers.

Bright red blood dripped from Mordecai's right nostril and puddled on the floor under his right cheek. They left Mordecai on the floor in the spreading pool without a backward glance.

Chapter 34

Fates Align

THE SCREAMS OF THE WOUNDED soared above the clang of metal on metal, a high-pitched counterpoint to the near rhythmic metronome of battle. The high mountain pass had opened into a sparse valley that clung to the side of the mountain, a saucer of greenery in a great stone cup. The verdant green was quickly turning to rust, as the churning of the horses' hooves trampled the grasses and flowers. A metallic taste hung in the air as blood was spilled, the blood of men and horses mixing with the anxious odours of sweat and urine.

Sharisha pulled her own short sword and dug her heels into the flanks of her mount. Her horse shot forward into the mix of Primordial warriors and legion soldiers. The men from the other side of the mountain were already blood-covered prior to the commencement of this surprise attack, and they'd hesitated before launching themselves out of the woods into battle. At first, she'd mistaken their wild shouts as cries of pain, rather than a war cry.

But now, she fought for her life. Soldiers fell on every side of her, but Sharisha's sole task was to protect the High Priestess, to whom she was bound. Her mount trampled two men trying to pull Marea out of her seat, and Sharisha stabbed a third through the throat as he grabbed the bridle of Marea's mare. The man's eyes widened in shock, and then he fell, slipping off the blade, hand frozen on the bridle, pulling the horse's head down with his collapsing body. The horse snorted in fear and bucked, clearing more men from the rear.

Sharisha reached over and pulled Marea off her mare onto the back of her horse, leaving the bucking mount to its crazed dance.

Sharisha sawed on the reins. Marea gasped and slumped against her back. Bright crimson ran down the High Priestess's arm, which encircled Sharisha's waist. With a snarl, Sharisha reared her horse, forelegs flailing, bringing it down on the two men in front of her. Then, she dug in her heels once again and her horse shot forward, bowling over men like stones on a game board. She cleared the main circle of fighting and whipped her horse with the loose ends of her reins urging her mount to greater speed, focused on the resumption of the path ahead. Her only thought was to get Marea away from the battle to find a safe place to tend to her wounds. Sharisha glanced over her shoulder and saw Marea clinging grimly to her, eyes flashing with fury. Her arm bled freely, but it did not look to be a critical wound. Sharisha dashed down the curve in the road, the cries of the battle receding. Just as she reached the edge of the clearing before the relative safety of the woods, a man rose from the bushes. Triumph glittered in his narrowed eyes, and then he grinned, lips stretching into a victorious, toothy smile. Raising his bow, he drew, sighted, and released the arrow with one fluid movement.

The impact was jarring, the arrow piercing Sharisha's right breast and driving straight through. Were it not for the fact that Marea clutched her around Sharisha's waist and held her upright, she would surely have tumbled from the saddle. Sharisha's horse ran on into the trees, now completely out of control, as Sharisha could no longer feel the reins in her hands. She tried to take in a breath, but it was agony. She coughed and blood bubbled to her lips. Spots danced in her sight and she sighed. *So, this is death,* she thought, watching as the light of the world shrunk smaller and smaller until it vanished completely. *I did want to see Avery one last time. There is something about that child.*

Sharisha slumped over the neck of her horse. A blue mist rose from her body and hung in the air, waiting to be claimed.

*   *   *

Cyrus lowered his bow and watched the Primordial women ride off into the woods. A clear trail of blood splattered behind them, obvious even to the poorest of trackers, of which, he was not. He gathered his horse, tucking the bow back into its scabbard and then remounted, following the trail. He cared not if his men survived. He only wanted the High Priestess, and now she was his.

He followed the trail for about half an hour, surprised to see that they had kept their saddle. He was sure he had killed the first woman, probably the High Priestess's bodyguard by the way she had come to the woman's defense. The High Priestess was also wounded. Would she stop to bury her guard, or would she shove the body aside and continue to flee? From what he knew of Primordial belief about the dead, he thought she would pause to offer prayers to the gods for the safe passage of the soul. How long she would pause, he was not sure, but it would afford him the time to kill her, if he was swift enough.

Sure enough, ten minutes of hard riding brought him to an ice-cold glacial stream. The trail led straight toward it and stopped at the edge of the water. He dismounted beside a hastily built mound, and laid out in Primordial fashion was the dead seeker. She'd been buried in the loose sand of the river's undercut bank, beneath a cairn of hastily scooped river rock, leaving her face uncovered, so that she could continue to commune with the spirits of the forest even in death. Her eyes were propped open, all the better to see the spirits when they paused to visit. The first of these ancient burial mounds he had come across had been in the foothills on a previous campaign, but he'd thought the bizarre practice had been long abandoned.

He placed his hand on the dead woman's forehead. The body was still warm. Cyrus shivered. *How barbaric! These heathens never change. They are an anthill that should be ground underfoot and stamped out of existence.* The Flesh Clans, at least, had adopted burning the bodies of the dead, if Alcina was to be believed, properly freeing the spirits from the imprisonment of the flesh, as was the way for those of Cathairian origins.

His eyes left the mound and he walked around, searching for the new trail. Horse tracks entered the stream, but due to the thickness of the undergrowth which hugged the shore, the path was obvious.

Crushed ferns provided a guidepost, and he picked out the continuance of the trail on the other side of the stream. The woman was alone now and easy pickings. He remounted and left the dead woman behind. She was nothing. His true prize still ran, and he would not rest till he caught her. With her as his prisoner, he would have all the bargaining chips he needed, especially if he caught up to the other woman they'd been following. He suspected it was their prisoner, escaped from the fiery hut. He would deliver two important gifts for his mistress of shadow. First, he would take this one, and then go after the other. If his men caught up to him, so be it. If not…well, they were a stupid lot and not worthy of accompanying him. Eventually, he would have had to dispose of them for learning what he was up to. He would overthrow Alcina or he would die trying. Too long he had laboured in the queen's shadow, while the goddess whispered to him of the rewards he would receive if he were the one to hand over the prophesied children. Alcina's blundering had cost them the boy. They had had him chained in the dungeon, for spirit's sake! Abruptly, Cyrus jerked his thoughts back to the search at hand. *Focus. I need to recover the woman. That is what I need to do.* With that grim thought, he booted his horse into motion and trotted swiftly down the trail, marking the dots of blood that occasionally dropped onto the forest floor.

*   *   *

Marea clutched at the bandage slipping down her arm. She'd wrapped it hastily with cloth torn from her underskirt and tied it off, but the knot had loosened with the hauling of the rocks she had used to bury Sharisha, and she had lost valuable time. Sharisha had been a loyal seeker though, deserving of the cairn for her final journey. She had protected her and honoured her in life, and now the bond had driven her to protect Marea from certain death. Sharisha deserved to be given the Welcoming Ceremony, the sacred sharing of the soul with the gods, and so Marea had halted beside the stream to let the horse drink, clean her wound, and bury the seeker.

The cut by the blade was deep but not long; however, it was jagged and located in the crook of her elbow. Every last movement of the arm opened the wound afresh, so that it continuously bled. It needed stitching, something she could not take the time to do, and impossible while jouncing on the back of a horse.

Marea pulled out an amulet tucked under her shirt and clutched it in her right hand, the hand of the bleeding arm. It helped to rest the arm across her chest and clutching the stone gave her something to cling to, to keep the arm as still as possible. The amulet of the High Priestess connected her to the temple, to the spirits of the temple, but it remained cold and lifeless in her hand. It had only sung to her one time, when she'd been granted access to the temple on that first occasion. She had picked up the necklace where it lay on a tray just inside the door. It had flared to life and forms had emerged from it, swirling around the common room and around her before fading away. It had not spoken to her since. Yet, she clung to the memory, to the fact that she could still enter even if the temple did not light up like it had for the girl.

Marea swayed in the saddle. Blood loss, she knew it instinctively. She would have to stop to rest soon, but there was no safety here. There was no place to hide. She was weak from lack of blood and weary, her body slowing down. She could not keep up the pace, yet she knew the soldier was still on her trail—she could sense it.

She closed her eyes and prayed to her ancestors, prayed as she had never prayed before. She reached out to the gods of her people. "Temple of the ancestors, I know I have not prayed to you in a long time and I have been negligent in singing your praises, but I pray to you now. Ancient Ones, if I truly am the anointed one, if I am truly chosen, then show me your will. Am I to die to make way for the girl? Help me...please show me my path! Show me your will!"

The amulet trembled in her grip and waves of energy vibrated so sharply through the stone that Marea's fingers numbed and she dropped it with a gasp. The amulet had never done that before. The crystal flashed a ball of blue flame which enveloped her, horse and all. With a clap of thunder, she was gone.

Chapter 35

Answered Prayer

AVERY FOUGHT THE DARKNESS that pervaded the room as she struggled within the Charun's slimy grasp. The stink of death surrounded the Charun, and she fought against the tug of the underworld. It pulled at her soul, at the essence of her being, dragging her down with the dry rattling breaths of one long dead. Avery fought the drag and the pull with every ounce of her strength.

Achak kicked and squirmed in the grip of the second Charun. Suddenly, it was enveloped in a skin of blue fire that slid Achak's entire body, encasing it.

Avery screamed as she writhed in the grip of the Charun, but Achak did not. Instead, he stilled, and the blue flames solidified and parted from his body to reform in the air above his head as a pure spirit phoenix. Its talons, beak, and eyes were ice blue flame. The feathers of the spirit guardian danced in an invisible breeze as the bird lifted into the air. The Charun gripping Achak hesitated, its focus distracted by the spirit bird.

The phoenix began to sing a mesmerizing song that froze the pair of Charun. They began to sway in response to the song, bewitched by the melody, and their grips loosened. With a jarring screech, the guardian dived at the Charun holding Avery and tore at its face with talons of ice that hissed and steamed. It screeched, the noise of good steel sharpening on a grinding wheel. Sparks flew from the Charun, and then it imploded, sucking the blackness back to the hell of its home.

Avery fell to the floor of the cave at the sudden release, and the phoenix swung back to the remaining Charun. Avery raised her head just in time to see Achak picked up by clawed hands as dark as night. The Charun raised Achak above his head and flung him at the glowing phoenix. He passed straight through as it had no corporeal substance. He struck the wall on the far side with a sickening crunch and a howl of pain. The phoenix flickered, then dived at the Charun, grabbing it by its exposed throat, and pulled. Black sulphuric blood bubbled and burned as it spilled onto the floor of the cavern and with a second bang, the Charun imploded.

"Achak!" Avery stumbled over to his side, avoiding the flashing ooze that pitted the marble floor.

Achak moaned, clutching at the leg crumpled and twisted impossibly against the wall. He looked at it and then swiftly away, as bile rose in his throat. He clung to consciousness by a thread.

"Shh!" commanded Avery, as she gently felt along the length of his leg. The femur was twisted under her hands, the sharp edges ridged under her fingers. It was broken in one, possibly two places. "Lay back. I need to splint this." She searched the interior of the cavern, looking for something to use, and her eyes fell on a several carved wooden staffs leaning against a wall in the corner. A straw mattress provided an aged blanket riddled with holes that separated easily in her hands. She tore it into long strips of cloth along the grain of the weave. Once she had enough strips piled in her lap, she retrieved a pair of staffs and ran back to Achak, who now slumped against the wall, unconscious. Avery dropped the staffs and wrappings, then laid Achak out on the stone floor. Straightening his leg, she coaxed the bones into alignment then placed the staffs alongside the break to judge the proper length. She pulled her knife from its holster and sawed at the wood, shortening staffs to the right length. The strips of cloth wrapped the leg from hip to ankle. Avery bound it so tightly that it could not shift. She crisscrossed the strips and tied off the tails, then stood to look at her work. Something about the cave prevented her touching the healing she was capable of. It was like there was a blanket over the cave, isolating it from the natural world around them, smothering her connection with the natural world from which she drew her power.

Rising to her feet, Avery walked to the entrance of the cave and peered out into the rift, to see who might be around. The passageway was empty. Silently, she moved along the path, listening for any indication that a guard remained, slowly edging her way to the opening of the bowl. A contingent of Flesh Clan warriors with their backs to her stood guard at the gap in the rock. Quietly, she withdrew, then spun around and ran back down the rift to Achak. She was about halfway back to the cave when suddenly the runes on her skin flared hot, and she cried out as the power of the temple surged within her skin. She lurched to a halt when with a flash of energy that made sparkling motes of light dance in her vision Marea appeared, swaying on the back of her horse. Marea gasped with shock at the sight of Avery, then slipped sideways and fell from her saddle, slumping onto the ground. Avery shuddered, rubbing her hands over the prickling tattoos to soothe her skin, then ran over to Marea and knelt beside her. She placed her hand on the woman's fevered brow. She was abnormally pale-faced, anemic with blood loss. Avery ran her hand over Marea's forehead and murmured under her breath.

Marea's eyes fluttered open. When she saw Avery, she reached up with her bloodied right hand and grasped the front of her tunic. "I beg your forgiveness, Mother! I have betrayed you! I was jealous. I wanted to hold onto power when I was only a caretaker. I realize that now. I prayed to the gods to save me, and they brought me to you." She sobbed. "Forgive me. You are the true High Priestess. Forgive me!"

"Shh, hush now," said Avery, prying Marea's stiff fingers off her tunic. "Shh. We are one people. Unity is what is needed. The past is done. I need your help to unite the people. Now lie still, and tell me what has happened."

"Sharisha is dead! We were attacked by a legion squad, and she died defending me. He shot her with an arrow." Her lips trembled. "I do not know how many have survived. Perhaps they are all dead but if not, Mother, they are coming this way!" The blood from the cut on her arm dripped onto Avery's lap as she helped Marea to a sitting position.

Avery grimaced. She had not trusted Sharisha, but she had not wished her harm. She had taken care of her in her own way. "Let me try to heal you. Here, lie still." She placed her hands over the wound and closed her eyes. She sensed the jagged edges of the cut where the flesh was torn and reached out with her mind to pull the raw ends together. Then with a flash of her own soul, she knit the flesh back together. Without conscious thought, she willed it to be whole. The skin wriggled and stretched, and then it was still. Other than the dried blood, not a hint of the wound remained.

Avery opened her eyes and sighed, tired from her struggles with the Charun and the exertion of healing the deep wound. Marea stared at the arm, a bemused but sad twist to her lips. "Sharisha was the most powerful with healing, but she could not hold a candle to you, Mother. Thank you."

Avery stood and pulled the older woman to her feet. She led the way back to the cave. Marea ducked under the threshold and gazed around with reverence. "No one has entered the Sacred Caves except for the guardians in eons. I've never been in the caves. The war with the Flesh Clans prevented any such thing." She wandered around the cave, a childish wonderment on her face. "I do not know what these objects do. Do you, Mother?"

"Yes," said Avery simply. "These objects of magic were placed here by my sister or sisters, a long time ago." Her eyes flashed. For a moment, an ancient knowing entered her gaze, as though she looked at the objects through a different pair of eyes. Marea dipped her head and did not inquire further.

"We are trapped here at present, Marea. There is a Flesh Clan contingent at the end of the passage." She gestured toward the bowl. "We need a distraction to draw them away from here. Do you think you could do this? It will be very dangerous. You have the advantage of them not knowing you are here. They will be surprised to see you exit this sacred place, when they did not see you enter." She reached into her tunic and pulled out the vial that Aossi had given her. "Perhaps this will help. It will hide you from your enemies. You must lead them away from the valley. Do not return for me. There is something I must attend to in here."

"What of Achak?" Marea wandered over to look at the injured man.

"He is needed here. I will heal him in time."

Marea nodded. "Then let me depart. I will create an illusion, a trick of the mind. They will follow me, thinking it is you."

"Go with my blessing, Marea, and thank you."

Marea lifted Avery's hand and kissed the back of it and then left the cave.

*   *   *

Marea exited the cleft of the rock and did not bother to disguise herself. The Flesh Clan warriors, on seeing her, quickly surrounded her and ordered her to halt. Marea reined in, and with an imperious tone commanded, "Take me to Hototo, now."

The warriors exchanged looks over their drawn swords. Clearly, they did not expect to be commanded, nor did they believe that Hototo wished to speak to a Spirit Clan priest. They made no move to lead her to her requested destination.

Marea sat on her horse like a queen, regally surveying the men as though they were her escort, part of her entourage. "Better yet, take me to whom Hototo serves. I would speak to his master."

A tall red-bearded man stepped forward, motioning toward the grey stones at the far end of the valley. "Follow me." He took the lead and Marea urged her horse into a quick walk, following Red Beard, the balance of warriors trotting at her side, easily keeping up to the pace of her mount. Her thoughts drifted back to the cave, and she glanced down at her blood-stained tunic. A flash of sorrow for the loss of her seeker—for the loss of her loyal companion, Sharisha, drifted across her thoughts—but then her will hardened.

You are far too trusting, Avery. I will not bow to you so easily. You know nothing of the politics of this world or who serves whom. You will kneel to me in time, as a chained and controlled servant of the temple. Spirit Shields should not be allowed control of world events. They are servants of the people, not rulers...not even one descended from the gods.

As she rode, her hand slipped inside her pocket, and she pulled out the vial given to her by Avery. With a derisive snort, she tossed it away onto the grass of the meadow. It tumbled and rolled and then made a *clunk* sound as it hit the base of one of the tall upright stones in the grass.

Chapter 36

Genii's Vision

GENII BENT OVER THE STONE SCRYING POOL, the waters dancing with internal light that bounced and shimmered off the stone walls and ceiling of the windowless room. He was watching a battle between the Charun, sent to restrain two intruders within the Crystal Cave, a woman and her companion. They struggled in the grip of the Charun, the woman familiar to him somehow. But it was the runes that covered her head and neck and the exposed portions of her arms that intrigued him. They were runes of power, runes of healing, runes of time and distance. Runes of nature and balance. He had never seen so many runes in one place, let alone on a person.

The man seemed to ripple and then a phoenix rose into the air, a spirit guardian of such rarity that it took Genii by surprise. Those creatures born of flame were usually associated with his mistress. To see one attuned to a mortal was highly unusual. Times were changing; Genii felt it in the air.

The phoenix attacked the Charun with blue-bladed talons of spirit. Spirit was the soft underbelly of the Charun, their one vulnerability. Being created from the souls of the dead, they could only be slain by another soul. *The phoenix is a worthy opponent, and my mistress would be pleased to hear of this.* But he did not call her. Instead, he wiped away the scene and returned to the image he had been watching earlier. He had not been sent to spy on the cave, but he had been curious where the Charun were being sent, seeing as everyone had been recalled and tasked to the creation of a lava idol. With the solstice only a day away, there was no time to lose and to spare even two of the Charun was startling.

The surface of the scrying pool calmed and reflected the image of Artio, riding at the head of a column of men and women, clad in Flesh Clan warrior garments. A covey of priests flocked around her, keeping a respectful distance from her side. Genii leaned in to better study her features. They had softened since the last time he'd seen her, some of the wildness of the bear fading into a hearty, healthy young female, but more muscular and shapelier than the Artio that stirred in his vague and scattered memories.

Straight-backed and fierce, she led her servants through a hilly terrain that resembled the early reaches of the sacred slopes. By nightfall, they would be nearing his mistress's realm. He felt a stirring in his chest that he associated with the human condition called fear and another that he associated with…love. He disliked the feelings intensely, yet he knew it was not for himself that he feared. Artio's return would not be greeted with warmth. He knew his mistress intended to slay the bear goddess once and for all. His fear thumped in his chest, gripping his imaginary heart in a tight fist. He could not let that happen. Artio must not be harmed. And yet, she walked into a trap. She did not know of his mistress's plans. But how could he warn Artio? He couldn't leave the caves. Frustration overwhelmed him. Angry at himself, Genii snarled at the image in the pool. At one point, Artio's head swiveled. For a moment, he thought that she saw him, that she was staring straight into his eyes…but then she looked away, expression unchanged.

His hand slapped the surface of the scrying pool, and the image transformed once again. This time his mistress came into view. Helga sat astride a midnight-black horse at the edge of the legion encampment, hidden by the deep shade of the tall pines. Face hidden in a matching-coloured cloak, she was indistinguishable from her mount. For one moment, she was barely visible, but then the illusion faded as black curls of smoke obscured her. She vanished, only to reappear without her horse inside a large tent. Fine furnishings decorated the tent, and a tall straight-backed chair with cushions sat on a raised dais. She stood frozen for a minute, observing the room, and then glided forward on feet that did not touch the ground to hover over a figure lying prone on the floor. Dressed in grey robes and laced boots, the man sported a long white beard. Blood trickled out of his nose and stained the rare and expensive carpet beneath him.

Helga lifted her imaginary skirts and walked around the wizard, examining him, then she paused and straightened, hearing activity in a curtained-off room of the tent. She smiled maliciously, then took her boot and roughly rolled the unconscious wizard over. A small bag with a drawstring tumbled out of his robes. She bent down and picked it up, loosening the fastenings to peer inside. A stone and a crystal were the only objects in the small bag. She pocketed them for later inspection.

On the ornate chair, she spied one of the items she had come for. She plucked the straw doll from the cushions where it had been tossed, and it followed the bag of stones into a deep inside pocket of her cloak.

Helga silently approached the partition of canvas that drifted softly in the air currents of the tent interior, and paused just outside the room. Inside, bodies writhed and danced in the age-old pagan ritual, entwined and absorbed and oblivious to the outside world.

Helga raised her hands and summoned a wicked obsidian knife, the blade twisted and razor-sharp, the glass formed of the very fires that fed the furnace under Genii's feet. Helga paused for a moment longer, listening for the guards, and then entered the room. She was still wreathed in shadows.

When she paused by the bed, a woman ceased her activities and cried out in shock, "Great Mistress!" She scrambled to separate herself from the man, but before she could move, the blade flashed and buried itself between Alcina's breasts. Alcina's face froze in shock, and then she crumpled sideways on top of the man. The man caught her, but before he could do anything further, before he could utter a sound, the blade slashed across his own throat. With a great gushing, Darius gurgled his last, his eyes rolling back into his head.

Helga stepped back to avoid the blood now flowing freely onto the feathered mattress and then wiped the blade off on the coverings pushed to the end of the bed. Once all blood was removed, she began to search the room.

She spied the other doll, her brother's doll, sitting on a table beside the bed, underneath a discarded garment. With a pleased chuckle, Helga picked it up and pocketed it, then left the room without a backward glance.

When she reached the wizard, the knife vanished, and she reached down to touch his shoulder. He became wreathed in the same smoke and both vanished, only to reappear on the back of her horse in the entrance to her abode.

So, Alcina has outlived her usefulness. Genii straightened and ran a hand over his nonexistent beard, a habit left over from his mortal days. What was Helga planning for the legion army? Surely, they would be thrown into disarray with the slaying of the former queen. Or maybe that was the plan? He pondered the events he had witnessed as he walked away from the pool and off to prepare chambers. It appeared they would have a guest...or two, very shortly.

Chapter 37

Stony Silence

HELGA SLID OUT OF THE SHADOWS at the edge of the Thunder Falls, a wraith transformed to human form once again. The unconscious wizard was draped across her saddle, but she would not remove him. She slung down from the saddle and, grabbing the reins, pulled Diablo into the mouth of her home.

"Genii! You have prepared accommodations? I have an unexpected guest, one I cannot say I am sorry to encounter! Where are you, Genii?"

"Here, mistress!" answered Genii as he came around the bend of the long hallway, hands tucked into his robes. "I have a cell prepared, mistress."

"No, no, a cell is no place for so great a personage." Helga dropped the reins and brushed past Genii. "Put him in the guest quarters overlooking the gardens. He is no threat to us now."

"Yes, mistress!" Genii bowed once more and then moved over to the side of the horse and hefted Mordecai's still form over his shoulder like a sack of potatoes. *Skinny wizard; he weighs no more than a starving rabbit.*

Genii straightened with his burden and headed down the side passage that had been travelled not long ago by Artio. Once he reached the bottom, he pushed his way through the dense copse of trees to series of doors that stretched along the stream. He entered the third one and then carried the unconscious wizard to the bed and rolled him down onto it. A bowl and a pitcher of water sat on a washstand under a dusty mirror. He picked up the pitcher and strode outside, dipping the pitcher into the stream and bringing it back filled to the brim with sparkling fresh water. He pushed aside a curtain that allowed light to filter in from the outside and lit a lantern hung on the wall. With one last look at the wizard, he left, pulling the door closed behind him.

*   *   *

Helga stirred the objects on the table with a long-nailed finger, pleased with the outcome of her raid on Alcina's camp. She had only intended to dispose of the woman, to sow seeds of confusion and chaos in the armies of men, but as luck would have it, she had also acquired control of two of her enemies. She chuckled as she picked up the doll of the wizard. To have control over one such as he, was a boon beyond measure. *You serve me better in death than life, Alcina. Your soul was already mine.* But what to do with the wizard? Helga pondered his uses, turning the doll over and over in her hands, examining how it was made. In the back of the doll, a coin was wedged. Although she could not see the significance of this, somehow it was tied to the wizard.

Helga set the doll down and picked up the second one, this one resembling Cayden, her dear reincarnated brother—but a human, no longer a godling. She snorted, amused at their attempts to play at being royalty and at being godlings. They had given up that power to her long ago. If it were not for the wizard's dabblings, their rebirth would have been impossible, but such as it was, they were nothing but annoying gnats that she would eventually swat out of existence, crushed beneath her will.

With this doll, I can make you dance to my tune, Little Brother, and dance you will, before the end. Before I am finished with you, you will wish you had never been reborn.

She flipped the doll over, and a quick search revealed it also had a gold coin tucked in the back of it. *So…the wizard and the boy are linked by the coins…how interesting.* She put the doll back down and then picked up the two other objects taken from the wizard. One was a clear crystal, oblong-shaped and smooth, and it fit easily in the palm of the hand as if made for it. She picked it up, and it immediately darkened. Grey clouds swirled through it, occluding the crystal, and it grew hot, very hot. Hastily, she dropped it, sucking her fingertips. Immediately, it cleared; so fast she blinked, unsure if her mind was playing tricks on her. She stretched out her hand toward the stone, caution slowing her reach, and as her hand hovered over the crystal it flashed again in warning. She frowned at it and instead reached for the second stone, a simple river rock, smoothed by water.

Leery of a similar reaction, she thumbed the rock. Nothing happened. She picked it up and turned it over in her hand. There were no special markings. There were no runes or painted symbols. She scraped a nail down it. Nothing happened. It seemed to be a rock and nothing more. She put it back down, puzzled. Why keep it in with the other crystal if it was of no importance? She frowned. She did not like mysteries, not at all, especially when they were related to magic. What she didn't know had the ability to become annoying and to interfere with her plans.

At that moment, Genii returned from depositing the wizard in the guest room. He stood hesitantly in the doorway, waiting for permission to enter, a good and loyal servant. Helga studied his body, silhouetted by the muted light of the hallway. So tall and handsome, he had been her mate for eons now. She could have asked for no better.

"Enter, my love." She beckoned him forward with a crook of her finger. "What do you make of these objects?"

Genii paused at the edge of the table, studying the objects. He did not touch anything. "The dolls are of Flesh Clan make, possibly Soul Fetches. The stones…they are wizard rocks. The crystal one is a focus stone, which tightens the will of the wizard when performing spells, amplifying his powers. The second…" His hand reached out to the rock but stopped short of touching it and let his hand hover above the rock. "This is a memory stone. I cannot tell whose stone it is, but it carries the unadulterated memories of someone. Possibly of the doll's hosts, but it could be anyone's. I cannot tell. Only the person whose memories reside in the stone can retrieve them. It is also an object of spirit and will."

"Thank you, love. You are such a good pet." She patted his arm as one would pat a good dog. "You will watch the wizard and stay with him at all times. I want to know everything he knows. Perhaps you can persuade him to cooperate with this." She picked up the wizard's doll and handed it to him. "But if you can do it by conversation, that would be better. He will need his strength for what I plan to do with him. His powers will be tapped to their fullest." She stroked the silent stone one last time. After a moment of consideration, she tucked it back in the bag. "Perhaps this stone would help to persuade him, but first I will see what I can learn from him. Work on him with the doll. Lie if you wish, use force if you wish, but find out what he is up to."

"As you command, mistress." He bent over her hand and kissed it. "So it shall be."

Helga patted his cheek, and he left like a good hound. She watched him go and a tiny frown wrinkled her brow. Genii was…different lately, ever since Artio's visit. At times, she thought he might have had a stirring of memory at the sight of her, that something of that distant past may have surfaced, but he never spoke of it. She wondered, not for the first time, if she should be watching him more closely, but then she dismissed it. He was the only one she truly trusted. *Paranoid—you are becoming as paranoid as the ones you manipulate,* she thought, as she picked up the focus stone with the bag it was carried in and then tucked Cayden's doll inside the bag for safekeeping. *But still, caution is warranted.*

Maybe I should not have trusted him with the wizard's doll. Caution is warranted. But what can he do with it other than torture him? Her frown deepened. She did not think he would be careless with the doll.

And she had other tasks requiring her attention.

Dismissing Genii from her mind, she stood up and wandered to the railing overlooking the grotto. A plume of smoke drifted cross the peak of blue sky that shone from the skyward opening, temporarily darkening the grotto. There was no way to mask her machinations beneath the mountain, no way to hide the tremors and quakes as they dug ever deeper into the earth. This time Helga meant to rule all, and no one would be able to resist, not even a skinny boy, now turned elderly wizard. There was no one left to resist. She smiled grimly down at the nearly pastoral scene below and then pushed away from the stone window and marched out the door.

Chapter 38

High-Flying Rescue

CAYDEN SOARED ABOVE THE TREES, scouting the landscape below for activity that might mean enemies lay ahead. Brimstone flapped his wings once, twice, and then spread them full, glittering black wing tips fluttering in the wind. He glided over the trees, hooves brushing the highest tips. Bursts of fragrant pine filled the air, and Cayden laughed. He felt *so free,* something he had not felt in a very long time. But the feeling of freedom was short lived. Memories crowded in, both happy and sad, triggered by his return to the air on Brimstone's back. The past year had changed his life completely. While he now knew the why and the how, it had also brought the weight of ancient responsibilities crashing down on his young shoulders.

They had made so many mistakes. They had originally gone about the investigation of the disturbances in the Highland Spine with an arrogant nonchalance *and innocence* that was shaming. Brimstone had fully restored Cayden's memory, complete with vivid flashbacks of that awful evening when *he had died…when they had all died, everyone except for Helga.* He could still feel the ripping pain of having his soul dragged from his being, of losing his immortality. If it had not been for Mordecai, that sweet boy of Hud's, darkness would have swallowed the world and all would be soul enslaved to Helga. Mordecai was an elderly man now, long-lived for a human as all wizards were, provided they survived the trials of the magic to live to full adulthood. It seemed strange to remember the boy who had been Mordecai. Cayden had so many memories to sort to reconcile with his current life.

As he flew, his eyes drifted toward the heavens to the planets of the distant cosmos where he knew the gods resided, his father Morpheus among them, having returned to the gods. Did he know what a mess his offspring had created on Earth? Probably not. Cayden doubted if his father ever looked at the world he had lived in so briefly. He certainly didn't check on them. Without their mother, he had no interest in the world. Helga had a point when it came right down to it; the gods cared little for the world. Although Cayden didn't agree that the worship of the gods should be completely abandoned, he could see Helga's point. Unfortunately, the power of the gods was necessary to keep the natural world in harmony and the spiritual world in balance. The power of the gods was the sticky and often-hated glue cementing the world, keeping it whole. Without the gods, it was possible to destroy the world from the inside out. Without the gods, the world would decay, rot from within, until all was consumed by the belly of the world, enslaved to the underworld and Helga's dominion.

Perhaps, if they contacted the gods and asked for their intervention, things could be different. Would they respond to the prayers of the people if they prayed? Would they even hear them? *Would they hear mine?*

From the vantage point of Brimstone's back, the peaks of the Highland Spine were ringed in smoke, reminiscent of that day so long ago when the world had nearly ended. The fiery hearths deep down inside the mountain stirred a caustic warning of doom's reawakening. And to the east, an army stirred, clouds of birds rising from the trees, heralding their passage. The Primordial clans were on the move. Cayden's eyes traced the path that would lead him to them, located deep within the Sacred Forest.

As Brimstone skimmed over a break in the treetop, his eyes fell on the remnants of a battle. The bodies of men littered the field below him. By virtue of the fact that there were no crows or ravens or vultures present, the battle could not be that old. *Maybe someone is still alive down there!* Blue mist rose from those who had recently died, their lost souls calling out to Cayden from the clearing. "We must land, Brimstone. Put us down, boy, but away from the worst of the carnage if you can. I don't want us to be shot down." Memories of Brimstone screaming in pain as his wing tore flashed across his mind. He gritted his teeth to stem the flashback. "Keep your eyes sharp!"

Brimstone circled, and Cayden kept a sharp eye, but nothing stirred. With a flap or two of wing and a light gallop Brimstone settled back to Earth at the edge of the forest. Cayden slid off his back and then pulled his sword, examining the scene before him. He grimaced at the sword, knowing he could not kill anyone even if they attacked, but perhaps he could incapacitate them.

The better part of one hundred bodies lay in the clearing, some Primordial, some bearing the insignia of the legion. He walked the battlefield as he had done a thousand times before, gathering the souls of the dead and sending them to the stream of souls that fed the well in Cathair. He was not even sure how he did it; it was just who he was. He could sense the stream of souls that fed the well, the conduits who ran in a hidden stream back to that central point under the castle in Cathair. He could sense the streams wherever they were, for they were a part of his soul and he a part of theirs. It was as if he was the heart and they the veins keeping him alive, and vice versa. He could feel the flow and as he focused on the stream closest to him, he frowned. It was a sluggish stream, as if it was blocking up, the walls narrowing.

Alarmed, he searched the killing field once more. He must find them all; they were his to gather, his to guard. Only the truly evil, the unredeemable, were sent to Helga's realm. They would not be reborn. Cayden cast around to check that he had gathered all the blue pinpoints of light. A blue light flickered on the edge of the clearing, and Cayden walked over to the fallen man. *Not quite passed from this life*, he thought as he approached the stricken man. He wound in and around the corpses, but when he reached the dying man he found two men, not just one.

Cayden tossed down his sword to gently roll over the first man and froze, shock tingling down his body to his toes. Cayden stared into Gaius's heavily scarred face, matted with blood from a sword cut across his forehead.

"*Father!*" he gasped aloud, and pulled him into his arms. "Father!" he repeated and then ran a hand down his arms checking for additional injuries. He couldn't find any, other than the forehead slice that was serious but shallow and had already stopped bleeding. He looked a mess, but Cayden didn't think his father was badly hurt.

Cayden took the sleeve of his tunic and wiped his father's face, clearing the blood from his eyes.

"Move one inch and this sword will have your head bouncing through the grass."

Cayden froze at the prick of a sharp blade against the side of his neck. *Not again!* he thought. *When am I going to learn to look before I leap?*

The blade circled around his neck as the man came into view. Cyrus stared at him, his gaze as cold as death. Pure, unadulterated hatred shone on his sweat-soaked face. His tunic was splattered with blood and torn by one too many blades that had come too close, slicing through the sleeve and breast of his coat. "Well, if it isn't the boy from the dungeons of Cathair. What a pleasant surprise. The Primordial bitch I chased escaped me, but instead I get you." He chuckled. "This is even better. You've caused me a great inconvenience. In a few short months, Alcina would have been dead by now and the throne mine, the last of that family line extinguished. With you out of the way, I would have had her murdered in her sleep, leaving my path to claim Cathair clear and unobstructed…but you had to ruin that, didn't you? You and that straw-filled scarecrow of a wizard. I should have strung the both of you up, not just chained you to the walls. Hung you from the belfry for the ravens to pick clean no matter what Alcina commanded." He paused in front of Cayden, blade sinking from throat to just over his heart. "But it matters not. You will never leave this clearing…and I will deal with Alcina later." He looked down at the two unconscious prisoners, and a look of malicious glee spread across his face. The stare made Cayden shiver to his boot soles. "But first, a taste of what it means to lose what means the most to you." He swung around to plunge his sword into Gaius's chest.

Cayden shouted, *"No!"* but before he could launch himself in defense of Gaius, Cyrus was snatched off his feet by Brimstone's teeth. He clamped on to Cyrus's cloak and jerked him with such force that the sword tumbled from his grip as he was swept screaming into the air. Brimstone screamed a counterpoint through his clenched teeth, the sound high-pitched and heady. His great wings battered Cyrus as he soared skyward, still gripping the struggling would-be king's tunic, climbing and climbing until they were but a pinprick in the sky. Brimstone banked then dived, flying directly at the stony face of the mountainside, diving as a kingfisher dives for fish. Cyrus's screams cut off abruptly as Brimstone released him, dashing him into the cliff face. He smacked the stone hard and plummeted hundreds of feet to the rocks below.

Cayden sank to his knees beside his father in relief and shock, sucking in great gulps of air as he slowed his racing pulse. His large hands trembled. *Too many shocks. I am becoming a nervous wreck! Get control of yourself, Cayden!* He took two deeper, steadying breaths, then pushed himself shakily to his feet.

Brimstone circled the clearing then landed a few paces away. It took Cayden three tries to finally gather enough moisture into his mouth to whistle to Brimstone. Crouching down, he scooped up his father and stood, only to find that his right wrist was shackled to another man's, a Primordial man who lay nearby. They were chained together. By the juxtaposition of the two men, they must have tumbled off their horses together. Cayden put his father back down and went to examine the second man. His chest rose and fell with his shallow breaths, but he appeared to be unhurt.

Brimstone danced excitedly over to Cayden and forcefully nudged him in the chest, snorting at the smell of death all around him, then snapped his wings, his black eyes narrowed and wild.

"Steady, boy," soothed Cayden. "We have a couple of passengers to take away with us. Can you carry us all?" Brimstone snorted again, and Cayden had the impression that he was being laughed at. Brimstone tossed back his head and pipped a high-pitched whistle, then started pawing at the ground.

The wait was a short one, for within a couple of minutes, Sandstorm and Moonbeam dropped down from the sky and trotted over to Brimstone's side.

"A much better idea!" With a rueful twist of lips, Cayden put his father back down on the ground and began a search of the fallen for a guard or someone who might hold the key to their prisoners. After ten minutes of grim searching he discovered a set of keys in the muddy grass. (At least, he hoped it was mud.) They had spilled out of the pocket of a Primordial warrior. It wasn't the only thing that had spilled out, but thankfully the keys were clean and dry. Cayden swallowed heavily then hurried back to his father, slipping in his haste. He fumbled the keys with shaking hands, presenting key after key to the locksets until finally he found the right one, and slid the key into the lock with a twist. It snapped open and the chain fell away. Cayden repeated the process with the second man, dropping the keys twice in the process. Once they were free, he scooped up his father and placed him on Moonbeam's back then returned for the second man and put him up on Sandstone.

"Now be careful, you two," he scolded the excited Pegasuses. "Don't let them fall off." The Pegasuses rolled their eyes, clearly annoyed with his mothering. They pawed at the ground, anxious to be away from the stench of death.

"Yes, I quite agree." Cayden sighed in relief, then swung onto Brimstone's back. "It is time to be gone." With a final searching glance around the field of death to be sure he had gathered all the souls remaining, he sent them on to the well in Cathair. Then with a light squeeze of his knees, he launched Brimstone into the sky.

Chapter 39

Tracks in the Sky

THE FLESH CLAN WARRIORS WALKED AMONG the bloating bodies, checking for survivors. Their Spirit-Clan brethren had lost a bloody battle, with no survivors. By the insignia on their vestments, they were of the temple guard, those bound to the High Priestess herself. But they could not locate her among the dead, nor could they locate her seeker. The rest of the dead were legion soldiers. Murmuring rose from the men. How had the legion soldiers slipped past their posts? How many more might be nearby? And where was the High Priestess? Searching for her made for a grim but necessary task.

"Marea is not here, immortal mistress. Whether she lives, I can't know for sure," Hototo, with forehead pressed to the dirt, informed Artio's feet as she strode by, knife in hand.

"Whose doing is this? Tell me all you know!" She gestured sharply to the festering corpses. "You've been gone far too long. I will hear all you have done since you left my presence. *Now speak*!"

Hototo kept his face pressed to the dirt, and his nose filled with earthy scents mingled with the stench of death.

"Mistress, I was on my way back to you when I came across this battle." He shuddered. "I arrived here shortly before you. If Marea has survived this battle, she will be on her way to the Shakra Caves. No High Priestess could miss the signs. The solstice approaches!"

"The Shakra Caves? What is this place?" Artio glared toward the smoking mountain, convinced she already knew.

"It is a cave of crystal, mistress, and full of sacred objects not touchable by human hands. The scrolls state that when the heir returns, the cave will give up its treasures and the secrets frozen in time. It is also said that only the gods can utilize the treasures within. We are simple guardians, mistress."

Artio snarled. *So that is what my sisters are up to. They are trying to steal my beloved's betrothal gifts.* Genii had showered gifts of magic on her, during their courtship. Rings and bracelets, music boxes and enchanted feathers, and she had kept every one of them in their special, secret cave. *Curse you, Helga! You sent me on this fool's trail when you know perfectly well that the answers lie where it all began. Caerwyn may be nearby, but it's Alfreda who holds the key…and by now my beloved's magical gifts!*

Not for the first time, Artio wondered at how much she still didn't understand about what had transpired that night, so long ago. *What were you up to that night, Helga? Somehow, all of you are tied together in this, and that leaves me with little choice but to go it alone. I will have my revenge! For myself. For Genii.*

"And you?" she snarled. "Did you reach the caves?"

"Yes, mistress, and the impostor you warned us about, the lady Avery, showed her face just as you predicted, but I captured her and sent her to the underworld! She is no longer a threat to you, mistress." He peeked out from under his arm at Artio. His back ached and he longed to sit up, but he had not been granted this boon.

Artio glared at the priest. "How could you accomplish such a feat? You have no powers except what we grant. What connection do you have with the underworld? Do not lie to me, Hototo." *Disgusting worm,* she thought.

She stamped down hard on his outstretched hands. He cried out as the bones ground together.

Gasping with pain, he blurted, "Mistress! They come to me in my dreams, mistress! The Charun! They are as black as night! They come and whisper things to me! It's how I knew how to summon you back from the stars, mistress!" Artio ground her heel on his hand, and he howled. The warriors searching the grounds glanced nervously over at the pair and then studiously ignored the goings-on. It was none of their business. "*She* told me!" he screamed as a finger snapped. "The great mistress of the dark! But I swear I only wanted to serve you! *Ple-e-e-ease!*" he cried as a second finger popped.

"She, being Helga?"

"Yes, mistress!" he sobbed. "The goddess Helga!"

Artio lifted her foot from his hand and strode off toward her mount. *As I suspected, none are to be trusted. Not one.*

As she crossed the ground, her eyes fell on a set of chains cast aside and almost hidden by the tall grass. She bent down and picked up the chains, and then her eyes fell on a long black feather. *A Pegasus feather! But where...how?* She straightened up, and her eyes searched the canopy, examining the sky, but found nothing. *So, Brother, you are closer than I thought. Good. It is time we met once again. Very good.* Artio's lips pulled back in a growl, teeth flashing, and she sniffed the air. *I smell you, Little Brother. I smell you on the wind. Do not think you can hide!*

She mounted her horse as the warriors scrambled into their saddles, and they fell into line behind her as she left the clearing, the bodies forgotten as soon as they faded from sight. She followed the unique scent of the Pegasus. They smelled like the rarefied air after a thunderstorm. It lingered in the treetops. If a smell could have a colour, it would have been golden. Artio's grin widened. She twisted the reins, pulling her horse around and followed the scent, tracking Cayden on the air.

*   *   *

Brimstone touched down in the clearing, followed closely by the other two Pegasuses. Ziona was crouched by the pond filling water bottles for the continued journey when she heard the whisper of wings announce their arrival. She stood abruptly and hurried over when it became evident that Cayden was not alone.

"Cayden! Who...? By the gods, is that your father? And an elder! Where did you find them?"

Cayden filled her in on his gruesome discovery as he slipped from Brimstone's back. He hurried over to his father's side, and together they eased the pair off the backs of the Pegasus and laid them gently on the ground. Ziona checked them over, running her hands over their limbs, thumbing back an eyelid, sniffing at their breath. "They have been hurt, but not fatally. Mostly they are drugged. Fortunately, I have just the thing." She snatched up her satchel and pulled out a packet of dried flowers. "Sharisha said this would cure anything." She took out a pestle and her bowl and ground some of the flowers up and added a bit of water to make a thin soup. "Cayden, lift their heads, one by one, and open their lips. I don't want them to choke. I need to get this potion into them." Cayden did as instructed, and Ziona fed each man two spoonfuls until the bowl was empty.

At first nothing happened, and then slowly their eyelashes fluttered as the cure counteracted the sleeping potion. Their bruises faded, and the gash on Gaius's head mended, now looking several days healed. They stirred, lifting hand to head with groans, the first movements they had voluntarily made since Cayden rescued them.

Gaius blinked once, twice, and then narrowed his focus to Cayden, who was bent over him staring anxiously into his face. Gaius's eyes widened on seeing his son, and he struggled to sit up. Cayden slipped an arm around his shoulders, steadying him.

"Cayden!" he gasped and tears sprang to his eyes. "I am so happy to see you!" They hugged as Elder Hania woke and slowly rolled over on to his side, pushing himself to a sitting position.

"Elder," greeted Ziona, "I am glad to find you alive, if not well."

"Seeker, it is equally pleasing to see you," he replied. He peered around at the campsite. "It appears our captors are no longer in control."

Cayden let go of his father. "They are all dead."

"Including Marea? Sharisha?" Elder Hania's voice was as hard as a stone.

"I didn't see them there. Were they trying to free you?" asked Cayden.

"No, they were our captors."

"What?" said Ziona, sharply. "Why would they restrain you?"

Elder Hania relayed the details of Avery's arrival at the temple and her subsequent reception.

"She is in grave danger then!" Cayden's fists clenched in anger. "We must find her and quickly!"

Ziona laid a restraining hand on his arm. "We need a plan, Cayden. We can't go running off without thinking this through. There is too much at stake. We know they are going to the cave. We can join her there, but who else might we encounter? We need help, some backup. We need Denzik and the rest of the Kingsmen. Then, we will have the might to confront whatever armies harry Avery."

"She has a young man with her. You remember Achak?" At her nod, he continued, "He has been sent as her protector. She is not alone."

Cayden stared at nothing, thinking. "She…Avery is going after the box…," he mumbled aloud.

"What box?" asked Ziona and Elder Hania in unison.

"It is…something of our past, a box of great evil. But there is only one who can control the magic of the box, and that is Mordecai. We need the wizard." Cayden stood up and walked away from them, thinking. *Mordecai said he could always find me via the stone. I wonder if works in reverse? He had it with him.*

Cayden closed his eyes and reached out to Mordecai. *Yes, I can feel him. It's faint, but I can point to where he is.* His arm raised of its own accord and he pointed. When he opened his eyes, it was pointed directly at the smoking mountain. "He is there. Why is he there?"

Ziona came up beside him and slipped an arm around his waist. "If Mordecai is there, it can't be good news. That is Helga's realm. No one comes out of there alive, not ever."

Cayden looked from the mountain to his companions and opened his mouth to speak. His words were interrupted by a whooshing sound, and the trees exploded above him. Debris rained down on them as the treetops burst into flame and fist-sized chunks of lava fell from the sky.

"*Go!*" Cayden shouted, grabbing Gaius around the waist and tossing him up onto Brimstone's back. He slapped Brimstone's rump, sending him skyward, then grabbed his satchel and flung himself onto the back of one of the pair of horses and dug in his heels, bolting for the uncertain safety of the woods in Mordecai's direction.

Ziona took to the sky on Sandstorm. Elder Hania grabbed the mane of Ziona's horse and swung onto its back, then bolted off after Cayden.

Moonbeam reared and followed the other Pegasuses into the sky. As the floor of the clearing caught fire, the grasses bursting into flame, Artio galloped into its midst. She caught a fleeting glimpse of the Pegasus disappearing into the smoke and saw two men on horseback swallowed by the trees.

"Helga!" she roared, cursing. Then she heeled her mount and took off after the two men on horseback. One was a young man and her brother would certainly look young at this time. *It must be Caerwyn*, she thought, following their trail on the ground. "He is *mine!*" she screamed aloud to the skies at Helga. For a second, back in the clearing a rippling reflection of Helga's face danced across the surface of the pond. The face laughed, watching Artio's furious passage out of the clearing with amusement. Then, the pond stilled and she vanished.

Chapter 40

A Matter of Age

MORDECAI WOKE WITH A START. The carpet on which he had recently lain had been replaced by a soft mattress, and a fluffy down-filled pillow cushioned his head. He frowned and cracked the lids of his eyes open the tiniest of increments in order to assess his whereabouts without alerting his captors of his consciousness. Instinct warned him that he was still a captive, regardless of the cushiness of his cell. Oil lamps with wicks trimmed low hung on wooden staves driven into chiseled holes and solid stone walls devoid of any human shaping draped with tapestries greeted his skinny-eyed appraisal of the room.

Definitely not a camp, then. So, if not a camp, then where am I? He could not see any guards in his room, which did not mean that he was not being watched. His hand twitched, and he opened his eyes wider and then sat up. No one came into the room. He swung his legs over the side of the bed then stood up on wobbly knees. He felt the doll's presence. It was nearby. But no one interfered with him right at the moment.

On a wooden stand under a cracked mirror stood an empty stone basin and a pitcher of water. Gratefully, he poured water into the bowl, then, dipping his hands in, drank thirstily. Next, he washed his face, scrubbing off the dried blood reflected in the cracked mirror above the stand with a rough towel hanging on the side. He rinsed the towel and then dabbed at the cut on his scalp that had bled.

Once his ablutions were complete, he followed the scent of food, his nose twitching at the smell of hot rolls and honeyed ham. He did not remember smelling them when he first awoke, but now hunger drove him toward the platter resting just inside the door. He picked it up and then headed back to the bed. He perched on the side while he wolfed down the contents of the tray. A brimming mug of ale accompanied the meal, and he drank it down in one long gulp.

Feeling much more human, he pushed the tray aside and decided to test the door. He reached inside his robes to touch his focus stone…only it was missing. Of course, whoever was responsible for his current lodgings had removed any objects of power they had found on his person.

I have a pretty good idea of who my host is…or hostess. Time to test the theory.

Mordecai strode over to the door and pulled on the handle. It swung open easily, and he stepped into a verdant green grotto. Bamboo and palm trees swayed in a gentle breeze. Bright parrots and lovebirds flashed from branch to branch, singing to each other. A stream burbled past, cutting the grotto in two. An arched wooden bridge crossed the span, and there, at a small table, sat a woman. On the table sat a pot of tea and two cups. The chair opposite the woman was empty, an invitation to sit implied in its positioning.

Mordecai sighed. *Out of the frying pan and into the fire.*

"Come, join me!" Helga gestured elegantly at the empty chair. "We have much to discuss, Mordecai."

Mordecai straightened his robes and then drew himself up to his full six-foot-plus height. *She is only a woman, if a godling. It does not make her a god. So what if she is older than you but looks like she is barely out of her teens. So what if she could snuff out your life just by thinking about it. Think, man!* Mordecai tucked his hands in the ends of his opposite sleeves, and his face stilled into the tableau of a wise one. His white mustache drooped and curled over his white beard, and his twinkling blue eyes, wrinkled with smile lines, darkened as he approached the woman.

"Tea? This is the last of my supply of oolong from the marshes. This was a particularly good year. I have had this tea for oh…about twenty-five years." A bitter smile creased her mouth and was gone. "I don't get out much, as you know, and all of those who would bring me such gifts have…faded from this earth. Mortality ends the most loyal of servants." She poured tea into his cup and then refilled hers, studying him as he eased himself into the chair opposite her. Her eyes travelled over his wavy white hair and the deep creases and the occasional scar, then drifted down to his hands, thin-skinned and heavily veined. "Age would appear to agree with you, but age, you do. Tell me, Mordecai, what is your plan for immortality? Do you pander to this reincarnation dribble, or do you strive to obtain a higher existence?" She took a sip of tea, sighed with remembered pleasure (for she could not taste it), and then returned the cup to its saucer.

Mordecai lifted his cup and took a deep draft. The tea was wonderful, full-bodied and fragrant. "Deep questions you ask, right off the top. Philosophers have pondered this question over the ages. In fact, my library back in Cathair is stuffed with volumes by wiser sages than myself. Why, I'd hardly know where to begin with such a subject. May I also compliment you on your apparent good health? I dare say you have not aged a day since we last met, and I was but a child."

Helga's dark eyes narrowed briefly, and then her face smoothed. The subtle reminder, that she was older than he sat like a burr under the saddle of a good horse. She struggled to keep the annoyance from showing on her face. Her lips widened into a smile that did not quite reach her eyes.

"Come now, you must have some theories of what immortality really looks like, immortality as enjoyed by the gods? For me, I have as close to immortality as one can have on this rock, but you?" Her eyes swept over him once more. "You are aging, Mordecai. Your body decays around you. Even with the fact that your life has been magically elongated due to being a wizard, you too will eventually die. You never married, did you?" She tsked as though he had overlooked the obvious solution. "No heirs? No one to carry on the wizarding gene? A trifle absent-minded, were we? What have you been doing all these years if not working on a way to elongate your mortal existence?"

Mordecai smiled and took another sip of tea. "Oh, a little bit of this and a bit of that. There is a lot to learn when you are one of the only remaining wizards in the world. There is a lot to record, a lot of information to preserve. Time does not exist in a vacuum. There must be ebb and flow for time to exist. As long as there are mortals, there is time. Time to learn what must be learned; do what must be done, undo what has been done, and take a stab at sorting out the future of time-marking mortals. Enough to keep me busy for another lifetime, I suspect." He drained his cup and set it down on his saucer.

"But I have found that when truly evil times exist, the fates provide for what is needed. It is never one man's victory or courage that wins a war. It is a hundred or a thousand small acts of bravery that carry the battle. No man is an island and their souls combined are stronger than any one foe. The ant surely knows this. Nature is a simple teacher of the complexities of life."

"You waffle, Mordecai. As always, you fill your mouth with useless words that buzz in the ear but say nothing." Helga reached into her pocket and withdrew two objects, placing them in the middle of the table. "I assume you know what these are?"

One was Mordecai's focus stone, his crystal. The second was the smooth river rock.

"A second direct question. Of course, I do. One is my favourite crystal, and the second is a stone I took a fancy to. I do love odd rocks. I have a whole collection back at the library."

"Liar." Helga picked up the crystal, and it glowed, heating rapidly. She dropped it before it could burn and the red blush vanished, returning to a nondescript crystal once again. "This crystal is a Soul Stone, a focus rock, commonly used by wizards to focus their own will. If I can make it glow, one wonders what it will do for you." She reached out and placed it in front of him. "I have no use for it, so I return it to you."

Surprised, Mordecai picked it up and put it back in his pocket. As he assumed he was not just a guest of Helga's, she could take it back at any time, so he did not challenge her on her choice of words.

"What I don't know is why you have this rock." Her finger stirred the grey stone.

Mordecai shrugged. "Occasionally, I pick up interesting stones to test. As I said, I thought it was an interesting rock."

Helga squinted at him, clearly not believing a word of what he said. "So, you would not care if I tossed it away, say, into my lava flow? It could be destroyed with no more interest than any other rock?" She slipped it back into her pocket, out of sight.

Mordecai reached out involuntarily before retracting his arm. "I would prefer to have the stone. They are difficult to find," he muttered weakly. Helga grinned back at him.

"So, it is more than a simple rock. Of course it is. I will keep it for now, for *safekeeping*, but should I decide that your answers and cooperation are less than stellar, we will see what happens with the rock.

"Now, there are these two precious bundles." She reached into her other pocket and withdrew the straw dolls. "Soul Fetches unless I mistake my eyes. One would appear to be yours. And the other…well, I can only guess. Perhaps you will enlighten me?"

Mordecai swallowed heavily. He'd feared that they were in her possession. His mind frantically searched for an answer, for a response that would waylay her suspicions. He settled on the fact that she could not know he knew who the doll was for.

"Alas, I cannot help you there, Helga. Alcina had just captured me with the doll, as you no doubt saw if you took me from the floor of her tent. I assume the other was taken from her tent? I have no idea who that doll binds." He kept his face still, eyes locked on his own doll.

Helga frowned at him, then twitched Mordecai's doll. "If you are lying, I will know it. You are going to be very useful to me going forward, Mordecai. Why, I might even grant you immortality if you please me well enough. You are now my soul slave, and you will do as I command or I will break you. One…bone…at…a…time…" She snapped a thread on the hand of the doll. Mordecai howled as his pinky finger on his left hand snapped. Pain shot up his arm. Tears sprang to his eyes, as he cradled the swelling digit. "Mine to command." She smiled, pleasure and promise in the threat.

"Genii!" Helga snapped.

Genii stepped from the shadows, or rather the shadows pushed him forward until he stood solid in the indirect lighting.

"Take our guest to the scrying pool. I want him to provide intelligence reports. He can begin to repay his lodging debt in this fashion. You will report back to me anything of significance he sees. Take this, and be sure he does not touch it." She handed the doll to him once more.

"Yes, mistress." Genii bowed, tucking Mordecai's doll into his robes, then grabbed Mordecai by the arm and dragged him from the room.

Chapter 41

The Task at Hand

AVERY SHOOK ACHAK, waking him. With that consciousness, he cried out, gasping as the pain of his broken leg overtook him. Avery tipped a cup of water, into which she had crumbled some powdered white willow bark, to his lips, as she murmured, "Drink this. Shh." He drank it down, some slopping down his chin at the angle. As she lowered the cup, his eyes darted anxiously around the cave. "They are gone," she said, lowering his head back down to the bench. "The phoenix did the trick. That is some Spirit Guardian!"

Achak groaned as he attempted to move his leg.

"I'm sorry," said Avery, grimacing. "I can't heal it within the cave. There is some shield that keeps my power from flowing here. I must move you outside to heal you. The guards should be gone now. Marea was here—Hey, lay still! It's OK," she said, restraining him as he tried to sit up. "She went to distract the guards away from the entrance. But first, I want to look over the other objects in the cave here. What can you tell me about these objects, Achak?"

Achak's eyes wandered the cave. "I am no elder, Mother. Elder Hania is who you want to speak to. The objects in this cave are rumoured to be usable only by godlings. They were created with the power and magic of the gods. But they are dangerous objects and so have been ever in this cave under magical protection. It is said in the ancient prophesies that these objects were placed here against man's most desperate hour. When war covered the earth, these gifts of the gods would hold the key to the salvation and preservation of the world." He peered around at the various alcoves and shivered. "I do not like being this close to the gods, even if they are no longer present."

"I do not believe these objects are of the gods, but only one god, my father, Morpheus." Avery wandered around the cave once again, peering into each alcove. "Yet I do not know what they do. To remove them would be to risk them falling into hands that should not have them. But to leave them is also to risk them being taken by those who should not have them. Which is the greater evil, do you think? Can we protect them if we take them?"

Achak's forehead wrinkled with thought. "There is only one place I can suggest that would be safe for these objects where we know no one else could access them—the temple. We should take them to the temple."

Avery swung back to Achak and smiled. "Yes! That is a fantastic idea! There is a room in there, and that is the safest place on Earth. That is what we will do."

Avery walked back over and sat down beside Achak. She pulled the box out of her pocket and sat it on her lap. It was as black as midnight, and all light appeared to be sucked into its depths.

"Tell me, can you hear anything?"

Achak frowned at her. "What do you mean? I do not hear anything. You mean from the box?"

"Yes."

"It's a box. What is it supposed to do? Play music?"

Avery shook her head. "No, it's...whispering to me. I can hear voices, but I can't make out what they are saying. It's very strange." She frowned at the box and went to put a finger on it but then changed her mind. She was loath to touch it. "I know this box. I have seen it before, but it was in the possession of a wizard last time I saw it. A young boy." Her eyes glazed as she pulled up the memory. Although it was the most recent of her past life, it was still a different existence and she found it difficult to reconcile. "I died the last time I saw this box. It is a god-killer."

"*A what!*" Achak struggled to sit upright, and his hand went to snatch the box away, but she grabbed his wrist, halting him.

"It was necessary," she whispered, her eyes still glazed in memory, "to stop a great evil. But we died that day. We must return this to the wizard. He will know how to use it. But I don't know where he is. Mordecai should be with Cayden, but I do not know where Cayden is. We are able to talk to each other telepathically, though. Let me see if I can reach him."

She closed her eyes and reached out to her brother. *Cayden, can you hear me? Where are you? I need you to come to me.* She sent the thought to him, praying it would find its way to him. The answer came back faster than she expected.

Avery! Where are you? I am coming to you! I have so much to tell you! Tell me where you are.

I am in a cave near…well, you will recognize it if your memory has returned, Cayden. It's at the end of a highland meadow, above Daimon Ford. Do you think you could find me if I described it to you?

I can find you easily. I can fly once again! Excitement tickled Cayden's voice in her head. *Give me an image of where you are, Avery.*

You can fly? Wait, how can you fly? What do you mean? Avery sent over the image of the caves and the meadow with the tall stones and waited for his exclamation of horror when he saw it, but it never came.

Cayden replied, *I'd rather show you!*

Avery had the impression that he was chuckling with amusement, like a kid with a new toy. *Fine, come show me,* she sent back.

You are in the sacred meadow with the monolithic stones, the place where we died. Yes, my memory has returned.

Avery shivered. *Yes, the place with the stones,* she sent back to him.

We are on our way, he sent back.

Is Mordecai with you?

No, but he should be along shortly. He had a…task…to complete.

I need to find him right away, Avery sent back to Cayden.

I think I can locate him.

All right, but hurry! A vague sense of acknowledgment reached her and then the link was broken.

Her eyes opened wide, slightly out of focus. "He is coming."

"Who?" said Achak.

"My brother."

"The new king of Cathair?" His eyes widened in surprise.

"He was my brother long before he was the king," she said ruefully, "but yes, one and the same."

Achak struggled to the edge of the platform and slid his wrapped leg out over the side, using both hands to ease it down to touch the floor.

"Help me up! I need you to heal my leg so we can begin packing up these items."

Avery slung an arm around his waist and he grabbed her shoulders for support and then stood. Achak's teeth clenched in pain, but he said nothing. He hobbled to the cave mouth then out into the passage. It was slow going as darkness was descending and little light filtered down to the base of the narrows.

As they came to the mouth of the passage, they slowed, and Avery crept forward alone to check that the way was clear. The clearing appeared quiet and peaceful, the sinking sun casting long shadows across the meadow. The ancient grey stones, missed on her trip into the cave due to being unconscious, now grabbed her attention. She could not suppress a shiver of fear that ran up her back at the sight of them. Tall and unmoving, they cared not for the scratching of the mortals that stirred the grasses beneath the stones, neither slug nor bear nor human. They grimly stood at attention, waiting patiently for the next chapter, the next page in the annals of mankind. Long fingers of shadow stretched from the bases, pointing toward them as the sun sank into the west.

Nervous of being exposed in the open, Avery dragged Achak into the closest copse of trees. Once far enough away from the cave and the rocks to feel relatively safe, she set him down on the forest floor.

"This is a serious break. I do not know if I can fully heal this right here, but I can get the process started." She laid her hands on the leg and closed her eyes once again, feeling her way along the leg. The break was severe, the bone splintered internally. Fractures spiralled within the bone. She drew on her will and the runes on her skin began to glow, pulling on the healing power of the temple. She moved her hands along the leg, her fingers twitching to pull at the sections of bone and align them. Sweat broke out on her forehead and began to run down the sides of her face. With a gasp, she opened her eyes, panting in exertion. The healing had caused Achak to faint, as it drew on his strength to cement the healing.

Avery manipulated the bones, and while it was not completely set, at least it was aligned. Rest would heal it the rest of the way; but the debilitating portion of the break had been fixed. It was all she could manage for the moment. Exhausted, she flopped onto the ground beside him.

The box vibrated in her pocket.

She lifted her head and stared at the stones. In the center of the ring, a light glowed. The light called to her, called to the box. A distant rumble echoed across the valley like great stones grinding together. The valley shook and lava burst from the mountaintop, small flaming pinpricks flashing into the clearing and then winking out.

Time is short. I must begin the healing of the land and its peoples before Helga breaks free, if that is what she is trying to do. But do I wait for Cayden? Do I dare wait for him? I cannot fail. This time the healing must be complete. Artio designed this circle to be a healing focus, and not just for physical injuries. The circle is linked to the temple and draws its power from the temple, and the celestial elements.

Avery read every level of rune carved into the great stones. As the last rays of the sun fell below the horizon, the top level of runes began to glow softly. The light of a full moon on the rise waxed as the sun waned. It was time.

Chapter 42

Anarchy

THE CAMP WAS A FROTHING SEA OF CONFUSION. The legionnaires woke in the morning to a numbing sense of having been asleep for many days and weeks, if not months. They rolled out of tents and began to wander around the main camp, not recognizing anyone. Strangers surrounded them, men who a few days ago they would have greeted as comrades.

One young officer entered the tent of the queen to find her and her lover dead in their blankets. They had been slain in the night, and whatever enchantment had lain over the men evaporated with their deaths and the rising of the morning sun. No one knew who she was or why they were there or who was supposed to be in charge. Their ranks meant nothing to them and the biggest and the strongest began to assert themselves, pushing and shoving at the weaker, taking whatever they wished and filling their pockets with supplies and loot.

Shouts could be heard and fights broke out over what belonged to whom. No one could remember, so each man grabbed what he wanted and tried to keep it from others. Before noon, several men had been left to die on the hard-packed dirt, each with a blade in his gut.

The men slunk into groups for protection. By midafternoon, those who were able to fight their way to a horse had left in mobs of ten or twenty, headed back toward Cathair. Roving bands of angry legionnaires on foot left the camp shortly thereafter, and by sunset the main legion camp was completely abandoned and empty except for the dead.

By nightfall, they had made their way to the plains with only one goal in mind: to return to Cathair and the homes they remembered to be there.

The only problem with this is that the homes they remembered were twenty years in the past, if they were not a recent addition by way of Alcina's recruiting parties.

Like a wildfire, they swept onto the steppe, crazed with flashes of memory, like a badly performed play of a past life they barely remembered. Wives and children and homes, fields and crops left behind. Disoriented by their incongruous thoughts, they marched for an unsuspecting Cathair, a plague of traumatized, battle-weary soldiers returning to homes that no longer existed, to families that had grown, to wives that had moved on to new husbands and lovers.

Lightning had struck suddenly and swiftly, in the form of Helga, and flames of trauma and revenge and need licked the heels of the deranged as they charged toward…home.

*   *   *

Artio sat her horse and watched the bands of roving ex-legionnaires descend onto the grasslands and set off toward Cathair. She held her hand up to prevent the Flesh Clan warriors from loosening arrows on the unsuspecting men.

"Let them go," she growled. Hototo cancelled the order to release arrows, and the men relaxed their draw on their long bows.

"As you wish, mistress. What is your command? I could send a team of assassins to wipe them out. They would not even know we were there." He bobbed his head as her eyes fixed on him, and his fingers throbbed in remembered pain.

"They run like children seeking their mother's pap. They are nothing, a mere distraction, which was no doubt my dear sister's intent. Ever she liked to sow anarchy. They are my dear brother's problem now." She twitched in her saddle, eyes dismissing the legionnaires, great head swinging back around to the forest into which her brother had fled. "Cayden, however, is here and headed straight into Helga's loving embrace. I am sure she has set a trap for him, a lure of some sort," she mused aloud.

Hototo, surprised that she would speak to him directly of her thoughts, bowed his head in acknowledgement but remained silent. He did not think she meant him to hear or cared about his opinion.

By holding my tongue, I might just keep it, he thought.

Artio checked the height of the sun in the sky and then swung her head back toward the mountainside. With a vexed snort, she brutally yanked her horse back to the trail and to the climb, past boulders and along thin ledges to the clearing she knew all too well, shrouded in low-lying clouds. *Which path should I choose?* She checked the height of the sun in the sky once again and cursed, tightening her hands on her reins. She did not have enough time to chase after Cayden and be at the clearing by nightfall. He had a head start, riding that cursed Pegasus and it would easily outrun her four-legged mount. Artio lifted her arm and stared at her hand. It was a curious thing how her body was reverting to her original appearance. A blessing of the approaching solstice, no doubt. She snarled. Time was of the essence. She needed the Primordial warriors and could not leave them behind.

Even though Cayden was on horseback, Brimstone was never far from him and could snatch him from the saddle at any moment. Artio shook her great mane of hair, arguing with herself. No, it was time to push on for the clearing of sacred stones she had erected so long ago. She walled away the tragic events of that day. They belonged to another Artio, another woman, another time.

She stared down at her arms and clenched hands, covered with light fur and grimaced. *This Artio, this half-breed godling, seeks only one thing. Revenge.* The beauty of her youth was gone. The woman she had been, was gone. In its place was this beast formed from her rebirth. Even if Genii lived, he would see nothing but a monster. It was a blessing that he had died. She no longer cared if she lived on, for she had lost all and being brought back had reawakened the pain of that cursed memory. While suspended amongst the stars, imprisoned by their failed experiment, she had neither felt nor remembered. But in being dragged back to this semi-human body, she was forced to endure the agony of a broken heart and mind once more. *This time though, others will feel it too. They will suffer with me for all eternity.*

The sun sank toward the horizon where no doubt her sisters were gathering. She yanked her horse's head around and set off up the trail, the Primordial warriors falling in behind her. They rode silently, following their goddess up the narrow, twisting path.

Revenge will be mine. I swear it on the departed soul of my love, Genii.

Chapter 43

Mordecai's View

MORDECAI BENT OVER THE SCRYING POOL and examined the scenes that rose into his view. A sheltered pond, encircled by tall trees and waving grasses, graced his sight, and a group of people suddenly launched themselves onto the back of Pegasuses. He tensed involuntarily in surprise then stilled, unwilling to give away the game to his companion.

I know those Pegasuses! Brimstone! And Moonbeam and Sandstone! They are alive! Mordecai could not make out the faces of the people in the clearing as they dodged the flaming tree embers and rock that fell from the sky. But where Brimstone was to be found, Cayden would not be far away. The Pegasus launched into the sky, and two men took off on horseback. The outline of a familiar mountain flashed by as he attempted to follow them in the scrying pool, and a peak wreathed in smoke slid through the image. *No! You must not come here, Cayden!* Alarmed, he sat back abruptly, breaking contact with the image and drawing Genii's attention. *What is that fool boy doing?* Mordecai thought furiously, concern for Cayden straightening his back and causing him to break contact with the pool.

"What did you see, old man?" Genii leaned over his shoulder, but only his own reflection stared back.

"This 'old man's' back is stiff from leaning over a scrying pool. It's time for a break. We have been at it all day." Mordecai punctuated his lie by standing and arching his back, then reached up over his head and stretched, letting out a long, relaxing, whistling groan.

Genii pushed him roughly back down onto the stone bench. "Visions, old man. Concentrate on the pool, and continue gazing into its depths. My mistress commands it. You will continue to scry until you provide some useful information." Genii reached over and rapped sharply on Mordecai's purple, distended pinky finger with the switch he carried in his hand. Mordecai flinched with pain. "I can stay here day and night. Time does not affect me. You can also stay here day and night. The choice is yours." He slapped the surface of the pool. As the waters stilled, a vision swam into view of a tall woman on horseback, rushing into the clearing Mordecai had seen before.

Genii gasped and tried to pull back from the pool, but Mordecai grabbed his arm and held him still. "You know this woman?" he rasped, now the one in command. Genii could not pull his eyes from the pool as the woman came into clearer focus. "She calls to your heart. I can feel it. Who is she?"

Genii shook his head and pried at Mordecai's fingers. "No, I do not know. This is your vision."

"It is not my vision. It's your viewing." Mordecai released him, but Genii could not pull away. He was frozen over the pool, staring at the majestic woman.

"She appears to be half-human. You have seen her before, haven't you?" Mordecai said softly. He straightened and crossed his arms across his chest and leaned back from the pool, eyes studying his companion's features. His white-winged brow frowned. "Have we met before?"

Genii's eyes snapped to his then back to the pool as though afraid the image might disappear, which was a real possibility. "I have no memories beyond this cave."

"We may not have met before," said Mordecai, "but I have seen you before, a long time ago."

This time Genii's eyes did leave the pool, and the woman vanished. "Where?" he demanded.

Mordecai began to speak, telling him of a time when he was but a child and of events that had transpired in a clearing not far from where they were currently sitting, of a man and a woman in love, but barred from being together forever by a small thing called mortality, of an attempt to circumvent death by binding the life of a mortal to the immortality of the moon, and a desperate attempt to beguile the heavens by a couple in love. Of a battle between godling sisters for the love of the same man and the battle that ensued, and of one godling left standing but bound to the underworld for all eternity in the backlash.

"What is your name?" Mordecai asked in a quiet, still voice, barely more than a whisper.

"Genii," he whispered back and put his hands to his face feeling the contours, the form he presented as the template of his body here within Helga's realm. As a wraith, he had no need of a solid form. Yet why he felt the need to project a form, he could not remember. "I have…small patches of memories…that may be what you speak of, but not enough to know it for truth."

"You would be of the right age in appearance," said Mordecai. "I was but a small child. But I witnessed the event." His eyes drifted back to the still surface of the pool. "I think that was…Artio?" His eyes caught the flash of recognition in Genii's eyes at that mention of the name. "Although how she has come to be in a mortal form again, I do not understand. She is not quite as she was, yet you recognize her, don't you?"

"Yes." The single word escaped on a sigh.

Mordecai leaned back over the pool, and Artio slid into view once more. "Well, it seems we are both interested in her, but I think for different reasons." Artio watched the Pegasus wing away and screamed silently at the air. "I have a suggestion." Genii frowned at her then passed the gaze to Mordecai. "I suggest we both bind our tongues in relation to this interest. I also suggest that maybe our interests are aligned closer than with your mistress."

"What makes you think I have any interest in anything outside of my mistress?" Genii hissed, pulling away from Mordecai. His face darkened like a thundercloud. "Helga commands my loyalty, old man, not you, and certainly not some vague vision of a forgotten past. Now, unless you wish me to snap a few more fingers the old-fashioned way, get to work."

He gripped Mordecai by the hair on the back of his head and pulled it back, stretching his neck as he tilted his face up. His other hand slid into a pocket of his tunic and pulled out a small vial of a dark amber liquid. A cork popped, and he emptied the vial of potion into Mordecai's open mouth. He continued to stretch his neck, and Mordecai was forced to swallow or drown. He swallowed the bitter liquid then Genii released his head with a shove. Mordecai gagged, leaning over the basin.

"Prophecy, wizard," commanded Genii. "Show us your visions."

Mordecai's vision swam, and the surface of the pool seethed and became a wild red tempest that sucked him into its swirling depths. Events past, present, and future jumbled together, and he was tossed from one event to another without any anchor and with no way of knowing the timeline. The pool was no longer a flat tableau but an angry three-dimensional funnel. The visions came fast and furious, and he cried out as heat washed over him like a wave. Fingers of flame licked his skin and crisped his brows, flashing them to dust on his face. The cry of battle assaulted his ears, and a sea of men and beasts clashed and writhed on the ground below him, the red of the flame surrounding him reflecting off rivers of blood. With a splash, he hit the quagmire, which flowed around his ankles, sucking him down into the river spilling over the edge of a cliff. He grabbed for anything to stop his tumbling progress and the only solid object became another body, and another, and another, until the surface roiled with the dead. With a cry, he was tossed over the edge, and he shrieked as he fell, a sick swooping tickle bringing his stomach into his throat.

The ground rushed up at him, and Mordecai squeezed his eyes shut. Before he struck the bottom, a Pegasus picked him out of the air and flew off with him toward Cathair, following a trail of men. Mordecai gasped and clutched at its mane, squinting down at the remnant of an army, screaming their madness to the plains. Burned farms and looted villages littered their path and ran straight as an arrow toward the heart of the kingdom, toward the capital.

The Pegasus disappeared, and suddenly Mordecai knelt in a tower room beside a Primordial princess, heavy with child.

"*Noooooo!*" he cried out and squeezed his eyes tight. He could not stand to lose her again, not like this.

When he opened his eyes again, he was in complete darkness. There were no windows, no door, and no light to define the space. He was laying spread eagle on his back with a stone floor beneath him:

cold, damp, and hard. He lifted his right arm and was jerked to a halt, inches off the floor. His wrists were encircled with manacles that fed into a set of heavy chains that rattled as he moved his arm. A similar set ran from his ankles. A rat squeaked…or at least he thought it was a rat. He could not remember ever being in such a predicament. He felt a pinch on his toes and kicked out, but the rat did not let go of his toe. It bit down harder, and Mordecai cried out with pain.

"Good, good. Now we are getting somewhere." The voice floated past his consciousness and was gone.

The scene shifted. A great bone temple, multiple stories tall, glowed as though alive, each of its frescoes flowing with movement. The temple groaned and the earth shook as it lifted from the ground and rose into the air to hover about the tops of the trees. The frescoes writhed and detached themselves from the walls, forming bodies of beasts and people and vegetation that could move under its own power. Blinding blue light shone from the windows like great fingers and stroked the air around the temple. Then two people stepped out onto the balcony at the very peak and walked to the edge of the railing, just as a bolt of lightning struck the temple. The flash of light blinded Mordecai, and he was flung back by the force of the vision, soaring through the air for real this time to land in a heap several feet away from the scrying pool, unconscious.

Genii bent and picked up Mordecai's wrist in his fingers. A thready pulse beat in it. He scooped up the wizard for the second time that day and carried him off to his chambers.

The scrying pool relaxed, and the surface stilled. Red and blue flames danced across the surface, and then were gone.

Chapter 44

Sheol Animus

CAYDEN'S WILD RIDE through the forest on his spooked mount brought welts and bruises from slapping tree branches whipping his arms and legs as his horse made the shortest possible dash away from the flaming debris. Burnt horse hair still wafted into his nostrils despite the movement of his horse. His horse was also of a mind to put as much distance as possible between him and the flaming forest.

Cayden's only thought at the time had been that he could not lose his father again, and the safest place for him was on Brimstone. Now he wondered about the wisdom of that decision, but done was done.

As the mountain calmed, Cayden was able to rein in his panicked mount, pulling it to a snorting, shivering halt that allowed Elder Hania to catch up to him. The sides of the horses moved under their legs, great bellows pumping as they pulled in lungful after lungful of air, shaking with exhaustion. Cayden's grip on the reins did not slacken. His head swivelled as he checked the progress of the Pegasuses in the air. It was just as dangerous to be airborne as galloping through flaming woods as he knew only too well. Memories of another flight flashed across his mind, a flight that had ended in the worst possible outcome. This time, at least, he was well aware of what the flaming balls of rock meant. Helga had a lot to answer for. How dare she disrupt the harmonies of the world? Gritting his teeth, Cayden glared at the mountain. Helga also held Mordecai, he could feel it. The how and why of it, he did not know. What he did know was that he needed the wizard. He had always needed the wizard, and this time, he would do the rescuing; this time he would be the one to spring him from his imprisonment. He could still feel Mordecai's pull.

"Where are you heading, my lord? Sire? I believe you are the king of Cathair?" Elder Hania gripped his reins as tightly, slumping slightly in the saddle, still weary from his recent abuse.

Cayden's nodded tightly in acknowledgment, and his frustrated glare swung to the elder and then softened. "I apologize, Elder." He bowed from his saddle. "You should be safe on the back of a Pegasus and winging your way back to your people." He frowned again, then his gaze swung back to the mountain. "I am about to pay a visit on a…relative. This is no place for you." His voice echoed weirdly, as he thought of Helga.

"You would be seeking the goddess who calls the mountain home, the goddess of the underworld. She is called amongst my people Shadow Soul, mistress of the dead." He nodded as if reaching a conclusion and straightened in his saddle. "I will aid you as I was aiding your sister Avery. You have returned as prophesied."

"You have seen Avery!" At his nod, Cayden exclaimed, "Is she all right? When did you see her last?"

Elder Hania shook his head. "No, she did not tell me. She was on her way to the Crystal Caves the last time I saw her. She may even be there by now."

Mordecai or Avery, who should I go to first? Who was the most urgent, the most important? Cayden pondered his choices, knowing that time was short and that possibly the fate of the world hinged on his decision. What was Helga's plan? Avery was free and Mordecai likely imprisoned. Avery's soul was free, and Mordecai's soul was imprisoned somewhere. Cayden prayed that Mordecai had been able to free him from the doll, but until such time as he was sure, he had to secure Mordecai's freedom, and that meant following the trail to Mordecai to get him back. That meant Helga's realm.

Elder Hania watched the play of emotions flit across his face. The struggle was a familiar one.

"We are wasting time, sire." He glanced at the skies and gestured at the sun, low on the horizon. "The day wanes. Time is making fools of us. What is the plan?"

Cayden's mount danced beneath his hands. "We free a wizard." His eyes locked onto the hazel eyes of the elder. "Failure is beyond comprehension. To be captured means death…for all. Are you sure you want to do this?"

"Yes." There was no trace of fear in the elder's steady gaze.

Cayden's eyes swung skyward. "Then come. Ziona tracks us from the sky, and my father is with her. We will see if four can storm an underworld fortress."

The elder squeezed the sides of his horse, riding up beside Cayden. "Just curious, have you ever been there before?"

Cayden glanced at him out of the corner of his eye. "Not even for tea," he said grimly and urged his horse forward onto the twisting path leading toward the summit of the mountain.

A raven circled overhead and with a sharp cry, wheeled back toward the mountain flapping furiously to stay ahead of the Pegasus on the same path. Gaining the shadow of the mountain, it dipped low over a stovepipe opening on the rocky face and disappeared inside.

*　*　*

Helga chuckled, as the raven settled onto her outstretched arm and she withdrew from sharing its gaze, releasing her control over the bird. *Come to me, older brother, come. It will be easier to instruct you once you are safely inside and ensconced as my guest. Why, it will be like a family reunion! You, me, and our dearest sisters once they arrive. How will I ever prepare? I don't think we have all been under the same roof since we were babes-in-arms. I might even find a place for you in my realm, once the peoples of this godforsaken rock bow in acknowledgment of me.*

Helga strode up the hall and called out to Genii. "Genii, come to me. A guest approaches." She paused at the top of the staircase, listening for his approach. She was greeted with silence. Where was the fool man? She leaned out over the short wall and noticed that the scrying pool below was still and abandoned. She continued along the hall, following its twisting path to the break by the waterfall. Cayden would arrive soon at this spot. She looked skyward. No winged shadow blocked the light. She settled herself onto a bench cloaked in darkness and waited, mulling over what she would say to Cayden when he arrived.

At that moment, Genii appeared, sliding out of the twist of twilight like the wraith he was.

"You called, mistress?" He bowed his dark head.

"Cayden approaches with another man. Prepare rooms for our 'guests.'"

"As you command, mistress." He faded back into the shadows and was gone.

Helga pulled out the mystery Soul Fetch and bounced it in her hands, thinking. She had a feeling that the doll was attuned to Caerwyn—Cayden, as he was called in this age.

I will rule supreme, Brother! The souls of the dead need not be tortured with a return to human mortality. They can serve me. Serve us. I am a patient goddess, and I will have your allegiance. We can be family, once again under my rule. There are enough souls for all of us, as long as you bow to me.

And if you refuse? Well, that is for you to decide what will be your fate. You and Alfreda—Avery, as she likes to be called in this age—hold the fate of the world in your hands, at least as it is currently configured. Without their Spirit Shield, there is no possibility of rebirth. Once your meddling is ended, the souls will truly be mine. I will choose who is reborn, and I will decide for how long. You may serve me and live or be converted into a loyal servant. I can always use more souls for my Charun army.

With one finger, she stroked the glossy feathers of the raven still perched on her arm without seeing it. It bobbed its head and cawed, flapping its wings, then it took off into the air to its roost in the tallest tree, closest to the rim of the opening. She watched it join its companions, the flock that scouted on her command. A shaft of sunlight blazed along the stone rim, announcing the hour, and she turned her back to the opening. The clatter of horses' hooves on rock sounded over the murmur of the falls. They were here.

The shrubbery parted and in rode two men on horseback. One was young, barely an adult, and the other an elderly man. They rode around the rim of the pool and toward her and then reined their horses at a safe distance.

Cayden swung down from his saddle and handed the reins to the elder man. His gaze fixed on the falls, and, staring straight at her, he called out in a firm voice, "Helga, I know you are there. Part the curtain, and let me enter." The elder slid out of his saddle and stepped up beside him, his eyes scanning the curtain of mist but seeing nothing.

Helga chuckled and waved her hand. The mist parted, swinging back on both sides like a curtain in truth. It created a dark tunnel of walled water, but the ground underfoot was completely dry. "Welcome, Caerwyn, welcome. It has been a long time."

Cayden gave his horse a quick pat on the neck and stepped forward into the tunnel, followed by the elder. However, when the elder attempted to step into the tunnel, he met with a solid force that would not allow him entrance.

"Your friend cannot enter. Only the dead or those who have the power over life and death can enter."

Cayden paused and looked back at the elder. "Sorry. I must go on, alone."

Elder Hania bowed and stepped back, worry wrinkling his brow. "Be careful, sire."

Helga chuckled from the shadows. Her voice echoed eerily down the passage. "I will take good care of him, elder. Return to your people. You have no place here amongst the gods."

Elder Hania gave a start at the sound of her voice. It was a cold voice, a howling moan, which reminded him of open graves and restless spirits. He'd not heard the original welcome to Cayden, and the sound of her voice sent a shiver down his spine. He clenched his teeth together then stepped back with a quick bow before returning to this horse. He mounted quickly, a touch of panic in his movements.

Cayden strode the rest of the way under the falls. With a wet slap, the curtain closed, and the fall resumed its normal flow. Cayden paused, allowing his eyes to adjust to the near dark. Helga stood up, filling the doorway to her home.

"So. The king returns. Welcome to Sheol Animus. Welcome to my home." She stepped aside to allow him to enter, then stepped up beside him. "I know why you are here, Brother. The wizard lives. He is bound to serve me now, as are you. There is no returning to the outside world, except as I command."

Cayden stiffened at her words, and his hand drifted to the sword hilt at his waist.

Helga laughed, amused. "There will be none of that. We both know that you cannot kill a soul. You may think that I have no soul to kill, and you would be right, so striking me down is impossible with such a weapon. Besides, it is a rude way to greet your sister. We are family. Come, we will have tea and chat about old times and what you have been up to since we last…met." Her lips twisted into a smile that did not reach her eyes. "We have plenty to talk about, you and I. And when we are through reminiscing, we can chat about these." She reached into her pocket and pulled out the two Soul Fetches. She saw his eyes widen with shock and recognition, then Cayden licked his lips nervously.

Cayden's mind spun furiously. Doubt and fear twisted his gut. *What have I done in coming here? Forgive me, Ziona! Forgive me, Avery! I have failed you both.*

*   *   *

Denzik and the raft of Kingsmen with him studied the Primordial host trotting along in the wake of the overly tall woman on horseback. That she led the band was clear by the deferential distance formed around her, as though she physically repelled them from touching her somehow.

Denzik scratched at the scruffy beard on his chin, thinking. They were headed in the same direction that they had tracked Avery—to the clearing where she and a companion's trail ended. They had been slowed by the disintegration of the legion, having run into band after band of half-crazed former soldiers. The first few instances had resulted in fierce battles that had wounded and weakened his men, a few had even died. Finally, they decided they would avoid any further confrontations and had begun a stealthy sneak through the thick forest, avoiding all forms of human contact. They could not avoid the creature contacts, but the creatures seemed to know that they aided Avery or were attempting to and left them alone for the most part. The legion soldiers were not so lucky and were harried out of the forests, which may have explained in part the crazed look in their eyes.

This band of Primordials, however, was neither crazed nor scared of the woods and moved with a purpose to where Avery was holed up. The tall woman bothered Denzik. She did not appear to be fully human. If not human, then what was she? It all smacked of the gods, and Denzik was no fool to stick his head into an immortal wasp's nest. If she was indeed of the gods, then he could best help Avery by choosing the time and location of the battle with care.

So, he continued to watch, and wait. The sun was setting, and the beginnings of a moon were in evidence on the jagged skyline. It looked to be a full moon. He and his men settled into hollows and into crooks of trees, with a view of the magnificent stone ring and the long valley. He pulled his curved pipe from his shirt pocket and clamped the stem between his teeth, but he did not light it. His thoughts organized themselves better when he had his pipe clenched between his teeth. Something was about to play out, and they had front-row seats. He just hoped it would be a show he wanted to see.

Chapter 45

Focal Point

BLOOD DRIPPED FROM AVERY'S FINGERS as she crawled through the brambles, the sharp points snagging her clothing and biting deep into the flesh of her arms and face. For once, she was grateful that she no longer had hair to tangle in the clinging vines, but that lack also meant that the rune-infused cap of skin covering her skull was shredding in equal measure. She blinked away a trickle of blood that insisted on pooling at the crook of her nose, and drew a sigh of relief on reaching the edge of the clearing. The brambles fully encircled the clearing. There was but one way to approach the clearing undetected. From this angle, she could creep over to the stones, their height and width hiding her approach from watchful eyes.

She hated leaving Achak behind. In truth, she hated being alone back in the woods where she had healed him, but there was no way he could keep up with a broken leg. She also did not want to expose him to what lay ahead. As he was unconscious, he should not be discovered.

The clearing was roughly two hundred paces in width, and about three hundred long. Four tall sentinel rocks ringed the clearing, each massive stone like a grey guardian towering over it. Each was decorated with a series of symbols, which Avery recognized, although some were faded to the point of being barely legible. The etchings themselves were not required, as the magic was set into the stone. It was equally obvious that they had not been used in a millennium. The glen smelled of decaying memory and stillborn traditions, abandoned by time and the mortals confined by it.

In the past, this glen had shuddered with power. Originally, this green meadow had been a gift from the heavens to the mortals they loved so dearly. This sacred clearing had once been the portal to the gods.

Now, the clearing was empty except for the stones. Long grasses swayed in the gentle breeze that sifted through the clearing. Buttercups dotted it, and a sense of peace pervaded the air. Avery sniffed the breeze and smiled. Relaxed, she walked up to the closest monolith, examining the carvings. The stones grew out of the soil, as much alive as the plants surrounding them, and indeed the bottom of the monolith was covered with carvings of vegetation. Sacred plants, plants long used in healing and nurturing. Great stalks of tobacco decorated the stone, and she ran her hand along the deep grooves. A waft of pipe smoke drifted to her nostrils, and she smiled at the memory it invoked. She glanced around and noticed that the other stones also carried carvings of plants, thin stalks of sweet grass, leafy sage, and fragrant cedar.

Stacked on top of the sacred plants were deeply carved reliefs of animals, all familiar to her. An eagle soared over the sweet grass; a buffalo chewed contentedly above the tobacco; a she-wolf stalking prey with her cubs above the sage; and a bear scratching at the ground where the cedar grew. Each animal was carved in a position of peace or contentment. Avery ran her hand over the buffalo. The face of the image looked at her, jaw ruminating.

Chiseled above each animal, an elemental was drawn, connecting through to the carvings below. The sun shone down on the buffalo and the tobacco; softly swirling currents of air carried the eagle over the sweet grass and encircled it; gentle rain bathed the wolf and cubs and watered the sage; and dark loamy earth fed the mighty cedar and the bear, scratching into the soil.

As Avery looked closer, she could also see the seasons carved into the four pillars. Spring, summer, winter, and fall were reflected in progression around the circle. Crocuses dotted the meadow of sweet grass; a thunderstorm threatened on the horizon behind the buffalo; the sage was partly covered by fallen leaves; and the earth had a slight crust of snow that contrasted with the russet ground.

The final carvings were spiritual and interpretive. The faces of the gods, those who were the elders in ancient times, stared down from the crest of the stones. A Spirit Guardian perched, overseeing the eagle, surrounded by a halo of carved eagle feathers. The second guardian's face was laughing and crying, the emotional guardian of the Primordial people. The third face was wise and caring, a consummate reflection of the guardian of wisdom and intellect. The final face was youthful with strong cheeks and a clear gaze, the guardian of the physical.

Avery swiped at the trickle of blood that once again attempted to block her vision, leaving a smear across the bridge of her nose.

This is the spot, the place I remember as a child. Papa used to bring us once a year to renew our vows to the gods.

Avery stepped into the center of the stones, memory guiding her to a spot equidistant to them, and knelt down. It looked the same as every other overgrown section. She grabbed great handfuls of the meadow grasses and pulled, uprooting them, and she pulled out the matted soil pack created by the webbing of roots, peeling back the sod like the skin of an orange.

When she had cleared an area roughly the size of wagon wheel, she stood up and dragged her boot across the partially cleared spot, pushing dirt back with it. Half an hour passed and the sun shifted along its axis, sinking closer to the horizon. Avery glanced up from her work and frowned. She had but an hour till the appointed time, until the rays of the setting sun were aligned as prophesied.

A niggling sense of panic wormed its way into her consciousness and she ran to the side of the clearing to search for a tool to use as a shovel, the box giggling in the inner pocket of her tunic. She cast her eyes over the ground, eyes searching for something to assist her with digging. A twig snapped in the woods and she froze, melting into the grasses to stare at what approached the clearing. One hand curled around the flat stone she had spied just before the sound. The other slid into her coat to clutch the handle of her throwing knife. Her eyes studied the edge of forest encroaching on the chest-high brambles. There was but one path into the site. All other approaches were on hands and knees, as she had entered, if one was to remain unseen.

No one could have followed her. No one would dare try. And if no one followed, that left one possibility. If someone was spying on her, they were already here. They already knew the location of the

Sacred Meadow. And the only one who would know this...she shivered at the thought. Avery suddenly felt very, very alone.

Cayden? she whispered in her mind. It did not matter that she knew it was in her head, the habits of a lifetime made her whisper, even there. *Are you coming?* She waited in silence, eyes still roving over her surroundings, searching for anything out of the ordinary.

Silence greeted her. Her mind remained silent too. *Cayden?* Her head swiveled. Tamping down her rising fears, she grabbed the stone and headed back to the center of the clearing. What choice did she have? The sun was going to set regardless of whether anyone was watching. It was now or never. Another solstice would not occur until after the doom had fallen. *No choice. None whatsoever.* Avery gritted her teeth and pushed aside her fear of whatever watched from the trees.

She knelt once again and took the stone in both hands, scooping the loose dirt toward her, moving around in a circle to drag back more and more soil all the time. She worked steadily for twenty minutes, sweat dripping off her forehead and mixing with the blood, stinging through the cuts even as it washed the blood away. She dared not swipe it away with her hands covered in dirt, and endured the stinging sweat.

The stone clunked and scraped against something solid. She paused, then dropped the stone and began to scoop away soil with her bare hands, clearing the area. Gradually, a white disk emerged, which glowed faintly in the waning light. Avery tossed aside the stone and began to scoop out handfuls of dirt, tossing them over the side and brushing the remainder off to the sides, smoothing her hands over the surface.

The disk was about three paces in circumference and made of a smooth stone-like substance that glowed softly in the fading light. The buttery texture was soft to the touch yet hard as steel. The scraping stone had not marked the surface, yet Avery swore she could have marked it with the edge of her fingernail.

Avery snapped her fingers and a flame danced to life. She held it over the disk and swept away the last of the dirt then bent to examine its surface. It was completely smooth and unmarked except for a hollowed-out bowl in the center and eight sectional lines, like small troughs that ran back precisely to where monolithic guardians stood.

The bowl was patterned with dots, some larger, some smaller. As Avery studied them, she realized they were a reflection of the heavens; the planetary bodies and the stars that would be visible at this time of day if the sun's light had not obscured them from human view.

Avery sighed with satisfaction, pleased that she had found the celestial bowl.

She glanced up to mark the placement of the sun. When she raised her head, it was met with the cool press of a blade at her throat. She sucked in a quick breath and froze.

"Hello, Sister. It is about time we met." Artio's blade forced Avery to her feet, and with a casual flick of wrist, she pushed the remainder of Avery's hood off her head. Their eyes locked for the first time in a millennium, sister to sister.

Avery's eyes widened in shock at her sister's bear-like appearance, and Artio's reaction was similar, if less intense. Artio's bladed knife dropped, while she studied her sister's tattooed form. She gripped the curved blade tightly in her right hand as though uncertain whether she was dangerous. The thought flashed through her mind that she should finish her right then and there.

Avery's eyes ran around the stones, searching for a path to freedom, but the Flesh Clan warriors surrounded them three deep. "Thank you for guiding us to the Celestial Temple," Artio growled. "I knew you remembered where it was. You were the one who worshiped Papa, you and…what does he call himself now, Cayden? You both worshiped the ground he walked on!" Artio chuckled as she strode around Avery, looking her up and down. "Of course, Morpheus was a god, but even so, I found your fawning quite revolting. But look at you! My, what a puny human you have become." Artio's hand shot out and grabbed Avery by the throat, lifting her up with one hand, so that her feet dangled inches from the ground. Avery gasped, choking, and grabbed Artio's hands with her own, pulling herself up to relieve the pressure on her throat, to little avail. Her eyes widened in fear, then flashed back to defiance. Artio threw back her head and laughed while Avery writhed in her grip. "I do believe I could snap your neck by simply squeezing, but you fight on! So, there is a remnant of the stubborn little girl in there." Artio tossed Avery to the side, where she bounced and tumbled through the grasses, coming to rest face down.

Avery sucked in a lung full of air and dirt, her hand rising to touch the bruise already forming around her throat from Artio's crushing grip. Avery heaved several gulps of air into her lungs and then sat up, only to be met by spears and knives before she could fully sit.

"Let her up, my pets. She has something of mine. A trinket box, promised to me by my beloved." Avery froze at the words. *How does she know? Have I been betrayed?*

The spears withdrew incrementally, and Avery sat up, gazing warily at her sister.

"You do not speak. Come now, Alfreda. This is a reunion! You should be rejoicing in our reacquaintance."

Avery stood up, testing her various wounds. Her head ached and her throat was on fire, but both of those she could deal with. With alarm, she found that her right foot tried to buckle under her. She had not even realized she had twisted it in the fall, but now it was well and truly sprained. Pain flashed as she tested it for weight, and she bit her lip to hold in the moan.

"I do not understand why you do this, Artio. You are Artio?" Artio nodded. "Cayden and I have never caused you any harm. We were your champions always, and especially after your disappearance! What has happened to you?"

Artio snorted and walked closer to her sister, her feral eyes absorbing the setting sun and glowing golden in the refracted light.

"Lies! You try to distract me from my purpose here tonight, but it will not work. Time is of the essence, and you would like to see the sun set on this day, true?" Avery's eyes widened involuntarily. "Yes, I know of the solstice prophecy, a prophecy that arose from my demise. From our demise, is it not? It promises that on this evening, the circle will be completed once more, and the healing of the stones unleashed. The Flesh Clan priests chatter on about how I will bring back the gods and that they will rule supreme under me." Avery shook her head but remained silent. She knew there was more to it than simply triggering the stones. "And I also know that my trinket box is key. You will now hand it over to me." The warriors grabbed Avery's arms and held her tightly, swords coming to throat again. "Go on. Remove the box from your pocket. My warriors have heard the stories of your cloak and know they will not be able to remove it from your person." Avery started defiantly back at Artio, not moving a muscle to comply with the order. Her hands clenched into fists, and she had to consciously relax her white-knuckled squeeze. She quivered with suppressed anger.

Artio's grin widened. "Oh yes, that is the Alfreda I remember. Defiant and stamping her feet to get her way. No worries, I have the perfect incentive for you." Artio snapped her fingers, and a man was dragged, screaming with pain, down the path and into the meadow. Achak was dumped, bound hand and foot, at her feet. He flopped face-first onto the ground, smacking his head on a rock, breaking his nose and gushing blood. He did not move.

Chapter 46

Daimon

ACHAK'S ARMS BENT to hands tied behind his back. His crumpled face pressed into the dirt, lips askew. His tunic was torn, and the wooden splint Avery had strapped to his leg with such care and attention was nowhere to be found.

Artio stepped forward and grabbed Achak by a fistful of hair, yanking his head back. One eye was swollen shut and his lips were split, blood dripping from his nose to join the blood flowing down his chin to. Artio pulled the obsidian knife from her leg and placed its shining edge against his jugular.

"Now," she spoke slowly and precisely, enunciating each word that followed, "you will place the box in the celestial bowl. If you do not do as I say, you will still place the bowl in the box, but it will be joined by pieces of flesh we carve out of his body. When we are done with him, we will start on you. If I put enough pieces of you in the basin, the box will be there too. This is your first and only offer, Sister. Shall I start sawing?" Artio lightly dragged the blade against Achak's skin, and blood blossomed along the cut, coating the blade edge with glimmering droplets.

"Wait!" Avery shouted. "What is your interest in the box? Why do you care about the healing of the world? You abandoned us to care for it. What does it matter to you if the world lives on? Why have you come to stop me?"

"Stop you?" Artio threw back her head and barked a laugh. "What do you think is in that box, Little Sister? I don't want to stop you. *I want to use you.* Only you can trigger what I need." Avery stared at her hard, reaching out with her mind. She could sense the truth in her sister's statement. That alarmed her more than Artio's threats that she was determined she use the box. Dread settled into her belly, a roiling cramp of fear sharp as a knife. *What has Artio done to the box? Or has someone else tinkered with it?* Not for the first time, she wished she knew what had happened after she'd died. *But what choice do I have? If I refuse, Achak is dead.*

"Enough delay! The sun fades." Artio's hand moved, and Achak swayed in her grip.

"*Stop!*" Avery shouted. Artio's eyes gleamed. Without another word, Avery limped over to Artio, reaching into her pocket and withdrawing the box. Artio released her hold, and the unconscious Achak slumped back to the ground. Artio took the box from Avery's hand and gently examined it. Avery's eyes darted to Achak. She could see the rise and fall of his chest, despite the blood staining his neck.

Artio's eyes glistened for a moment and then hardened. Avery thought she saw tears, but in an instant they were gone.

Artio handed the box back to Avery. "Place it in the basin, and speak the words."

Avery took the box and hobbled back to the disk, placing it in the center of basin. She closed her eyes and pulled from deep within her most ancient of memories, words she has spoken long ago, during a ceremony in this very spot. Their father, Morpheus, had been with them that time, holding both girls by a hand, one on either side.

He had thrown back his head and prayed to the gods as the box flashed with a wild blue light. Avery echoed those words, only now understanding their power, sending her prayer to the heavens.

"Blush of blood, barely born,
Sacred spirits eternally sworn,
Flesh of man's fading form
Magic's bonding, magic torn.

Torn from time, never mended
Crumbling oaths of faith upended
Abandoned of the gods descended
Shield of spirit, creatures blended

> Time eternal, gods forsaken
> Reign of man, dominion shaken
> Sibling wars, the cause mistaken
> Runes align, the world awakens
>
> Strife consumes, unwary foe
> Minds controlled, a killing blow
> Long forgotten, flaming woe
> Time divided, slowing flow
>
> Carry away the cursed one
> Bring an end to father's son
> Wild magic's cast begun
> Sacred creed, moon undone."

With an audible click, the lid popped open, just as the last rays of the sun settled into the clearing. The beams struck each pillar precisely on a guardian that began to glow, then the light travelled internally down through the columns of stone lighting them from within. The stones trembled and from each level, triggered by the guardian, waves of healing shot out from the monoliths and encased all who were within the circle. The beams touched everything and everyone, and every physical injury healed in that instant. Aging ceased and time rewound and flesh mended. But something more than flesh and blood began to heal.

At the same time, whispers of shadow snaked from the trinket box, twisting and gathering into dense black ropes that thickened and rose into the air. The ground shook and the ropes became a coil that expanded and solidified at an alarming rate. The healing waves rebounding around the clearing collided with the smoke, and the twisting forms resolved into bodies, both human and animal.

At first Avery though she recognized them, but as their features grew sharper, more defined, she knew she did not. Grotesquely deformed creations were being mended, healed back into existence by the healing portal. But these creatures were never meant to be. They were the result of an experiment gone wrong, the creation of a sick mind. Banished by the gods, torn apart in defeat and ashes scattered to the netherworld, they were never again to see the world of the living. Yet Avery could not deny the evidence before her eyes. *They are here!*

Someone has gathered the remains of the Daimons and secured them in the box! And I have released them right over the heart, the source of their strength, Daimon Ford. How could I have forgotten the events of that night?

And now, they were reforming. Not just released, but *healed and alive!*

Artio threw back her head and roared her pleasure. The Primordials at her side shied back, muttering amongst themselves in confusion and fear. A keening cry rose from the swirling mass, the horrible screech that was the ancient speech of the Daimon hordes. The sound was the last straw, and the warriors raced from the clearing, abandoning Artio and Avery to the dervishes forming in the night. Artio did not even acknowledge the abandonment, so focused was she on the rebirth of her true army. She raised her arms to embrace the daimonic spirits, the firelight dancing across her body, flickering in the depths of her eyes. Her only thought was of the revenge she would wreak on the world. How she would avenge her true love. *I have stolen your army from you, Helga! They are mine to command! I will have my revenge at long last!*

Avery dropped to her knees and crawled away from the portal, over to the still form of Achak. She ran her hands along his leg, checking the break, but she already knew he would be fully healed. She rolled him over and shook him awake, wincing at the high-pitched squealing that ramped higher and higher behind her, all the while keeping an eye focused on the hellish rebirths. Their non-corporeal bodies blurred into a tornadic swirl as the sun dropped below the horizon.

The energy of the sun's rays was no longer needed, for now a light glowed from the center of the swirl, blood red and volcanic. The white disk at its center flared a blinding white, and then melted into a blinking morass before her eyes. A rift opened up along the fault lines leading back to the monoliths. Magma pulsed up out of the fiery cracks and bubbled, hissing, into the bowl. The figures drew on the coursing lava and thin fingers of flame trailed up and over their bodies, igniting muscle and bone. Wings unfurled from backs, and demonic faces began to glow, their eyes a burning flame.

"Achak! We must go. *Now!*" Avery hissed, tugging on his arm. His eyes snapped open, widening in horror at the hellish vision greeting his groggy mind. He scrambled to his feet, swaying, and his foot kicked a glass vial. Avery spied a bottle rolling away, full of potion and quickly snatched it up, amazed at their luck. *Aossi's potion!* She popped the lid off, drank half and then passed the other half to Achak. He tipped it back, and they both faded from view. Hands linked, they both bolted for the cover of the brambles, caring not for the fresh scratches and injuries inflicted as they crashed through the underbrush. The earth quaked, and they staggered as they ran. Their one thought was to put as much distance as possible between themselves and the abyss forming in the sacred clearing and the monster rising from its midst.

A great keening rose on an unnatural wind, spawned of the blistering breeches, as the formerly peaceful meadow flashed into flame. The tall grasses were consumed with the ferocity of a grasshopper plague, and onto this crackling inferno stepped a hideous obsidian Daimon of unbelievable size. Twenty feet tall, the shining rocky goliath towered over the burning carpet. Its clawed feet puffed swirls of sparks into the air as it took its first steps out of the circle. In its massive hand, it gripped a flaming sword as tall as Avery. More rock Daimons followed it, spawned of the goliath, but Avery was no longer paying attention.

Avery dragged Achak behind her. "Move faster!" she screamed, launching herself over a log in their path. Achak's laboured breathing assured her that he was right behind her as they reached the cover of the trees, fleeing from what was surely death.

Artio's chilly laughter chased them as they fled. "You can run, Little Sister, but there is no place to hide."

Avery and Achak dropped behind a rock as Artio's words reached them, pressing their backs against the stone and gulping air. Avery peered around the side of the rock, horrified at the monsters erupting in the clearing. The flames of the meadow reflected off of the varied planes of their obsidian bodies and refracted in all directions, multiplying the crazed dance of demons so that was impossible to track with the eye. She could not count them because her human eyes could not focus on one long enough to register it as an individual. Only the tallest one, with glowing pits in its face where its eyes should have been, gave it away as a sole being, that and the great horns curving from its skull. It was similar to the Daimon from Artio's demise, and yet unlike the original beast of Daimon Ford. This version was refined, its face hot with an intelligence that flickered in its fiery gaze. This Daimon had been altered; improved, blended.

Avery shuddered and grabbed Achak's hand once again and started running. As they dashed away, Artio's words chased them. "We will meet again, Little Sister, on the plains of Daimon Ford. There, you will meet your doom. There, you and Little Brother will face Asag, champion of the underworld, and there, *you will die.*"

Asag! Avery shuddered. How had the Daimons been summoned? This had all the hallmarks of Helga's doing, but how had Asag come to be bound to the box? Avery did not pause to challenge Artio's statement. She knew they would die now, if they stayed any longer.

They ran.

Chapter 47

The Plan

IN A CAMP FAR AWAY from the sacred clearing, Avery sat on a log in front of a small fire, sipping at tea from a large pottery bowl. Across from her sat Denzik and Achak, both men mirroring her actions, letting the silence stretch.

Nelson appeared out of the dark, carrying three large bowls of steaming stew—goat, by the aroma—with potatoes and a wild edible orange root that was native to the area. He set the bowls down in front of them and straightened. "Two Primordial strangers have approached the camp kitchens. They are friends. I think you know the one woman, Avery. Her name is Ziona. The other is an elder. Your father Gaius is with them."

"My father! Is he all right?" Avery gasped and began to rise to her feet, but Nelson pushed her back down with a firm hand on her shoulder. "Stay and eat. They are bathing and will join you shortly. Eat!" he commanded and then disappeared back into the dark.

"Amazing news! What luck that they have found us! Or is it luck?" Denzik shovelled a mouthful of hot stew past his lips and chewed vigorously at the tough meat. He waved his spoon at Avery. "If you don't eat your meat, you won't get any dessert." His mouth twitched with a smile. "And around here, no one wants to miss dessert."

Avery pouted but complied, eating the hot stew as quickly as the heat would allow. The warmth of the meal spread through her belly and dispersed the chilly horror that had dogged her ever since their narrow escape from the clearing.

Her connection to Cayden was silent, as though he was no longer in this world. She frowned at the thought, and worry paused her spoon part way to her mouth. "Why doesn't he answer?" she murmured, unaware she had spoken out loud.

A hand fell on her shoulder, and her father said, "Because he cannot."

Avery bolted to her feet and flung her arms around him, hugging him, her face buried in his chest. A tear slipped out from between her tightly scrunched lashes as she choked back a sob.

"Avery, I'm OK. There, child, do not cry." He rubbed her back as he had when she was a child, passing a hand over her bald head. He sighed and hugged her tight, then placed a kiss on the top of her head, a father comforting his only daughter. She was still his child and always would be, regardless of the demands of the gods. After a couple minutes, she pushed back, swiping a hand across her cheek to dry her tears. Avery's eyes searched him, checking him over, looking for injuries.

Gaius smiled. "See? I am in perfect health. Ziona took care of me."

"I thought I'd never see you again." She hugged him tight once more, just as Ziona strolled into the firelight, followed by the fat baker Fabian, balancing a tray of sticky buns on his shoulder.

Sniffs and sighs greeted his arrival as he placed the tray next to the tea and settled himself to a cup of the hot brew. Nelson returned with the remnants of the stew and settled himself down too, filling a cup with the fragrant tea.

Once everyone was assembled, they shared their collective experiences, bringing each other up to speed on the events of the last few weeks.

When silence descended once again, Ziona cleared her throat and stood. "Cayden is there." She pointed, straight as an arrow toward the summit wreathed in smoke, the underside a red glowing smear. "He went after Mordecai, so Mordecai must be there, also. I can feel him, weakly, like the brush of a breeze on my mind. He is there one minute and gone the next. That"—she pointed at the smoking mountain—"is Helga's realm. I can only assume he is in Sheol Animus, the underworld." Her voice hitched and then firmed. "No one returns from the underworld. No one."

"Nonsense." This time the voice was Elder Hania's. All eyes swivelled to his. "You only say that because no one ever has...and because those who go there are usually dead. Do you think he is dead?"

Ziona frowned, examining the feeling in her chest, then shook her head. "No, I do not think he is dead, but we must be realistic."

Denzik spoke up, "The king is not dead. I can't believe it. He has a plan, and he has the wizard."

Gaius smiled weakly. "That wizard is too stubborn to die anytime soon. I also believe they are alive."

Fabian shoved a sticky bun into everyone's hands, and they stared at the dripping sweet in bemusement. Fabian waved his through the air and said, "Then we are decided. We carry on with our plans. Nelson, the Kingsmen, and I will return to Cathair to sort out the former legions and regain order. We will return with a bigger, better army. I know that there is a well-trained force of knights waiting to avenge the king's honour, Ryder will have seen to that training and be chomping at the bit to see some action, especially when he learns of Cayden's capture.

"Avery, Achak, and Elder Hania will return to the temple of the Primordials and explore ways to fight the Daimon running loose under Artio's command and see to the uniting of the clans. We must have unity if we are to take on the underworld." Heads nodded in agreement.

"Ziona, since she can still sense some of Cayden's essence, will join Gaius and Denzik to go after Cayden and Mordecai. They can figure out a way to assist them in their escape from Sheol Animus. Only freed can they fight for the souls of the world, for the preservation of the souls of the living, and for life as we know it.

"With luck, we will see each other once again." Fabian raised his sticky bun in salute. The others mirrored his movement. "Let us toast to the end of Helga's interference, once and for all." His eyes swept the flickering faces. One by one they nodded and raised their buns in a sticky toast to success.

"I promise a dozen sticky buns a week for life to the one that brings me the rock Daimon's head!"

Denzik chuckled. "A reward worthy of a king. I accept your challenge!"

"Hear! Hear!" they shouted, challenge accepted, their hearts lighter than they had been for a long time.

Trials lay ahead, but they went to their beds with the focus of a plan settled, with goals set. The path would not be easy. In truth, the real trials were about to begin. But they had hope, and hope could make all the difference between good and evil.

Epilogue

DEEP UNDER THE HIGHLAND SPINE lay Sheol Animus. Miles down in its dark depths, a second scrying pool ripped with images. This pool did not show current events however, like its cousin at the lip of Sheol Animus. This pool was located beyond the boundary of the living, bound to the souls of the dead, and as such reflected the future from the perspective of the dead. With the accuracy of a mirror, those who looked into the pool would see deaths to come, deaths in the future. Only those who were about to die could see their reflections.

Helga rarely used it for obvious reasons. Everyone around her was already dead, until now.

Four Charun dragged two unconscious men down to the poolside and dropped them on the slippery rocks at the edge of the steaming water then drifted back into the shadows at the edge of the circle of weak light. Curls of vapour drifted off the surface of the cloudy, sulphur-smelling water. The odour of rotting eggs dragged them back to consciousness, and they gagged, choking on the stomach-curdling smells.

Cayden rolled over and dragged his torn sleeve across his mouth and nose, attempting to block out the smell.

Mordecai did much the same thing, only he had no robe to use. He pressed his bare, bony arm to his nose, eyes watering.

Helga stood over them, disgust evident in every bend and curve of her face. "Look into the pool and tell me what you see."

Cayden eyed the putrid pool, suspicious as to what it held.

"What is it you expect us to see?"

She shook her head, bemused. "Look into the pool," she commanded again.

Cayden glanced at Mordecai, who was weak beyond belief. The years were catching up to the old wizard.

Cayden stood up and cautiously approached the pool and bent over the edge.

Grey clouds rolled across the scene. Rocks and landscape were obscured by what they took at first to be a huge storm. Lightning flashed and the ground shook, but the closer Cayden looked, he could see the rocks were actually men and beasts, dead for as far as the eye could see. The storm clouds roiled and flashed and suddenly he realized that he was flying toward tall plumes of smoke. Whole villages and towns were burning, along with their associated crops, and the fire was everywhere—every town, every village. He began to recognize the landscape the closer he flew to Cathair, until the great walls that had withstood every external siege ever thrown against it came into view. A glow, like an early sunrise, rose from behind the walls, and more smoke rose from the interior. He was swept along in the vision. As he came closer to the outer crenel wall, he was swept up to a tower he knew all too well. There, at the top of the tower, stood a figure. Tall and imposing with his back to him, he flung fire down on the outlying villagers and back into the castle keep, casting a ring of flame and death.

"No!" Cayden gasped as he swooped closer and closer. At the last minute, when it appeared he must collide with the figure, it twisted to face him. *"Nooooo! By the will of the gods, no!"* Cayden wrenched himself away from the pool and collapsed to the ground, weeping.

The man atop the tower wore his face.

"This has gone too far! All will perish!"

Other Books in the Spirit Shield Saga

SOUL SURVIVOR
SEER OF SOULS
SOUL SANCTUARY

Thank you for reading!

I hope you have enjoyed this second installment of The Spirit Shield Saga.

If you have enjoyed this novel, please leave a review at your favorite online retailer. This is the best way to support indie authors, and to let the world know your impressions of your book! Reviews are the life blood of an author.

Please visit my website for details on the other books in The Spirit Shield Saga. There are links under the books to every retailer that carries this series! http://susanfaw.com/spirit-shield-saga/

About the Author: Susan Faw

Professional by day, book nerd and fantasy champion by night, Susan is a masked crusader for the fantastical world. Championing mythical rights, she quells uprisings and battles infidels who would slay the lifeblood of her pen. It's all in a night's work, for this whirlwind writer. Welcome to the quest.

VISIT SUSAN ONLINE:

http://www.susanfaw.com
http://www.facebook.com/SusanFaw
http://twitter.com/susandfaw
http://www.pinterest.com/susandfaw
https://www.bookbub.com/authors/susan-faw
https://www.amazon.com/Susan-Faw/e/B01BW8MPDS/ref=dp_byline_cont_ebooks_1

FIND OUT HOW IT ALL BEGAN! DOWNLOAD THE FREE PREQUEL, *SOUL SURVIVOR*, AT THE LINK BELOW!

http://susanfaw.com/soul-survivor-prequel-free-download/

JOIN MY STREET TEAM FOR THE LATEST NEWS!
10 new releases are scheduled for 2017!
https://app.convertkit.com/landing_pages/98068?v=6

COMING SOON!
THE HEART OF THE CITADEL, A NEW FANTASY SERIES!